THE FINAL CROSSING

A tale of self-discovery and adventure.

VINCE SANTORO

The Final Crossing
Copyright © 2022 by Vince Santoro

Tellwell Talent
www.tellwell.ca

ISBN
978-0-2288-7185-9 (Hardcover)
978-0-2288-7184-2 (Paperback)
978-0-2288-7186-6 (eBook)

Acknowledgments

THE POET JOHN DONNE WROTE, "no man is an island." We are all connected to one another, and that connection allows us to thrive.

I would like to thank Elizabeth, my life partner. From reading my early drafts to keeping distractions at bay, she spurred me on with her unwavering help and encouragement. Thank you, Bella!

I am forever grateful to my family, my children, Julia and Philip and friends for their support during my journey. They nurtured my drive never to give up.

Then there are those who took time from their busy lives to read my manuscript, in various revisions, and gave me their honest feedback.

I am especially grateful to my editor, Aaron Redfern, from Historical Editorial for his guidance and keen eye on what it takes to make a story better.

This is why no man is an island. My connections with all these wonderful people and others who have known about my writing venture and who have given me praise along the way, are the reasons why I thrive.

To all of you, my heartfelt gratitude!

THE YEAR IS 1800 BCE, during the reign of Pharaoh Amenemhat III. He has brought prosperity to his kingdom, marked by numerous monuments and buildings, decorated temples, an array of pyramids, and a canal system to regulate the inflow of water in much needed areas.

Few military activities have allowed for a peaceful reign and for the opportunity to exploit the mineral wealth of his quarries. From Nubia to Byblos, he is honoured and respected. He has allowed foreigners to live and work in his country, among them the heqa khasewet, 'rulers of foreign lands'.

But his rule begins to blemish. His massive building projects and several low Nile floods are exhausting his coffers. It is the beginning of the decline of a great dynasty. Neither foreigner, nor slave, nor free man can escape the decay.

PART ONE

Chapter 1

The sound of dragging footsteps along the pebbled path grew louder. The morning heat would soon turn into an inferno and drain any enthusiasm from the simplest of pleasures. But it was not enough to hamper a hunting expedition.

"Finally," Nenshi said as he bent down to grab his bow and arrows nestled between his feet. "Must you always be late?" He looked up to the sky and squinted to get a reading of the sun's position. "I don't have all day. Unlike you."

"Don't scold me like a child. I keep forgetting," Hordekef replied and wiped his clammy hands on his shirt.

Nenshi shook his head. "You keep forgetting you're a free man and I am not?"

Hordekef shrugged his shoulders and turned to look down at his hunting dog. "Precisely," he replied as he tugged at the leash to nudge the dog to come closer. It refused. "I have known you as a nobleman's son, not a servant."

Nenshi frowned, hated to be reminded of his status. Unlike most servants, even raised in nobility had its burdens. Hordekef gave the leash another tug. The dog still refused to budge. "Perhaps one day you will call me to celebrate your freedom rather than go hunting."

There was silence, save for the sound of the dog's pant.

The yearning for freedom had grown over time but the longing was not enough to set Nenshi free. Even though it was uncommon for servants to ask for their freedom, if warranted, in time, it would be granted. But Nenshi could not wait to be accorded such benevolence.

"Well ... when will you ask your master to grant you your independence?" Hordekef asked. "You have told me, repeatedly, you would."

Nenshi was reluctant to answer but felt the obligation to provide his friend with an explanation. "I have tried, several times. Something always gets in the way, his work, visits from old friends. I don't know what else to do. He has been good to me. You know that. I don't want to disrespect him."

"Tehuti is aging. After he enters the underworld, you will still respect him. Unfortunately, your status will not have changed."

Nenshi remained silent. The dead air surrounding him fell on his shoulders and caused him to be still, immobile. The heaviness could only be shaken with distraction. "Let's go, we're wasting time," he said, tipping his head sideways in the direction of the wasteland. "I didn't come here to talk about my woes."

"What's the hurry?" It was a casual question as Hordekef ambled without a care, his body swayed to the rhythmic tunes from a lute played in his mind.

Nenshi glared. "I still have tasks to finish. It seems Tehuti needs to remind me about my status. I never understood it. He has afforded me privileges yet he keeps me in servitude. Let's not waste any more time." He sighed as he raised his bow and arrows and motioned to begin the trek.

The insistence didn't spark Hordekef to move any faster which frustrated Nenshi.

"Is this your way of protesting any desire to go hunting?"

Hordekef lifted his head. His chin tilted slightly upward. "My skills are no match for your ability with those weapons. At times I think it would be better to meet you at the tavern and quench my thirst rather than fight the heat and go home empty handed, as usual."

"Perhaps today will be different," Nenshi said as he looked behind him where three servants stood. The same three Hordekef had always chosen to carry water, food and hopefully the spoils. "Must you always bring them?"

"Who? Them?" Hordekef pointed with his eyes. "Of course. Who else will carry the rewards of our adventure?"

"We will. We're strong enough."

"That toil is beneath me."

"That's obvious. Sometimes you're like the rest of them. You take advantage of your position. You can't even enjoy a day hunting without dragging servants to appease your whim."

Nenshi turned towards the helpers. One was just a young boy who could barely hold his own weight let alone carry spoils. Luckily the other two, stronger and much older, were accustomed to the ordeal.

"Have they had anything to eat before you left?" Looking at their bodies slouched forward, Nenshi sensed a lack of energy. Or perhaps they were bored of the same routine.

"I don't know," Hordekef replied. "They prepare my meals. I don't prepare theirs."

Nenshi shook his head and reached into his sack. He pulled out some dates, figs and bread and gave them to the servants. At first, they were reluctant to accept the offering. Nenshi smiled and gestured to take them. Hunger quashed hesitation and they accepted the food, given by a privileged servant to servants in need.

Nenshi turned to Hordekef and said, "Let's go. I have a feeling today will be a good one."

"You always say that. But wait. Brave One looks hungry."

"So you care more about the dog's hunger and far less for that of another man." Even though Nenshi objected to the delay, he realized it was prudent to be patient and wait when Hordekef was ready rather than end an excursion that had not yet started. After all, the servants were fed so why not the dog.

The sun's heat began its daily onslaught. Nenshi wiped the sweat as it rolled down his forehead. Pensive, slouched forward with his hand to his chin did little to calm the intensity nor mollify his mind, heavy with languor. Cramped thoughts swirled. He watched Brave One as he licked his paws. The dog was free to roam the fields yet the servants were chained to their life of servitude. Hordekef lived as he chose and Nenshi lived as a servant dispensed with privileges. The leap to ask for freedom was within reach. Yet at times, he was no closer in taking that step. Raised in nobility had given him insights into what it would be like to be a free man. The tantalizing possibility pulled at him, a request he thought would take less effort than removing the droplets that edged down his temples.

The morning sun moved across the sky. Its rays pierced and became increasingly relentless. Eyes, glazed in thought, Nenshi's heart pounded to gain control. He tore himself away from the grip, the same grip that often held him captive. He stood, focused, pulled back his shoulders and clenched his jaws. The drumbeats in his chest softened. A gentle smile replaced the anguished stare as he scanned the desolate arid land where he came to hunt and seek solace.

The wilderness had become his sanctuary where no man dared to take root; where the gods had forgotten it exists. The same wasteland mirrored his temple; a shrine that sustained a dream, immune from the memories of a life in want of change.

Sand, rocks and scarce vegetation shrouded his world which reminded him of the burden of his status, a class he did not choose. For now, his favourite pastime shared with Hordekef would make him forget about his lot in life.

"We should really move on," Nenshi insisted. "The day's heat is creeping up quickly."

"This won't take long," Hordekef said and reached into a sack and took out a piece of meat specially prepared to the hound's liking. "Mmmm ... smell this." He raised it towards Nenshi's face but Nenshi gently nudged Hordekef's hand to the side. "It's goat," Hordekef added.

"I know what it is."

"Brave One likes goat." His eyes then shifted towards his servants. "I would never feed him figs and bread."

Nenshi shook his head. Annoyed at the humiliating remark, he gripped his bow and arrows.

"Did you bring him to eat or hunt?" Nenshi asked.

"He's too old to give chase. Look, he's like an elder statesman, content and passive."

"Or he has just become lazy. He knows to stay close to the hand that feeds him rather than chase down animals."

Hordekef clenched his jaws. Nenshi ignored the reaction. The bickering killed the joy in hunting. It had dried up and they both knew it. The simple pleasure in competition between friends turned into a rivalry, an ordeal, as challenging as the hunt itself.

They reached an oasis that sprang from the desolation. There was life even in the desert. The three servants took their usual positions. They stood next to one another, well behind the two hunters. Nenshi grasped his bow in one hand and an arrow in the other. He closed his eyes for a moment and relished the freshness of a rare gentle breeze as it filled his lungs. A soft sigh broke the stillness.

"Must we always go hunting? We can also go fishing." Hordekef said, lips taut as he pulled out a cloth, tucked in his waistband, and dabbed his forehead. A deep breath could not relieve him from the angst, nor from the air, as dry as the bones of a boar's carcass.

"Here, take some." Nenshi offered his water-filled flask in the hope it would quench his friend's thirst and soften his mood. "I know you prefer to fish rather than hunt."

Hordekef grabbed the container, raised it over his head and let the water pour out. It ran down his chin, his neck and on to his silken shirt.

"There's fun in fishing." Hordekef said. "It reminds me of our childhood. Remember when we would play at my house. My mother would say to my father, *Nenshi might as well live with us. He spends so much time here.*"

Nenshi nodded and smiled at the recollection. "We can go fishing sometimes, but there's no challenge in it," he said and wiped the sweat from his face with his hand and waited for the flask to satisfy his own drought.

"I welcome the day we fling spears instead of arrows." Hordekef took another sip from the flask. But there was no competition between them in hunting. Hordekef knew he was not as good as Nenshi with the bow and arrow, even though he always tried to find a way to top him. There was no embarrassment in fishing, no opportunity to be outdone.

The heat crushed any desire to engage in a debate about the virtues of hunting. It was Nenshi's simple preference to be away from the River Iteru. There were too many people on both sides. Most took advantage of the grassy swales and ponds that gave way to lush green hills and provided an abundance of life. Instead, Nenshi favoured the remote areas - home of wild animals, low shrubs, and scattered trees, nurtured by the occasional rain. It was here, in the wilderness, that he would come to slay a beast and forget about his lot in life.

Finally, the flask was handed over. Nenshi lifted it with care, making sure not to spill a drop. While the sight hound rested on his belly, ears bent back, Nenshi cupped his hand, poured water into it, and gave it to the dog. The thirsty canine lapped it freely. Nenshi stroked his long head and rubbed his even longer muzzle. He then lifted the flask towards the servants as a gesture of offering. They smiled, bowed, and pointed to their own flasks.

"Brave One," Nenshi called. The dog knew the sound by which he had always been summoned. He lifted his head and turned his eyes upwards. Nenshi passed his hand along the hound's slender and flexible spine feeling the smooth coat. The caress revealed a feeble dog whose legs, no longer muscular, certainly were not able to propel him and reach great speeds in pursuit of a fleeing animal. Even his eyesight now betrayed him. At one time he could spot a hare in thick grass farther than an arrow could travel. Now they were of little value. Only his keen sense of smell and acute hearing were left.

"I remember when you would chase down an antelope, bite its hind leg and not let go until it dropped to the ground," Nenshi said. Brave One turned away as if embarrassed by the memory. Nenshi patted him again. Just then the dog pivoted his head towards bushes in the distance, next to a pond. Nenshi turned in the same direction.

"What is it?" Hordekef asked, stretching his neck to get a better look.

"Shh ..." Nenshi held up his hand. "It's time."

"How do you know?"

"Brave One just told me."

Hordekef's eyes narrowed. The dog's sudden resurgence of life, for shifting favouritism from a mere stroke of the spine, displeased his master.

The three servants took a few steps back. Eyes locked on what lay hidden in the bushes. Perhaps a lion waited for the right moment to attack. Many hunters, along with their party, had not returned from their favourite pastime. Often, they would become the hunted.

Hordekef quickly positioned himself with his bow and arrow. Was this an opportunity to outdo his friend? He aimed in different directions like a blind man with a cane trying to decide which way to go. A bird flew out from the thickets. Hordekef swung around and released the arrow. He frowned and glared down at the hound. "He can no longer tell the difference between a bird and a beast."

Nenshi smiled. Still crouched next to Brave One, he prepared his bow and arrow. The scarce high grass, some of it browned by the lack of water and hot sun, stood tall. He managed to peer over them as he rose. His thighs bulged with every lift. The bushes rustled for a moment. An absent wind could not have caused the sway, for the air was calm.

The ridged tips of a gazelle's horns, sharply bent backwards, could be seen. A male. Its light pale colour was visible only through the branches and leaves. The white and brown stripes between the eyes and mouth stood out even more. For a brief moment Nenshi remembered a key lesson taught to him by the great masters of hunting, afforded only by the affluent. His teacher would tell him, *squeeze the bow tightly as if you were strangling a serpent. Pull back on the bowstring, make sure your elbow points out and does not tremble. Pull back until your thumb touches your ear, that way you know you have the right tightness. This will also help you aim more accurately.* Nenshi did exactly as he had been taught.

As he clutched the shaft of the bow, the muscles in his outstretched left arm swelled. The gazelle stopped chewing. His nostrils expanded detecting an unwanted scent. Both man and beast were motionless. In an instance, the arrow struck. A cry of death broke the silence. The servants exhaled as if the weight of the animal was lifted from their shoulders. Once again, Nenshi's prowess with the bow and arrow prevailed. It was also a reminder of Hordekef's shortfalls. The pang of envy spread, like a fruit gone rancid through the contamination of a worm. Another hunt had ended with reward and rejection.

They stood over the dead beast. "I was certain the gazelle had seen you," Hordekef said. "You were motionless, like a statue. It was a fatal move, the twitch of the beast's muscle was your signal - as if the gazelle had surrendered its life to you."

"One of us had to make the first move." Nenshi smiled and pushed back his shoulders as if he had just defeated an army, single handed. He wiped the sweat from his temples with his finger and flicked the drops to the ground. He brushed back his wavy dark hair which exposed his high forehead and dark eyes.

"Not bad ... for a house servant," Hordekef jabbed, the compliment withdrawn.

Nenshi's excitement waned, his lips tightened, his fist clenched. The words cut deep. "I didn't need to be reminded," he said, flinging his own heartless tone.

As they approached the mansion Nenshi looked behind him. The servants had slowed their pace to create more distance, wary of becoming the target of the discord between friends. And to be out at the peak of the day's heat was ludicrous. It was not the weight of the dead beast that slowed them to a crawl.

The bloodstained throat of the gazelle hung upside down. Two servants carried it by its legs and neck tied to a long thick tree branch at each end. The third, luckier servant, carried the bows and arrows. The dead animal reminded Nenshi of Hordekef's failures. He now regretted having killed the beast.

"Your aim is better than the last time we hunted. Maybe you just need to practice more." Nenshi's attempt to bridge the friction did not go unnoticed. Hordekef's demi-smile veiled his feelings.

"I don't need more training," Hordekef said, with indifference.

"Then perhaps you need some good fortune. But remember, good fortune is not something that just presents itself. It must be created."

"And what good fortune have you created for yourself? To be free."

Hordekef was right and Nenshi knew it. To talk about freedom was one thing. To act on it with conviction was another.

The relentless heat, the still air and the thought of not having pleaded for his freedom made the walk home seem longer. If the leaves from the top of a tree swayed it was only because of a bird jumping across from one branch to the other. Surely not from a sudden gust of wind.

"Sometimes I think the comfort in my life has overshadowed everything," Nenshi said. "Riches have fogged my dreams. They are a blessing and a curse. I don't see myself as a servant. But there are times I wish I could change everything and live as a servant. Then I would not hunger to be free."

"Look at it this way - you are practically a free man. You come and go as you please. You have the education of a nobleman's son." Hordekef's attempt to mollify a growing concern had little satisfaction.

"What good is it if I can't use it?"

"There are many servants who would give their right hand to have what you have." Hordekef raised his voice to reinforce his message.

"Yes, I'm grateful. I come and go as I wish. I don't have a sibling to compete with. But I want more."

"Not enough? You have everything and that is not enough?"

"You don't understand." Nenshi's face reddened, not from the heat.

"I may not fully understand," Hordekef said, apologetically. "But gratitude starts from within. Those were Soreb's words not mine. Your tutor, remember?"

"If only Tehuti had chosen not to buy me from those slave merchants."

"If he didn't, someone else would have and it might have turned out very differently."

"Then why has he not made me his son, through the courts?"

"Because only those who could not have children could adopt, you know that. Tehuti had a son."

"That excuse is too convenient." Nenshi had grown tired of trying to justify his master's lack of initiative. "Meti should not have died." He took a deep breath to quell the frustration building inside.

"But sadly he did, and you had become like Tehuti's adopted son."

"There were plenty of opportunities for him to grant me freedom. And now with the country almost in ruin, it will be more difficult to get a favourable judgement."

"Ruin? What do you mean?" Hordekef's face crunched. "Egypt is the greatest of all lands."

"It's not just my opinion. I've heard it from Tehuti. He has seen things with his own eyes. You know how much Pharaoh is consumed with erecting buildings, temples. Tehuti had been commissioned to design some of them. There is no money left for Pharaoh to manage his kingdom and take care of his subjects. There is even talk of threats of invasion. The decline is seeping deep. Some even question the existence of an afterlife, including me."

"Times do change, and people like to talk about it. But you are fortunate to have Tehuti's support. I'm certain he will not abandon you."

"I suppose. I have privileges yet I am deprived. But I must demand my freedom."

"And he will grant it. I know it."

"I hope you're right."

As they sauntered back home, they joked and laughed leaving behind the acrimony of changing times - left in the wilderness, perhaps to wither away.

"Don't forget," Hordekef said, "You promised to meet me at the market tomorrow."

"I'll be there, even though you haven't told me why."

Hordekef grinned and nodded his head like a playful child. They parted ways.

As Nenshi approached Tehuti's mansion, the uneasy feeling returned. It felt like the sun's heat, unbearable - a burning desire to be rid of a life he didn't choose; one he didn't want. He walked through the lavish garden towards the mansion, a stark reminder that a servant raised as a nobleman was less than a man. And now his yearning for freedom loomed in the wake of a country on the wane and rumours of foreigners at the doorsteps of his homeland. The night would pass with spiralling thoughts of confronting his master.

Chapter 2

NENSHI KEPT HIS PROMISE AND met Hordekef at the market. They meandered through the narrow paths where tents were quickly and perilously assembled. A careless bump would cause them to collapse. Merchants guarded their tables, overflowed with goods, in case a thief unsuspectingly grabbed something and ran off. Experienced buyers strolled with calculated intentions and chose only what they needed.

A lackluster stride reflected Nenshi's interest in being here. A gaze at the sky, a pensive stare at objects for sale, only bolstered his eagerness to return home to speak with his master. The sun moved away from its morning position and yet it seemed to have stood still. If only he hadn't promised Hordekef to come to the market. Instead he would have been pleading for his freedom rather than dodging carts.

A familiar sour odour warned that stalls reserved for fishermen and their catch were not far off. Nenshi spurned and held his breath. As they passed a stand, a merchant called out to them while he waved samples in the air. Behind the trader, on a long table, fish were being cleaned - perch, moonfish, eels and catfish. Blades slashed and cut through them with precision. Some of them still had hooks made of bone and shell hanging out from pierced mouths.

"Walk faster," Nenshi insisted. "The stench is turning my stomach."

"Follow me, over there," Hordekef pointed. Luckily a gentle breeze blew the odours in the opposite direction.

There were fewer stands in the market, an unusual emptiness. Where once tents outnumbered people, now unfilled carts and abandoned donkeys occupied their places. There were more soldiers too, patrolling the streets. It was Pharaoh's order. Stories of unrest from afar spread like the flooding of the River Iteru. Merchants feared their goods and livelihood could easily come to an end.

"The market seems more empty than usual," Nenshi said.

"There are still too many people for my liking," Hordekef replied.

"It's not the same."

"You trouble yourself too much."

"You know what I'm talking about."

"You mean the *heqa khasewet*."

"Yes. Rulers of foreign lands, as some prefer to call them." Nenshi slowed to inspect a gold amulet as he passed a table overflowing with trinkets.

Hordekef waited for him to catch up and said, "But didn't Pharaoh allow these people to live in Egypt?"

"Pharaoh is only interested in what they can produce for him. He has ignored the state of his land. The people in the outer regions have little to eat. And nothing is being done about it. It seems our ruler merely wants buildings, temples, palaces and gold." Nenshi stopped and turned to face Hordekef. "Can't you see the unrest is spreading, even reaching Thebes?"

"And what of it? It means nothing to me," Hordekef said and nudged Nenshi to resume walking.

"It means everything to me!" Nenshi said as he took hold of Hordekef's shoulder and stopped him in his tracks. "In short time these people will become tired of being puppets at the hands of Pharaoh. They'll take advantage of the unrest and who knows what they'll do next. For now, they are wanderers. One day they may be our masters."

"Until then, I'll continue to do as I choose which includes what I'm about to show you. Walk faster, we're almost there."

Nenshi quickened his pace to catch up, wondering if it was a deliberate act by Hordekef to end the conversation.

They passed more stands where everything from crops to clothes and even services from a doctor could be bartered. There was always a buyer, no matter what was sold.

"Here it is!" Hordekef's eyes, child-like, shined with excitement.

"This is what you dragged me here for? A flute?" Nenshi had anticipated something more masculine. He picked up the instrument and examined it. "Cane," he said. "It's made of cane." He counted six finger holes and wondered why there weren't more holes, for all the fingers. "Why didn't you tell me we were coming to look for a flute?"

"If I had told you, you would not have come," Hordekef said and took the handcrafted wind instrument from Nenshi. "I've wanted a double flute for a long time."

"Why is it so special?" Nenshi took a closer look.

"I can blow through it from the side or from its end." Hordekef closed his eyes. "I can hear its sweet tunes played by Osiris to enlighten the land."

Nenshi smiled and couldn't help to tease. "Perhaps it's easier to master the flute than a bow and arrow."

Just then a voice called out. "Hordekef". They both turned.

"Sia ..." Hordekef blushed, lost for words. Nenshi folded his arms, waiting to see what Hordekef would do or say while holding a musical instrument rather than manly hunting tools.

Sia smiled and glanced at Nenshi who returned the gesture. He poked Hordekef's rib with his elbow.

"Oh ... forgive me ... this is my friend, Nenshi."

Nenshi respectfully bowed his head.

Hordekef had never mentioned her before. Perhaps it was a new relationship and he had kept it to himself until he was certain of a commitment. Nenshi understood the attraction. Sia was captivating, a beauty that radiated like a shining star. A long strapless sheath made from the finest cotton reached her ankles. Soft leather sand-coloured sandals adorned her feet. The long tunic, tightly worn, accentuated her sensuous body. Her eyes, inviting, were framed by light green *kohl*, shadowed on the eyelids. A gold necklace rested just above the cleavage of her breasts.

She turned to Hordekef. "I never thought I would see you here." Her eyes pointed to the table packed with musical instruments.

"I've been looking for a flute, a special one, and now I found it."

"There are so many different types." She picked one up and observed it.

Nenshi took the opportunity to nudge Hordekef to the side and whispered, "I didn't know you were courting someone."

"She's a friend. If I was courting someone, you would know." His voice was low enough for Sia not to hear.

Nenshi smiled, open to the possibility of exploring his intrigue. He stood next to her.

"Have you found anything interesting?" he asked.

"No." She looked up at him and imparted a casual smile, a careful gesture not to surrender herself. "Do you collect instruments as well?"

"My only instrument is my weapon for hunting." He placed his hand on his side and pressed it against his dagger.

"Did you come to buy something special?" he asked.

She chuckled. "I came with friends. I rarely come to the market. I don't like the crowds, the stench, the ruffians."

"Are you calling us scoundrels?" Nenshi teased.

"No ... no," she asserted. "I wasn't referring to you or Hordekef."

Nenshi smiled which seemed to set Sia at ease. "I have an idea," he said. "Let's go hunting."

"Hunting?"

"Something for you to buy. You don't want your friends to see you empty-handed. A beautiful woman of your stature must uphold her reputation."

"But you know nothing about me."

"Then I need to find out." He smiled and shrugged his shoulders. She accepted the invitation with a gentle nod. He then turned to Hordekef. "Take your time here. You might find another instrument you've always wanted," he said and walked off with Sia. Hordekef frowned, defeated again.

They sauntered through the market, a casual stroll, as if it was not their first acquaintance but rather one of friendship rooted by a natural bond.

"Do you like to barter?" Nenshi asked.

"Isn't that what the poor do?"

Nenshi furled his brows, never having considered that only the less fortunate had the need for such negotiation. He overlooked her dismissive tone. Fortunately for him, she would not know by his attire that he was a servant. He wore a soft linen loincloth, woven into pleated decorative panels, wrapped around his hips and left his knees uncovered. The kilt accentuated his lean body - strong, muscular and in proportion. And the way he presented himself - educated, refined, athletic – gave sign that he stemmed from affluence.

"Bartering is like a game," he said. "You can get anything you want, if you know how to play it. I'll teach you."

They stopped in front of a table. A portly man with an intimidating frown kept an eye on them. His focus shifted to Nenshi who was examining the countless pieces of stones, rings, bracelets and charms. Then his glare turned to Sia who was also looking at jewellery. Nenshi was drawn to the ones made of lapis lazuli, copper, gold, and turquoise; an abundant supply in every imaginable colour and style.

"Is there something that interests you?" The merchant said as he leaned forward to appear more intimidating than his heavy stature suggested. It was a customary approach. If anyone stole from him, they would certainly have to deal with the brute. The man stepped back and forced a smile.

"My name is Nenshi. What's yours?" The game began with an introduction and a connection made through a name. The lure with honey is more successful than one with vinegar.

"Hasani. My name is Hasani."

"Ah ... appropriate indeed, as is the meaning of your name. Sia, don't you agree, this man is handsome?"

Sia struggled for a response, smiled and nodded. Hasani blushed. Could even a beautiful woman find him attractive? On the contrary he was quite gruesome. A sparse beard painted over his acned face. His blood-shot eyes added to his repulsive image. As he spoke, he revealed a mouth full of crooked and discoloured teeth. "I beg you, if you wish to buy something please hurry. I want to pack up and go home." Another tactic to hasten a sale, perhaps.

"Leave? So soon?" Sia asked. "The day is pleasant. What possible urgent business does a merchant have other than to sell his wears?"

Nenshi smiled, realizing her beauty was matched by her intelligence, having picked up on his tactics and challenged herself to use them.

"I've been here since sunrise. I'm tired," Hasani said and scanned the area around him. Nenshi turned to look behind him and considered the rumours of invaders. Hasani silenced himself. Potential buyers could easily be scared away.

Sia then reached down and picked up a pendant, adorned with gold leaf beads and copper ornaments. It felt heavy as if it was made for an obese woman.

"It comes from Nubia," Hasani said.

"I know of this land," she said as she examined the necklace. "My father told me it's a place for criminals, punishment for their crimes.

Two of our servants were sent there for taking bread to their quarters. We have to be wary of those who offend our laws."

Nenshi shunned. Hasani agreed. "Indeed. If it were not for villains, we would not have gold." He let out an uncontrollable laugh. "These criminals are sentenced to work in the gold mines to produce what we sell," he said. Nenshi grimaced. He could have walked away from both of them and left them to their world of intolerance. But he didn't. He hoped Sia did not share all of her father's beliefs.

"I'm looking for something simple," Sia said and handed the necklace back.

"Perhaps this is more to your liking." Nenshi picked up a pendant strung on a beaded locket. The small beads were made of lapis, malachite and turquoise. Sia smiled.

"What's the price for this?" Nenshi dangled it on his finger suggesting it had little value. Hasani took it, pretended to evaluate it and gave it back to Nenshi.

"This comes from traders along the caravan routes," Hasani said. He raised his left hand, an enormous hand, and displayed four digits to indicate the price.

"Four *shats*?" The obvious disappointment meant nothing to Hasani since he didn't even react to Nenshi's tone. Sia scrunched her face. The price was too much. Sia took the necklace from Nenshi and handed it back to Hasani.

She turned to Nenshi. "A friend told me about a stand at the other end of the market with fine pieces ... for a lesser price." A casual wink signalled her understanding of the ploy in bartering.

Hasani was now even more determined to sell the necklace and certainly not to have a sale rejected by a woman. "What do you offer for it?" He proudly held it to the sun's light. It glittered with royalty.

Nenshi put his hand to his chin. He slid his other hand down to his side and felt his empty pouch, one he wore only to give the impression he was like everyone else, that he belonged. He had come to the market to accompany Hordekef, not to meet a girl, unexpectedly, and venture to buy a necklace.

Hasani shrugged his shoulders and waited for an answer. Nenshi acted quickly and removed his own amulet from his wrist.

"I'll trade for this."

Sia tugged on Nenshi's shirt, but he pretended not to notice.

"This amulet was made to protect those who wear it. It's infused with power." Nenshi held it up to Hasani. "Take a close look. Can you see the carving? Look at the falcon with outstretched wings. Horus."

"Horus, our god of power and strength," Hasani said. His intrigue crested with excitement. His eyes, wide as the river, coveted the amulet. A quick examination convinced him of its authenticity. Both Sia and Nenshi realized they had the advantage.

Sia reached to take Nenshi's amulet away from Hasani and reminded him, "As I said ... we can go elsewhere if you're not interested."

Hasani pulled it back. "No, no," he said and then as Sia reached for it again, Hasani belted out, "I'm interested. I just need a closer look." He studied it from different angles and scratched his head. Nenshi reached out to grab the amulet. Hasani grunted and pulled it towards him.

"I'll take it," Hasani said. "The necklace is yours."

"I'm certain you will not be disappointed." Nenshi handed over the amulet and scooped up the necklace. "Come Sia, it's getting late." They briskly scurried away.

"Why did you give him your amulet? I could have paid for the necklace myself."

"I've wanted to get rid of that old thing for a long time."

"You bartered well for it. Even I believed your story about the amulet's power."

"And you learned quickly, the art of bartering.

They chuckled. Their eyes met. Nenshi's heart beat faster. He wanted to kiss her and she would have let him. But kissing her would have been deceitful.

"Besides, the necklace looks better on you than the amulet does on me."

"The band is strong. Even you could wear it," she said as she held it close to his chest. He took the necklace from her and placed it around her neck. Reaching behind to tie it, his cheek touched hers. The smell of the soft fragrance of her aromatic perfume - traces of lily, myrrh and cinnamon - evoked the scent of love. He stepped back to admire how the necklace adorned her.

"I like the yellow stone. A symbol of eternity," he said.

She smiled. "Then I will make this my stone, for eternity."

They walked together. Providence prevailed and their worlds collided through a timely excursion.

"So, will you come back to the market, now that you have learned how to barter?" Nenshi asked.

"I still have much to learn. You're a good teacher."

"Then we have an agreement. We'll meet here again."

"I would like that." Her acceptance came without effort. "I must go now. My friends are probably wondering what happened to me." She smiled, turned and walked away. Nenshi's face lit up as her elegant strides filled the excitement of newfound love.

Nenshi and Hordekef went to a familiar tavern near the market. Nenshi wasted no time in interrogating his friend.

"Why haven't you told me about her?"

"Who, Sia? I met her a while ago through a friend," Hordekef said, as he poured beer into two cups. "Besides I don't have to tell you everything."

"That's obvious," replied Nenshi as he glanced at Hordekef's flute on the table.

"Are you smitten?"

"She's beautiful ... elegant ... charming ..."

"You can run after her if you wish. I have no interest."

"Really? How could you not?"

"I have too many women to consider."

"Then tell me more about her. Tell me everything you know."

And so, he did. Hordekef told him she was the daughter of an aristocrat, Anpu, a successful and skilled sculptor. Her mother had died from a boating accident. While on an excursion she fell into the River Iteru. She couldn't swim. Her frantic attempts to rescue herself caused more than just the curiosity of crocodiles hidden among the reeds. In an instance, she became their meal and left a young girl without a mother.

As for her father, everyone who knew him said that Sobek, the god of crocodiles, did Sia's mother a favour - relieved her of her life with her husband. His cantankerous personality instilled fear. Patience was the ultimate virtue for those who dealt with him.

Sia never personified her father's irritable habits. The loving and patient hand of her surrogate mother, Ankhet, helped to shape her since childhood. Her father had decided to hire Ankhet to help raise his daughter. Ankhet never had a family herself, not able to have children, and explained her infertility as being visited by Serqet, the goddess of Scorpions, during her sleep one night. When she had awakened the next morning, in a sweat, she was convinced the goddess had left her with a spell for life.

So Ankhet had devoted herself in raising children and had become good at it. She was well sought after and only those, like Anpu, who could afford her services, reaped the benefits.

This bode well for Anpu because as a sculptor, his skills were renown but as a father, incompetence prevailed. No doubt he tried on many occasions to remarry but no woman accepted the invitation. No amount of money could entice a woman to become his wife. But for

Sia, having Ankhet in her life was a blessing from Wadjet, the goddess of protection. Like a true mother, Ankhet made sure Sia was loved and all her needs taken care of. Sia became close to Ankhet. She confided in her on many subjects. After many years of devotion to Sia, Ankhet succumbed to her age and died. Sia felt the loss, for days on end.

"At least we have something in common," Nenshi said.

"And what's that?"

"We both lost our mothers at a young age and we were raised by a surrogate. In our own way we are trapped within the confines of nobility."

Hordekef wrinkled his forehead and shook his head. "Trapped? Hardly. She's a free woman. She carries her own coins. You are an entitled servant with an empty pouch. Will you tell her this?"

It never occurred to Nenshi that love had restrictions. It was too soon to tell her. If she found out now, she might cut the delicate threads that held them together and accuse him of some criminal act. The possibility of loving a woman with whom he felt so natural to be with, now began to fade.

"If you're thinking of getting involved with her, I suggest that you tell her who you are, instead of it coming from others," Hordekef advised.

Nenshi remained silent, pensive, and then said, "You're right. I must tell her about my status and how I feel about her." He knew Hordekef had his best interest in mind. But he also realized that love indeed had limitations. And he knew the difficulty that lay ahead. Facing the unknown in the wilderness was one thing. But now, was he willing to face uncertainty for the sake of love?

Chapter 3

As Nenshi walked along the garden path towards the gates, his mouth became as dry as the air that lingered. A muscle, at the corner of his left eye, twitched, against his will. His life hinged on facing his master.

Servants, tasked to manage the garden, worked nearby. They eyed him as he approached and greeted him with a smile. He stopped to help them pick up fallen branches and debris. His place among them was as natural as the privileges he had been granted.

The gates opened followed by the sound of heavy footsteps. It was Hordekef. Nenshi expelled a sigh of relief, not to have to confront Tehuti. The twitch settled, a temporary reprieve. The thought of asking for his freedom had echoed in his mind ever since he was allowed to leave the compound, trusted to return. Often his lips whispered the words he would use to make his plea. He was prepared and yet he doubted any master in Egypt would graciously free a servant.

"You look as if you've been bitten by an asp," Hordekef laughed.

"Have you seen Tehuti on your way here?" Nenshi ignored the scorn.

"No. Is that why you're so edgy? Have you finally decided to ask him?"

"Yes, but I haven't seen him all day. He slips in and out like a snake."

"Then I'll wait with you and help catch the old snake."

They laughed. Nenshi clasped his hands and dreaded what he was about to do. He had mastered the art of hunting, had faced whatever charged towards him. But this was different. No one had guided him through the path of seeking freedom. As he paced back and forth, each step disturbed the biting flies in his stomach, gnawing to get out.

Hordekef pointed. "Who's that? A thief?"

Nenshi stretched his neck and recognized the frail figure standing by the doors of the mansion. The sun cast a long shadow of his body.

"It's Tehuti."

They both stared at Tehuti-em-Heb. He stood on the porch and squinted from the intense light of the afternoon sun as he gazed through the palm trees and garden shrubs towards the gates. The house lay hidden in the farthest corner of his estate behind dark foliage, vines, and his favourite trees - fig, pomegranate, and palm. A brownish brick wall pierced by two granite doors surrounded the entire abode. His house was the epitome of his craft as an architect, uniquely designed to suit his every need. His garden was his treasure that engulfed the house with sweet fragrances, fishponds and trees of every imaginable type. He had put more effort in designing his house that in creating some of Pharaoh's buildings.

Barefoot, Tehuti contested every reluctant step on the hot white marble porch. Nenshi chuckled as Tehuti moved like a rat in search of shade. Luckily, one of the four enormous pillars that embellished the porch and supported the house, offered relief. His aging hand wiped the sweat from his forehead. With the same continuing motion, he combed back his greying hair and gazed at the top of the motionless palm trees.

"He appears distracted," Hordekef said.

"I've gotten used to his unusual demeanour," Nenshi said as he moved under a palm tree to shade himself from the sun.

"What do you mean?"

"When he's distressed about something, it's hard for him to let go."

Such was the time when Pharaoh had decreed an increase to the levy on grains. It angered Tehuti for weeks on end. It was a sign of uncontrollable greed and he warned that Pharaoh's actions would create harsh consequences. Weeks later, fewer merchants had sold grain. The less they sold, the less they were obligated to give to Pharaoh. He had become displeased with the protest, and so had ordered the mills to produce more grains or everything would be confiscated.

"I don't look forward to what's ailing Tehuti this time," Nenshi said as he squinted to get a good look at the image. His plan to ask for his freedom had been dampened. How much longer could it be delayed? When would Tehuti be in the right frame of mind?

Nenshi strained to follow the figure as it paced back and forth like a cat with infinite patience waiting for a rodent to come out from its hiding place.

"He works too hard, especially for his age. Sometimes I worry about him."

"I don't think that will change," Hordekef added.

"I agree. The devotion to his craft is admirable. It's unfortunate that his experiences with the country's administrators have made him less tolerant and more cynical."

Hordekef waved his hand over his head to get Tehuti's attention. Nenshi shook his head.

"Don't bother. He has difficulty seeing things from a distance."

They watched Tehuti turn and gingerly walk inside. Nenshi's opportunity had slipped away like an abandoned boat floating aimlessly, waiting for a current to corral it back to shore.

"Before we go to the house, I have a challenge for you," Hordekef said. "Do you have your bow and arrows with you?"

Nenshi looked at Hordekef's empty hands. "And where are yours?"

Hordekef would not let it go, determined to demonstrate that he too was skilled. "I'll prove that I'm as good as you."

"You don't have to prove anything to me."

But it was proof for himself that Hordekef sought. A testimony that would relinquish him from years of being second best.

"Are you ready for a challenge?" Hordekef asked, confident of his skills.

"It seems I have no choice."

Hordekef set the stage. A long empty water jug lay on the ground. He took it and placed it upside down in front of a pomegranate tree so that the bottom of the jug became the top where he placed on it a fallen pomegranate and then surrounded the fruit with leaves. At twenty paces from the target, he placed Nenshi's bow and arrows on the ground. At ten paces to the right of the target he placed some stones and branches, large enough to be hurled. With his hands on his hips, he faced Nenshi and smiled. He stood, like an intimidating statue at an entrance gate, set to ward off strangers.

"Now listen," Hordekef said. He deliberately spoke slowly, as he detailed the challenge, to make sure there would be no confusion, no misunderstanding. "We'll both stand with our backs to the target, which is the pomegranate hidden behind the leaves. When I give the signal, you must run to your bow and arrows. At the same time, I'll run to those stones and branches. The first to hit the target is the victor."

Nenshi put his hand to his chin. He surveyed the stage Hordekef had created.

"You have a good imagination," Nenshi said. "But I'm at a disadvantage. You don't have to take a bow and arrow and carefully aim at the target which, I might add, is difficult to see and with those big hands of yours, you can pick up as many rocks as you can and fling them all at once at the target. And, may I add, you only have to run half the distance to get to the rocks than I do to get to my bow and arrows."

Hordekef crossed his arms, stern, soldier-like, impervious to the complaint.

"That's the test my friend. A test of speed and accuracy. Besides your legs are longer than mine, therefore my distance has to be shorter."

Hordekef was certain to win. His smile made his oval face and predominant cheekbones, hidden behind his long and straight black hair, appear larger, an expression of anticipated victory. Nenshi shrugged his shoulders.

They stood a few feet from the target with their backs turned. Hordekef gave the signal. The two ran and got to their weapons at the same time. Nenshi quickly picked up the bow and an arrow and once he placed it in position, he aimed at the target. At the same time, Hordekef picked up a large branch with one hand and several stones with the other. He drew the branch over his head and tightened his muscles, ready to thrust it at the target. As he was about to bring his arm forward, he heard the sound of an arrow whistle through the air and then saw it pierce the fruit and penetrate the tree immediately behind it.

His jaws tightened, he lowered his arm, his muscles relaxed and the branch fell to the ground. He walked over to the target, tore away the leaves and pulled the arrow out from the tree with the pomegranate still pierced by the arrow. His eyes bulged, his mouth dropped, he stared at the fruit as he held it close to his face.

Meanwhile, Nenshi quietly picked up another arrow and slowly placed it in position. He raised the bow and arrow with the same mastery as when he had struck the gazelle. He took a breath, held it and then released the arrow. He shot the fruit right out of Hordekef's hand. Hordekef jumped in fear and looked over to Nenshi whose laughter bellowed and caused birds to fly out from among the trees and bushes.

"Hordekef," he called out. "With that mouth of yours looking like that of a hungry hippopotamus, I thought you were going to eat that rotten fruit."

Hordekef scowled. Nenshi walked over to him and put his hand on his shoulder.

"Now I didn't want you to get sick, in case you were to bite into the fruit, so I had to shoot it out of your hand," he said and laughed again.

Hordekef frowned. What could he possibly do to get the upper hand? If the situation presented itself, he would undoubtedly take advantage.

When Nenshi and Hordekef reached the steps of the house they were met by a servant, short and stocky.

"Master wishes to see you," Bata said, his anxious gaze stirred concern.

"Did he give a reason?" Nenshi asked.

"No. There's no purpose for him to tell me." Bata furled his brows and shook his head and left the room. His job was done, to deliver the message. He could not control the whims of entitled youth.

"I sense you're anxious about speaking with Tehuti," Hordekef said.

"Anxious hardly describes how my stomach is churning right now," Nenshi said, clutching his hands.

"I have never known you to be like this. Are you afraid that your request will bring trouble?"

Nenshi couldn't remember the last time his actions caused trouble in the household. That usually came at the hands of careless servants who would forget to lay out the appropriate kilt for their master or fail to cook meals to their master's palate.

"Perhaps I'm afraid of rejection."

"I haven't known you to be afraid of anything. You face whatever confronts you. Do you remember the other day when we left the tavern and a drunken man tried to lure you to a fight?"

Nenshi chuckled. "He took a swing at me, missed and fell to the ground. It wasn't much of a challenge."

"He reminded me of our tutor Khenemsu with his long pointy nose."

Nenshi laughed. "You mean the crusty old man who tried to teach us how to use symbols for counting?"

"Now, now, let him be with the gods."

"He's better off in the other world than in a teaching room."

"Have you forgotten your irate confrontation with him?"

"You mean our debate about reality and imagination?"

"Yes, that one," Hordekef laughed.

At the time, Khenemsu had pointed out that imagination was nothing but a poet's poem, a singer's song. Daily life required strictness. *Precision is reality*, he would say. But Nenshi would have none of it. He was impetuous, even back then and deviated from what others had followed. His imagination and his dreams were more important.

"Dreams are like pieces of wood that kindle the fire. Take away the wood and the fire dies. Dreams have a way of becoming reality," Nenshi had said to Khenemsu.

"No!" shouted his teacher as he approached the undisciplined student. Nenshi stared at his teacher's piercing eyes. Whispers and fear grew among the other students watching the ordeal unfold.

Khenemsu continued. "Reality exists in what you see. Reality is not measured by dreams but through the stylus you hold in your hand."

The young and rebellious Nenshi became annoyed by his teacher's insistence and stood to challenge him.

"Tell me master, what exactly is reality?" He fought back a calm respectful tone. The grey-haired teacher frowned and answered indirectly but without hesitation.

"The very subject I am teaching is reality."

"You are teaching the use of symbols."

"That is correct," Khenemsu said, convinced he was starting to get through to his pupil. "Symbols are real," he added as he reached to grab a sheet of papyrus. He took his stylus, dipped the tip of the split nib reed into a small cup of black soot. With a swift stroke, he drew two lines.

"Those are a symbol of something," Nenshi pointed. "Alone they have no existence."

Now it was the tutor who became annoyed. He wrinkled his reddened face. A silence, as desolate as the desert, filled the classroom. Students sat motionless, dreading what Khenemsu would do to the defiant student. Khenemsu's contemptuous eyes glared at the outspoken and pugnacious youth who repeated his disparaging argument.

"Symbols are not real. They were created from our imagination. Those lines are not real. They do not exist."

Khenemsu would not be outdone by any student, least of all one who hid behind the façade of nobility. He grabbed Nenshi by the arm and dragged him out of the room.

"Go to your master," he said, incensed by the insinuation of the fallacy of his teachings. "Tell him there is no place for an insolent servant in my class."

Hordekef laughed, as Nenshi retold the event.

"And did I ever tell you what Tehuti had done when I got home?" Nenshi tried to control his laughter.

"No! What happened?"

"He forbade me to leave the house for a full moon and burdened me with chores I didn't even know existed. It was awful. I paid the price."

The incident was not only a lesson for Nenshi, but it also marked the day that Hordekef began to compare himself to him, and aspired to be like him, emulate his confidence. It was the day when the envy began and the resolve to be just like his friend.

Just then a voice echoed from across the room. They didn't know that it came from Tehuti, for the sound reverberated against the stone walls, giving the impression of a bellowing thunderous voice. He stood like a stone pillar with his hands on his hips.

"You tell Bata that you will see me, yet you move with the speed of a tortoise. And don't cower at my presence. You are not a child."

Bata ran into the room, alerted by the sound of Tehuti's cry.

If there was an opportunity for Nenshi to approach Tehuti and discuss his desire to be free, it had been washed away by his master's harsh and sudden appearance. Nenshi also wanted to be alone with Tehuti. Hordekef, in his usual casual way, had not yet left. Nenshi decided to hold back and wait for a better time to approach his master.

Tehuti sauntered down the three marble steps with calculated moves to keep his balance. His knees creaked. He threw a glance at Hordekef.

"Greetings," Tehuti said.

"Good day, noble Tehuti." Hordekef bowed his head.

Tehuti turned to Bata. "Bring us some beer," he demanded. "The throats of these young men are dry, and my mind is tired."

Bata nodded repeatedly and left the room. Tehuti walked past Nenshi and Hordekef who resembled two frightened children about to be scolded by an irate parent. His voice softened.

"You must be tired. How was the hunt?"

Nenshi and Hordekef looked at each other, confused. Their last hunting excursion happened two days ago but Tehuti spoke of it as if they had just returned from it.

"It was good," Nenshi said. It was pointless to correct Tehuti's memory.

"Nenshi struck a gazelle," Hordekef said.

"I'm not surprised," Tehuti smiled.

Bata returned with the drinks, served them and left the room.

Tehuti gulped down mouthfuls of the bitter brew. "Ah ... this beer from the east can loosen one's tongue and make one say regrettable things. However, I'm in my own home and I can do and say as I please. And before this beer softens my memory, I remind you Nenshi that I will take leave for two days to tend to some work in Memphis."

The beer not only loosened his lips but seemed to have given him the energy matched by young men. He appeared to move about without concern of pain or age as he went to sit on his divan.

"I prefer to be here. There's too much uncertainty," Tehuti said.

"What do you mean?" Nenshi asked.

"As I have said before, the state of Egypt is delicate. This is not the time for me to go anywhere. And yet it may be too late to do anything about the country's affairs."

Nenshi's ears perked. If the country's situation was more dire than he was aware of, it now made him wonder what it meant to him. If a decline was imminent, why had Pharaoh concealed it?

Tehuti reached out for more beer. Nenshi gladly obliged, with a gentle grin. Tehuti took a sip, smaller and more controlled and continued.

"Egypt is strong and dominant. It has conquered peoples, taken lands - all with ease."

Leaning forward, Nenshi wondered where the soliloquy was headed.

"Many people believe they are superior to others and so they show no sympathy for those who remain deprived of their land and homes," Tehuti continued. "Politicians, I call them charlatans, prance in the streets to remind everyone about prosperity and about what great warriors they have been."

"You can't deny Egypt's significant progress," Nenshi said.

Tehuti could not refute the accomplishments made by Pharaoh. Egyptian influence expanded into Nubia and beyond, to the east. The Walls of the Prince protected his people from invaders and trade had reached Byblos, Crete and Punt.

Tehuti grinned. "Sometimes our eyes lead us down the wrong path. Successes can make one feel secure and think that there is no end to either success or security."

A pause allowed Tehuti time to drink until the cup was empty. Nenshi and Hordekef looked at each other and shrugged their shoulders.

Tehuti continued. "Pharaoh has reclaimed the desert into a field of blossoms. The Fayum was built - that massive palace at It-Tawy with its three thousand rooms. Perhaps because of this, Pharaoh had decided to move the capital from our great city of Thebes to It-Tawy. But Pharaoh's accomplishments have produced a financial strain on the country. Word is out that he is not well."

"I haven't heard this," Hordekef said.

"Pharaoh may not have made it known publicly but perhaps someone within his circle has loose lips."

"If this is true, who will lead the country?" Nenshi asked.

"Leaders seem to rise out of the right set of circumstances," Tehuti said as he leaned forward. "Opportunity for themselves, that is. More importantly, where will the money come from when it will be most needed? The wind whispers words of threatening invaders, the *heqa khasewet*, the mighty Hyksos, rulers of foreign lands. Ah, but the Walls of the Prince will hold them back, so it is believed. Yet these walls are made of mere bricks and wood, guarded by soldiers whose numbers have decreased. Are the walls strong enough to protect us? I'm not sure they will protect us from the blight of thousands of barbarians or a bunch of churlish sand dwellers. I have worked too hard for my successes. I am not about to hand everything over to colonizers or invaders."

"If what you say is true, what does it mean for us?" Nenshi asked. His fears over the state of the land were playing out as he had imagined.

"We must remain vigilant, be prepared for anything. If necessary, move to where it is safer, perhaps Memphis or It-Tawy. Who knows,

Pharaoh may suddenly have a revelation, see the deficiencies of his ways and restore the country before he goes to the other world."

Nenshi's jaw clenched. It seemed that now was a good time to speak about his freedom. But he needed to speak with Tehuti alone. Hordekef was still there. He might interrupt, add his opinion, albeit for a good reason and thwart any chance at convincing Tehuti.

The thought of what could happen was unsettling. Nenshi mused. If the barbarian hordes eventually attacked, what would happen to him? A slave at the hands of invaders will change everything. And then who would take care of his master? Would Tehuti not fight for his home, the house he had built? What if Tehuti died before all this occurred, would Nenshi be servant to another master? If so, as Hordekef had said, Sia would find out from others that Nenshi was not a free man. The deceit would shatter their relationship.

Tehuti walked to the window. He managed to control his steps, not from the effects from his declining years but from the libation. It now replaced the energy with fatigue. "I can't drink as much as I used to," he said. His eyes were reddened by the elixir.

Nenshi and Hordekef chuckled. Tehuti smiled. "Yes, keep smiling and laughing. Life does not have enough of either."

The empty cups peeled back the hardness in Tehuti. It brought back the gentle side that Nenshi hadn't seen in some time. Tehuti stood in front of the window. As the sun behind him began its descent, it cast a lasting glow around the feeble form.

Tehuti turned to the two puzzled young men. Words of encouragement to face an uncertain future was all he could offer.

"Always be on your guard but don't let fear overcome your thoughts and actions. We don't know what lies before us and don't let this weigh you down. We cannot solve the country's problems. We can only control our own actions."

He walked over to Nenshi. "Your tutor Soreb had taught me a poem." Nenshi smiled with fond memories of his sagacious tutor.

"Recite it to us," Nenshi implored. Tehuti smiled and cleared his throat to deliver the poem.

Do not sleep in fear of what tomorrow may bring.
When the sun rises, what will the day be like?
No one knows!
What men say will be cast aside,
But the actions of the god remain.
Do not think of yourself without fault.
Do not endeavour to quarrel or defend.
For all that is wrong and all that is right,
The god knows.

For a moment the poem lifted Nenshi's hopes. He could hear Soreb's voice in his mind echoing hidden truths once shared, never lost. Reciting the poem also seemed to soften Tehuti's demeanour. It was the opportunity Nenshi needed.

"Master, I wish to speak with you," Nenshi said and glanced over to Hordekef and tilted his head to the side in a gesture for him to leave. But Tehuti interrupted.

"Not now. Unfortunately, I have little time to get ready. You'll have to wait until I return from Memphis."

Another opportunity strangled by misfortune. Nenshi had no choice. Sia would have to wait too, he thought. Once she knew he was a servant and his master had agreed to grant his freedom, she would be more accepting and forgiving. Or would she?

Chapter 4

WHILE WAITING FOR TEHUTI TO return from Memphis, Nenshi passed the time ruminating how to approach his master. Knowing Tehuti well enough, there was only one way – to be direct. It was also during this time that Nenshi had not seen Sia. He couldn't stay away from her forever. A fire wanes and eventually dies if the embers are not kept alive. He was excited to meet her again in the market, as they had planned.

Nenshi and Hordekef meandered through the passages, some narrow, some wide enough to parade animals for sale. There was a different mood among the merchants. Nenshi noticed the acrid atmosphere. An unsettled sensation lingered, like a haunting image from a nightmare. The acrimony spread like the annual flooding of the River Iteru - the sorrowful tears of Isis for her dead husband Osiris.

But Nenshi could not let things go unsaid. At the very least to make sure Hordekef was aware of it all.

"Something is very different today," Nenshi said.

Hordekef surveyed the surroundings. "All I see is the same greedy merchants selling the same worthless merchandise to the same rude buyers." He grinned and then pushed a short man aside who stood in his way. The man turned and raised his hand to strike but realized the difference in size and strength. He casually submitted to the titan and moved aside.

"Look around," Nenshi said. "Tehuti may be right, the *heqa khasewet* may be closer than we think."

Hordekef laughed. "You are obsessed with this notion of invaders." He refused to let Nenshi's preoccupation ruin his day. "If they're as close as you suggest, the marketplace would be empty."

"Don't you see there aren't as many merchants."

"That doesn't mean an attack is imminent."

Even though there were fewer merchants, the market was still busy. A sea of sellers and buyers overflowed the narrow paths. Merchandise of every kind, from near and far, strewn on tables, hung on ropes, were on display to attract customers. Merchants added their own special calling, chanted or yelled, to solicit a sale.

Nonetheless, Nenshi remained vigilant. Unlike raids, common in small towns, he knew attacks in Thebes were never anticipated. And like many others, he had been lulled in the belief that the Walls of the Prince, there to protect the people, were impenetrable.

"This is the perfect stage for an attack," he said. "A large unsuspecting crowd is fodder for mayhem." But he was hardly heard, drowned by squealing flutes, competing with thunderous drumbeats. He shook his head and motioned to keep walking.

"There she is." Nenshi smiled. Twenty paces in front of him was Sia.

"Thank the gods," Hordekef said. "Now I don't have to listen to you talk about attacks. I thought you were going to meet her in her garden, as you have secretly done before."

"Not today. I prefer the market."

"Where we could be attacked?" Hordekef laughed. The irony did not go undetected. "And may I remind you that Sia still doesn't know you're a servant."

Nenshi had no response, only silent agreement.

"You told me that you're in love with her. I hope you're not deceiving her or yourself. I hope she's not just the spoil of another hunt."

Nenshi's fear of being rejected was greater than the fear of telling her he's a servant. "You're right," he said. "I'll tell her."

Hordekef smiled. "Now go before she disappears into the crowd." He rested a reassuring hand on Nenshi's shoulder and then reached into his pouch. "Take these," he said. "Just in case you need to buy something. You're running out of things to barter."

Nenshi marched towards Sia. Every beat of his heart, quickened his longing to be with her and yet it also questioned his judgement, cloaked by emotion. The risk of being caught increased with every encounter. The infallibility of young love showed no boundaries.

As he got closer, he stopped when a young boy approached Sia. Frail and gaunt, the young beggar held out his hand. She gawked at his desperation, unmoved by his plea. She placed the back of her hand on the boy's arm and nudged him aside. The boy, too weak to keep his balance, fell. Sia tilted her head, imparting a look of regret. She took a step towards him but then, as if embarrassed by her action, she turned away.

Nenshi's eyes widened, his jaw dropped. Perhaps Sia, eager to meet him, had overlooked the young pauper. But he knew that the elite demeaned the less fortunate. As witness to both servitude and privilege, he had become intolerant of the mistreatment of the impoverished. Now he couldn't help but wonder if she even shared the same empathy as his for the poor and oppressed. If she were to discover that he was a servant, would she treat him with the same denigration? Watching the boy's neglect left an indefinable impression, one he chose to keep to himself.

Nenshi lifted the frail boy to his feet with no effort. He weighed less than what his meagre body suggested. The boy held up his arm, afraid of being struck. Nenshi reached into his pouch, pulled out a coin and placed it into the boy's skeletal hands.

In a gentle voice, Nenshi said, "When you put your hand out for offerings, keep your distance. That way you can't get knocked down."

The boy smiled, thankful for the advice, even more grateful for the gold coin.

Nenshi ran to catch up to Sia. She stood by a stand that displayed an array of earthenware jars, pots and beer vessels. There were funerary gifts made to look like the gods, complemented by a collection of animal-shaped objects. The merchant made it a habit to set up at the same location every day.

Nenshi was excited, in eager anticipation of being with Sia. He kept his eyes on her, through every step, as he weaved his way among the crowd.

"Finally, you're here," she said with a smile that glowed with delight like a blossomed jasmine. She stepped forward and wrapped her arms around him.

"Did you come alone?" Nenshi asked.

"No. My friends are at the other end looking to buy jewellery. It seems that's all they want to do."

"That'll keep them busy. Are you hungry? Can you smell that? Roasted duck."

She inhaled the scent. "Are you sure it's not just burning wood?"

"Did you ever roast duck on a skewer?"

"No. I just eat it when it's brought to me."

"One day, I'll roast one for you."

"That's a task for servants."

Nenshi forced a smile. Just the sound of the word *servant* passing through her lips made him question their bond. They have met enough times for the infatuation to carry them away into a world of illogical passion. His desire to be with her every moment, at any cost, cast a delusion. But he didn't care. His love for her would take on any risk, including to tell her about his status.

Hordekef was right. Nenshi had been taking too many chances and Sia needed to know that he was a servant before she heard it from others. Yet his thoughts were still clouded with doubt, with the fear of being rejected outright. What if she changed her mind about him? She may be infuriated with his deception and have him beaten. The scars would remind him of his empty and miserable dishonest life. Yet he knew he needed to tell her everything.

They followed the trail of smoke that led to a spit. Nenshi held Sia's hand squeezing it, gently tugging her along. "Is everything all right? Why are we walking so fast?" she asked.

"I haven't eaten all day."

Her eyes narrowed in disbelief. She tugged back on his grip and stopped walking. Her intuition was not to be discounted.

"What's on your mind?" The corners of her eyes wrinkled, wondering, searching for an answer.

As Nenshi moved closer, the throb of anxiety replaced love's pulse. Waiting was no longer an option. The inescapable truth had to be revealed. He took a deep breath and looked into her eyes. He felt the heavy beat of his heart trying to burst out from his chest. He had repeated the words over and over again in his mind and was now ready to deliver them.

Suddenly, screams drowned his heartbeat and jolted him. His eyes darted in every direction, overwhelmed by the cries of women and children who scurried in panic. Men grabbed their sacks of purchased items and dashed out of sight. Merchants collected their wares and haphazardly packed them away. Bedlam ensued. A voice yelled, "Run for your lives ... we're being attacked!"

Sia's face filled with fear. Nenshi pointed to a path. An escape. A grip of her hand and a tug was just enough to start moving.

Unrelenting screams pierced their ears and awakened a primal need for safety. They fought through the hysteria in search of shelter. Terror overshadowed the frenzy. Men charged in Nenshi's direction. A wave of blades cut through the air; bows prepared to release its arrows. He put his arm around Sia. Together they crouched to the ground, ready for the onslaught.

Several attackers stepped closer towards Nenshi. Their clothes and features told him they were not Egyptian. Could they be the invaders Tehuti had described? If so, perhaps it was just the beginning, a test by the small group to determine the strength of those that one day could be conquered.

Nenshi slid his hand down to his waist. His fingers traced the form of his dagger, the only weapon he had to stave off the barbarians. On the ground, several bows and arrows were abandoned by their merchant owner. Instinctively he picked up a bow and a few arrows and strapped them over his shoulder.

Then three men ran towards him. If only Hordekef was here to help, he thought. The men carried long thick clubs and swung them with stern intention hitting defenceless men and women in their path. One of the attackers moved to strike a woman from behind. He raised his club over his head. Nenshi reached for an arrow. With one quick move, he placed it in position and released it. It whistled through the air and struck the man in the shoulder. Sia stood motionless, her jaw dropped.

The other two attackers, alarmed to see their fellow warrior fall to the ground like a sack of grain, raised their clubs. They let out a war cry, pointed at Nenshi and ran towards him. The injured man groaned as he pressed his hand on his shoulder. Blood oozed between his fingers. Nenshi took another bow and squeezed it in his hand. His arms tightened; his muscles bulged. It was enough to scare the soldier away. Nenshi relaxed his grip.

Sia, frantic, turned in every direction. Nenshi remained calm. He grabbed her hand and pulled her away. They went behind tents to an opening away from the confusion. Here, out in the open, he was alone to defend himself and protect Sia. The men moved in. Nenshi guided her to a wooden pillar used to support a tent that fell during the attack.

"Stay here," he ordered. She nodded, repeatedly.

Nenshi stood between the two men as they circled around him waiting for an opportunity to overtake him. One man ran forward from behind with his club ready to strike.

"Nenshi ... behind you!" Sia screamed.

He turned with the speed of a leopard and positioned himself between the two men. The other attacker grinned. His hand crawled towards his hip to pull out his sword from its sheath. The louder the scrapping sounded, the bigger the grin became. Meanwhile, the man with the club prepared to lunge forward.

Nenshi glanced over his shoulder and saw Sia pick up the leg of a broken table from the ground and moved behind the assailant. Her face tightened as she raised the piece of wood as high as she could and with one swift motion, she hit the man on the head. Like a falcon struck in flight, he dropped to the ground.

One man remained. His weapon, a sword, was more perilous than a club. Nenshi glanced down at his bow and arrow. They were of no use. The assailant was too close for Nenshi to shoot an arrow so he pulled out his dagger. They sparred back and forth taking swipes at each another. The man landed a hit with his sword and cut Nenshi on his left arm. Blood soaked his sleeve. The man lunged and Nenshi stepped back. The man pounced again. Nenshi grabbed the man's arm and squeezed it as hard as he could. With his other hand he pierced his dagger deep into the man's chest. The lifeless body fell with a thud.

Sia ran to Nenshi and put her arms around him. He grunted. She stepped back.

"So much blood!"

"I'll be all right." He tore off the other sleeve and wrapped it around his arm. "There, that should do it, until I get home. Are you hurt?"

"No."

"Thank you for saving my life."

"You saved mine."

"I guess we saved each other."

They smiled. They kissed. Unlike their other kisses, this one was long, reflecting a passionate hunger for the love just threatened. They held each other tightly, the warmth of their bodies pressing, not wanting to let go. Their lips parted long enough for Nenshi to look into her eyes, seeing the reflection of her heart. She then closed them, inviting another kiss. With a tender touch, Nenshi's lips met hers. Their mouths began to sway like a gentle wave coming to shore. They savoured the immersion of their love.

The war cries had stopped. Out of nowhere Hordekef appeared. Dishevelled, with his hands on his hips, he seemed amused by the devastation. Tents flattened, looters ran frantically, women screamed and two dead men lay at the feet of a couple, kissing.

"Is this what you do amidst all this commotion?" Hordekef asked. "I've been looking for you."

"Your timing is impeccable," Nenshi said.

"It appears you have done all right without me. Your arm looks better than those men."

The turmoil had subsided and Sia and her friends were well on their way home. Tehuti's prognostication about invaders proved true and Nenshi, falling in love with a free woman, made matters worse. His yearning to determine his own road in life matched his burning desire to love.

Thoughts of his past surged and took hold. If only Meti had survived, things might have been different and there would not have been a need for Tehuti to bring Nenshi into his home. If his own parents were still alive things might have been different and he would still be with them today.

The life of a peasant, educated only by hard work and the need to survive, seemed more appealing than a tranquil life guarded by the wealth that surrounded him. His new life with Tehuti had shaped him into what he was today, a noble servant. But it was time to take hold of the fire within and draw on its energy. His tenacity, a trait perhaps from one of his parents and his impulsive ways, the yields of entitlement, were enough to seek what he wanted most. The emptiness returned. The angst prolonged. It was now time to ask his master for his freedom - to demand it.

Chapter 5

IN HIS WORKROOM, DEEP IN thought, the aging architect stood over his oversized granite worktable. His fragile hands rested on its smooth finish to support his weight. It wasn't long before stiffness set and, as he had become accustomed to its call for relief, he reached behind him and placed his hand on the small of his back. A good stretch was just enough to loosen the tightness. He leaned over the table. On it was a long papyrus roll, weighed down with small statues to prevent it from curling at the ends.

Nenshi's eyes dampened, his face wilted, as he witnessed his master at work. Standing by the entrance, he wondered how much longer Tehuti would be able to endure the long hours he had devoted to his projects. But now there was something more important at hand. He walked into the room.

"Master, I apologize for intruding. May I speak with you?" The trembling voice drew attention. Tehuti peered up, unmoved by the request, he returned to his work.

"Master." Nenshi raised his voice.

"Yes ... yes ... just a moment." Tehuti swung his finger back and forth, pointing, across the sketched papyrus. "Look at this. What do you think?"

For a moment Nenshi thought Tehuti was avoiding him, intuitively sensing the inevitable. He remained patient. For a moment, it was safer to let Tehuti bask in the glory of his work, than to challenge him with his demand for freedom.

"Well? What do you think?" Tehuti repeated.

It was one thing to look at lines on a sheet of papyrus, another to visualize the completed work. Nenshi didn't know what to think. Tehuti went on to describe the mansion, proud of his latest design. In his mind, it was practical to incorporate the key elements of an estate all under one roof.

"Your projects have always intrigued me." Nenshi said. Eager to discuss the reason for his interruption, he kept his remarks brief so as not to engage in long conversation. Tehuti took his measuring stick and pointed at his work, to the design of the estate's supporting pillars.

"I designed the peaks of the columns to be in the shape of fully opened papyrus buds. I want to project that when the sun god is overhead, his beams are productive of life and energy."

Nenshi now regretted coming to his workroom and wondered if he should have waited until Tehuti was resting on his divan instead.

"And look ... here. These are six thin pillars," Tehuti continued. "A canopy is draped over them to shade those beneath it from the hot sun. Even I would enjoy sitting here, breathing the sweet air of the north wind. I would drink beer while admiring the flowers and trees in the garden." He smiled and raised his head. "So, what is it that you want? And what happened to your arm?"

The sudden shift caught Nenshi by surprise. He had forgotten about his injury. He put his hand to his arm, wrapped with a fresh cloth. Some blood still leaked from the cut.

"I was helping to remove a diseased tree and a branch struck me," Nenshi said, hoping it was a convincing alibi.

Tehuti nodded. "Sometimes the unexpected can scar us for life. So I take it you have not come to talk about your hunting expeditions or fallen branches."

Nenshi took a deep breath. His heart pounded in his throat. He chose his words carefully.

"Master ... I wish to speak to you about my status." There was no need to skirt around his purpose. As he remembered, a direct approach with Tehuti was always best. He continued. "I'm grateful and fortunate for the life I have with you. Most servants can only dream about it."

Tehuti's eyes drooped with waned energy. Nenshi's tone, resolute in his conviction, was evidence of an imminent plea.

"Despite everything I have, I don't have freedom." Nenshi paused for a moment. The simple expression said everything. The saliva in his mouth wasn't enough to wash away the dryness. The tightness in his chest did not fade. Then he added, "I respectfully ask you to grant me independence."

Tehuti put down his measuring stick. A somber gaze overshadowed his proud moment as an architect. He walked over to the other side of the table.

"Freedom. What does it mean to you?" he asked.

Nenshi had no interest in a debate. A simple yes or no would have sufficed. Yet he reflected for a moment, searching for the words that would capture his thoughts, to satisfy the question.

"Freedom is knowing who I am, not what others think I am." He paused to gauge his master's reaction. The corners of Tehuti's mouth curled but Nenshi didn't know whether this was a smile or a sneer. He continued. "As a boy, a young servant, I couldn't distinguish the difference between who I was and whom I was supposed to be. As I grew older, I struggled with what I had been given and what I didn't have. Soreb tried to help me through my turmoil. *You must make your own decisions*, he would say. *Solve your own problems*. But I can't do that without the freedom to act as I will, as I choose."

Tehuti walked away from the table, towards the window that overlooked his garden. Before he had turned to face the garden, Nenshi caught a glimpse of Tehuti smiling. "Soreb had led you down a righteous path," Tehuti said. "It appears the fruits of his guidance have been fulfilled."

"I'm grateful to have had him as my tutor."

Nenshi went to stand next to Tehuti and he too looked out the window. It was always a welcoming distraction for Nenshi during situations of uncertainty. A light breeze pushed the fragrance of blue lotuses towards him. He wondered if Tehuti knew that this day would come. If he did, he could never have prepared for it.

"We take freedom for granted," Tehuti said. "At times, we even abuse it. Are you ready to accept the responsibilities of being free? Are you honest with yourself to want this freedom?"

Nenshi had never given thought about the misuse of freedom. He needed to be free in order to keep away from threatening invaders; to carve a life not affected by his country's tenuous state; and, to be with Sia. These thoughts swirled in his mind, all knotted in servitude. His future lay in the winds, unless he took control of his life.

He thought about what Tehuti had asked him – if he was ready to accept the responsibilities of being free. Nenshi believed that the only obligation in freedom was to make mistakes from which its lessons helped in life. In servitude mistakes brought the master's wrath.

He took a deep breath. The anxiety lifted; his confidence regained. His eyes, clear as the azure sky, demanded the resolve he had longed.

"Master, the time has come for me to be free."

But concession did not come easy. "I will consider it. I make no promises," Tehuti said. "Whatever the decision, it will be for the right reasons."

Consideration was a rejection. Nenshi scowled, expected more. Thoughts spun in his troubled mind. Running away might have been easier. But he remained calm and chose not to push for an explanation. Instead he accepted Tehuti's choice, for now.

"There are many deserving reasons to grant you freedom," Tehuti said, offering words of comfort. "I don't want to cast you into the world with newfound privilege only to have it drag you to where many have gone. Freedom is to be cherished and used for goodness and not as a tool to enslave others. This may sound strange to you, coming from someone who has servants. But as you know my servants help me do the things I cannot. They are not pawns, whose dignity and brute strength have been slowly battered for the sake of selfish desires. I want to be sure you are ready." He then smiled and embraced Nenshi. The trembling arms of an aging father did not want to let go.

Nenshi left the room, disappointed but not without hope. He was one step closer to getting his freedom. Now it would be easier to tell Sia the truth.

It was early morning. Nenshi hurried to the marketplace in the hope of a rendezvous with Sia but she wasn't there. After her experience with the skirmish, she may have been afraid or even forbidden to go.

He left in a hurry, headed to the only other place where they agreed to meet - in her garden, a most daring yet familiar encounter. They began meeting here since the beginning of the lunar month, the inundation of the River Iteru. Now, having past the time of the river's low water, the trysts outnumbered the seasons.

Nenshi peered through the gates. Among the shady trees an array of flowers surrounded a rectangular pond, stocked with fish and water lilies. Roses, irises, jasmine, and small yellow chrysanthemums emitted their intoxicating fragrance.

Encircled by nature's beauty, Sia sauntered, humming an old song her surrogate mother had taught her. She bent down, every now and then, choosing flowers for a bouquet. It all made for a perfect secluded and romantic place for lovers to meet.

Nenshi rustled a bush to get Sia's attention. Her head lifted. Perhaps it was a bird. The sound repeated. She knit your brow, realized it was Nenshi and went to open the gate. She opened it just enough for him to squeeze through.

"What are you doing here?" She scanned the garden.

"I didn't see you at the market." The expectation was clear.

"We never planned to meet there today. Is everything all right?"

Nenshi wrenched his hands, clammy, as awkward as his presence. A sudden breeze shook the leaves from a nearby shrub and startled him.

"Are we alone?"

"Yes ... I think so."

"You're not sure? Where's your father?"

"I haven't seen him this morning. He may be at the quarry. Come, let's sit over there." She pointed to a stone bench, secluded, off the garden path. "You surprised me." She placed her hand on his. "I was thinking about what had happened in the market."

"You were brave to do what you did."

"You mean to hit that man on the head? Sometimes there's a fine line between bravery and an urgent need to act."

"I never looked at it that way but yes, you're right."

Nenshi put his arm around her. She may have noticed the slight quiver from his hand on her shoulder. He was too nervous to realize it himself but the trembles in the pit of his stomach could not be overlooked. Each shake tightened the entangled fibres between the knowledge of his status and his growing love. Only a kiss could calm the tremors. Sia welcomed his lips press against hers. When the moist touch separated, their eyes opened and locked.

"There's something I need to tell you," he said. She pulled back, puzzled, the same look she had the other day when Nenshi was about to reveal his secret but, without warning, the market was attacked. "You must keep this between us ... for now," Nenshi said.

Sia frowned. The unforeseen visit came with unexpected news. Her stare implored an explanation. To meet in her father's garden came with irresponsible risk.

Nenshi took a deep breath. He bit his lip to stop the shake. The fear of rejection was something he wasn't used to, a trepidation that left him wondering how she would react once he revealed his secret. He put his arms on her shoulders and gazed into her eyes. They pleaded for him to speak, to explain himself. Another deep breath injected courage, ready to tell her everything. But the sound of footsteps broke his thoughts. A voice called out. A housemaid.

"Sia ... Sia."

Nenshi quickly crouched behind a henna bush and managed to hide behind countless pink flowers.

"Sia ... there you are." A housemaid appeared out of nowhere. "Your father is looking for you, to speak with you, right away."

"My father? He's at the house?" Her voice pitched higher; her face bent with fear.

"Where else would he be? Are you not feeling well?" The housemaid surveyed the area. A simple garden snake would cause the fear in Sia's eyes. But there was no snake.

"I'm fine. I just thought ... well ... it doesn't matter," she said as she moved to stand between the maid and the henna bush. She pointed to flowers further down the path. "Help me pick them. And here ... take these," handing her the bunch she had previously collected.

As they walked towards the house, Nenshi slipped out from his hiding and fled. The shrub rustled. The housemaid turned and took a long suspicious look. Sia kept walking, humming.

Nenshi walked alone. His plan was thwarted by an intrusive housemaid. The pleasure of the tryst emptied, replaced by a failure about what he was about to tell Sia. Now the urgency to let her know his secret grew stronger. The past needed to be explained; how he had been transformed from servitude to nobility. He needed to tell her that he had asked his master for his freedom. But since she knew none of this, he felt like a coward. The agony in misery had overcome him. If she found out from someone else, she might reject him for being deceitful. She would be humiliated for allowing him, someone from a lower class, to kiss her and exchange words of adoration. Would the love between them be enough to overlook his station in life? The sleepless night brought no resolve, yet the next day would reveal Tehuti's decision.

Chapter 6

A FRANTIC AND SWEATY BATA waited as Nenshi and Hordekef walked up the stairs to the estate's entrance. Out of breath, he resembled an impatient mother fussing over her children. As he followed them into the house, Hordekef chuckled. Bata flung a scowl at him and held his tongue in obvious displeasure.

Turning his attention to Nenshi, Bata asked, "Where have you been? Master Tehuti wishes to speak with you. He's in his study with Intef."

"Intef? What's he doing here?"

"Who's Intef?" Hordekef asked.

"A friend of Tehuti's. A litigator. Wait here. I'll be right back."

Hordekef sighed and made himself comfortable on a cushioned chair.

Nenshi walked to the study, wondering why Tehuti wanted to see him in the presence of a litigator. Did it have something to do with the attack in the market? If so, Tehuti may have decided to ensure his legal matters were in order, all in preparation to leave the city. Nenshi wondered if his penitence for obsessing over invaders and matters of the country may have caused Tehuti to act needlessly. The remorse reawakened the churning in his stomach, consuming any hope to be set free.

Stopping just outside the room's entrance, Nenshi overheard voices. The echo that swirled in the hallway made it difficult to understand the conversation. He walked in.

"Master Tehuti, forgive me for interrupting but Bata said that you wish to see me."

"Ah ... Nenshi ... come in, come in. You remember my friend Intef?"

"Yes, I do." Nenshi turned to Intef and bowed his head to hide the apprehension in his eyes. Intef smiled. As Nenshi looked up he noticed papyrus sheets, a stylus and ink pouches on the table. Intef casually moved to obstruct Nenshi's view.

Tehuti continued. "The other day we spoke about the possibility of your freedom. I spent countless hours thinking about it. I shared my thoughts and concerns with Intef."

The corner of Nenshi's eyes crinkled. He wondered if the papyrus folios were more than just about Tehuti's personal matters. Litigators can be convincing, Nenshi thought. Who knows what Tehuti's advisor has led him to believe?

Nenshi couldn't help but remember when some time ago Tehuti had need of advice over the commissioning of the design of a mansion. Shortly after the work had begun, it had stopped and the project abandoned. The proprietor had told Tehuti that he did not have sufficient funds to continue and asked Tehuti to relinquish the design to him until such time he could resume work. Tehuti agreed. Shortly after, the owner handed Tehuti's drawings to another architect, who made slight modifications and work resumed to build the mansion.

Tehuti was never compensated for his work and sought guidance for recourse. At the time of Tehuti's inquiry, Intef was not in Thebes and assigned an associate to advise Tehuti. The associate litigator had told Tehuti there was nothing he could do. Even though the modifications were minor, it was best to let things go, for it would take years to contest the matter through the courts. Tehuti submitted to the ill-advised counsel. When Intef had finally returned and heard about the resolution, he was disappointed and embarrassed that his associate did not even attempt a compromise.

Nenshi questioned a litigator's ability to advise.

Tehuti took a deep breath and smiled, a rare smile in recent days. "There comes a time in a man's life when he realizes there are fewer days ahead of him than those that have gone by."

The look in his eyes, the tone in his voice, caused Nenshi to rethink his purpose. He looked at Intef and then back at Tehuti. "What are you saying? Are you not well?" Concern for himself had now become secondary.

"No ... no. It's not that," Tehuti replied. "Oh, I admit I am not young but there is still plenty of life left in me. Don't you think, Intef?"

"Sometimes I wish I had the energy you exude," Intef said. His voice was low, calm, friendly.

Nenshi was relieved. "I'm glad for your good health although at times I worry about you when I see you move slower than usual."

"I have my good days and bad ones," Tehuti smiled.

Again, Nenshi glanced at Intef and then asked Tehuti, "Why have you asked to see me?" If it didn't have to do with Tehuti's health nor perhaps his legal matters, what need was there for a servant to meet in the presence of a litigator? Nenshi fidgeted with his shirt sleeve.

"It's time to put my needs aside and reflect on the desires of others." Tehuti paused and cleared his throat.

Nenshi noticed his master's eyes begin to swell with tears. He remained patient, waited for an answer to his quest for freedom.

"Nenshi ... I have decided to grant you your freedom," Tehuti said, as a joyful tear rolled down his cheek.

Nenshi's eyes widened, almost bulged like a bullfrog staring up from a pond. The dark cloud that loomed over him for days on end, lurked no longer. His eyes too filled with tears. His mind spun with elation, almost in disbelief in what he had just heard.

"Master ... I have no words to express how I feel."

"That's unusual, coming from you," Tehuti said. "Save your words for others when you share the good news. I can see in your eyes, the joy that is in your heart. I can't give you this house, nor my wealth or my belongings but I can give you freedom which is worth more than all my possessions."

Nenshi reached out and put his arms around Tehuti and whispered in his ear, "Thank you."

Servitude would soon vanish, leaving no trace in its wake. He would be free at last.

"Master, forgive me for being so forward but when will this happen?"

"Soon, I hope. And you won't need to call me master any longer."

Nenshi fought to hold back the tears that would wash away the anguish of a life not of his choosing. Nobility provided benefits from which he reaped and yet it was the same lifestyle that caused his struggle. He was anchored, for so long, at a crossroad, without the power to choose his direction. Now he would be freed from the shackles of a life confined within the walls of servitude. Now his path, wide and endless, was his to discover.

He looked at Tehuti, seeing both happiness and sorrow. As Nenshi straddled between freedom and servitude, so did Tehuti between the fear of losing another loved one and doing what was righteous. It was better to have freed him in life than in death.

"The petition is ready," Intef said.

"Now I understand your presence here," Nenshi said.

"I am glad to be of service to a good friend."

Nenshi then turned to Tehuti and once again embraced him - father and son, who not of flesh and blood, have given of each other, to each other and were bonded by their hearts.

"I must tell Hordekef!" Nenshi's face lit up like the night sky flooded with a sea of stars. "After all, as you said, I must share the good news with others." Like a roaring lion, from the top of lungs, he called out for Hordekef. He ran into the room.

"What is it? Are we being attacked? Is everyone safe? Tehuti ... has he fallen?"

Nenshi laughed at the comical hysteria. Hordekef's face reddened from the embarrassment of his display of panic. Nenshi then told him about Tehuti's decision. Hordekef's face stirred with excitement. As Tehuti and Intef were discussing the last additions to the scroll, Hordekef leaned over to Nenshi. "I told you this would happen." He then cried out, "We must celebrate! The tavern awaits our valued patronage."

"Not just yet," Tehuti said. "Intef is putting the final touches to the petition."

Nenshi impatiently clasped his hands while Tehuti added his sign to the plea. Intef waited until it dried and then rolled and tied the papyrus with a twine made of reed. Proudly he held it with both hands as if Egypt's declaration of peace with its neighbouring enemy had just been read to the populace. With a stern voice and legal expression, he cautioned the young men.

"I know you're both excited about this good news. But neither of you must speak of it to anyone until a decree has been made by the courts. Do you understand?"

They didn't understand. They shrugged their shoulders. Foreheads, wrinkled with lines of confusion, entwined within each other. Faces pleaded for an explanation.

"The courts are filled with all kinds of protests these days," Intef continued. "Once I hear back that the scribes have received and registered the plea, I need to find out who will preside over the hearing. Knowing if it's a favourable or unfavourable Vizier will help me with my approach, how to present the plea. There have been times when petitions like this have been intentionally routed into the hands of those whose prejudiced minds have no desire to set men free, regardless of the circumstances. Litigators have been surprised by decisions and if they had known who was to make the verdict, they would have been better prepared. I trust no one in the courts. Now do you understand?"

Nenshi and Hordekef nodded. Tehuti reinforced the demand. "I want both of you to promise you will not say a word. Is that clear Nenshi?"

"Yes."

"Hordekef?"

"Yes ... yes ... I promise."

Intef smiled, confident that his plan would not be made public.

"I must go now and take these to the courts. I hope my weary bones can move fast enough before the scribes leave for the day. Once they prepare the petition for its hearing I can plea the case in the Audience Hall."

"I can take them," Hordekef said. "It's on my way home. I can get there in no time."

Nenshi put his hand on Hordekef's shoulder and nodded in agreement. Tehuti looked to Intef who shook his head, reluctant to agree. But the day had been exhausting. He reconsidered.

"Very well, take these and go." Intef handed the petition to Hordekef. "Remember, not a word to anyone."

Hordekef tucked the rolls under his arm and dashed out the door but not before he finished the last of the beer in his cup.

Nenshi's face exploded with the smiles of a thousand children. Tehuti extended his hand to Intef. "You have always been a trusted friend."

"May Renenutet bestow her fortunes upon both of you," Intef said. He then collected the rest of his belongings and bid farewell.

Nenshi walked into the salon to find Tehuti sitting on his divan smiling in the comfort of his decision. The sun's light began to fade.

"It's getting late," Tehuti said, as he stood. "You must go and get ready to accompany me to Anpu's house."

Nenshi tilted his head back, his palms felt clammy. Another surprise, yet of no lesser significance. Nenshi often accompanied Tehuti on many social occasions but this was different. This meant being in the same room with the woman he loved and with her father, who knew nothing of their secret affair. Although he looked forward to seeing Sia, what made matters worse was that she still didn't know that he was a servant. If things unravelled, the possibility for irreversible repercussions was waiting to run wild.

"Did you say Anpu's house? This evening?" Nenshi asked, as he wiped his hands on his sleeves.

"Yes. Don't waste time. Go get ready."

"What's the occasion?"

"Anpu and I have been commissioned to work on an estate. I'm designing the house and he is providing the statues. He needs to examine my plans to make sure the stone carvings are the appropriate sizes for the rooms, terraces and entrances. And I also need to see his plans. Now go. We've been invited for dinner."

Nenshi had no choice but to obey. Murky thoughts swirled about what it would be like to be in the same room with Sia, her father and Tehuti. He felt like an unneeded colour on a tomb's wall.

Hordekef approached the entrance to where Viziers' scribes worked. He held the rolled petition close to him. A sense of power and control lifted his spirit. In all the years he had tried to be better than his friend, to prove his worth, there had never been a more opportune situation than what had just presented itself.

There was no resistance from Nenshi to deal with, no prowess with a bow and arrow to overcome. The edges of his eyes curled with a satisfaction to be had. Envy seeped through his veins again. Like the vindictive thoughts of a demoralized prisoner, he mused over the idea not to deliver the petition.

Perhaps I should keep them for a day or two, he thought. Nenshi has been a servant all his life. Another day would not make a difference.

As he squeezed the petition, just enough to confirm his control, he could now demonstrate that he was better than his friend, a mere servant. The power to delay delivery would prove to himself that he was no longer second best. He tucked the petition tightly under his arm and walked home.

Chapter 7

AT THE GATES OF ANPU'S house a servant greeted the guests. It was a familiar sight - a familiar garden filled with secrets of lovers' encounters. The usual scent surrounded Nenshi. The display of an extravagant variety of flowers, whose fragrance engulfed him every time he met her, once again played on his senses with the intoxication of love. He cast an eye at the fishpond, flaunted with every imaginable fish. Their eyes, just below the surface, seemed to gawk at the familiar young man as he walked by.

Once inside the house, another servant led the guests to the greeting room. Nenshi scanned the room, several times, thief-like. He wiped his clammy palms on his shirt.

"Are you not feeling well?" A puzzled Tehuti threw a stare to examine a bewildered face.

"I am well. I was just admiring the handcrafted vases."

The alibi wasn't convincing. Tehuti shook his head. Nenshi shrugged his shoulders.

They were led to another room where an overweight Anpu sat in a high-backed chair carved from wood. He struggled to rise and greet his guests. An uncaring face forced a smile as he raised his hand in salutation.

Tehuti introduced Nenshi, by name only. Anpu's cordial gesture invited Tehuti to sit on a thickly cushioned divan, but he gave Nenshi a cold nod, merely to acknowledge his presence. It proved that Anpu shunned at the undignified practice of an invited guest taking the liberty to be accompanied by someone from their household. Nenshi's awkward and nervous smile added to Anpu's annoyance.

Nenshi understood his place and remained standing while the two statesmen exchanged pleasantries. He fidgeted with his shirt sleeve and with the sash around his waist. He noticed Anpu watching him as he would a suspicious thief. It confirmed the uneasiness Nenshi felt whenever he visited Sia in her garden. He was certain that he had been seen by one of Anpu's servants who in turn reported it to his master.

The architect and the sculptor eventually got around to discuss the design of the house to be built overlooking the River Iteru.

"My designs for the statues are complete," Anpu said. "They are the best that I have ever made. My preferred one is that of Pharaoh which will be placed at the mansion's entrance. It's a fitting symbol."

Tehuti nodded. "I understand," he said. "I have no doubt your plans reflect the embodiment of our king and the mansion's owner. But I will need to see your designs to ensure they complement mine."

Anpu frowned. He was not used to having his statues questioned. "I will have the plans delivered to you. They will convince you of their merit."

It was an unlikely collaboration between two men who respected each other and their work, yet how they expressed it had created a strain between them. To Anpu, Tehuti conveyed radical trends. One who made architecture something less of what it deserved. To Tehuti, Anpu's statues were like their creator, cold and lifeless. But a joint commission brought them together on this evening. It was certainly not a visit between old friends.

A young helper, feeble and tired, appeared. He fanned his hand across his chest and pointed towards the dining room.

"Come gentlemen," Anpu sprung to his feet. "I'm hungry and hope you are too. I believe my daughter is waiting for us."

The dining room, like the rest of the house, reflected its owner, lacking warmth and character. Servants brought in saucers made of pottery and stone, filled with castor, linseed and sesame oil. A braided line floated in them and when lit they served to light the room.

As they entered the dining area, a warm flush passed through Nenshi's body when he saw Sia. She stood beside a chair; her hand gently rested on its backrest. His heart pounded. Every beat grew louder and muffled his hearing. He took a deep breath to regain his composure, as best he could. He casually turned his head away from her with a hint of a smile.

"Ah, Sia ... I hope you haven't been waiting long?" Anpu smiled for the first time since his guests had arrived.

"No, father. I have just come in." Her voice was soft like petals of freshly blossomed daisies.

"This is Tehuti, the architect commissioned to design the estate that will showcase my sculptors," Anpu introduced. "And this is Nenshi," he said, with an intentional flippant tone. Heads bowed and Sia acknowledged the gesture with a smile. Nenshi and Sia glanced at each other for a brief second, long enough for them to say with their eyes what was in their hearts.

"Anpu, my compliments, you have a beautiful daughter," Tehuti said. It was easier to complement Anpu's daughter than his sculptures. Tehuti was mindful of her blush. "No no, my dear. Don't feel embarrassed. The gods have bestowed you with the gift of beauty."

She had taken the time to prepare herself. An aura about her radiated elegance. Her enchanting smile complemented her grey eyes, accentuated by the green paint made from the ore of copper put on the corners of her eyes and brows. Black painted lashes and red lipstick matched the colour of her fingernails. Her hair, shoulder length and black like the night, flowed like a satin scarf in a gentle wind. She wore a pleated gown to the ankles with a low neckline. Over this, she had a robe that gathered around her left breast.

Nenshi craved for a long look. Even an attempt would have been improper. He wanted so much to tell her how beautiful she was.

The servants brought food to the table. Distinct and pleasant odours permeated the room. Earthenware pots were filled with boiled poultry, stewed meat and waterfowl garnished in peas, beans, onions and garlic. Fresh lettuce and leeks were just as appetizing. There were breads of various shapes and pastries covered with honey. Decorative bowls overflowed with dates, figs, grapes and pomegranates. There were jugs filled with date juice, wine and beer.

During dinner, Anpu talked about his favourite subject, life after death. His obsession about plans for his afterlife was evident. He took pleasure in sharing them with anyone in his presence.

"The day of my departure from this world will be a most glorious one." It was as if Anpu had predicted the very day of his passing. "Preparations are complete. The ceremony itself will be quite lengthy and elaborate. Some of my closest friends will read selected chapters from the Book of the Dead. My journey to the other world will be a safe one. I believe I'm worthy of acceptance by Osiris and the Scales of Toth."

It was quiet, except for the clatter of ladles, knives, and spoons. Nenshi took it upon himself to respond. For a moment he had forgotten his role and didn't ask for permission to speak, having no qualms about sharing his thoughts. Soreb had always encouraged it. *As a man thinks, so he acts,* the tutor would say; words never to be misconstrued, even if challenged by an outspoken adolescent. Yet at times Soreb would have to rein in Nenshi's indulgence in speaking out. Nenshi would be reminded that a man's thoughts should be filled with good will and then live according to them. Soreb would tell him that expression is one thing but a voice without thought can bring regrettable action.

"I trust that after death, everyone goes to the other world, regardless of what they have done," Nenshi said, as he eyed Anpu, who reminded him of an opportunistic jackal, Anubis, god of the dead.

Anpu frowned at the insult of the contradiction to his beliefs. Coming from an impulsive and unwanted visitor made it more offensive. What exasperated Nenshi was Anpu's lack of knowledge of changing religious beliefs. Anpu was stuck in old principles, like an unmovable pillar dug deep into the desert sand, evidence of a stubborn and intolerant man. Many in Egypt had begun to stray from the views that had been entrenched since the beginning of time. Now, there were signs that the popularity of the adoration of Osiris and that of Amun were meshing to create an all-powerful god. Yet this only proved to Nenshi that religion was as fickle as the malcontents, Pharaoh and citizens alike. Nenshi played with Anpu's beliefs where gods promised stability in one's earthly journey and an eternal life beyond the grave.

"You believe that the other world is filled with happiness and pleasantries," Nenshi continued.

"It's not only my belief," Anpu assured.

"But neither you nor others of the same belief have considered the underworld could also be dark and gloomy where vague and dim shadows of dead spirits move about in fear of not being fed or given a drink."

Anpu's disconsolate glare confirmed Nenshi's intention. The description played on his mind. His face reddened, angered by the bleak possibility. The thought, as Nenshi described, of malignant and cruel gods waiting to devour those who should enter, had bolstered his distaste for Nenshi's description of the afterlife.

Tehuti now showed concern. As did Sia. The conversation was headed in the wrong direction. Tehuti cleared his throat in an attempt to signal Nenshi to pull back on his comments. But it was Anpu who didn't hold back, especially not towards the impetuous youth.

"You can paint a dark world for yourself if you wish," Anpu said. "Things will not change for me. I will continue to do the things I have been doing here. I'll still yacht on the Iteru, spearfish in the marshes and even watch as maidens dance for me. It is all prepared. I'm aware of the pending perils awaiting my journey. I have consulted with the priests who have taken extreme care to choose the rituals and magic spells that will keep me safe. In all, a good man deserving a better life after death."

"I do not disagree with you," Nenshi replied. "In the end we all must face the final test as we stand before Osiris and Toth. The weight of our hearts and how we have lived will determine if they balance favourably on the Scales of Toth. Would we be able to say for certain that we have lived a life of justice and equality to balance the scales?"

Sia leaned forward. "So you are of the same belief in the afterlife as my father's."

"Not exactly," he replied. "Life after death is a principle our people have cherished for countless years. And yet not everyone believes in it."

The room went quiet again. Even the monotonous melodies from the crickets and cicadas in the garden stopped their serenade. Anpu had underestimated Nenshi's shrewdness and intelligence.

Anpu leaned back and crossed his arms. Nenshi knew by the language of the body that his own unorthodox view of life after death had caused Anpu to wonder if the gods would find him worthy. Anpu grimaced and gulped back his drink to help wash away the trepidation. He tipped his body forward, ready to put the entitled young man in his place, only to be interrupted.

"I am not obsessed about life after death," Nenshi said as he reached to take a sip from his cup. "Nor about the gods who await to judge us, if you believe in such gods. You can probably tell that I don't share the same sentiments about religion as others. I do not disrespect anyone else's beliefs. I'm not convinced the religion of our land will sustain us."

Anpu looked down at his empty plate and squeezed his knife. It was blasphemous to doubt the belief in Osiris and Toth. And for a loose-lipped escort, to indulge in wine in the midst of a delicate discussion, was just as offensive.

Nenshi continued. "I wonder whether, at the end of our days on this land, we can say that we have been unbiased. Have we treated everyone with equal consideration?"

Anpu still had his head down. And now Sia interjected, knowing that her father's patience would soon explode. She asked, "Are saying that we should all be the same, be regarded the same?

"Yes," Nenshi replied. "And sometimes I think religion gets in the way, inhibits us from treating everyone the same."

Sia put her hand to her chin. "If I understand you, religion should free us from our prejudices but if it continually changes, as you have described, it's purpose undermines the core of who we are."

"You have expressed it better than I." Nenshi smiled. Sia returned the gesture. But her interpretation of Nenshi's opinion failed to mollify her father's annoyance.

"I hope you are not as impressionable as it appears, denouncing our beliefs," Anpu said, glaring at his daughter.

"Father, I have made no such claim. Impressionable women believe they have no voice in discussing religion or anything else for that matter. That woman, I am not."

Nenshi looked at Sia who was visibly upset by Anpu's insinuation of his daughter as a malleable woman. To embarrass her in the presence of guests was a meagre attempt to promote his own beliefs. Nenshi wanted to lash back and pounce on Anpu for his inconsiderate disparagement. Instead, to avenge the insult, he chose to continue the discussion. One final jab.

"Remember this, noble one. As our kings have gone to their tomb, so will you. Your house will no longer exist, and you will not hear the voices of friends. So, feast now, for once you are gone, you will not come back again."

A deafening silence paralysed Nenshi. Did he speak out of turn? Would Sia now think of him differently?

Anpu rose from the table, seethed by Nenshi's remarks. He replied, "Such words from the mouths of insolent youth is not welcomed in my house."

Nenshi's eye's bulged. He should have known better than to challenge religious views of conventional thought. Tehuti was also disappointed. To take the conversation to this end was disrespectful.

"Nenshi, wait outside," Tehuti commanded.

Nenshi walked out wondering if his impetuous comments might have caused Tehuti to reconsider the petition.

After the guests had left, Sia approached her father. She was annoyed with him from the embarrassment of painting her as naïve and gullible. And for dismissing Nenshi as he did, an invited guest, was rude.

"Don't you think you were a little too harsh with Nenshi?" she asked. The question came across more accusatory than inquisitive. Anpu smirked causing Sia to become more irritated.

"Harsh? You think I was too harsh?"

"He was merely expressing his opinion, as you did yours. Just because you don't agree doesn't mean he should be treated as a commoner. He was a guest in this house. And to react to my opinion, as if I didn't matter, was suggesting to our guests that I should be submissive. I am as capable of expressing my own thoughts as any other man or woman." Her voice elevated, reverberating in the room.

"If I didn't know better it appears you were impressed by him, even fond of him." Anpu's observation caused Sia to hold back her displeasure for fear of raising suspicion of her relationship with Nenshi. "Besides, I'm not convinced Nenshi is Tehuti's son."

"What do you mean?"

"Tehuti did not introduce Nenshi as his son. He just mentioned him by name."

Sia recalled the introduction but dared not acknowledge her observation. It never struck her that Nenshi may not be Tehuti's son. Now she questioned how little she knew about him.

"If he's not Tehuti's son, then who is he?"

"Perhaps he's a servant."

"A servant? How could that be?"

"It's customary for servants to accompany their masters to social functions, to large gatherings, or even to dinners."

It all seemed credible but Sia was not going to give in to her father's insinuations. She needed to find out for herself, from Nenshi.

Chapter 8

THE NEXT DAY, WHEN HORDEKEF heard about the dinner he could hardly contain his laughter. "Sia sat across from you? Her father and Tehuti were in the same room? You must have been out of your mind to go."

"I didn't have a choice."

"Did anyone suspect anything?"

"No. But I was surprised to hear Sia express her opinion on equality."

"Oh ... I imagine that didn't go very well. From what you told me about Anpu, a topic like that could incite his wrath."

"And that it did. I felt like strangling him when he chastised her. The look on her face, the hurt in her eyes ... I wanted to jump at the bastard."

"Good thing you didn't. You don't want to pay the price for striking a free man. And what about Sia, how did she react to seeing you there?"

"I sensed her anxiety. I'm sure she was aware of mine. And for Tehuti to dismiss me and ask me to wait outside. Was that necessary?"

"He didn't belittle you. He put you in your place. I would have done the same thing. You know what I mean."

Nenshi nodded in silent acquiescence. Hordekef offered a strand of support.

"Soon it will all pass, and you can tell Sia you're a free man."

"I wonder how long it will take before a decision is made?"

Not delivering the plea was now becoming problematic.

"As Intef had said, the ways of the courts are mysterious," Hordekef said and then changed the subject, a hopeful distraction. "So, tell me more about what happened at Anpu's house?"

"No. I must tell you about a dream I had. Such a peculiar one. Maybe caused by the uneasiness during the entire evening."

"Or perhaps something you ate." Hordekef laughed again and then sighed. "Go on."

"I remember standing in front of a window looking out. I held a cup filled with beer and when I drank it ... it was bitter and warm. I saw water ... a river ... and an image of a man standing on its banks. Then I went outside. The man was a dwarf and he looked like me! Suddenly I ... or the dwarf ... turned and dove into the water. Yes, it was me. I dove into the water. The current pulled me in every direction. Then I woke up ... in a heavy sweat."

"What do you think it means?"

"I have no idea. Our tutors had never taught us how to interpret dreams."

"Not even Soreb?"

"No. I had asked him about such things. When I was very young, I had dreams about my parents. All he said was that visions can be very telling and one day he would talk to me about them. I guess at the time, he didn't think I was ready."

"I've heard there's someone in the city who interprets dreams."

Nenshi frowned at the suggestion, but his strange dream aroused enough curiosity to want to find out what it meant.

"Who is this person?"

"She goes by the name of Sheikha."

"The name is not Egyptian."

"I know but she has lived in Thebes for many years."

"If Soreb did not want to teach me about dreams, why would I trust anyone else? Besides so-called divinators are appointed by Pharaoh. Anyone else who claims to have such power is an imposter, so it is said."

"You're always sceptical. Of course, there are imposters who will take advantage of the weak-minded, but we're not fools. We would know in an instant what genuine divination looks like. And I've heard that this woman is competent in her own right. Give it a try. And don't worry, I have coins for her service."

"Maybe she can also tell me when my plea will be heard. I still wonder why there has been no movement. I hope the scribes have not intentionally delayed sending it to the courts. In any case, I wonder if this woman is probably more clever than skilful. Yet, I am curious."

"I'm hoping she's beautiful."

"Let's see what she is all about. Soreb had always said not to underestimate the power of a dream."

"Or that of a beautiful woman."

They laughed and off they went.

In an unfamiliar part of the city, in a district where the most undesirable lived, they meandered through the streets and dodged people and dogs. Eyes stared from every crevice. These two young men, finely dressed, certainly didn't belong here. A beggar approached and Hordekef fanned his arm across his body to move aside.

Nenshi watched children as they played - raggedly dressed and barefoot. He saw men, some alone, wandering aimlessly. Some were huddled in conversation to pass the time. Women carried baskets, in their arms, on their heads. It occurred to him he could have been one of these people, destitute and alone rather than a privileged servant. He mused at the thought that his fortunate life in servitude was better than the poverty of free men and women.

"I never knew this place existed," Nenshi said, as he twisted and turned his head in every direction to capture the decrepit life everywhere.

"I heard it mentioned but I never expected this," Hordekef said.

"We better remain alert. We are fodder for someone's desperate means for survival."

"Agreed. Let's walk a little faster. From what I was told we're almost there."

"I hope we can get out of here before sunset or we may not get out at all," Nenshi said and moved his hand until it reached his dagger on his hip.

They reached a dilapidated house. Hordekef put out his hand. "Stop. I believe this is the place." He stood at the entrance and looked at an icon on the door.

"What is it?" Nenshi asked.

"I'm not sure. I was told to look for two stars on the door. I can't tell."

"Let me see." Nenshi nudged Hordekef to move aside. "They are faded but I can see two signs. They look like stars."

"That makes sense. A divinator would look to the stars to predict the future just as priests look to the stars to foresee the outcome of a battle or guide Pharaoh in uncertain times. We have arrived."

They walked in. The house appeared empty until they heard the eerie sound of footsteps skimming along the floor. Out of the dim light, a voice cackled from behind a partition. An unusual odour pierced their noses. It smelled like the stench of an animal's carcass left for days, picked at by vultures.

"Let's get out of here," Hordekef whispered, holding his nose.

"What? Why? This was your idea!"

"I know but I don't like this place."

The voice called out, "Come in and sit down. If you are here to rob me, I will set forth an army of locusts to devour you while you sleep."

No thief would dare risk the affliction of such a spell for the sake of a few coins, Nenshi thought.

"Maybe we're in the wrong place," Hordekef said.

"You made me come here. We're staying." Nenshi grabbed him by the arm and with his other hand moved the partition to one side. Hordekef tried but couldn't pull himself away from Nenshi's grip.

They entered a small dark room. There was just enough light to discern the image waiting for them. A woman sat at a round table. There was no beauty to be wooed by, but they would soon learn that her power to foretell through dreams would not be underestimated.

The table was too small for three guests. Nenshi and Hordekef sat, shoulder to shoulder, in the comfort of their fear. A candle, that had almost reached the end of its life, didn't produce enough light to fully reveal the image behind the voice.

The shadow created by the dimness flattered the threatening figure making her appear bigger than her frame suggested. A black garment covered her, too big for her small stature. A black veil cloaked her face and her hands rested on the table. Prominent veins protruded from the crevices of her wrinkles. Nenshi wanted to reach out and pull away the woman's covering. But the thought of locusts swarming his body while he slept made him think otherwise. He stared into her eyes. The reflection of the candle twinkled. She didn't even blink.

A scullion in ragged clothes appeared and offered the guests a drink. They hesitated to take the cups. The servant didn't say a word but casually pushed the tray closer to the fearful two. Nenshi's suspicion grew, wondering if the beverage was made of a concoction that would cause them to fall sleep; a common trick followed by an act of robbery. Hordekef took a sip, slow and measured. Nenshi didn't drink. The servant shook his head and grunted, waiting until Nenshi succumbed to the persistence. Finally Nenshi took a small sip. Satisfied with his success, the helper walked out.

The woman placed her hands on the table, palms open. There were no sticks to shake to be interpreted nor a cup with leaves to decode their meaning. She would gaze into fearful eyes and examine faces of uncertainty. Then she would implore Shai, the god of fate, to voice through her. She used skills fostered from her birth country along with Egypt's gods to foretell what was to come.

Her eyes squinted and then opened wide. Silence and a stare signalled Nenshi to explain why he had come. A flush ran through him. He found it peculiar that she looked to him to speak. What power did she have from the underworld or was it her good fortune that she chose the right one to face, to speak; the one who had the dream?

Nenshi was reluctant to say anything. There was nothing unusual here; the dim room, the potion, a woman who may have just memorized prayers. Not even her helper was out of place. Up to now, it was all too predictable. Would her interpretation of his dream be more of the same, he wondered?

Nonetheless, Nenshi described his dream in detail and when he finished, Sheikha spoke. Her voice, deep and coarse, echoed with a chill that reverberated through his bones.

"Before I begin with the divination, I warn everyone who comes here that I say all that must be said. I'm not interested in your fears, hence I omit nothing." She took a breath to clear her throat. Silence followed for a brief moment. She gurgled again. "After you woke from your dream did you recite the prayer to the goddess Isis?"

Nenshi frowned, a supplication he had not heard in years. Nor would he tell her what he thought about Egyptian gods. If he had shown any signs that he had distanced himself from the gods, practically denounced them, such a revelation might prompt her to cast a more horrifying spell. He was careful not to divulge that he had outgrown Egyptian gods, created by Pharaohs and priests to gain favour from the people and the dominant forces around them. He had kept his views to himself.

"Repeat these words after me," she said.

She recited the prayer. She paused after every few words for Nenshi to repeat.

"Come to me, come to me, O mother Isis! Behold I am seeing things which are far from my dwelling place! Here I am, my son Horus. Let there come out of you what you have seen, so that the afflictions pervading your dreams may go out and fire spring forth against him who frightens you. Behold I have come to see you, and to drive forth your evils, and root out that which is horrible! Hail to thee, O good dream, seen by night or by day! Driven forth are all horrible things, which Set, son of Nut, has made! Even Ra is justified against his enemies, so am I justified against mine."

An unnerving stillness gripped Nenshi as if the elixir gained its effect. His eyes watered but no tears dripped down his cheeks. Several times he gasped for air, as if he was held down, his mouth wrapped in linen. His heart beat slow, rhythmically, like the beat of a drum leading a procession of priests during the Opet festival in Thebes, in honour of the god Amun.

Nenshi stared at Sheikha, her trance-like pupils, dilated, held him captive. His senses regained enough to hear her speak.

"There are clear signs of what is to come. You said that you stood in front of a window. This is a good sign. It means you are open to new ways. Do not give in to the fear that is in your heart for a god will hear your cry and will walk with you as you confront this menace." She stopped, cleared her throat and swallowed whatever she collected in her mouth. She continued.

"The warm beer you drank is a sign that you will witness suffering and you too will suffer. Endless sand will cover you. Blood will be spilt. You said you plunged into a river. Its waters will cleanse you from all the evils that have afflicted you. The dwarf you saw means that life, as you know it, will change. It will be cut in half. You will discard the half that you have lived. As for the other half, you are destined to know it. That is all."

Nenshi listened intently. An earnest stare questioned whether to believe the decrepit woman who knew nothing about him. She had mastered her trade. Her undertaking was convincing to match her cunning delivery. She had been doing this sort of thing longer than he had been alive. Who could attest that her divination had truth? She spoke well, in her garrulous manner. And what if her words held a grain of truth, what could he do about it? She had not given him any advice. He wondered why he agreed to come at all.

She slid her opened palm towards Nenshi. He turned to Hordekef who nervously reached into his pouch for the gold coins promised. Nenshi took the coins and placed them in her hand. It felt cold, as the touch of death. A chill brushed the back of his neck, causing him to coil his shoulders, to break the shudder. He then reached over and grabbed Hordekef by the scuff of his neck and dragged him out.

"Like a fool, I allowed you to bring me to this horrible place," Nenshi said, his voice stern as if scolding a child for stealing bread. "She has probably used the same interpretation for all dreams. This is what she does to survive, take coins from the weak, the insecure, and make them believe her readings."

"Don't be angry with me," Hordekef protested. "I didn't believe a word she said."

"Look at you. Your face is as white as your shirt. You believed every word."

"I feared a curse, but..."

"And my life ... cut in half ... what does that mean? I'm more confused now than before I heard this feeble woman speak. She is good at what she does and what she does is all about performance. Let's get out of this dreadful place."

They walked through the busy streets and sidestepped people and carts everywhere. At a house under construction, weary slaves raised massive stone blocks, attached to heavy ropes. They were used and reused continually at each level as the house took shape. Yet they were seldom checked to make sure they could still withstand the weight of the blocks.

Four slaves pulled and pulled. No one realized that the fibres of the rope had loosened. It snapped in two. The men fell back and hit the ground as they held the rope at one end with nothing attached at the other. The long cry of a slave warned the passers-by of the falling rock. Nenshi and Hordekef stopped. They looked up in horror as a block plummeted down.

With the speed of a leopard, Nenshi stretched towards Hordekef and pulled him away from the block's path. As they stumbled over debris, they lost their balance and fell to the ground. The falling block landed beside them with a thunder and shattered pieces flew in all directions. One of them struck Hordekef.

Nenshi rose to the sound of Hordekef as he gasped, writhed in pain, and grabbed his leg, struck by a large slab.

"Help me!" Nenshi called out.

Workers ran to them. As they raised the rock, Hordekef struggled to breath and then lost consciousness. Four men lifted and placed the motionless body on a cart and took him away.

Outside Hordekef's room Nenshi sat distraught. With his hands cupped to his chin, his elbows rested on his knees, he reflected and blamed himself for having told Hordekef about his dream. And he should have refused to seek the interpretation of a witch. The remorse strangled every thought, every breath.

The physician walked out from the room accompanied by Hordekef's parents. A look at their faces, their eyes, revealed their pain from the deepest recesses of their hearts. They gave no sign that the worst had passed. It was left to the physician to opine.

"His injuries are serious," he said, in typical physician's fashion. "His leg is broken. Internally, he is bleeding. He's in significant discomfort. I have given him a sedative and a potion to help stop the haemorrhaging. The hours ahead are crucial. I will remain and keep watch."

Hordekef's mother wept, stricken by the accident. His father questioned Nenshi. "Why would you go to that part of the city? Didn't you know it's not a place for our kind, nor yours?"

The accusation cut deep. "Forgive me," Nenshi said. "We should not have gone there."

Hordekef's father shook his head and walked away. Nenshi turned to Hordekef's mother. "I must see him?" His eyes begged for the visit. She understood the friendship and nodded.

The physician put out his hand. "Be aware that he is under heavy sedation. He may not recognize you or even acknowledge your presence. Please be brief."

Nenshi sat by the bed and stared at his friend, immobile and peaceful; a sign the sedative took control. Hordekef's leg and lower abdomen were wrapped to prevent movement. His sallow face invited death and his breathing became slow and rhythmic. Nenshi wiped the tears from his cheek fearing Hordekef would open his eyes to see his friend, broken.

He held Hordekef's hand. The touch, warm and comforting, caused it to twitch. Hordekef's eyes opened, as slow as the morning sun peered from the horizon. His pupils were dilated, his senses fogged. A short smile acknowledged Nenshi's presence. Hordekef's lips quivered, wanting to speak, wanting to tell his friend not to worry. They exchanged a glance. For that moment the sedative had paused from its purpose, long enough, to allow friends to greet each other. Then Hordekef closed his eyes. Serenity accompanied his long and deep breaths.

Nenshi took a damp cloth and dabbed the perspiration from Hordekef's forehead. A tear fell and landed on Hordekef's hand. Nenshi gently wiped it with his finger, then rose and left the room.

If only Nenshi had turned around just before he exited, he would have seen Hordekef open his eyes again. He would have noticed his friend struggle to speak and raise his hand. He would have noticed Hordekef point to the corner of the room, to a wooden chest that rested on a small folding stool. In it were the documents, the petition intended to set Nenshi free.

Chapter 9

THE NIGHT SKY WAS ABSENT of its usual splendour of bright stars. The light of the crescent moon, low on the horizon, cast bleak shadows. An occasional cool breeze swept over the trees through the stillness. An eerie feeling engulfed Nenshi and all he could think of was Sia, to tell her what had happened.

Along the way Tehuti's acrimonious criticism of the Egyptians and their way of life played on Nenshi's mind as did his own disbelief in the concept of life after death; that life passed but once and never repeated; his unusual dream and Sheikha's divination; and he reflected on how he had saved Hordekef's life or had he? He thought of Sia and the disparity between two classes that had prevented him from expressing his love. Now he longed for her warm embrace, for only in her arms could he forget his burden.

He hurried to get to the garden. Once there he climbed the usual tree and perched himself on a supporting branch. He moved leaves away from his view. There was no sign of her, so he made the distinct sound of a songbird to draw her attention, the one that signalled his visit. Sia had opposed the suggestion, saying it was too risky. But lovers take risks. He had devised the signal and the new plan after he was nearly caught by a housemaid the last time he had visited.

Sia walked through the garden, a leisure stroll not to raise suspicion until she found Nenshi.

"You know I don't like meeting like this," she said as she held his hands, cold to the touch. "You look startled. What is it?"

He told her about what had happened to Hordekef, told her about his dream, about Sheikha and the interpretation. Her eyes, watered, fixated on Nenshi, frightened as a child shaken from a nightmare. She cupped her hands around his face. His pain passed through her.

"Hordekef is a decent man," Nenshi said. "A good friend. He doesn't deserve this."

"It's not your fault. He will heal. Only the hand of Sekhmet delivers suffering."

"A goddess of vengeance has no place in the lives of good men."

Sia then took him in her arms. Her embrace soothed him. The sorrow lifted, even if it was just for a moment.

He stroked her cheek with the back of his fingers. Her soft and supple skin felt good. He brought his lips to meet hers, gentle petals of a rose in full bloom. The long kiss ended as their mouths, warm with passion, unwillingly separated.

But he had more to share in this rendezvous, something left undone, to reveal a hidden truth.

"There's something else you should know."

Sia smiled, waiting to hear the words expressed to a woman in love, anticipating hearing him speak with his heart. But suddenly their tryst was interrupted by a sound from the shrubs behind them. Nenshi's ears perked.

"Are we alone?" he whispered as he scanned the garden.

"Yes. I heard my father order a servant to take him to the city. Let your mind rest."

They embraced and their lips met again and their heated bodies pressed against each other. But there was still uncertainty. She tilted her head back.

"What is troubling you?" she asked.

As he was about to reveal his truth, once again, a sound behind them caught his attention and he turned. Out from the dusk Anpu flung in a rage and pulled Nenshi away from his daughter. There was no time to react. The sudden appearance pierced through them. The fear in their eyes held them motionless.

"Filthy scum!" A shaking fist exuded an uncontrollable wrath. "I suspected this for a long time, you undeserving wretch!"

"Anpu, let me explain. I..."

"Explain? I've seen your explanation. You will be severely punished for this!"

Sia stepped between them. "Father, he's done nothing wrong."

"I'll deal with you later." Anpu raised his hand and slapped Sia across the face. She screamed, put her hand to her mouth to control her tears.

Servants, who had heard the commotion, ran to the scene. Nenshi looked at Sia and became infuriated to see the cut on her lip. He reached to wipe the blood with his hand.

"Leave her alone. Your trouble grows by the minute." Anpu's command resonated with a scorn reserved for criminals.

Nenshi ignored the order and finished wiping the blood. He turned and walked towards Anpu. With clenched fist Nenshi swung and knocked him to the ground. Three servants helped their overweight master to his feet. He held his hand to his mouth and pressed to stop the bleeding. Four more servants suddenly appeared, swarmed Nenshi and held his arms tightly behind his back.

"You're a stupid child!" shouted Anpu as he wiped his bloody mouth with his sleeve. "You have just committed a crime from which no one, including Tehuti, can save you. The consequences await you and count the days of your life." He then turned to his servants. "Throw this ruffian out of my property." He grabbed Sia by the arm and pulled her away.

Sia and Nenshi could not take their eyes off each other as they were dragged in opposite directions, perhaps the last of their encounters.

Chapter 10

TEHUTI WAS EXASPERATED. "INTEF ... there must be a way to remedy this."

"The matter is complicated," Intef said. He looked down to the floor, as if in search of a solution. "I'm still waiting to be called to present the petition to free Nenshi. Learning about the assault on Anpu may have caused the authorities to reconsider it."

All the while Nenshi stood against the wall, leaned back, hands clasped in front of him, listened in silence. It was all he could do. It was pointless to let frustration govern his thoughts. He waited to hear what the litigator had to say before he spoke.

Intef turned to Nenshi. "You must remain in the house until all of this has been resolved. You are fortunate that you have not been shackled and put away," he said and chastised him over his persistence to meet with Sia.

"I have rights," Nenshi reminded the litigator. "Even as a servant," he added, annoyed for the child-like treatment.

"True but there are limitations. If you disobey and leave this house you will be considered a runaway criminal. The authorities will hunt you down and punishment will erase all petitions."

"You must listen to Intef," Tehuti insisted. Nenshi frowned. The helplessness dug deeper.

In a battle against time, before Anpu could unleash his wrath, Intef worked feverishly to finish the second petition that would hopefully get Nenshi out of trouble for striking a free man.

"These two matters need to be handled separately. With any luck they would be adjudicated by two different viziers," Intef said.

The seasoned litigator sat to complete his work. After he set aside the papyrus sheet, he reached into a small wooden box for soot. Sap was added to it, made from a papyrus plant. When the mixture blended to his satisfaction, he dipped a stylus into it and meticulously wrote on the scroll. He then inspected everything to make sure the signs were correct. He held the finished work to the light. The ink was dry.

"It's complete," Intef said as he showed the petition to Tehuti, sitting on his divan. "Remember, Nenshi is subject to all laws that govern servants."

"He's no ordinary servant!" Tehuti's assertion needed no explanation, at least not to Intef.

"Even though to others he appears distinguished and respected, like a nobleman's son, under the law he is still a servant."

"Nenshi had stopped being one a long time ago."

"We're dealing with two different matters. The strategy to resolve these is most critical. When I learned of the incident, I realized that Anpu is concerned only with Nenshi's continual visits with his daughter. There's no law against that. It's only Anpu's prejudices getting in the way. What worries me is that he is capable of making matters very difficult, even to the point where he'll point out the lack of control of a servant." He looked at Tehuti when he said this. "You may end up with very few commissions and a bad reputation. So, I have offered a solution, a compromise, if you will."

"And may I ask what is that alternative?" Nenshi asked. Now he needed to intervene. Intef fell silent. Litigators were rarely questioned by those they represented. Even Tehuti sided with Nenshi.

"Yes, we should know what you are proposing," Tehuti said.

Intef's reluctance to explain the proposal was obvious. He retrieved the petition from Tehuti and turned to his writing kit beside the papyrus. Fastidiously, he cleaned the palette and brush holder. With less consideration he emptied the water cup, picked up the papyrus and carefully folded it. He added his official seal and tied a string around it.

Nenshi moved to stand in front of Intef. "May I ask, what do you want the courts to do with my life?"

Intef glanced over to Tehuti who tilted his head to one side in anticipation of a response. "I have offered the opportunity for you to become a temple servant," Intef said.

"What? A temple servant?" Nenshi fumed. The fury streamed through his veins.

"Go on. Explain," Tehuti demanded.

"I'm asking the courts to accept Nenshi as a temple servant for a period of two floods of the river. I have also assured them you will pay a stipend for this privilege."

"Privilege? You call it a privilege to be a servant?" Nenshi said, the fury seethed. Intef ignored the incensed comments and continued to address Tehuti.

"I've detailed Nenshi's writing abilities. Being able to write in both cuneiform and hieroglyphics is a highly sought-after skill. His knowledge of foreign languages is also of value."

"If Soreb was alive he would have regretted teaching me all this," Nenshi remarked. "And in which temple have you offered my services?"

"At It-Tawy of course."

"The city near the Fayum?"

"Yes."

"You have sentenced me to death, not to serve Pharaoh. I'll never be able to come back." Which meant he would never be free and never be with Sia.

Once again Nenshi was ignored. Intef turned to Tehuti. "Nenshi's abilities will be well received. Serving the temple will be his penance for the wrongdoing."

"I've done nothing wrong!" Nenshi said. The bold tone echoed through the room.

Tehuti held out his hand. "Enough! You will do as you are told!"

In silent acquiescence Nenshi folded his arms. Tehuti turned to Intef and softened his tone. "If the request is accepted, what happens while Nenshi works as a temple servant?"

"It will give me time to find out what has happened to the petition for his freedom."

Tehuti's face went barren of expression. Nenshi abandoned his silence, questioning the litigator's value.

"You have done all this without our agreement? You have written a petition without consideration?" Nenshi asked.

"I'm trying to keep you from harsh punishment. It's the only solution, for the time being."

"And what makes you think this strategy will work?"

"We both know that Pharaoh's affinity for erecting massive building are exhausting his coffers. A number of low floods in the past have added to this seepage of funds. Workers who have come from afar to settle in our land are becoming nervous for lack of food and labour."

"You mean the Hyksos, settling everywhere, wanting everything." It was a stark reminder of the potential overthrow of power.

"That remains to be seen," Intef said. "Nonetheless the palace would welcome a well-educated servant, someone who can read and write in the languages that threatens Pharaoh. The Temple Priests will know how to take advantage of your knowledge. Besides, you would be spared forced labour."

"Any idea how much the payment will be?" Tehuti asked.

"That will be up to us to decide," replied Intef. "It's an integral part of the contract with the Temple Priests to allow Nenshi to work as a temple servant. We must make the payment attractive, in light of Pharaoh's financial constraints. Any payment from any source will help reduce taxation on the people. It will not only pay for the privilege of becoming a temple servant but also protect Nenshi from harsh labour."

"Very well. You have my approval. Take the petition to the courts," Tehuti said as he lifted himself from his seat.

"One more thing," Intef said. "I managed for only the two of us to attend the hearing."

"Me and you? That's unheard of. It's usually the accused that must stand to defend himself." Tehuti's high pitched tone raised another concern.

"It's been done in the past. You are known in Pharaoh's circle, in It-Tawy, in Thebes, in Memphis. No doubt whoever presides over this matter will know of you and you are the best one to speak of what has happened."

"You want me to speak, to present the case?"

"You must trust me on this."

"Very well."

"Good. I must leave now. We'll give the scribes at least three days to move the petition forward. I'll send word to let you know when to meet me for preparation." Intef gathered his tools, rolled up the papyrus and marched out like a soldier prepared to do battle.

Nenshi shook his head and looked around the grand room, filled with the finest furniture, lavish frescos. He then thought of the temple palace in It-Tawy. Would the home he had known since childhood be replaced by an asylum so far away? The pit of his stomach churned with anguish. And was this litigator, Intef, insane, to allow Tehuti, who had no knowledge of the ways of the courts, to present a case as sensitive as this one? The torture of servitude, inflicted by his own hands, was now left in the hands of the unknown.

Chapter 11

IN THE HALL OF JUSTICE Vizier Kheti sat on an Acacia wood chair. He shuffled his weight to allow the open back to give a comfortable support. The chair's lion-shaped legs were inlaid with paintings of a lion's wildlife setting and its sides were engraved with lotus flowers. The cushioned seat matched the one under his feet. A rug gifted from the east gave accent and attention to the royal chair. Upon it sat the second most powerful man in the land. The Vizier, Priest of Maat, with baton in hand, was ready to hear petitions and protests. His eyes closed for a brief moment to feel the flow of a gentle breeze from the plume of his fan-bearers.

Tehuti took a long gaze and squinted, as the Vizier sat majestically and adjusted his long white robe to make sure the strap over one shoulder was positioned properly. A slow wave of his hand gestured for the hearing to begin.

"It's Kheti," Intef said, stretching to confirm it was the most high Vizier. "He normally presides at Pharaoh's palace in It-Tawy."

"Then why is he here?" Tehuti became suspicious. Disputes and petitions of a minor nature were heard in the lesser court, in an antechamber next to the Hall of Justice. The accusation against Nenshi paled, compared to crimes against the state, against Pharaoh or the gods.

"If Kheti is here, shouldn't Nenshi also be present?"

"No. Sometimes the mere presence of an accused servant would cause a vizier such as Kheti to rule harshly."

Tehuti took a long look to read the Vizier's expression that might suggest benevolence. But all he saw was a pale face. It was not a sign of illness but rather reflective of the little time the Vizier had spent outdoors. A forced smile reflected too much time spent on his royal chair in a judiciary capacity as part of civil administration or overseeing the running of the country on behalf of Pharaoh.

Tehuti turned to Intef. "Is he not a member of Pharaoh's family?"

"Yes. A cousin, perhaps. I'm not certain but royal he is."

"Does it make a difference who judges over our petition?"

"A great deal. Kheti has left many destitute for the benefit of others. I think Henenu had something to do with the Vizier's presence here."

"Who's Henenu?" Tehuti asked, feeling the anxiety of courtroom tension.

"Anpu's litigator. He's the only one who could have persuaded his long-time friend to come to Thebes. That explains why it has taken so long for this matter to be called by the courts, to give Kheti enough time to get here from It-Tawy."

"So Anpu and his litigator have worked to thwart our attempt to prevent punishment. What does that mean for our petition?"

"We don't change our plan. Sometimes the road to justice is long and tiring. Only bribery or flattery could curtail it."

"Henenu has probably delivered both," Tehuti replied and released a sigh to settle his nerves. "It's wise that you got approval for Nenshi not to be here. Sometimes his opinions and beliefs cause impetuous conduct."

Leaning next to one of the pillars near the entrance of the hall, stood Henenu, arms crossed. He watched and waited. Vizier Kheti opened the session.

"His royal highness, the great Pharaoh Amenemhat III, has appointed me Judge over this *kenbet*, district council of Thebes. I will listen to matters and make judgment."

The Vizier's assistant then motioned to Henenu to come forth and present his case. He was a masterful speaker, Tehuti noted. His presentation was brief, highlighting the main points of the accusation; the law doesn't condone a servant striking a free man. He then sat in his place.

Tehuti grinned and leaned over to Intef. "He didn't have to say much. He said everything, in private."

The Vizier's assistant then motioned to Tehuti to speak. Intef sat and listened to Tehuti present his case. It was an impressive dissertation about a young servant, intelligent and educated that neither scribe nor huntsman could claim to match. Tehuti also referred to Nenshi as his son, explaining what had happened to his wife and the loss of his own young son Meti. And in the spirit of impartiality Tehuti balanced his discourse with a confession about the strike on Anpu by clarifying how a young man, whose judgment, clouded by passion, caused a most regrettable act. Intef made sure Tehuti would say this, being well aware that Vizier Kheti had the entire *kenbet* at his disposal. If he had ordered an investigation, it would have uncovered the same truths.

Vizier Kheti listened with the patience of a feline and waited for the right moment to speak. He cleared his throat. Tehuti leaned forward in his chair. Intef stood, just as anxious, to hear the verdict.

"I have heard your plea and I have seen the records of the incident. Maat, our goddess of truth and justice gives order to our land and our people. There is little stability when a servant administers his own law."

Tehuti's head dropped, disappointed that the Vizier did not demonstrate a strand of benevolence. Perhaps an adjudicator from Thebes might have seen things differently. And perhaps if it wasn't for Henenu's far reaching influence and lack of moral precepts, the words might not have been as painful. But the courts uphold the law and consideration is granted only to those who, behind closed doors, can persuade a different outcome.

Vizier Kheti continued. He raised his voice so that everyone in the Hall of Justice could hear. "There's no place in Pharaoh's palace for a servant without order, no matter how many languages he speaks, no matter how accurate he is as a huntsman." A silence weighed down on the audience as if Anubis, god of death and dying, sucked the air out of the chamber leaving everyone helpless. No one moved as they waited to hear the verdict.

"As judge, appointed by his majesty, I declare the servant by name of Nenshi, belonging to the house of Tehuti-em-Heb, guilty."

Tehuti looked up. His eyes swelled. His lips quivered. His heart sank to the depths beyond the darkest reaches of death. And there was more from the Vizier. The final blow.

"I command the servant to be exiled from his homeland. I sentence him to labour in Nubia. There he will serve Pharaoh best." It was a simple judgement with far reaching implications that neither Pharaoh nor Vizier cared to consider.

To toil in the gold mines in Nubia was an unfathomable life. And the petition to free Nenshi had still not been heard. As Tehuti and Intef left the chamber, Henenu grinned, relished his victory.

Tehuti realized that he needed to relay the verdict to Nenshi for he might never see him again.

Chapter 12

NENSHI SAT ON THE STEPS of the porch. The sound of songbirds echoed a reminder of his visits with Sia. Memories of forbidden love could not lift the anxiety of any undeserving verdict. He understood the world in which he lived, both in servitude and in privilege. Soreb had taught him well - to see both sides of the human condition; of those who take and those who give. Nenshi was prepared to accept punishment for his wrongdoing but not prepared to be the victim of values that favoured the privileged.

Where were the gods and goddesses that ruled over the world, Nenshi wondered? Where was the goddess Maat and her reign over justice? Nenshi didn't share the beliefs where only worship and sacrifice would lead to a favourable afterlife. He cared for life in the present and hoped the barriers between the divisions of people that fractured a society would ultimately crumble.

The notion of running away to escape from whatever punishment awaited him crossed his mind. But he didn't run. He couldn't. His respect for Tehuti was too great and it would not overcome the shame in dishonouring him.

His ears perked when he heard the sound of the gates open. He ran to meet Tehuti in an anticipation of a decision and even willing to accept becoming a temple servant, if that be the verdict. One day, upon his return to Thebes, things would change.

Tehuti walked to a bench along the path and motioned Nenshi to sit next to him. The canopy of a tamarisk tree offered much needed shade. As Tehuti rested his hands on his knees, Nenshi noticed the tremble. He wondered if it was a sign of his age or of bad tidings.

"We had an audience with Vizier Kheti," Tehuti said.

"Vizier Kheti? Pharaoh's Vizier from the palace?"

"Yes."

"Why would Pharaoh send his Vizier to administer over such a petition in Thebes?"

"Sometimes the ways of the courts are least understood."

A brief pause seemed like an eternity. Nenshi tried to read Tehuti's eyes for a clue of what the Vizier had decreed but Tehuti's evasive shifting left no indication. Nenshi's patience expired.

"Master ... I need to know."

Tehuti gave a slow nod. His eyes swelled. "Your life is spared but you are exiled to toil in the gold mines in Nubia." He laboured to hold back the tears.

There was no expression that could explain the shock that Nenshi felt in his heart. His body was numb as if he was mourning his own death. Once a servant, he was now a slave.

"Nubia ... not the temple palace in It-Tawy?"

"The Vizier didn't even consider it. The petition was read in private and he ignored the benefits of our request." Tehuti omitted telling Nenshi that Anpu, through his litigator, had a hand in the decision. There was no need to fuel a fire already out of control.

Tehuti continued. "The work in Nubia will be hard and the years long. But remember, you are still alive." His words were of little comfort.

"A life in exile is a death sentence in itself," Nenshi said.

No longer a servant to Tehuti, he had now become a slave to Pharaoh, and he might never return to those he loved. Nenshi looked at Tehuti, whose dejected gaze spoke to his pain, pierced with the guilt of not having freed his servant in years gone by.

"Forgive me. I have failed you." The measured words parted from Tehuti's lips. Nenshi put his hands on Tehuti's shoulders. The frailness attested to a passage of time, a passage that neither of them could bring back.

"There is nothing to forgive," Nenshi said with a tender smile. "You made me your son. I am your son."

Tehuti's eyes swelled again but this time he could not prevent the flood of tears. They embraced, father and son. Nenshi stepped back and wiped his own tears.

"I will ask Bata to prepare the few belongings you are allowed to take with you."

Nenshi nodded. He cared not for belongings. "Am I permitted to visit Hordekef before I leave?"

"No. It was made clear that you must leave when the sun rises. Hordekef is hanging on to his own life. If he survives, I will tell him."

"And Sia ... she must know ... I must tell her."

"No. You cannot. You will not. You will leave." It was not a request but an order, his last command to his servant. "She knows. She was waiting outside the Hall of Justice. I told her."

"What did she say?"

"Nothing. Her tears spoke for her. She gave me this, to give to you. She wants you to wear it, to remember her."

Tehuti reached into his pouch and pulled out a necklace.

"This is the one I gave her. The one we bargained for at the market."

It would serve as a memory of the natural and tenuous simplicity of the love they shared. Nenshi now realized that his life in Thebes, as he knew it, had ended. What awaited him would be of greater significance.

The time had come for Nenshi to leave. He stood at the gates of the mansion with Tehuti. On the porch servants with disheartened expressions gathered, as if to grieve the death of a friend. Bata waved and wiped the tears from his eyes. Soldiers waited to escort the servant out from the land.

Tehuti fought through the sadness of his heavy heart to speak. "Nenshi, my son, this is not the end for you. Remember Soreb's teaching; when your road is made impassable, look for another way to reach your destination."

The words were carved in Nenshi's mind. He tried to fight back the tears. Tehuti then took Nenshi into his shaking arms. As he held him, he sobbed. Nenshi pulled back and wiped Tehuti's tears with his hand.

"You will always be with me," Nenshi said. "If gods exist, I pray they hold you in their favour. If ever a man is fortunate to learn the value of life, then that fortune is mine for I sprang from your love and your guidance. From this I will draw my strength. And if I shall one day die after long suffering, I will accept my death knowing that I have loved you and was loved by you, my father."

Tehuti managed a smile. It eased the pain to hear Nenshi refer to him as his father. "This is not the end for me," Nenshi said. "I will return. I will find a way."

With those words, Nenshi bid farewell to his father, Tehuti-em-Heb. They embraced one last time and parted not knowing whether the tides of time would allow their lives to meet again.

Chapter 13

SAD AND IMPOVERISHED FACES OF men sitting across from Nenshi confirmed they were all victims of unfortunate circumstances. They stared at him as he pulled at the shackles around his ankles. They were heavier than he had imagined. He looked up and glanced at the lives that had been hardened by their own indiscriminate acts of crime. A glimpse of their probing eyes made him wonder how they judged him; one stricken with ill misfortune or one caught during a lawless exploit? It didn't matter. He, along with the others, were all considered criminals destined for Nubia.

The River Iteru, known for its splendour and source of life, now had another purpose - to deliver a floating sarcophagus filled with men condemned to a world of the living dead.

Nenshi turned and looked towards the shore, in the distance, beyond the city, beyond the hills. The wilderness, the wasteland that served as his sanctuary, where he ventured to forget about his status, called out to bid him farewell. Now, the shackles that bonded his legs and his life, were all that remained, a permanent reminder of his sentence.

The ship's captain, a stern and uncompromising man, made his usual casual walk up and down the ship. He stopped in front of Nenshi who couldn't be bothered to look up to see who was blocking the sun's light. A weathered face and eyes, darker than the night, who had seen thousands of criminals in his time, studied Nenshi from head to toe. Nenshi felt a hand on his shoulder, as if shaking him to wake up. Nenshi looked up, shielding the sun with his hand. The captain offered a gentle smile and nodded. Nenshi knew he didn't belong on his ship but it was pointless to engage in a conversation and try to convince the captain. Now, seen as a criminal, Nenshi was like all the others, an opportunity for profit. The captain walked away.

Nenshi looked down and examined the shackles again. A strong tug to release them from their grip was futile. And there was nothing he could use to pry them open. There were only rats, Ra's abomination, darting across the floor, a nuisance to all those who set eyes on them.

As Nenshi fidgeted with the restraints, a man, sitting across from him, seemed amused by the obsession. Nenshi looked up and the man shook his head as if he had also tried the same thing.

The ship was released from the dock. An unexpected gust of wind propelled it down the river. Nenshi stood and leaned over the rails. It was better than looking at the castaways across from him. The river was crowded with merchant ships and small boats whose owners came to enjoy the day. Close to the shore a nobleman slept on his moored boat while his servant fanned him. Further along, Nenshi saw slaves draw water to irrigate the fields. Its riches would fill their masters' coffers. The unfortunate life of many hardened his belief that man's insatiable appetite for oppression matched the gods' reluctance to intervene, if indeed gods existed.

He had seen enough. He sat, slouched back to make himself as comfortable as possible on a splintered wooden bench and fell asleep. Thebes disappeared into the horizon and along with it the hope of his return.

The ship finally reached its destination. A sudden jolt shook Nenshi from his sleep. They had docked. He stretched out his arms and yawned, then stood, placed his hands on the ship's rail and looked out. The most unforgiving site lay before him, the most desolate terrain he could have imagined. As the sun began to set, it cast eerie shadows over the land, as if entering the underworld. The hinterland, where he used to hunt, paled in comparison to what lay before him. He had only heard of this place, filled with gorges, rocks that were as numerous as the stars and caves as deep as the bowels of the land. He had learned about the military campaigns aimed at extending Egypt's dominance and wondered if those who had survived the wars would seek revenge on a boat filled with Egyptian criminals. Nenshi shook his head and tugged at the ligatures. He needed to find a way to escape.

PART TWO

Chapter 14

THIS WAS NUBIA, THE LAND of gold, hidden beyond the arid desert in the forsaken mountainous region of the dynasty, where its riches belonged to one man - the Pharaoh of Egypt.

Nenshi stood in a line, with the rest of the outcasts, criminals and slaves sent to labour in more than one hundred mines. One at a time, they were led into a tent and then escorted out through the back. While he waited to enter, Nenshi checked to see if the necklace was still where he had hidden it. He had rolled the top of his loincloth, just enough to tuck it in. Touching it reminded him of Sia. He wondered if her heart was as heavy as his.

As he got closer to the entrance, a groan echoed from inside followed by silence. The procedure was repeated to each one that entered. Nenshi had no idea what was being done until it was his turn.

He walked in. The heat from a burning fire hindered his breathing. Two soldiers, the size of pillars, stone-faced and arms crossed, waited for him. A third soldier kneeled next to the fire, from where metal sticks protruded. The smell of burnt skin was evidence of what was to come.

As the soldiers approached, Nenshi tightened the muscles in his arms, not to resist, but to prepare himself for certain pain. The soldiers grabbed him, held him tightly and positioned his right arm for the procedure. One of them pulled Nenshi's sleeve, up and over his shoulder. With a thick cloth, the soldier that was kneeling, wrapped it around a thin long iron blade and drew it from the fire. Nenshi noticed two circles at the end of the rod. He bit on his lip. His face and eyes contorted. The man waited until the rod had cooled yet it still hot enough for him to perform his duty. He then pressed the tip against Nenshi's skin. A groan tried to control the pain, instead, the pain controlled him. The burn seared through his arm, up through his shoulder until he felt as if his entire body had been doused by the fire.

Three soldiers succeeded in bestowing Nenshi with his new status - branding him with the markings of a criminal. Then he was taken to another tent to rest. He was given a damp cloth to help soothe the soreness. In time the circles would harden to form a permanent scar.

He sat on a wooden cot, hard as his heart had become, hard as his existence. The cloth, soaked with his blood, had dried. A gentle pull caused his skin to tear and bleed. The circles would remind him of his new status and they would be the motivation to recapture the life he had treasured.

On the ground was a stick, the length of an arrow. He picked it up and held it with the same firmness as when he would prepare to slay his prey during hunting expeditions with Hordekef. It made him wonder if his friend was still alive.

On the tent's wall hung a metal disc. He squinted and could make out the image of the sun god, Ra. Its figure had faded over time, now a mere outline of what it used to be.

His eyes burned as he stared at the object. An irreverent glare confirmed the faith he had shed when he was old enough to question the purpose of the gods; old enough to seek the knowledge that would provide answers to the mysteries of life.

His grip on the stick tightened while he focused on the disc. With a quick sweep, he raised his arm, drew the stick behind him and flung it. The target was stuck hard, and it fell with a clangour. The sun god had been defeated. He reached under his waistband and pulled out Sia's necklace, now his own. He clutched it in his hand, laid down and went to sleep.

The next day at sunrise Nenshi was awakened by the crack of a whip. The end of a baton pressed against the backs of each man sleeping. Nenshi reached for his necklace and hid it underneath his cot before he was nudged to get up.

Outside, he was thrown into the routines of the labour needed to make gold. He followed men inside the belly of a mountain. The light from oil lamps fastened to the walls reflected against protruding veins of quartz that contained gold in its raw form. An overseer gave Nenshi a two-handed stone hammer and pointed to where others worked. He watched as workers pounded to loosen the gold-filled stone from the walls. His jaws tightened as he gripped the shaft of the hammer, ready to perform his first task. The thought of the endless toil stirred anger and as he hit the fractures in the rocks. He imagined every strike against the Vizier who judged him according to the whims of corruption.

Later, working with the same group of men, he filled baskets with the fallen rocks. One after the other, in a long line, the group resembled black ants, scenting their way to the exit. Some men stumbled along the way, fell to the ground and let out a scream as their knees hit a sharp-edged boulder. They stood, wiped the blood with their dirty hands and continued. Nenshi felt powerless. He wanted to help but whips cracking in the air ordered him to carry his load. By the end of the day, Nenshi's bruised shoulders ached. A night's rest was a much-needed respite.

The next day Nenshi was taken to one of the shafts where, near its opening, quartz was heated until it became brittle enough to be separated from the rocks. Here Nenshi was shown how to use a one-handed hammer. A simple lesson - repeatedly strike the quartz until it was reduced to pellets, the size of lentils.

He eyed children as they painstakingly carried the cooled chunks to tables. They knew no other life. Their feeble bodies, overcome by the weight they carried, crushed his heart. They were born from the loneliness of the men and women, slaves and criminals, who had married among each other. There was no formal ceremony, only the simple commitment to devote the rest of their enslaved lives to one another. As soon as their children had become of age, they too were forced to work.

The children had no place here, Nenshi reflected, convinced that the despot Pharaoh relished in the atrocity of the mines. Soreb had said that man was indeed cruel and thoughtless and wished only to inflict pain on others.

Nenshi turned away for a moment and thought about the gods. If they existed, how could they have permitted this to happen? Is there not one true god who defends peace and justice? The questions were left unanswered. He squeezed the shaft of the hammer and struck the pellets with a vengeance.

Later Nenshi was summoned to move to the next station where the pellets were ground into dust. He saw a woman unload the pellets on a table that was set on an angle. An old man poured water over them to wash away the dust and quartz particles. Only the heavier gold remained. As the water cleaned away the dust, the endless drudgery washed away their lives.

Another day had passed, only to add to his aching body and drain his mind from any notion of a better existence. Like the pellets, he felt beaten by the hammer of slavery.

On the third day, he was taken to the last step of the purification process. It was the most dreaded. Large vessels that contained gold, sat over burning fires for five days. This allowed the gold to separate from other substances. The heat of the day, as unbearable as that from the fires, rendered its own punishment. Nenshi recoiled at the sight of a man being carried away who screamed from the burns to his hands and legs caused by the spillage of an overfilled vessel. No one else paid attention to the daily occurrence.

When the gold liquefied and then shaped into rings, they looked like the kind of charm an affluent woman wore on her wrist. They cooled and soon hardened. He had not only learned how the gold was produced but like the hard gold rings, he too had become hard, contemptuous.

The early evening brought relief from the day's drudgeries. The sun's red glow seemed to hold its place in the sky long enough for Nenshi to tell a story. Children waited for him in a remote area not far from the dwellings. They were always in awe of his stories and revered the storyteller himself. Through his tales he seized their imagination about lands unknown; challenged them to solve mysteries; and, brought characters to life as if they were sitting among them.

And so, they gathered for another story. Their aching bodies rested while their imagination was captured by new and strange images. Nenshi smiled as he looked at them, some lay with their eyes closed, others sat with eyes wide open eager to absorb what was to come.

"Many say that what I'm about to tell you is true. Many say it's a meaningless tale." Nenshi paused. Anticipated whispers grew. "What's this I hear?" he continued. "You first want to know if the story is true or not?"

Heads nodded.

"Ah ... but I can't tell you that. Let me first tell you the story and in the end, you can decide for yourselves the answer that will quench your thirst."

They looked at each other. Some shrugged their shoulders; others scrunched their faces, but they were all eager to hear the story.

"There once lived a very strong and handsome man. The gods were proud of this young man and of all the good deeds he had done. They were so proud of him they decided to bestow upon him the gift of everlasting life. But the man wasn't satisfied with just being given eternal life. He wanted to know its secret. He wanted to know where it came from."

Eyebrows raised; mouths opened to a sliver.

"So, the young man went on a long journey in search of an old ancestor who might know the answer to his question. When he found his relative, he asked, O wise man, you who are of my blood, answer me - what is the secret of life? It wasn't until after a long conversation with his kin that he finally answered the question."

Lying bodies sat up and joined the others eager to hear the revelation.

"The old man said, Many years ago I lived in another land. Like you, I too became the favourite of the gods. They had told me that the secret of life was not in the land where I lived. And so the old man searched and searched and searched."

An impatient girl called out, "What did he find?"

"Wait and I will tell you but you must first know that on his journey the old man had seen many good deeds and many bad ones. The ways of the people were like a boat on stormy waters swaying back and forth not knowing where it would settle."

Shoulders shrugged again and more faces scrunched.

"The old man said, When I returned to my homeland, I realized that the secret of life was not in any land at all."

A long pause. Children waited to hear more. There was no more.

"And that my friends, is the end of the story."

Whispers grew. The same girl spoke out again. "But Nenshi, did the man find the answer to the secret of life?"

A boy asked, "Is the story true?"

Puzzled faces looked on. Nenshi leaned closer to quench their thirst. "The secret of life is not in any place but in your heart. And that is true." They giggled and chattered amongst themselves.

"It's time to go now," Nenshi prodded. "Go rest your body and think of the story. There's a lesson in it for each of you to ease your mind and withstand the days ahead." Their babble slowly diminished as they walked back to their camps.

Nenshi sat quietly for a while also reflecting on the story and how he ended up in this land of the oppressed. The adversity of being a slave made him stronger to overcome the hardships of life but in that life he realized it was only what was in his heart that true happiness dwelled.

He rose and began to walk back. He could see the children in the far distance and hear their prattle and laughter. Tomorrow would be another day like all days but perhaps a little lighter for the children. And perhaps a little lighter for him too. He realized that he was not alone in the world. Every step he took, knowingly or not, touched the life of someone else. And the deeds of those who entered into his world, knowingly or not, touched him. Was this the lesson he had taught the children or what they had taught him?

Now, with strong mind, strong body, and what was in his heart, he could find a way out from the mines. This, he was determined to do.

Chapter 15

Several weeks passed and every day had been the same as the one before. The only reward came in surviving the toil of the day and avoid being one of many whose lives ended for the sake of the effulgent stone.

It was a day of rest and Nenshi strolled to a nearby river to shed the week's drudgeries. The warmth from the morning sun against his skin was a welcomed feeling. His body had grown stronger; shoulders round and brawny, his arms robust and forceful.

The land cut by flowing waters had become his sanctuary. It had replaced the wilderness. The water, used to quench the thirst of overburdened slaves and to clean the gold, now washed away his pain.

He sat by the edge of the water whose rippling flow overshadowed the cries of battered slaves etched in his mind. Carriages stood still. Hammers lay on the ground resting from the monotonous and continuous pounding against rocks. Women tended to their children's needs instead of those of thirsty workers. Soldiers put away their whips until the following day - the next thrashing against flesh. The temporary tranquillity of a place usually filled with perpetual torture was a welcomed distraction.

Suddenly he heard a voice call out to him from a distance. He turned and recognized one of the boys from the mines. Halim panted heavily; his pale face burst with fear.

"Nenshi ... Nenshi ... Dedi ... he fell ... he fell into the cave!"

Nenshi placed his hands on Halim's shoulder to calm him.

"Slow down ... tell me what happened."

Halim took a few deep breaths. "We were playing near the caves. Then I heard rocks falling and a loud scream. When I turned around, he was gone. He was calling me but I couldn't see him. I went to look for him ... I saw him in the cave. He fell in."

"Show me where he is and we'll get him out. Don't be afraid."

"But Nenshi, the cave is deep and Dedi is lying on a ledge. If it breaks, he'll die. How do we get him out?"

"We'll get him out." The confident, soft-spoken words eased Halim.

The dilemma, tenuous at best, seemed precarious. The deep and natural cave penetrated the base of a mountain. Children played in the area, against their parents' wishes. It left to wonder that no one had fallen into the hollowness until now.

Nenshi walked around the opening. He positioned himself to allow the sun's rays to cast a light into the cave. When he bent over, he saw Dedi crouched on a fragile ledge. Nenshi's shadow against the wall startled Dedi and he screamed.

"Dedi ... it's me ... Nenshi ... up here."

Dedi looked up. His face shook with terror.

Nenshi examined the opening, wide enough only for a child to squeeze through. Removing some rocks around the hole to enlarge it would be too risky. It might cause debris to fall through, land on the ledge and be the end of it all.

He knelt over the hole. "Dedi ... are you all right?"

Dedi tried to stand. His body shifted and caused the ledge to loosen and small rocks plummeted into the darkness.

"No! No!" Nenshi shook his head and held up his hands. "Don't move! Just answer me ... are you all right?"

"Yes," echoed the voice from below.

"Good. Now listen to me and do exactly as I say. Stay still. Don't move and we'll get you out. Do you understand?"

"Yes," Dedi said, his voice shook, his body trembled.

By now, other children had gathered and Nenshi held out his arms to keep them away. "Don't get close and don't say anything!" They were quick to follow his orders.

It would prove futile to send Halim or one of the others for help. Without warning the ledge might collapse. Nenshi scanned to find the tallest boy. "Dhutnakat ... come here."

A boy with spindly arms and legs approached. Nenshi placed his hands on him and felt the bones and small muscles and wondered how this fragile child could be of use. There was no other choice but to make the best of it.

"Will you help me?"

The lanky Dhutnakat nodded his head, eager to help.

"Listen. I'm going to lower you down as far as possible. If Dedi can reach, he'll grab your ankles and hold on. Then I'll pull both of you up. Do you understand?"

"You mean you will use me like a rope?"

"Yes. Can you do it?" Nenshi needed the assurance. Dhutnakat nodded.

Nenshi crouched over the opening and explained his plan to Dedi. Dedi signalled with one slow nod that he understood.

Nenshi stood over the hole with his legs apart and placed each foot at the widest part of the opening. He reached to his loincloth and wiped his sweaty hands. Dhutnakat noticed and did the same to his hands. Nenshi pressed hard on one foot, digging it into the soil to secure his footing. Then repeated the action with the other foot.

He reached over and took Dhutnakat by his hands and wrists just tight enough not to hurt him. Dhutnakat gingerly stepped closer to the opening and was slowly submerged into the dark hole. Dedi raised his arms but could barely touch Dhutnakat's feet. Nenshi bent his knees and lowered himself more. He squatted with his legs apart, his arms between his legs, while he held Dhutnakat just tight enough to secure his hold. But Dedi still couldn't reach.

Nenshi's shoulders and wrists began to ache. He imagined that Dhutnakat's were too. Dedi shifted his body, ever so slowly. The ledge remained stable. Nenshi twisted his head until he could get a glimpse of what Dedi was doing. Dedi needed to grab on to Dhutnakat's ankles before the ledge loosened. Nenshi slowed his breathing to save his strength. He looked below again and saw Dedi get on his knees. This time the ledge moved a little. Dedi stretched out his arms but still couldn't reach. As he shifted his legs, the rest of his body followed, and he managed to keep his balance with his arms stretched out while he raised himself.

The ledge moved again. Nenshi shook his head as if trying to tell Dedi not to move. He glanced down again and saw stones fall into the darkness but did not hear them land. Dedi's sharp effort to try to stand shook the ridge. Nenshi felt the quiver in his feet, up through his legs and body. He now feared it would collapse. Then with one quick move Dedi jumped and grabbed Dhutnakat's ankles. The ledge collapsed and plunged into the abyss.

Nenshi felt a sudden pull downwards and almost lost his balance. Dhutnakat let out a scream from the tug in his wrists, shoulders, and legs. Nenshi took a deep breath, straightened his legs and pulled up until Dhutnakat appeared out from the hole. But Dedi had not yet surfaced. If Nenshi lost his balance, he would lose both boys. He looked at the other children. His eyes pleaded for help. Two boys swiftly ran to him. They knelt and reached in to grab Dedi. One managed to put his hands under Dedi's arms while the other grabbed his waist. They pulled him out.

Nenshi, Dhutnakat and Dedi lay on the ground. The children cheered, jumped up and down and hugged one another. Nenshi was relieved, Dedi safe and Dhutnakat, a hero.

The news had spread how Nenshi and Dhutnakat had saved Dedi's life. The overseers, masters in mobilizing the workforce, used the event to maintain a high morale; an opportunity to lift spirits and produce more gold.

An overseer approached Nenshi. "It's been reported that you rescued a child in the caves," he said.

"Yes. With the help of that brave young boy." Nenshi looked towards Dhutnakat.

"Your act of bravery has been good for morale."

"Morale is short lived in a place like this."

"Nevertheless you have been granted the opportunity to accompany a shipment."

"Me? Why me?"

"It's a small reward. Since the day of the boy's rescue more gold has been produced."

"Don't thank me for that. Maybe you should send everyone to accompany the shipment."

The overseer laughed. "Do you want to go or should I find someone else?"

"What will be my task?"

"A simple one," explained the stone-faced officer. "You, and others chosen for this trip, will cook, keep the mules moving, gather sticks for fire, fill water jugs and obey orders from any soldier during the journey. Do you accept?" Nenshi nodded.

The officer then added, "I must also tell you to always be on your guard. At times we have been attacked. We do not have enough soldiers here to accompany the caravan and so we have asked for additional soldiers from a nearby camp. We usually prefer to travel on the river to avoid being attacked but some ships are in need of repairs. The caravan will go to Edu but will stay on the east side of the River Iteru, across from the port town, to be safe. After a day's rest the shipment will be transferred to vessels for the trip on the river to Thebes and then on to It-Tawy. Now go and be ready to move when called."

Nenshi bowed his head and walked back to his camp. The corners of his mouth tilted upward. His eyes sparkled. The mention of Thebes piqued his interest. Thoughts ran through his mind. It was a welcomed chance to be away from the mines. It also ignited thoughts of an escape once he got to Thebes and hide in the nooks of the big city. Regardless of whether his attempt to escape would be successful or not, he didn't want to return to the mines.

He will miss the many he had come to know and help and certainly miss the children. They will miss his stories of his parting wisdom and friendship. And he would not forget the strong ties he had made with the pitiful lives of slaves. Nor would he shed his disdain for those who could not find it in their hearts to forgive the men and women for their crimes or, at the very least, abbreviate their punishment.

He thought of Tehuti, Hordekef and Sia. The longing to be in their company shifted from being a dream to the possibility of its reality. He waited to be summoned to join the caravan.

Chapter 16

IN THEBES, HORDEKEF HAD SURVIVED his ordeal from the injury. His leg, although still tender, grew stronger each day. His limp became hardly noticeable. But his guilt had not healed from holding back the petition to set Nenshi free. It remained hidden and now, with Nenshi in exile, his reluctance to confess for his transgression intensified. He couldn't even face Tehuti. There would be no forgiveness, only embarrassment. He had paid the ultimate price for the envy that had consumed him. It had caused him shame and perhaps his friendship.

Nenshi's absence stirred a determination to make up for his indiscretion. Hordekef had one last chance, to take the petition to the Vizier. But so much time had passed. What if the court dismissed it without even reading it? What if freedom was disallowed? After all, everyone knew about Nenshi's punishment for striking Anpu. But Hordekef had the resolve, the fortitude, to personally deliver the petition. He had even brought the walking stick he had used during convalescence from his injury and feigned a limp; a dramatic touch to help a friend.

With the petition in one hand and a staff in the other, he made his way to the court's administration building. He frowned at the line-up of those who came to submit their pleas for anything that needed the court's decision, from a complaint about someone infringing on property to accusations of robbery.

Hordekef's impatience to wait in line motivated him to exaggerate his injury. He leaned heavily on his staff, wrinkled his face, as if in uncontrollable pain, and emitted a groan loud enough that those in front of him turned to see what caused the fuss. The man before him, motioned Hordekef to take his place.

"Thank you," Hordekef replied, loud enough for the others to hear. "Maat, our god of justice, will show goodwill over your plea."

Soon, one by one, they allowed Hordekef to move forward in the queue. His injury was of less concern than the blessings for a favourable decision.

A scribe, sat at a table receiving petitions. He looked up. Hordekef imparted an amicable smile in the hope of drawing out the scribe's good nature.

"I'm here on behalf of the litigator Intef, to submit a petition," Hordekef said, with the confidence of a litigator's assistant. The scribe appeared puzzled and took the petition. "Everything is in order," Hordekef added, in a calm tone, not to raise concern.

"Intef, the litigator, you said?" asked the scribe.

"Yes. I assume you know of him."

"He has already presented a petition. I was here when he delivered it. This isn't the same one, is it?" The scribe leaned to one side to look past Hordekef at the long line-up. Hordekef looked over his shoulder. He didn't think he was going to be challenged and needed to think quickly.

"No, this is not the same plea. You know litigators, they're always looking to fill their coffers. What easier way is there than writing petitions and attend court proceedings, representing the innocent and the guilty? Litigators profit and so do I, if you know what I mean."

The scribe unrolled the petition. "This refers to the same person as the previous one that I received. I recall the name." Again, he leaned over. The queue was getting longer. Some began to grumble.

Hordekef reached down with his hand and gently massaged his leg. His eyes squinted, feigning pain. The smile didn't work, perhaps pretending to be in discomfort, might. The scribe waited for an answer.

"Yes, it's about the same person."

The scribe turned to look at the queue, now even longer.

"Let me explain," Hordekef continued but the scribe interrupted and looked once more at the line-up. Complaints were getting louder. He then rolled the petition and registered its acceptance.

"No explanation is needed. You may go."

Hordekef gave a respectful nod and walked away. He continued to feign his exaggerated pain and once outside the building he picked up his staff and his gait and happily went home. His redemption had been released in the hope that the petition would bring Nenshi home. He was ready to come to terms with the envy that caused the schism between him and his best friend. Repentance would be realized in Nenshi's presence, face to face. The healing had begun, haunted no longer by the demons of resentment.

Tehuti and Intef ambled along the polished grey granite floor of the long corridor that led to the entrance to the Hall of Justice. Statues of the gods lined both sides of the passage - Anuket, Osiris, Isis, Maat.

Tehuti whispered to himself, rehearsed his presentation. "I hope not to disappoint you," he said.

"Don't be nervous," Intef said. "You'll do fine. Remember, Vizier Kheti is not presiding."

"I'm not sure that makes it any easier or makes a difference." Tehuti took a deep breath to calm his nerves. With impeccable confidence he had presented his architectural designs to noblemen and priests alike. But this was different. It involved Nenshi's life. Drawings on papyrus, once rejected, can be discarded. A life, its freedom rejected, is destined to wither. If I fail, my life will also fade, he thought.

"Just repeat the key points as I instructed you," Intef encouraged.

"I will do my best."

"Good. Follow me, the entrance is down this corridor."

As he walked towards the entrance to the Hall of Justice, Tehuti was astonished at what he saw. The hallway was filled with people ready to be called upon to plead their case. "Why are there so many?" he asked.

"In times of uncertainty many come to complain about tomb robbers or bad neighbours, all looking for something to gain." Intef explained. "Luckily for us there is no one here today to make a case for manumission. Follow me, our hearing is at the far end."

Lesser Viziers of the nome of Thebes were stationed in the hall, dealing with protests, and making judgments. Tehuti held out his hand to stop Intef from walking as they passed one station where a decree was being heard.

"One moment," he told Intef. "I might learn something."

A man had been accused of stealing grain from a neighbour. He protested and when the *kenbet* found no proof during its investigation it was left to the Vizier to make judgment. The Vizier waved his baton and summoned a priest who stood behind him. This meant that the Vizier was in no position to decide and so reverted to the gods to intercede. The priest took a small statue of the god Maat, placed it on his shoulder and walked towards the accuser and the accused. The priest then stopped in front of one of them indicating the god's favour. The Vizier declared the man innocent.

"Is this how our gods are used?" Tehuti asked, his forehead furrowed.

Intef smiled. "The deities have power even to administer our laws."

"I hope our judgment will not be made by a priest carrying a statue," Tehuti said, shaking his head.

"That remains to be seen," Intef said.

"I'm beginning to understand why Nenshi questioned some of our beliefs. And I have learned nothing from this exchange."

They reached their station in time where a lesser Vizier sat, ready to hear the appeal. He called upon Intef.

"My lord, I implore you to listen to Tehuti-em-Heb, master of Nenshi, his servant for whom a petition to grant freedom is before you. It's only through his words that you will come to understand his desire and through the goddess Maat you will, with impartial judgment, award the request." Intef stressed the word *impartial* hoping this Vizier would not follow in Vizier Kheti's footsteps.

The Vizier nodded, agreeing to hear Tehuti's testimony.

As Tehuti stood, Intef whispered to him, "Remember how to begin, how I taught you."

"My lord," Tehuti began. "You who are greatest of the great, you who are the guide on the sea of truth, hear me as I praise you and the judgment you command. Behold, I have a heavy weight to carry. My heart is troubled. I am in sorrow." Tehuti waited and gaged the Vizier's response. A nod expressed pleasure of the address.

"I remember the first day Nenshi had arrived at my estate," Tehuti continued. "From the top of the steps, a frail ten-year-old boy climbed each step with difficulty. I held out my hand and he reached up to take hold. Two years before that, my lord, my wife had died. We had a son, Meti, who cherished his mother and had become disheartened by his loss."

Tehuti went on to explain that he had need of help in his household and fortuitously had bought Nenshi from slave merchants. His prayers to Renenutet, the cobra goddess of good fortune, had been answered and the two young boys, of the same age, had become close companions.

But the same goddess of nourishment had abandoned Tehuti. Meti had died. A serpent had bit him. The venom had gone deep into his leg and doctors couldn't save him. Nenshi had lost a friend, a brother.

"Your worship, the death of my son and that of my wife had left my home empty. Nenshi had filled the void. I had decided to raise him as my son. I afforded him with the best tutors. I am grateful to one in particular, Soreb, who had taught him more than any father could ever have taught their son."

On hearing the tutor's name, the Vizier's eyes lightened, as if he had known the sagacious teacher. If so, the Vizier would have known that Nenshi would have been taught the lessons he needed to live as a free man.

Tehuti continued. "Nenshi had become my son and in the selfish years that followed I did not adopt him nor grant his freedom when his age was appropriate."

Tehuti's eyes filled with tears. He cleared his voice from the acrimony of his thoughtless past. "I am old," he said. "Nenshi has a life with dreams to fulfil. By the good graces of Pharaoh, through you, his steward, I humbly request to grant freedom." Tehuti bowed his head, signalling he had finished presenting his plea.

The Vizier motioned for Tehuti to take his seat. As he did, he felt his body shake. He wiped his eyes and took a deep breath. Silence begged to be broken, waiting for a decision. The Vizier took his time assessing what he had heard. Tehuti wondered if the delay held an inauspicious outcome or it suggested that the Vizier actually considered the plea. The Vizier then took the baton that had been resting on his lap and held it upright. He was ready to announce his decision. Both Tehuti and Intef stood.

"I have heard the plea as presented by Tehuti-em-Heb," the Vizier began. "The life of his servant has been one of privilege and schooling by a distinguished tutor. I am also aware of the unlawful act of this servant against a free man for which he has been sentenced to labour in Nubia. In light of this testimony, as judge, appointed to preside over this case, I declare the servant by name of Nenshi, belonging to the house of Tehuti-em-Heb, be granted his freedom. I also give pardon for his unlawful act. The time he has spent in the mines has served as his punishment."

Tehuti's eyes bulged in disbelief. His heartbeat quickened with excitement. "My prayers have been answered," he whispered. A new life has begun. The uncertainty of Nenshi's freedom has been washed away. Heka, the god of magic, poured its potion over Tehuti's grief and made it disappear.

Tehuti turned to Intef, grateful for the service of a trusted friend and able litigator. "What's to happen next?" Tehuti asked. "How much longer before I see him?"

Intef replied, "I will send a message to Nubia to notify the officials that Nenshi is to return to Thebes immediately."

"At last, the day has come."

Chapter 17

THE SUN'S GLOW ABOVE THE horizon signalled for the caravan's journey northward to begin. Countless donkeys carried sacks filled with gold. Soldiers smugly marched in unison; their armour glittered in the sunlight. Children gathered along the roadside, waved and shouted their farewells to Nenshi. The mines faded in the distance yet the sense of bondage did not.

Nenshi pulled at the reins of two overloaded donkeys and struggled to keep them in line. A soldier, riding alongside on a camel, was amused.

"You have your hands full," he said.

Nenshi turned and found himself staring at the beast. Its droopy eyes and snout decorated with big lips, gave the impression it was bored from another trek through the desert. Its long eyelashes flapped a few times to keep the blowing sand away. As Nenshi stepped closer, examining the animal as if it was a rare beast, its jaws began to work, gnawing at something. Its cheeks filled and bulged.

"Move back!" the soldier shouted. Not knowing what to expect Nenshi ran to the side of the camel. To his surprise it spat out whatever was in its mouth. The man laughed. "They tend to do that when they're bothered."

Nenshi turned his attention to the stubborn donkeys. They continued to wonder off and Nenshi fought them at every step. They chose their own path.

"Perhaps it's easier to carry the load myself," Nenshi said. He had learned how to scribe and take measurements, but his tutors had never taught him how to deal with donkeys.

"This must be your first time," the soldier said. "It gets easier. Don't pull on the reins. Relax. Let them hang. If you walk in front of them, they will follow."

"It's worth a try. And yes, this is my first time."

"What's your name?"

"Nenshi ... and yours?"

"Muzzafar," he said as he kicked at the camel's side with his heel and rode off. Nenshi heeded to the advice and soon the donkeys learned to follow his lead.

The sun had set, and fires burned throughout the campsite. The first day seemed endless. Men and beasts deserved the rest. Nenshi devoured his meal and rested under a tree when Muzzafar walked by.

"Thank you again for the suggestion," Nenshi called out.

Muzzafar turned and shot a puzzled look.

"The donkeys ... my ordeal with them ..." Nenshi reminded him.

"Ah yes ... you're Nenshi."

"Yes."

"May I sit with you?" It was an unusual request from a soldier. Nonetheless Nenshi welcomed the company. Muzzafar removed his cloak.

"I've never seen you before ... I mean, at the mines." Nenshi said. "After a while one becomes familiar with faces."

"I'm not from Nubia. I'm part of a platoon sent to accompany this shipment. It's not the most exciting task but it's my duty."

"Is it also your responsibility to teach others how to train a donkey?"

Muzzafar chuckled. "I did it for me as much as for you. The sooner we get to Thebes the sooner I can visit my friends."

The mention of Thebes stirred excitement. Nenshi's thoughts drifted for a moment and he could see himself with Sia in the garden.

He envisioned hunting with Hordekef and having a philosophical discussion with Tehuti. All of this he kept to himself. Any sign of eagerness to return to Thebes might cause Muzzafar to keep a close eye on him.

"So, what crime have you committed?" Muzzafar asked.

"Are you always interested in knowing the crimes of those who deliver gold to Pharaoh?"

"No need to be defensive. You don't strike me as a criminal."

"Why not?"

"Murderers and thieves know only how to spit and use vulgar language. I doubt you do either."

"I'm neither a murderer nor a thief."

"Then what crime have you committed deserving of punishment in the mines?"

"I struck a man, the father of the girl I love."

"I see. But there must be more to it than that."

Nenshi realized that Muzzafar was no fool and had a talent to see through people. Or his amicable demeanour with strangers caused them to relax, open up and reveal things that otherwise remained secret.

"I'm also a servant to a nobleman."

"Ah ... I understand," he nodded. "So you were handed the penalty of hard work rather than the alternative, life in prison or perhaps even death. How did you manage that?"

"My master, who raised me as his son had his hand in the matter."

"That explains why you act like a nobleman."

"I've been fortunate. And what about you? Are you from Thebes?"

"No, my home is in the Fayum, or rather my birthplace. My home is wherever I serve Pharaoh."

"Is that why you are sitting with me and not your fellow soldiers? You move from place to place and don't get to know anyone?"

Muzzafar chuckled at the observation. "Not at all," he replied. "I know most of these soldiers and I know their stories. I have heard them all before, over and over. I find speaking with those whom I have never met before satisfies my curiosity about the ways of the world. And I can assure you that those ways are sometimes so twisted it's a wonder how we have all survived."

Their conversation lasted well into the night. The soldier had nothing to fear. He trusted the noble servant, punished for a love affair gone wrong.

The next day the caravan passed through small towns. It stopped at sunset to set up tents on the outskirts. Those who had become ill during the day remained behind. Once recovered, they were either escorted back to the mines or sent ahead to catch up to the group.

Nenshi's excitement grew as the convoy got closer to Edfu. There they would load the cargo on a ship and be off on the River Iteru headed for Thebes. It had been a long journey; men were tired, the beasts even more so. The march was silenced by exhaustion. The caravan finally reached Edfu and camp was set up on the east bank of the river. Soldiers patrolled the area to keep out intruders during the night.

The following morning began with the usual collection of belongings and preparations made for the next destination. Nenshi was eager to move on. He made sure his chores were completed to avoid any delay. The caravan was on its way.

At the peak of the day's heat a flurry of screams broke the stillness, releasing pent up fatigue. "Sand dwellers!" someone yelled. Nenshi had heard of them. Bedouins living in the desert.

Swords and spears swayed violently as robbers swept over the sand dunes. Long black cloaks flapped uncontrollably, appearing like an army of wasps, a pestilence that had been unleashed at will and swarmed towards the caravan. Soon the clatter of bloodstained sabres spread over the silence of the desert.

Muzzafar rode on his camel, slashing to stave off attackers. Nenshi was alone, defenceless, trying to hide behind mules. As the enemy approached, Muzzafar rode up beside Nenshi and tossed a dagger to him. Two men set their eyes on Muzzafar. One of the men remained still while the other circled behind. As the ploy unfolded, Nenshi anticipated the next move and ran towards them. He faced the man who stood behind Muzzafar.

Nenshi's dagger was no match against a sword. The robber lifted his weapon to the sky, ready to strike on the downtrodden slave. Instincts took over and just as the gazelle had exposed its weakness during his hunting expedition with Hordekef, so did the attacker. Nenshi lunged forward and stabbed the assailant.

As Muzzafar fought with his enemy, Nenshi realized he had an opportunity to get away. He kneeled over and took a goatskin flask from the dead man. He shook it. It still had water. The man's black cloak was also of good use. Nenshi then tied the flask around his waist and began to run from the battle scene. At that moment, Muzzafar, who had just killed his enemy, looked up and saw Nenshi running. Muzzafar abandoned his obligation to go after him. Nenshi turned. Muzzafar smiled and waved his sword in the air to bid farewell. Nenshi returned the gesture and kept running, until he disappeared.

Chapter 18

THE NEVER-ENDING ROAD STRETCHED TOWARDS the horizon in a void barren of life. Edfu can't be too far away, Nenshi hoped. Yet in awe of the vastness that surrounded him, he felt a sense of freedom, a slave to no one, a master only to himself.

In the distance, the sounds of battle lingered. The clattering of swords, the cries of death grew dim until a calmness spread like the serenity of a waking child after a night's sleep. The haunting echoes faded, and the only sound came from Nenshi's footsteps, as they pressed against the gravelly path. He moved off the road to avoid being seen. He had fought the enemy, now he was fighting against the sand, planting his feet, struggling to move forward. Sand dunes and salt marshes outnumbered the few streams of fresh water. Nature's whim unleashed a dust storm only to be followed by unbearable heat and stagnant air.

The joy, once held in hunting, had been replaced by the fear of being hunted. Where at one time there had been no end to water carried by servants, now every sip from the flask had to be measured. Where he had relied on a friend to keep him company, now he put his faith in his instincts to survive. His place of learning had transformed - the desert became his teacher, albeit unforgiving and hostile.

After he assured himself, he was far enough from the battle scene, he returned to the road. He travelled for a day, staying on the east bank of the river. He filled his flask, drank freely and refilled it, as he looked for a narrow passage to get to the other side to Edfu. A man walking alone would be questioned, more so after word got out about an attack on Pharaoh's caravan of gold.

Nenshi stayed as close to the river as possible until he thought it was safe enough to cross. But another sandstorm raged. From the wrath of the gods, the wind screamed, collected clouds of sand, and then released them over the land. Nenshi covered his face. He felt as if he was being stung by countless mosquitos. His vision obscured; he slowed his march. When the gods tired, their wrath subdued, the storm relinquished its assault. Now Nenshi only had to deal with the heat. It soaked the little energy he had and caused him to be disoriented. His head hurt as if it had been hit by the hammer used to strike the rocks in the mines. He strayed and walked further away from the river. Now lost, in the land of emptiness, he didn't know how to reach Edfu.

His flask soon dried up. His thirst begged for a spring, a pond, or an oasis. He didn't know where or how to find such refuge. The burning sun parched his lips and caused them to bleed every time he stretched them. He licked away the blood. The little saliva he managed to collect in his mouth helped moisten his lips and wash down the trapped sand. Salty sweat trickled down his forehead into his eyes; an unbearable sting.

He bent down on one knee to rest for a moment and wiped his face with his sand-covered forearm. As he looked up, he saw in the distance, images in long dark robes. He had little life left in him. His skin, no longer a golden brown, shared the colour of sand. Death loomed to claim him. He squinted, hoped he would recognize them, but the exhaustion overpowered him. He walked aimlessly towards the sounds of people and animals. His vision, blurred, he couldn't make out the faces or even know where he was. If someone chose to attack, he was too weak even to defend himself. As he got closer a Bedouin approached. Nenshi collapsed at his feet. The man flung back his charcoal grey robe and reached for his dagger. He gingerly removed it and poked at Nenshi's shoulder. There was no reaction.

"Zayid ... come here," the man, Rashid, called out. Zayid stepped down from his camel and walked towards what had aroused Rashid's curiosity. Zayid plodded his sandals against the sand. He held his head high and pushed back his shoulders. His arms swayed back and forth, causing his robe to flap - all signs that he had mastered the gait of a tribal leader.

"Who is this?" Zayid asked, pointing to the body on the ground.

"He's not one of us," Rashid replied, as he bent over to get a closer look.

"He wears a desert robe," Zayid said. "There's too much sand on his face. I can't tell which tribe he is from. It appears that he has returned from a *ghazwas*. The raid must have failed. Bring him to the camp."

In a tent isolated from the rest of the camp, Nenshi lay flaccid on a rug. A guard stood by the entrance, watched, waited, for the motionless body to show a sign of life. A tribeswoman, familiar with the ailment, walked in carrying two bronze cups of boiled milk and honey. She hummed a tribal incantation and Nenshi responded to it, turned his head, slowly. He then felt her hands on his shoulder, shaking him until he was fully awake. He turned over to find the woman sitting next to him. She placed a hand behind his head and began to treat him with the remedy. As she finished Zayid and Rashid walked in.

Zayid gestured to the guard to leave. As Nenshi rose to greet him, Zayid motioned to remain seated. Zayid then sat and crossed his legs.

Nenshi looked at the distrustful faces. No doubt, they were sand dwellers. He had learned enough about the Bedouins and their customs.

Some tribes were peaceful; some were not. He wondered to which group this one belonged. Many had become a constant menace to Egypt, capable of havoc. Over time, the sand dwellers had gained knowledge of the routes that led into Egypt. Nenshi remembered Tehuti talking about the Walls of the Prince that were built to protect Pharaoh's kingdom. Now, as their confidence grew, so did the thieving ways of the wilderness wanderers. It was a matter of time when they would set their eyes on Memphis, Saqqara and even Thebes.

Rashid pulled back Nenshi's head cloth. As suspected, his features betrayed his origin.

"I knew it. He's Egyptian!" Rashid said with a disdain that ran deep in his blood.

"And what of it?" Zayid asked, knowing Rashid made confrontation his duty.

"We must kill him!"

"No. If I wanted him dead, I would have given you the pleasure when we found him. You would have enjoyed watching vultures tear apart his body."

Nenshi listened as the two debated what should be done with him. They acted like two children who had stumbled upon a lame leopard cub and one wanted to keep it while the other wanted the satisfaction of killing it. Nenshi watched Rashid as he walked back and forth, shaking his head in frustration. Zayid folded his arms, relaxed.

"What do you have in mind for this single Egyptian?" Rashid asked, in a deliberate mock. Nenshi saw the hatred in his eyes and was glad he was not alone in the tent with him.

"I'll tell you later. Besides, you must remember our custom. All strangers are guests in our camp, whether they have been invited or not."

Respect for traditions was a good reason to trust Zayid, Nenshi thought. Zayid was also the obvious choice with whom to seek alliance if he was going to get out of the Bedouin camp.

"But his people have killed many of ours!"

"And we have done the same to his. For now, he's our guest. Say no more."

Rashid's furled brows and taut lips expressed obvious disappointment. He grunted. Nenshi ignored him and turned his attention to Zayid who had removed his robe and white tunic. He then combed back his thick short hair; the colour matched his black penetrating eyes.

"It's our custom, our sacred duty, to show respect and hospitality to strangers, even if they are our enemies," Zayid said. Nenshi appreciated the tradition but not the inference.

"Thank you for saving my life. But I'm not your enemy."

"Everyone has an enemy." Zayid scrutinized his captive to try to discern a reason for him being alone in the desert. "My name is Zayid and this is Rashid."

Rashid, like a spoiled and bitter child, didn't acknowledge the courteous introduction. Nenshi looked at their faces, rugged and worn, a testament to their adeptness in living in the wilderness.

"My name is Nenshi. I come from Egypt." To conceal his identity would only elicit more hostility.

"Tell me, how did you get the garments of a Bedouin and how did you learn our language?"

Nenshi was careful not to reveal his past. A fabricated tale might satisfy their curiosity. "I come from Thebes. My father is a trader. He's getting old and I want to follow in his footsteps."

"Why did you leave Thebes?" Rashid stepped in and asked with the challenging tone of an interrogator.

"Some time ago I joined a caravan to gain experience how traders conduct their business. It was my father's idea."

Zayid's brows raised. He smiled and nodded. "And you have been tutored to speak other languages." Zayid, said.

"Practical experience goes a long way when travelling with a caravan, learning languages, the ways of other people, how to barter."

Once again Rashid interjected. "But you were alone in the desert. What happened?"

"The unexpected," Nenshi replied, without hesitation; the approach to sound convincing. "The caravan was raided. I ran for my life." He wisely omitted the part where he had killed a Bedouin.

"Perhaps running was not the best option. Is that what your father would have wanted you to do?" Rashid asked.

"I had never been taught to use a dagger, a bow and arrow or a spear. My father would like me to return home, alive."

"But you still haven't told us how you got the clothes of a Bedouin."

"During the skirmish there were bodies everywhere. I was afraid for my life. I panicked and took the clothes of a dead attacker so they would think I was one of them and they wouldn't hurt me."

"That was clever," Zayid said. "I guess there's a place for caravans to teach how to defend oneself without weapons," he added and chuckled. But Rashid didn't relent and continued to probe.

"The necklace," he said. "I noticed it around your neck when I found you. Is it yours or did you steal it?"

Nenshi put his hand to his collar, feeling the necklace that Sia had given him. He remembered, after the raid on the caravan, taking it from where it was tucked securely in his waist and placing it around his neck. The reminder of Sia and his longing to return to her had given him strength to march relentlessly through the desert.

"It was given to me by my mother," Nenshi said. "She made it for me. She gave me a prayer to recite while I hold it close to my heart. She said it would help guide me through my journey."

Rashid frowned. "And what is that prayer?"

Nenshi smiled, happy to deliver one of the many he knew, and Bedouins did not. "Mother of Horus cover me with your kindness so

I may sit among the stars and never die," he said. "It's a simple prayer, don't you agree?"

Rashid shirked and turned away.

Zayid walked to the tent's entrance. "Follow me," he said. "I have heard enough."

Nenshi hoped his stories convinced Zayid that he was not a threat. On the other hand, he knew there was nothing he could say to convince Rashid. Zayid's face lit up and he turned to Rashid.

"Tell the women to prepare a feast. I'm certain our guest will enjoy a meal and entertainment."

The thought of food clouded Nenshi's assertion of the sand people. Perhaps these ruffians were not as ruthless as they appeared, he thought. True, they raided caravans and killed to survive. Egyptians were just as brutal.

It was midday. Zayid and Nenshi walked side by side. Rashid followed behind them. As they sauntered, Nenshi saw a man gently tap his camel's neck to make her kneel and then he coaxed her to lie down. He then lay beside her and closed his eyes.

"Why doesn't he rest in his tent?" Nenshi asked.

"A man who rests with his camel, while a breeze cools his tired body, is blessed," Zayid replied. "And he would never trade places with a king."

Young boys dashed back and forth, chasing each other, laughing. It reminded Nenshi of the children in the mines. He thought of Dedi and Dhutnakat and the stories he had told the children.

Desert faces of men and women, shaped by a lifetime of the harsh land, stopped from their daily chores to peer at the stranger who moved about in Zayid's company.

"You will stay there for the night." Zayid pointed to a tent. "Someone will bring water for you to wash and prepare for the feast. There's time. If you wish you may stroll nearby. I'm certain you will not wander too far. I have men surrounding the camp. When you are ready, one of my men will escort you to the festivities. We'll continue our discussion later."

Nenshi walked into the tent. Zayid honoured his guest with a respectable place in which to rest. But what discussion did Zayid have in mind?

The evening air, fresh as the running water from a pond, brought relief. The stars lit the sky with a soft glow. Nenshi hoped that now only good fortune would come his way, a sign that he had been absolved of any transgressions he had committed.

As he walked outside, he heard the cry of sheep from behind a partition. An unfortunate one had been snatched up, silenced and prepared for the festive meal, in honour of the guest. Further along, his senses awakened. The sharp fragrance of roasted green coffee beans pounded in a heavy brass mortar, brought back memories of the kitchens in Tehuti's grand house.

On the ground lay some discarded articles taken from caravans. They served no purpose for these backward people. Nenshi crouched to have a closer look and saw lapis lazuli that rich men in Thebes bought for their wives or lovers. He saw a small container filled with the cosmetic compound women used to colour their eyelashes. Another canister stored *kohl* used to paint their eyelids. They reminded him of Sia, when they first met, captivated by her perceptive eyes framed by a light green colour on the lids. He continued looking and found leather goods from Byblos, vases from Crete, Phoenician dye-works and an assortment of trinkets from Tyre.

Only the men from the tribe gathered for the feast. Women celebrated in an adjacent tent. Nenshi could hear their ululation, a curious cry he had not heard before. Was it a call for celebration or war?

A handful of sticks were tossed into the fire to kindle the embers. Flames came to life and more twigs were added. The air warmed enough to take away the night's dampness. Nenshi saw men perform their customary ablution. Since water was scarce, needed for drinking and cooking, they took a handful of sand from the ground, and cleansed their hands. They repeated the ritual to their foreheads. Nenshi knew he could not partake of the festive meal unless he also did the same to himself with the symbolic sand.

"Tagabbil Al-ilah, may the moon god accept your prayer!" Zayid cried out. The incantation amused Nenshi. Now, in the desert, the Egyptian moon god, Khonsu, had been replaced.

Two boys struggled to carry a clay bowl, filled with meat, rice, spices and bread. They placed it near Zayid, the signal to move closer for the communal meal. Nenshi sat waiting for permission to eat. Insatiable appetites and eating habits, alien from his own, left him wondering what to do. Zayid nodded for him to join the group.

Hands plunged into the bowl and grabbed the sticky rice. They shaped it into lumps big enough to fit into their hungry mouths. Zayid distributed select pieces of sheep that had been cooked over a fire pit. Later, a young boy brought a dish of sweet dates and bowls of fresh camel's milk. Zayid did not eat. As the host, he waited until his guest had finished.

After the meal, they sipped coffee from small cups, spiced with cinnamon. A serving of tea and more coffee followed. During the meal, hardly anyone spoke but afterwards, with plentiful of hot drinks, loud and echoing voices filled the tent.

Zayid motioned to Nenshi. "Come with me."

A partition separated the tent and opened to a smaller section. The large pillows, the rugs, and the fire made the prearranged setting a pleasant meeting place. The sand beneath them still held the warmth from the day's heat. They faced each other.

"I hope you enjoyed the meal," Zayid said, as if he had just entertained an old friend.

"It's been a long time since I had such good food and so much of it too." A courteous response might secure his safety.

"I know that cleansing before a meal is not an Egyptian ritual. I'm grateful for the respect you have shown."

"Customs are deep-rooted," Nenshi said. "My father had taught me that tolerance fosters peaceful relationships."

Zayid nodded. Was it a polite gesture or shared wisdom? Nenshi studied Zayid to discern a greater revelation about his character. But Zayid was cunning and wouldn't allow his façade to be penetrated.

Nenshi too was cautious. His storytelling and shrewdness were enough not to cause suspicion. He continued to appease Zayid through conversation.

"We may not accept what others believe but we can try to understand," Nenshi said.

"What things do you wish to understand?" Zayid asked.

Nenshi was caught by surprise. "Well … I'm interested to learn about your moon god."

"None of my visitors have ever asked me that. But since you are intrigued about these gods, I will tell you about them." Zayid twirled his moustache and continued. "Al-ilah is one of our gods. The most powerful one."

"Every nation has a most powerful god. What others do you have?"

"We pray to the god of the land, the sun, the plants ..."

"Plants?" Nenshi smirked. "But we're in the desert. Where are the plants?"

Zayid paused, his lips tightened, rejected the inquisitiveness of someone who should have known better to challenge his tribe's beliefs.

"Don't you pray to the goddess of frogs?" Zayid cast his own sarcastic tone.

"Yes ... Heket ... the symbol of new life. Egyptians pray to the gods that have the most meaning for them."

"Even so, they are frog-looking," Zayid grinned. "To Egyptians, who live in palaces, we may appear as a lost and backward people. But desert people, as you call them, have a knowledge and wisdom beyond the entrapment of mortared dwellings."

He spat on the ground, into the sand. The boorish act brought the conversation to a close. A discussion about religion will only bring out a person's true character.

A welcomed interruption set Nenshi at ease. A woman carried a tray of coffee. She filled the cups and left. Zayid held a cup with both hands and took a sip. As Nenshi lowered the cup he noticed Zayid staring at him.

"Why are we here ... alone?" Nenshi asked. Time had ended frivolous conversation. "I know you want something from me or you would have killed me by now."

"You're no fool. I can see that. I've given you food, drink, and your life. Now you will give me what I want."

Nenshi was not surprised by the sudden shift. "Whatever it is, how can you be certain I will accord your wishes?"

Zayid smiled, a crooked smile of a man in total control. "You're alive only because of me. You will return the favour."

Nenshi could no longer deflect Zayid's persistence; the determined sand dweller would not accept anything less. Nenshi took a deep breath and looked down into his cup. He took a long sip to gather his thoughts. Zayid's words were as bitter as the drink.

"If you want me to join you and raid caravans, I admit I'll be of little help. I have told you what had happened to me. Besides my father ..."

"No ... no," Zayid interrupted and laughed. "My plans are greater than an attack on a caravan. Listen and take heed to what I say. I'll bring together capable men. With your help, we'll penetrate the Walls of the Prince and enter into Egypt."

Nenshi controlled his anger. His face was calm but the blood in his veins seethed. He needed to find a way to save his life and those that had been targeted for the onslaught.

"We've attempted to pass through the walls many times," Zayid continued. "But our numbers were few and the gates were well protected. Spears and arrows rained down on us like an unexpected storm. The only way to succeed is to attack where the entrance would be most vulnerable."

There was a long pause. Nenshi reflected. He remembered that he had told Zayid that he had been travelling with a caravan and now needed to use that alibi in response.

"I need to think about this," Nenshi said. "I know of the walls. I may have passed them at some point with the caravan."

Zayid leaned forward, his gluttonous eyes ripped through Nenshi and he said, "I will give you time to think and to remember what you know and have seen about the walls. You will tell me everything. It will be our best chance, how to get past the walls. If you fail to tell me, you will be returned to the desert accompanied by Rashid, to do with you as he pleases."

"You speak as if I should know these things ... walls ... gates ..." Nenshi was a good storyteller; the children in the mines would attest to it. But he was not a good liar. He wondered if Zayid would see through him.

"The desert has been my home but I'm not a beetle burrowed in the sand," Zayid said. "Many Egyptians have crossed my path. I'm no one's fool. Surely, there must have been times when you heard your people speak about the walls that defend your land."

Nenshi's silence gave him time to think. Creating a ruse might be the only way for him to escape from the clutches of an obsessed Bedouin. He had to be careful. Zayid was as cunning as a scorpion buried beneath the sand waiting to spear an unsuspecting prey with its poison. And Nenshi didn't want to be a prisoner at the hands of Bedouins nor did he wish to die among scorpions.

Nenshi lifted his empty cup. Zayid politely refilled it. "I do recall a time when our caravan passed the walls" Nenshi said. "But it's a little vague and I need time to piece things together."

"The things we see never leave us. You'll have time to remember."

"Perhaps. But I have gone through a great deal – trying to learn how to conduct business, learning new languages, attacks that have nearly cost me my life. I have been shaken. I don't know what I can remember anymore."

Zayid's impatience took control. He crouched and scooped up sand. His hand opened just enough to allow the grains to trickle through his fingers like a gentle waterfall.

"May I remind you that your life is in my hands. It can pass as fast as this sand passes through my fingers."

Nenshi reached over and cupped his hand below Zayid's to catch the falling sand. He made a fist and raised it in front of Zayid's face. His voice stern, his manner undeterred, he said, "You will not kill me! I hold the key that opens the doors to your riches."

Zayid pulled his hand away and the remaining sand fell to the ground. He no longer had the advantage. He had never come close to penetrating the walls and he knew this was his best chance. He was forced to bite his tongue.

"I understand," he said, with a deliberate calmness in his voice. "Let us both reflect on our desires. The night is young. Come ... dancers wait to entertain us, and wine is plentiful."

Indeed there was an abundance of wine. Dancers were a much-needed distraction and Nenshi wanted to forget, for the time being, about the walls and how to avoid being a traitor to his people.

The wine was strong, masked by a hint of sweet berries. Soon Nenshi's mind, body and senses gave way to the sounds and sights before him, all to his delight.

Ten young women in colourful costumes formed a half circle in front of him. They clapped and chanted in their tribal dialect. The barefoot dancers held long sticks over their shoulders to resemble *khanjars*, the ritual daggers. They brandished them, warlike, as they performed to the beat of various drums - the *al-kasir*, the *al-rahmâni* and the *ad-daff*. The high-pitched sound of the flute, the *al-qassaba*, accompanied them. The instruments, spoils from caravan raids, were so different from one another. Over time, men from the tribe had taught themselves how to play them with precision and simplicity.

The dancers' steps were just as complicated. The random hand-moves and the gentle and playful hip-moves made the dance more appealing. It was all part of the tradition, the embodiment of the tribe's courage, strength, and hospitality.

The women dropped their sticks and walked off the centre of the floor. A new set of performers appeared. They took several steps towards Nenshi and began their dance of the belly. Their moves transformed into quick shoulder-shaking and handclaps in different rhythms. The simple synchronized movement became each woman's attempt to capture the imagination through poetic flirtation.

The evening ended with intoxication from wine and celebration.

When Nenshi awoke the next morning, his head hurt, and he had little recollection of what had happened. He tried to get up but couldn't. His muscles were heavy, like grain-filled baskets. When he realized he couldn't move his hands and feet, he looked down and saw that he was tied like a beast, being prepared for the slaughter.

"I had no choice," Zayid said, as he walked into the tent. Nenshi fought with the ropes. "I didn't want to make a scene last night during the feast so I thought that a little wine would relax you and make you more agreeable to be escorted here. You're valuable to me. I can't risk you leaving us, not now."

Rashid walked in. "The other tribes will soon receive your instructions," he told Zayid and then looked down at Nenshi. "Now this is a more fitting sight - our enemy in captivity, instead of enjoying our food and wine."

"I'm certain this pleases you," Zayid said. "But he's still a visitor, an important one at that. So leave us and go about your tasks." Rashid nodded and left. Zayid approached Nenshi. "Remember ... the Walls of the Prince can be penetrated. I'll be back later to discuss what you remember about them."

As Nenshi lay strapped on a cot he thought about what Zayid had demanded of him. If Zayid had plotted to invade Egypt, Nenshi would now need to have plans of his own. He decided he would tell Zayid where to penetrate the walls. But he would not disclose what he and his men were about to face on the other side.

The sound of footsteps entering the tent caught Nenshi's attention. He raised his head and saw Rashid at the foot of the cot. He came alone. Nenshi remained calm, helpless, at the mercy of a crazed man who would disobey orders for the sake of his own obsession.

"Are you not afraid of me, Egyptian?" He twirled his dagger with his hand and wrist. "It's so easy for me to kill you. But I won't ... I can't ... not now." He taunted Nenshi. "Our plan is set. Our people are ready. Fear not, I won't harm you, even though it would bring me great pleasure." He walked to the side of the bed. "I have never spent as much time as this, alone, with an Egyptian. I have battled them and I have killed those who fought against me."

He stepped closer. With a quick, sweeping motion, he leaned over and slapped Nenshi across the face. Blood spewed from the brute force.

Nenshi grimaced from the pain. He collected the blood in his mouth, took a deep breath and spat in Rashid's face. Rashid stepped back from the unexpected retaliation and wiped his blood-soiled face. He lunged towards Nenshi and struck him again.

"You are brave, Egyptian. Perhaps when I return you will still be here. Then we can settle this ... to the death."

Nenshi held back his anger; it was futile. If he could tear away from the ropes that bound him, he would strap them around Rashid's neck until he no longer breathed.

As Zayid's plan was in motion, so was Nenshi's.

Chapter 19

IN THEBES, TEHUTI WAS IN his garden admiring the lush foliage and flowers. Suddenly Intef appeared.

"Tehuti, I need to speak with you, immediately," Intef said, panting.

"What's the matter? Sit here. Catch your breath." Tehuti's face soured with unwanted news. Something was wrong. A litigator doesn't come looking like he was being chased by a lion, to deliver good tidings. Tehuti waited until Intef was ready to explain his unexpected visit.

Intef took a deep breath and exhaled. "I received word that a shipment of gold on its way to Thebes was attacked. At first ..."

Tehuti interrupted, puzzled why Intef came to deliver such trivial information. "It's not the first time a caravan has been attacked, nor will it be the last."

"Let me finish. The message I had sent to the mines didn't get there in time. Nenshi was chosen to accompany a shipment of gold destined for Thebes and en route the caravan was attacked. My message reached the mines one day after the caravan had departed."

"So Nenshi is not in Nubia?" Tehuti was miffed by how such a thing could have happened. "Is he alive? Do you know? Does anyone know?" Almost panic-stricken, he stared at Intef, waiting for a response.

"It's unknown. Bedouins attacked the caravan and a skirmish ensued. As you might expect, there was great bloodshed and obviously, some of the gold was taken. Nenshi was among those who didn't return to Nubia."

Tehuti felt the air drain out from his lungs and left his head to spin in a cacophony of images only seen in nightmares. "Are you telling me that he died during the attack?"

"No. He was not identified as one of the dead."

"That doesn't mean he's still alive. Maybe he was injured. You know what it's like out there. A sudden windstorm can bury everything in its path leaving no sign of its destruction."

"You must remain positive. Even if a report about Nenshi may not exist, it doesn't mean that he's injured or dead."

The compassion and sliver of hope didn't soothe Tehuti. He covered his face with his hands. The gods who had heard his prayers had now deserted him.

"So Nenshi doesn't know that he's a free man." Tehuti sighed. He sat next to Intef on a stone bench. He slouched forward and released the hopelessness in his heart. Once again, an unknown force controlled time and circumstance. The opportunity for freedom had been crushed by bondage. Time became the impediment, the enemy, and not even Isis, the patron of nature and friend of the oppressed, could intervene. Nor could she bestow her magic to reunite a father and son.

"Something must be done," Tehuti insisted. "I want to know where he is."

He walked towards the house. Every remorseful step brought pain to his heart and a helplessness that spanned to the end of the great River Iteru. He hoped and prayed for Nenshi's safety.

Chapter 20

THE SUN HAD JUST RISEN when Nenshi was awakened and untied by Rashid. Zayid waited by the entrance of the tent.

"Come with me," Zayid said. "We will eat before we complete our plans."

As they walked through the campsite, Nenshi saw women yanking up tent pegs from the ground. The tribe was preparing to move. Perhaps there was an opportunity to escape. But he reconsidered it. He wouldn't get too far before they caught up to him.

"Everyone is getting ready to leave," Nenshi said.

"Not everyone. Some will go ahead and look for a suitable place for our next encampment. We have time."

Women called out to children, playing nearby, to help pull out the heavy pegs from the ground. It was another ritual; the dismantling of tents and later the same women would pitch them and anchor the ropes into the ground. As the sun rose and set, the cycle would repeat. It seemed that these people were never content to remain in one place. It was not their land, according to them. It belonged to their god, Al-ilah, who allowed them to use it. He provided them with a place to rest their tents.

Another group of women gathered and bound the tent poles that would burden camels. Children stuffed sacks with everyday items and placed them nearby for their mothers to load. When the party was ready, some climbed up on the camels and made sure the sacks were secure. Men mounted only with their swords.

"The women work hard," Nenshi said.

"Yes, and when they reach the new camp site, they will build up the tents and prepare the meals."

"And what will the men do?"

"What they usually do."

Very little, Nenshi thought to himself. He moved aside to make room for the travellers. A woman walked by. There was no camel for her to ride on. She walked behind her husband while he rode a camel, his arrogant posture insensitive to his wife's needs. As she passed Zayid, she grumbled, several times, in protest. Zayid grinned and held back his laughter.

"Forgive me," Nenshi said. "I don't see the humour."

"There's a proverb; a woman who sighs has a bad husband."

"We also have a saying. A man who does nothing, is nothing."

Zayid frowned. Nenshi smiled. There was no such Egyptian proverb.

Nenshi was then captivated by women picking something from the ground, from bushes and twigs. "What are they doing?"

"Come ... I'll show you." They walked to where the group was busy collecting the substance. "We call it *mann es-sama*," Zayid said. "Bread, which comes from the sky."

"Bread ... from the sky?" Nenshi shook his head.

"At daybreak, it falls and hangs in beads like dew on desert shrubs," Zayid explained. "It is sweet like honey and it sticks to your teeth. Look at it, there, on the ground," he pointed with his dagger. "It's white but soon it will become yellowish brown." He bent over a shrub and pierced at a few pieces. "Have some."

Nenshi pulled a piece away from the dagger and put it into his mouth. He smiled. "So, it is possible to survive in the desert if you know where to find food."

"And look over there." Zayid stood looking towards two women assembled underneath a makeshift canopy. "They're kneading the *mann es-sama* until it's smooth and thick." He called out to one of the women and ordered her to bring a bowlful of the puree. "Eat it," he said to Nenshi. "It's good." Nenshi took the bowl and dug into the crushed bread from the sky and ate it heartily.

"Does it stay on the ground all day?"

"No, that's why we gather it early, at sunrise. The sweetness will soon attract ants and they'll devour it in very little time. It's a miracle, isn't it? It's Al-ilah's gift."

"You say that Al-ilah sent this ... miracle of food ... from the sky?"

"Yes ... we submit to him and he rewards us," Zayid declared.

It was a subject not be pursued. Nenshi remembered their last discussion about the gods - Egyptian gods that resembled frogs; those of the Bedouins that looked like plants. Nenshi didn't care for either.

"What's that road, over there?" Nenshi pointed.

"It leads to a town, Marsa Alam, by the great waters of the red land."

"Have you been there?"

"Not often." Zayid said then changed direction. "Let's go where there is shade, in the tent," he pointed.

Once inside they sat on rugs, facing each other. Nenshi looked around. The tent was larger than the one he stayed in. In the centre a large poll reached to the top where it supported the tent roof. This is an unusual place to have a discussion, Nenshi thought. Just as the previous one, the setting had been pre-arranged.

Zayid was forthright. "Tell me, what's the best passage for us to enter into Egypt?"

Nenshi had prepared himself for the inevitable discussion; a detached approach would not give Zayid reason to worry. Nenshi delayed his response, scratched his head and forced a nervous smile.

"You do know how to enter into Egypt, don't you?" asked Zayid, his puzzled look gave cause for concern.

"Yes ... yes I do ... but ..."

"What is it? What's on your mind?" He curled his moustache at one end, a sign that his patience was being tested.

"I have a request."

"I'm not surprised. What is it?"

"After I tell you what you want to know, I want to be set free."

Zayid didn't react to the request. He kept his head down. "Why should I do that?" he asked. Nenshi was silent. He knew he had little leverage with which to bargain. "Perhaps you can't remember anything about the walls, and you take me for a fool," Zayid said, with a harsh tone. He stood, went to the tent's entrance and peeled back at the opening. Two men walked in, one holding a whip.

Nenshi tried to remain calm but the muscles in his arms tightened at the thought of a beating. "That's not necessary," he said, calmly.

"It's your choice," Zayid said.

"I will tell you what I know."

Zayid smiled and waved the men away. He sat down. "I think we have an understanding. I'm listening."

"I still ask to be set free, after I tell you."

"Anything else?"

"I will need food and water."

Zayid nodded. "The price is fair. But first you will tell me what you know and if I'm satisfied, I'll give you what you want."

Nenshi had no choice. All he had left was his skill in persuasion by creating a believable ruse. He proceeded to describe, in detail, what he led Zayid to believe he had heard during his travels with caravans in and out of Egypt. He explained how the Walls of the Prince were constructed and how they protected Egypt. Zayid had always prided himself in the knowledge he had gained over time about his enemies. But it seemed there was more than what he knew.

Zayid questioned. "You're certain about all this? Yesterday you had told me you had little recollection about the walls. Now you give me great details."

"Yesterday my mind was like a tempest. This desert life is new to me. Food from the sky. Gods I had never heard of before. I told you I needed time to reflect."

Zayid pushed one more time. "And you're certain that the place you described is defenceless."

"The entrance is well hidden and rarely used. And so there are few soldiers stationed there. You can overtake them with ease. I swear this on my father's life."

Nenshi succeeded with his embellishment of the walls. Zayid called for the guards to enter. Nenshi stood, clenched his fist, fearful of what might happen.

"You are going to have me beaten, after I told you everything?"

Zayid laughed. "No … no …," he said and then turned to the men. "Take him back to his tent. Tie him up. His story still needs to be proven."

Zayid stepped outside and waved to Rashid who had been waiting at a distance. They spoke, whispered, for several minutes. Nenshi wondered if his tale had failed and now raised suspicion. Rashid walked away, mounted on his camel and rode off. Two other men followed him. Nenshi wondered where they were going.

The next morning a tribesman untied Nenshi. Even in the mines he never had to sleep tied to a post. His life seemed to have greater value to the Bedouins than to Pharaoh. He rubbed his wrists and stretched out his arms to loosen the tightness in his body.

Outside he noticed Rashid and Zayid in conversation. Men in their black cloaks scurried to get to their camels. The flurry of activities meant it was time to march into Egypt.

"We're ready," Zayid said. He stood proud, ready to lead his men. "It appears that what you described has truth," he told Nenshi. "Rashid and his men went to survey the entry point. It's where you said it would be."

Nenshi was relieved. His knowledge of the walls had proven beneficial. Tehuti had often spoken about them, in great detail. Now Nenshi's chance of escaping was getting closer and he was careful not to show anticipation or the slightest excitement. If his ruse were discovered, Zayid would unleash Rashid.

"We must leave soon," Zayid said. Nenshi took this as a signal for him to get ready as well. After all, he had an agreement.

Nenshi went inside the tent and put on a dark robe. He tied it below the collarbone. He covered his head with the familiar Bedouin head cloth and went back outside.

"Where is the food rations and the flask of water you had promised?" Nenshi asked.

"Did you think I was going to let you go before the raid? If we're successful, when we return, you will be freed." Zayid's tone was stern, confirming his authority. Nenshi's jaw clenched, his face threw a dirty look at Zayid and then he spat on the ground in protest.

"Tie him up," Zayid ordered. Two men dragged Nenshi back into the tent.

The army of sand-dwellers were ready to march towards the Walls of the Prince. From inside the tent Nenshi could hear swords rattling and the excited cries of warriors, cries that would meet an unknown fate.

Bedouins scattered everywhere, some on foot, others on camels. Final preparations to move into Egypt were complete. Some waved their daggers in the air like a scorpion that swayed its poisonous tail just before stabbing its victim. They were excited and anticipated a glorious assault and spoils to be taken.

Zayid shielded his eyes from the sun with his hand. He squinted and looked to the sky for the sun's position. He calculated, with precision, the march towards Egypt. He was skilled in battle. The element of surprise was his reason for success.

Zayid commanded his men to move forward. His orders spread throughout the camp as fast as a desert snake that disappeared into the sand. After several hours, just as the sun rested on the horizon, the army reached the Walls of the Prince. A signal from Zayid motioned his men to pass through the gate that Nenshi had described. Cautiously the group began to pass through them.

"Who goes there?" A voice echoed. Twilight prevented a good look at the intruders. The voice called out again. No response. Trained soldiers took no chances. Arrows with flamed tips shot through the sky lighting up the land below to reveal unexpected visitors. Countless Bedouins. This time the voice made a different call. "Attack! We're being attacked!"

Within minutes a sea of Egyptian soldiers appeared on scaffolds that were attached to the wooden walls. Eyes, innumerable as the stars, looked down at the intruders. Bows were raised, arrows pointed at them.

Zayid exuded horror. Did he misinterpret Nenshi's instructions? Were these not the gates he had described? Zayid had little time to deal with his confusion. Arrows and spears whistled through the air towards the sand dwellers. Cries of death reverberated. Bodies fell. Zayid ordered to retreat. Those that managed to get out headed back to the camp.

The sand dwellers were losing the battle against the onslaught from the Egyptians. Zayid cried out to Rashid to fall back. Zayid grabbed the reign of his camel and swung around. As he retreated, an arrow whistled through the air and pierced his back. He cried out in vain. Rashid turned and saw a fallen Zayid, motionless on the ground. Enraged, Rashid clenched his fist. His eyes seethed with vengeance. He had only one thought - to go back and deal with Nenshi.

It was chaos at the camp. The men who had retreated from the unsuccessful raid had already spread the word. Women wept for the loss of their husbands. The injured were treated for their wounds. When Rashid arrived, he ran to the tent where Nenshi was being held. The veins on his arm protruded from gripping a dagger as tight as he could. He pulled back the opening. At the foot of the pole lay the cord that bound Nenshi. He was gone.

Rashid ran outside. There was no sign of a runaway Egyptian who had betrayed his leader. With everything lost, there was only one thing he could do - find Nenshi and kill him.

PART THREE

Chapter 21

EVERY ANXIOUS STEP WAS MET with a feeling of being pursued. But it was better than being tied to a pole waiting to meet his death. While the Bedouins were attempting to pass through the walls, Nenshi had been helped by the woman who had treated him earlier. She had walked into the tent and found him tied to the post. He feigned illness long enough to gain her pity and treat his ailment. As she untied him, he released himself from the rope. His quick movements frightened the woman. But she didn't scream for help. He noticed a bag with food and a flask of water that she brought with her. He took them and left.

As he ran, he passed Zayid's tent. He quickly went inside to see if there was something useful to take with him. He spotted a pouch, picked it up and shook it. Coins. He remembered Zayid had described the way to Marsa Alam. A scan of the campsite confirmed he wasn't being watched and so he headed straight for the road.

During the entire walk, Nenshi often looked behind him. An eerie sensation that he was being followed brushed against the back of his neck. He recoiled at every unusual sound.

The coins he had taken from Zayid's tent proved useful to pay for a preferred seat aboard a ship, headed north. He kept to himself, spoke very little and managed to stay out of harm's way. They passed Quseer and stopped briefly at Safaq where affluent dealers accompanied by their personal guards boarded with sacks filled with hand-crafted jewellery and emerald gemstones.

Two days later they docked near Maskuta, the most northern point of the sea. As Nenshi disembarked, he asked one of the merchants where to find the best caravan route.

The merchant pointed. "Some call it the Incense Road. Caravans cross it all the time. Where are you going?"

No reply. Nenshi headed for the road.

After a night's rest at a local inn, compliments of Zayid's generous coffer, Nenshi went to the town's market, bought food, filled his flask and went on his way. He was convinced he was headed towards the River Iteru. It was only after a few hours that he realized the path of the sun was not what he had expected. He was travelling in the opposite direction. He chose to continue, hoping a town would soon appear and he could rest and figure out how to get back to the river.

Away from the road, makeshift tents sprang up and a few fires burned to create a temporary resting place for a caravan travelling through the area. Nenshi approached a man and asked where they were destined.

"Hebron," he answered. "Perhaps a day or two away."

Nenshi had not heard of Hebron. If it was the caravan's destination then it would be a major stop and he could plan his way back to Thebes. He asked the man if he could join the group.

"Can you pay?"

"Why should I, if I'm walking?"

"I thought you might want to ride a camel. I have two."

The man brought Nenshi to see his camel. He was reluctant to get close, remembering his encounter when Muzaffar's camel spat at him. He stayed far enough to get a good look at the animal's face, melancholy, eyes drooping, its mouth chewing from side to side. He reached into his pouch and showed the man three coins. The man's brows furled.

"I have to eat," Nenshi said. The man took the money.

On the outskirts of Hebron, Nenshi left the caravan. It was better to be on his own rather than be the target of a barrage of questions: Who was he? Where was he going? Why was he alone? Where did he get the coins?

He realized he needed to replenish his empty goatskin flask. But he did not want to risk the unknown, so he stayed away from the town, even if it meant being without water. Luckily though there was a communal well on the town's fringes.

He waited behind a fig tree until he felt it was safe enough to go to the well. He lowered a bucket into it and pulled it back up as fast as he could. The cool water was refreshing. As he filled his flask, he heard footsteps. He remained calm. As he turned, he saw an old man approaching. They exchanged a respectful nod. From the corner of his eyes Nenshi watched the old man study him. No doubt the well would be a place to stop for many travellers on their way to the next resting place. And the old man could afford the time to examine each one as he passed through. Old men and their suspicions always looked for fault.

"Where are you from?" The old man spoke in dialect. His raspy tone reminded Nenshi of Sheikha, the one who interpreted his dream in Thebes. The old man repeated his question but Nenshi refused to answer.

"How far is it to the next town?" Nenshi asked as he flung his flask over his shoulder. Perhaps the man might know how to get to Thebes.

"You have strong legs," the old man said. "You should get to Uru Salem by sundown. And you may even find time to stop by the Salt Sea to rest and bathe. Don't stay too long there, no birds fly over the waters and no animal is there to be hunted."

"Why is that?"

"It's a bitter place. As if demons took over the waters and not allowed life to surround it or birds to fly over it. You can bathe in it though. I have, many times, in my youth of course. But as I said don't stay too long. You never know if the demons will devour you too."

"Have you ever seen these demons?"

"No … perhaps it's just a tale to keep people away."

The old man scratched his head. His bony fingers plucked out a head bug and squeezed it. He then reached into the bucket that Nenshi had pulled up from the well and cupped out water with his hand, sucked it into his mouth and spat it out. Nenshi was glad he had already filled his flask.

"You appear to be in a hurry. Are you in trouble?"

"No." Nenshi remained calm but felt the need to come up with an alibi at the whim of the old man's meddling. "I'm meeting a friend near … ah … Uru Salem."

"I see. Will this be your first time, to Uru Salem? I can tell by your broken language that you're not from this area."

"I've never been there before. My friend usually comes to visit me."

"And where's that?" The old man's questioning was beyond being nosy. It had now become an interrogation. A stranger with an unfamiliar accent and unusual appearance was suspect of an offense. Nenshi began to walk away when the old man repeated the question. "I asked you, where are you from?"

While walking backwards Nenshi said, "I come from a land that you can only see in your dreams." The old man was left standing by the well, speechless and crabby.

Nenshi reached the Salt Sea, the place the old man had described - a place to rest and bathe. It was also a place where no fish lived in its waters, nor did coral or seaweed exist.

The shores were desolate, covered with sand and rocks unknown to man's footsteps. A mild breeze carried a strange odour. Oily patches randomly appeared on the water. Nenshi looked up at the blue sky. Just as the old man had told him, no birds flew overhead. They were unable to reach the other side. Those that attempted the flight would stop, without cause and fall to their death into the sea.

Nenshi knelt by the water and eyed the slow-moving waves. After each wave reached the shore, it retreated into the sea and repeated the timely beauty with uninterrupted motion; each wave did the same as the one before. Within minutes the salt, contained in the water, dried and coagulated on the rocks. As far as the eye could see, the shore, touched by the sun's rays, sparkled like countless stars that fell from the sky.

The strangeness and lifelessness of the water had an inviting beauty and mystery of its own. Without hesitation, Nenshi took off his clothes and jumped in. No sooner had he plunged in, his body was pushed up to the surface with a force he could not control. He made no effort to float. The sea did it for him. He lay on his back and smiled. He thought of himself like a water lily resting peacefully on a pond. He wanted to stand, convinced he could walk on the water. People would say that only a man with powers could perform such a feat.

He swam back to the shore. No demons appeared to devour him. While he walked to get his clothes, the intense heat penetrated his skin and instantly his body was completely dry. The salt from the water dried and formed a thin crust over his entire body. He was amused by it all. He took his head cloth and rubbed off the salt.

It was late in the afternoon when Nenshi came upon the city of palm trees, Uru Salem. He stood on a hill that overlooked its vastness, surrounded by massive walls. Within it, towers sprouted from the fertile earth. Countless houses, filled with people from surrounding lands, huddled together as if to protect this special place. Camels carried spices, gold and precious stones. Obedient oxen pulled its plough. Men and beast worked to provide sustenance to a growing nation.

Indeed, this was a unique place, different from Thebes. He expected it to be like Thebes. After all, they were both major centres for their nations, the only difference would be language and customs. But he sensed something different about Uru Salem. The lure of what was known and what was not seemed to attract many to this place. An unseen force drew man to explore the greater power beyond the land, the sun and the stars. It was a place that had been touched by a power, waiting for others to follow.

The sensation extolled by the city went deeper. The lessons from hard work in the mines; fighting for his life in the market in Thebes; and, escaping death at the hands of Bedouins - have brought him closer to understanding the fragility of life. He looked closer within himself to balance his world as a servant who sought freedom and a world within him that sought harmony. As Nenshi gazed upon the splendour of Uru Salem, he was drawn into the mystery that lay behind the walls. There was a sense of belonging, a pull to be part of this new world.

He walked through the streets which by day saw townspeople and merchants busily going about their affairs. Now, as the sun's bronze glow rested on the land, the city was empty. Dogs barked incessantly to warn their masters of the stranger. Clamorous voices, innocuous laughter and music echoed all around him. He walked, cautiously, through the labyrinth of narrow passages. They were like rivers that meandered through a valley and led to a lake. The streets eventually emptied into a large square, the centre of the town. Even Uru Salem had a place of refuge for those who sought shelter.

In an apparent sea of confusion, merchants dismantled tents with calculated swiftness. Makeshift counters were removed with less care. Traders sat and counted their earnings while others cursed those who didn't buy anything.

A short man carried long rolls of fine cloths and fabrics. The scowl behind the stubbles of a beard was evidence of his annoyance. The heavy load blocked his view. He staggered like a drunken man trying to find his way home after a long night in the tavern. He swayed back and forth recklessly and had little concern for those around him. Men shouted and cursed at him angrily as he knocked over several stands. He continued, unconcerned by the verbal abuse.

He walked, scowl-faced, towards Nenshi who tried to avoid him. Stepping from side to side failed to bypass the short man. Nenshi bumped into him, causing him to lose balance. The rolls of fabric flew into the air, unravelled, and fell to the ground, along with the man.

"Many pardons," Nenshi said as he held back a burst of laughter.

"You clumsy fool! Have you no eyes to see where you're going?" asked the man with an expression that made him look more comical than upset.

"Forgive me ... I didn't see you." Nenshi helped the man gather his goods.

"I don't need your apology. I have no time for it ... move aside." He collected is wares and walked away in his drunk-like fashion. Nenshi followed him.

"Let me help you. Your load is heavy," Nenshi offered. The man stopped and turned. His face was red, not from anger, but from the weight of the goods he carried.

"Is this your way of stealing from me?"

"If I helped you, perhaps you could return the favour."

It didn't take long for the man to have second thoughts. A heavy load can make anyone submit to almost anything. He handed the goods to Nenshi.

"Follow me. And don't drop anything. If you try to run and steal them, I'll chase you like a hyena after a helpless sheep." Nenshi examined the plump figure; hardly capable of catching anything let alone run like a hyena.

"Or perhaps bump into clumsy fools like me." Nenshi tried to make light of the incident. But the wit went unnoticed.

"What do you want? I'm not rich and I can't pay you for your help."

"I don't want coins. I'm a stranger here. I only want to know where I can eat and rest for the night."

"You're not the only one. It will be difficult. Are you familiar with caravans and trade?"

"Ah ... yes ... but not of this kind."

"Then what kind? It doesn't matter. I don't want to know. Tonight is my last night in this city of prayers. Tomorrow I leave for Damascus. For that, I rejoice. I ... the subject of all misfortunes ... I loathe caravans!"

"Then why are you here?"

"As I said, I'm the subject of misfortune. My brother took ill on the day the caravan was to leave Damascus. He asked me to come here and sell his goods for him. We all pay a price in this world. Some more than others." He paused for a moment to catch his breath and then continued. "But you don't care about caravans and misfortunes. All you want is food. Listen, I'm in a hurry and talking to you is a waste of my time. Help me pack my goods and I'll give you food and shelter for the night."

"You're a generous man."

"Don't be mistaken. This isn't charity. You must earn your keep."

Several hours later Nenshi finished packing all the rolls of fabrics. To his delight, he soon found himself sitting in front of a warm fire enjoying a plate of roasted goat. The aroma from the herbs and spices spread like an early morning fog. Passers-by stopped and took a deep breath and relished the distinctive smell. Stray dogs circled the campsite, instinctively keeping their distance, yet ready to pounce on discarded scraps and bones.

"My name is Babak. What's yours?"

"Nenshi."

The fire crackled and the song of cicadas echoed in the background. It was a familiar sound that reminded Nenshi of the garden where he and Sia often met; the place that had nurtured love and had also betrayed it. Yet he would still go back there, a hundred times, if it meant he could be with her. He was still determined to find his way back to Thebes.

"Forgive me for the way I spoke earlier," Babak said. "The day has been long and the sales have been few." Nenshi nodded his head. He was too busy enjoying his meal to offer a response.

"You said you're a stranger here. Where do you come from?"

Nenshi stopped eating to gather his thoughts. "The west," he said.

"Where in the west?"

"Beyond the Salt Sea."

"I understand ... you don't want to tell me. It's not important. I was trying to make conversation. Your name is unfamiliar to me and I was curious where you call home."

Nenshi hesitated. The barrage of questions was enough to withdraw and silence himself. But then his tale might be too unbelievable and hence would be easily dismissed.

"I come from Egypt," Nenshi said and swung his head in different directions. The feeling of being followed returned.

"So that's where you've learned to speak our language and those of others, I assume."

"Yes."

"And what brings you to a place like this?"

"I got lost. I thought I was on the road back to Egypt. Instead, it led me here."

"It's quite a ways to Egypt. And I'm not sure what you can find here to sustain your stay. If you want, you can come with me to

Damascus where there is life and opportunity. Uru Salem is a place for worshippers."

The words exploded in his mind with thoughts of how it was like to be free, to make his own choices - what he had always wanted. And even though he still longed to go back to Thebes, at least Damascus could give him temporary refuge. For all he knew the Bedouins were still on his heels determined to avenge the death of their leader. Also, by now the administrators at the mines would have realized that he was not among the survivors of the attacked caravan. Nor was his body found. They could only conclude that he ran away. Nenshi saw himself as a fugitive, sought after by his own country and sand dwellers. He was without a home and for the time being Damascus was his only alternative. His body and mind needed rest, after which he could plan his way back to Egypt.

"Very well," Nenshi said. "I accept your offer."

"I have offered you nothing but the means to get to Damascus."

"Yes, but how a hunter hunts will bring him bountiful spoils or empty hands."

"Oh ... and you have the gift of the tongue as well. You're wiser than you appear."

"I have more knowledge than I have wisdom. Knowledge comes from learning, wisdom from living."

"Enough ... enough of your eloquence. My head is beginning to spin. We must get some sleep. Damascus ... I'm coming home."

Chapter 22

DAMASCUS EMERGED FROM THE HORIZON. Behind it, the snow-capped Mount Nebo stood majestically. From afar, walls jut out from the foothills of the mountain giving the impression of a mother's arm stretching to embrace her child.

As Nenshi and Babak approached the main entrance to the city, their senses were awaked by the fragrance of olive groves, mulberry plants, apricots and almond trees, all in their maturing and blooming stages. The freshness of life was a stark contrast from the staleness of the road they had travelled.

"This is Damascus," Babak proclaimed with a smile. "We call it Es Sham, the beauty spot."

"Come with me, I'll take you to meet my brother."

"The one who was too ill to sell his goods?"

"No. My other brother, the owner of a tavern. You can stay with him. You can work for him and earn your keep. He always complained about not having enough help."

"You never told me this was your plan."

"You didn't ask." Babak grinned. Nenshi shook his head.

"How are you certain he'll allow me to work for him? He doesn't even know me."

"Leave it to me."

"Wait. Then I should tell you something." Nenshi didn't want to reveal anything about himself but if he was going to stay in Damascus for a while then he needed to trust someone.

"Ah … I see … everyone has secrets."

Nenshi paused, as if waiting for an enlightenment from the gods to begin the discussion. "I'm not sure where to begin."

"It's always good to begin from the beginning," Babak said with a grin.

"Very well. I was a servant in Thebes, sent to work in the gold mines in Nubia. I escaped and …"

"Stop, stop! Say no more," Babak interrupted. "If this is what I think it is, why do you tell me?"

"You had said you wanted to know my past, my secrets. To do that, I have to be honest."

"I see. Very well. Go on. What crime did you commit?"

"I fell in love." He reached into his waistband, pulled out his necklace and placed it around his neck.

"Oh … love … yes … it can free you or imprison you … in more ways than one. Did she give that to you?"

"Yes. To remember her." Nenshi smiled and told him everything.

"Now I know why you always keep looking behind you. Living as a renegade can cause one to see and hear things that are not there. But you must be careful about your honesty, be more mindful to whom you tell the truth."

"What do you mean?"

"Every fugitive has a weakness. Yours is love and freedom. There are men that would turn you over to the authorities if they knew what you have told me. There are runaway slaves and prisoners from many lands seeking refuge in places like this. Some pay a high price for their capture."

"But I've just told you everything. How do I know you'll not deliver me to the authorities for a few measly coins?"

"Don't worry, your secret is safe with me. I have no interest in a reward at the expense of your misfortune."

"Then perhaps I should say that I'm a poet," Nenshi said with a chuckle.

"A poet?"

"Yes, a poet. A poet on a mission."

"What sort of mission?"

"The great Pharaoh is fond of poetry. I have been commissioned to travel near and far in search of the most eloquent words to make his life pleasant. Is that believable?"

"You'll be surprised at the things people believe, especially when one speaks of Pharaoh."

Babak flung open the door of the tavern and stomped in.

"Saulum ... where are you?" he shouted. Patrons turned, startled by the roar that interrupted their meal. Saulum appeared from behind a partition. He looked fatigued. He was younger than Babak, yet his tired face and overworked body made him appear older.

"Babak, you've returned, so soon! Welcome back," he said, always glad to see his brother. "How much have you sold? Never mind, it's not important. You must be hungry and thirsty. I'll bring you food and drink but first I will tend to the patron behind you." Saulum looked behind Babak and tilted his head upward, pointing to Nenshi. "He will pay, you won't."

"He's not a customer," Babak said with a grin. "This is my friend Nenshi. We met in Uru Salem. He's a poet from Egypt, the Pharaoh's poet." Heads turned to look at the so-called poet from Egypt. Blank faces, foreheads furrowed, reflected their disappointment. A beggar was better dressed. Babak raised his voice for everyone to hear. "He's travelling in search of words that will bring pleasure to the great one.

And there is no better place than Damascus to find such words." Everyone cheered.

Saulum glanced at Nenshi and then looked at Babak. He knew his brother well enough not to believe him and wondered what he was up to. He motioned Babak to step closer and whispered, "Even if he is a poet, it means nothing to me. I don't sell words. I sell beer, wine and food."

Babak put his arm around Saulum's shoulder and gave him a little squeeze. "My dear brother, he's my friend and needs a place to stay. He'll work for you. You always told me to let you know if I found someone to help you. Well, here he is."

Saulum looked at Nenshi and then at Babak whose eyes bulged. Babak nodded his head like a dwarf frog bopping in and out of the water looking to swallow a bloodworm. It signalled his approval of Nenshi. Saulum could either continue to do what he had been doing with no help or try to find a helper himself for which he had no time. Even if Babak was wrong, his intentions were always honourable. Saulum turned to Nenshi.

"Words I don't have but work I have plenty. Come with me, I'll show you where you can stay."

"You can show him later," interrupted Babak. "Night has fallen and we must have something to eat." He grabbed Nenshi's arm and pulled him towards the door.

"Where are you going?" Saulum asked. "There's plenty of food here."

"Not tonight. There will be plenty of days for that. Besides, you don't have dancers here. If you want more customers, you must get dancers. I told you that many times."

"I don't need dancers and I don't need more customers." His eyes widened in obvious anger. "I'm busy enough as it is. Don't waste any more of my time. Go to your dancers." He then turned to Nenshi, lowered his tone, and said, "Be ready to work tomorrow, early."

Babak led the way through the streets, their path paved by the moon's light. At every turn, they heard the soft tapping from the feet of hungry dogs, prowling for food.

"Saulum is a good man," Nenshi said.

"He's a hard worker. Not a peddler like me."

Babak picked up his pace. Hunger caused him to move like a leopard. Nenshi had difficulty keeping up. The sound of their footsteps replaced the pitter-patter of stray dogs. Nenshi grabbed Babak's arm and forced him to stop walking.

"What is it?" Babak asked. "Am I going too fast for you?"

"Shhh ...Quiet!"

"What is it?"

"I thought I heard something. Footsteps."

"The only thing I hear is my stomach, growling."

They waited for a moment. It was quiet. They moved on.

Suddenly a figure ran out from the darkness and collided with Nenshi. They both fell to the ground. It was a young girl. He lifted her up and began to apologize. She merely stared at him.

"Are you here alone?" he asked, leaning closer to the dirty face, covered by unkept and tangled hair.

The girl didn't answer. She was expressionless like a child's old doll. "Where's your home?" Still, no reply. Confused, Nenshi looked to Babak.

Babak folded his arms and shook his head. "It's no use," he said. "She can't speak. She can only hear. And she is without a home. She sleeps in the streets and begs for food."

"How do you know this?"

"Her name is Aziza. Everyone knows her. She's been this way for most of the fifteen years of her life."

Nenshi looked at the torn clothes and at the despondent look in her eyes. She reminded him of the children at the mines, malnourished and deprived of their youth.

"I'm certain that if someone showed her a little kindness, she would return it," he said.

"All she knows is how to steal or beg for food."

"Food ... that's it ... food. She must be hungry. She'll come with us." Nenshi smiled and hoped the girl would recognize the gesture.

"Are you mad?"

Nenshi ignored Babak. With a gentle motion he brushed aside strands of thick black hair away from her face. She turned to avoid the contact. Nenshi cupped her chin with his hand and drew her to look at him. She furled her brows and moved to take a bite of his finger, but she didn't. Nenshi looked into her eyes, letting his own speak to her, to let her know she was safe.

"You have a right to be angry," Nenshi said. "You've been treated as a castaway, something I know all too well. I won't treat you that way."

He hoped the gentle touch, the soft voice soothed her anger, tempered the hardness in her heart. Nenshi took her by the hand and said to Babak, "Lead the way. We're your devoted servants."

"Hmm ...you look more like two stray cats," Babak muttered.

The commotion in the overcrowded inns was a welcomed ritual for its owners. Patrons, mostly traders, indulged to satisfy their hunger and ate abundant quantities of meat, poultry and fresh fruit. Wine and beer flowed freely over boastful conversations. Innkeepers relished nights like this. The more tumultuous the chatter, the more they drank, the more they spent.

Aziza focused on a dish of braised mutton. Her eyes widened like a preying hungry lioness preparing to attack. Out of self-preservation, she pulled the plate closer towards her and ravenously shovelled the meat into her mouth.

"She's like a wild boar," Babak said.

"She probably hasn't eaten in days," Nenshi said as he filled her cup with water.

"Maybe so," pitied Babak. He stared at her while she ate. He shook his head. "So, what will you do with her, now that you have rescued her? She'll become like a lost puppy and follow you everywhere, the hand that feeds her."

"I don't know." Nenshi said. "This food looks good and a good meal makes problems bearable."

There was little conversation at their table. They preferred to fill their stomachs and let the other patrons satisfy the room with laughter and rant. When they finished their meals, they listened to amusing tales of merchants' gains and modest acceptance of losses.

"I know what to do," Nenshi said.

"I'm afraid to ask."

"She can help me at your brother's inn. If he permits it, of course."

"You had too much to drink. First you want to feed her, now you want her to work with you."

"Saulum won't have to pay. He'll be getting two workers for the price of one."

"A mad poet, that's what you are. But knowing my brother, he'll probably allow it. He doesn't know how to refuse anything."

Aziza listened. Her head pivoted back and forth as the two exchanged words. Her eyes lit up as if to express thoughts of being in a tavern, eating and drinking all she wanted.

They stood outside the inn, lethargic and satisfied. The night's warm air added to their sluggish stroll. Babak walked up to a juniper shrub growing in a planter near the entrance door of a house. He looked around and then plucked a long needle-like leaf from one of its stems and used the stiff end to loosen a piece of meat stuck between his teeth.

Nenshi looked behind him to Aziza. She maintained a safe distance. There was opportunity to run away. But she didn't. Nenshi smiled, turned and kept walking. Aziza followed.

Chapter 23

BABAK WAS RIGHT. SAULUM DIDN'T refuse and allowed Aziza to help out. But there was a condition. She could stay only as long as Nenshi worked in the tavern. If he decided to leave, the girl would have to go too.

The first few days working together proved to be difficult for the two outcasts. Communicating with a mute was much more challenging than Nenshi had thought. He had learned to speak languages of different lands, now he had to learn a different kind of language; one using hands. He thought of symbols he had learned to draw on papyrus and how they were used to represent words and sounds. If he could do the same, without speaking or drawing, and use his hands instead to describe what he saw and heard, then perhaps Aziza would understand.

It took time for them to learn how to exchange words, thoughts, and expressions with one another using only the language of signs. Eventually she would no longer silence her hands and regress, emotionless, into her world.

Nenshi knew she trusted no one. He had learned the same mistrust himself. He gave her sustenance and she took it; food satisfied her basic needs. She wouldn't go to sleep until she was certain that Nenshi was fast asleep and in the morning, she was the first to wake. Nenshi wondered if she ever slept at all.

On a busy day in the tavern Aziza, inexplicably, chose to work at a slower pace than usual. Customers waited a long time for their orders and when the food was finally brought to the tables, it was cold.

She sat in the kitchen for much of the time as Nenshi and Saulum scrambled back and forth. Saulum walked by, his hands full of dishes and drinks, and commanded Aziza several times to get up and help. She didn't budge. Nenshi was too busy to say anything. It wasn't until the end of the evening, when he was tired and frustrated, that his patience gave way. He grabbed Aziza by the arm and dragged her outside to the back of the tavern.

She tried to loosen the grip, but to no avail. Nenshi scolded her, repeatedly. But this made her more obstinate and her defences turned into outbreaks. Her attempts to claw and scratch her way out of Nenshi's hold failed. The more she tried, the more he tightened his grasp. She managed to free one arm, reached up and pulled at his hair. He cried out in pain and grabbed her hand, squeezed it, until she let go of his hair. Her eyes swelled with tears. She covered her face.

Nenshi understood her pain, not from his grip of her hand. It came from deep inside – a broken heart, a lonely life. He reached out and put his arms around her. She didn't resist.

"I know your pain," Nenshi whispered. He had no sign to express his words, only an embrace. The comfort was welcomed, desperately needed, to feel accepted by someone who cared.

That day changed things for both Nenshi and Aziza. He had learned that a simple embrace could tear down walls, even for a young homeless child. For Aziza a new beginning, full of dreams and hope, was on the horizon. Now smiles and laughter replaced apprehension and suspicion. Nenshi trained her to use her hands and arms to express her thoughts in ways that she hadn't known before. She even taught herself to make sounds to complement her gestures. They spoke to each other in a world without words.

The tavern was empty, except for a few regular customers who sat sipping on warm beer, waited, hoped, for a breeze to cool their clammy bodies. Babak walked in, fatigued from the heat. He scanned the room.

"Ah, there you are," Babak said and waddled, his legs grew heavier with every step. Nenshi sat alone, glad there was no one to serve. Babak grunted in relief.

"I want you to come with me tonight. I have friends you should meet."

"No ... I can't. It's been a busy day and there's still much to do."

"It can wait. You can get up early tomorrow and finish it. You've been caged in this prison too long."

Nenshi threw a scornful glare.

"A poor choice of words, I know," Babak said, apologetically. "How much longer are you going to burrow yourself here?"

"I'm not hiding. I'm working."

"But you must come with me tonight. There will be women too." Babak insisted.

"Women? Now what will you do with a woman?" Nenshi mocked while he loaded a tray of empty mugs. "You're too old. Do you even remember what a woman looks like?"

"Huh ... I can teach you a few things young man." Babak's ego refused to be insulted. "When I was your age fire came out from my feet, the room filled with smoke, as if announcing the arrival of a handsome prince. Women everywhere danced around me."

"That was the dust that you kicked up with your big feet, not smoke. The women didn't dance, they were running away from you." Nenshi laughed, lifted the tray and went to the kitchen. Babak shook his head.

Just then a stranger walked in. He stood at the entrance. Babak was alone and welcomed the customer. "Come in and be seated where it pleases you. Someone will be here to serve you in a moment."

The man's face was concealed, half covered by his traditional garb. His body hid behind a long and dirty black cloak. Babak had seen many strangers pass through his brother's tavern. He was always curious where they came from and where they were going. Those travelling alone were of most interest. But this stranger seemed different. He remained statue-like except for his eyes darting in different directions surveying the room.

"Take your time to choose your table," Babak said. "I'll bring you some water." The man didn't respond.

"Saulum, come here... you have a customer," Babak called out. Saulum appeared from the kitchen wiping his hands with a cloth.

"Come in sir. It's my pleasure to serve you."

"I'm looking for someone," the stranger said, his voice dull and deep, rumbled across the room.

Saulum turned to Babak. They looked at each other and simultaneously shrugged their shoulders. Based on the stranger's clothes, he could not have been a tax collector. Some of the patrons took notice and a few paid for their drinks and casually walked out. Saulum lifted his chin, signalling to Babak to say something, do something.

"Many people pass through here," Babak said, hoping his calm tone would appease the man. "Perhaps we know your friend. What's the name?"

At that moment, Nenshi came into the room. The stranger stood by the door. At first, Nenshi made nothing of it until he looked closer at the man's robe, a familiar attire. Their eyes met. The hostile stare was also familiar. The stranger then removed his tunic and pointed.

"I have found him."

Babak looked over to Nenshi. "You know this man?"

The stranger pushed Babak and Saulum aside as he walked between them towards Nenshi. A table toppled over. Aziza ran in from the kitchen, having heard the commotion.

"What do you want Rashid?" Nenshi asked, as he tried to think of his next move.

"So you know each other," Babak said. "Oh my." His jaw dropped.

Rashid circled Nenshi. Nenshi followed him with his eyes. "So, this is what has become of you, a servant in a tavern," Rashid said with a smirk. "What will your father think?"

"Is Zayid here with you?" Nenshi asked. "If he's outside, he can come in. I will explain everything."

"Zayid is not here. He's dead. At the hands of your fellow Egyptians. And so are many of our men."

Nenshi closed his eyes for a moment. Was there another way to escape from the Bedouins, instead of creating a ruse, he thought? His deception caused the death of many, including the tribe's leader whose guidance and wisdom are lost forever and his people now without direction.

"I never meant for any of this to happen," Nenshi said. His apologetic tone had no effect.

"Your words are empty," Rashid said. His stone-faced glare, eyes filled with rage, showed no consideration. "You must pay for your deception."

"Rashid ... listen ..."

"And you thought I would never find you. You thought that hiding in a hole like this, like a beetle burrowed in the sand, would keep you safe. I know this land better than you. It was only a matter of time before the beetle was discovered."

Rashid looked at Aziza. "And who is this?" he asked and stepped closer to her.

Nenshi moved between them. "What do you want?" he asked.

"You took something from me. Perhaps I will do the same," Rashid replied, with eyes on Aziza.

Nenshi's protective instincts heightened. "She has nothing to do with this. It's between you and me."

Rashid grinned. Nenshi gestured Aziza to move away. Rashid removed his cloak and threw it to the floor. His hand slid down to his waist and he drew a dagger. Nenshi raised his defenceless and empty hands. Aziza moved to jump at Rashid but Babak held her back.

The dagger's sharp blade cut through the air as Rashid slashed several times at Nenshi's face. Nenshi stepped back with each failed attempt. Rashid jabbed and this time he made contact. The thrust found its mark. The blade cut Nenshi's leg and he fell to the floor shrieking in pain. He pushed hard against the wound to stop the bleeding. His hand reddened.

Babak picked up a vase and was about to strike when Rashid turned and stared Babak into submission as he waved his dagger in the air. Rashid then turned and charged towards Nenshi. While on the floor, Nenshi reached over and picked up a chair. He swung it across Rashid's legs that knocked him down. The dagger flew out of his hands.

The combatants were on their feet and exchanged tremendous blows to the face and stomach. Blood rolled down Nenshi's leg. Aziza's eyes drew together, her face hardened with anger and she was about to jump on Rashid when Babak grabbed her again. She scowled, tried to fight him off but he held her tightly and shook his head.

A hard blow struck Nenshi in the face and blood spewed from his mouth. He fell to the floor. He saw the dagger close to him, picked it up and stood to face Rashid. He leaned forward to strike him, but Rashid grabbed Nenshi's wrist. They pushed each other in all directions and they both tumbled. They rolled endlessly, their arms and legs in a tumultuous wave until a loud grunt ended the battle. Nenshi lay on his back, motionless. Rashid was on top of him, motionless.

Aziza gasped, still held tightly by Babak. Saulum looked numb, helpless. Rashid raised his head and turned towards them. He lifted the upper part of his body to get up. But he couldn't. He then dropped back down. Nenshi rolled over and pushed the heavy body to the side. His hands were covered with Rashid's blood.

Chapter 24

"THE BEARD SUITS YOU WELL," Babak said.

"It makes me look like a Damascene." Nenshi rubbed his furry chin. Babak tilted his head to get a look at both sides of his face.

"It's a little sparse here and there but it'll do."

"You're too generous with your compliments."

They wrangled back and forth at nothing of importance, as they often did. Nenshi enjoyed bantering and Babak relished in the attention.

"We must celebrate your stay in Damascus."

"It's only been eight full moons."

"That's long enough for a celebration. You must admit your alibi as a poet has served you well. You're safe here."

Nenshi smiled. It seemed it was only the beginning of the hot season when he had met Babak in Uru Salem. As Soreb would say, time flows faster than water through the dry lips of a thirsty man. But Damascus could not replace Thebes. Acceptance does not always bring happiness.

"If you're looking for a reason to celebrate, then let's commemorate our friendship," Nenshi suggested.

"Any excuse to celebrate is fine with me."

They laughed. "Go and find Aziza," Nenshi said. "I'm certain she'll want to join us and perhaps you can make sure she wears something special."

Babak left and Nenshi was alone. The thought of friendship made him think of Egypt. He still longed to return to his homeland. His country was often on his mind and Sia was still in his heart. He remembered the fateful night in the garden. He held her in his arms. He felt her lips press hard against his. It was a night when time stood still, blessed by Hathor, the goddess of love. They feared nothing and chanced everything for the few stolen moments of intimacy.

Nenshi relived his rage as Sia, in tears, had been dragged away from him. The memory, etched in his mind, carved in his heart, haunted him. He often wondered if more time away from Thebes would ease the pain and the anguish. It didn't.

His work in the tavern afforded him the opportunities to witness countless caravans pass through the city, even those from Egypt. During their stopovers, Nenshi was often tempted to introduce himself to the visitors, but he never did. The risk was too great. He feared that if he revealed his identity he would be brought back to Egypt and face an even greater penalty, perhaps even death.

It was Aziza that kept Nenshi abreast of events from his homeland, whenever she happened to be around Egyptian caravans and overheard conversations. She would parrot, in her usual way, so that Nenshi clearly understood, everything she had heard. He valued any news, good or bad.

He was not surprised to hear that Egypt was still in moral decay and corruption. He remembered Tehuti's description of impending invasions and now wondered if the intruders finally infiltrated the land. Those who had ruled the country would have become victims of their own immorality. The words of his teacher Soreb resonated - the work of the great god is powerful, so is that of the tyrant.

Babak and Aziza returned. Nenshi wiped his hands on his apron, eager to get away from the day's drudgeries. Aziza smiled as she untied a string around a loosely wrapped fabric and revealed her new outfit, baggy and comfortable trousers and an equally loose-fitting red and white blouse.

It delighted Nenshi to see her hold it in front of her, close to her body. He realized how much she had matured.

"Aziza, that's beautiful!" Nenshi said. "Don't you agree, Babak?"

"Ahh ... I imagine it suits her." Babak approved, in his own way.

"Did Babak buy this for you?"

Aziza nodded with a smile longer than a scribe's never-ending stroke of his brush. She had never dressed as a young lady should.

"I told you that I didn't want to be embarrassed," Babak said.

Aziza walked over and hugged Babak. He resisted, slightly. "Get away from me you ... you..." he grunted and nudged her to step back. She squeezed harder. "Enough ... enough," Babak said. "I must go get ready before she drowns me with her affection."

An Egyptian delegation came to Damascus. The pageantry and excitement filled the streets as the entourage boasted at every opportunity to demonstrate what Egypt had to offer in the hope of increasing trade.

Aziza had been parading in her new outfit near the tavern, waiting for Nenshi and Babak, when she heard men talking about special visitors to the city. She moved closer to them to get every detail. When she realized who the visitors were, she ran back to the tavern, stormed through the doors, and scurried to find Nenshi.

"I'm almost ready," he said, puzzled at her sudden appearance. "Why are you out of breath? There's plenty of time to celebrate ... no need to hurry." Aziza paid no attention to what he said as she gestured with her hands. "What are you so excited about? Is there a lion in the streets?" Nenshi was amused. She moved her hands and arms frantically. "Slow down. What are you trying to say?"

She finally controlled herself. With deliberate and distinct motions, she relayed her thoughts. Nenshi interpreted her signs, repeatedly, to validate them with a question or comment. Aziza responded with a nod or shake.

"There are strangers ... not from caravans?"

Aziza nodded her head.

"That isn't unusual." Nenshi paused and focused on her gestures.

"There are beautiful men and women carrying swords. Hmm ...that is odd."

Aziza shook her head violently, angry at the misinterpretation. She tried again.

"Oh ... the women are beautiful, and the men carry swords." Aziza nodded. "And they have brought many gifts. Who are these people?" He waited for Aziza to respond. "They're from ... from where? They are ... my people?" His eyes widened; he was uncertain of his interpretation. "They are Egyptians?" Aziza smiled. "Aziza, are you sure they're not part of a trade caravan?" She nodded, repeatedly. "What are you doing?" She grabbed his arm and tugged him towards her. Nenshi pulled his arm back and forced Aziza to sit down. "Aziza, stop. I'm not going anywhere. Listen to me." She took time to calm herself again. "I know you want me to go out there and see these people. If these Egyptians are not part of a trade caravan, then they're here for a very different reason."

He wanted to rush to be with his fellow countrymen, the only connection to his homeland. Alone in Damascus, isolated from Egypt for so long, was all he knew. He could sit among them, drink beer, share stories, and even help him get back home. On the other hand, making himself known to them might result in imprisonment and more punishment. He tried to explain his dilemma to Aziza.

"Do you remember when I told you about why I left Egypt?"

Aziza nodded.

At that moment, Babak ran into the room. "Nenshi," he stopped to catch his breath. "There's an Egyptian delegation in the city."

"Yes ... I know. Aziza just told me. Do you know why they're here?"

"I'm not certain. This type of visit is not unusual even though we don't see it as often as caravans. I think they have come to make sure Egypt maintains good relations with its allies. As you know the trade routes are important to them. I've also heard that some members of the delegation have been told there's an Egyptian in the city. One who is favoured by Pharaoh to perform a specific task for the great one. That's you!"

"Perhaps it wasn't a good idea for me to have told others I'm a poet."

"The delegation had no knowledge of such a commission." Babak paced back and forth. "I imagine they will remain on alert."

"That's not good." Nenshi's hope to meet with the Egyptians faded. He feared returning home in shackles. And even if they didn't find him, his identity would be revealed and everyone in Damascus would paint him as a liar.

"How long will they remain in Damascus?" he asked.

"A few days, I imagine. And you can't stay here. I'll take you to my house until they're gone. I'll speak to Saulum to be vigilant and let us know if they make any inquiries. There will be no celebration tonight." He gestured the same decision to Aziza. She frowned in disappointment. She wouldn't be seen in her new outfit.

Nenshi tried to mollify the fears. "There's no need to be concerned, I promise to keep out of sight until they're gone."

"That's not the only thing that concerns me." Babak didn't conceal his dislike for colonizers. "Don't be offended but this type of delegation has a purpose other than a friendly visit."

"What do you mean?"

"I don't believe they're here looking to simply share their way of life with ours. Their intention is purely to exploit. They bring us gifts to demonstrate their benevolence - nothing but a stunt, a mask to conceal their purpose."

Nenshi was surprised to hear such a view come from Babak. Did all Damascenes think this way, he wondered?

"So what is their purpose?" Nenshi asked. The question held a defensive tone rather than one of curiosity.

"Egyptians have come here more often than other foreigners. It's a reminder of their formidable existence. We've been the focus of many because of where we are situated, a crossroad to the trading routes."

"But that's what has made Damascus prosperous."

"Yes, we have flourished from the influence of other nations. But we would have done so without their impact, nonetheless. Egyptians and others have rendered their mark and departed. We were left to undo what the vultures left behind."

Nenshi became defensive, compelled to stand up for his homeland. But deep inside he agreed. He also thought of his people, cruel and opportunistic, as Babak had described. Now, to have others speak of his country with the same sentiments, only confirmed his beliefs.

"Not all bad things have come from Egypt," Nenshi said, trying to soften the discourse. "After all, it is my home."

In the heat of the moment, Babak snapped back, like the sharp bite of a jackal. "You have no home." The piercing words penetrated Nenshi, and he tried not to show the hurt.

Babak realized what he had said. "I'm protective of you. I suppose I want to shelter you even from your own people. Forgive me."

Nenshi forced a smile and wondered if he could still call Egypt his home.

"Now listen," Babak added. "If you don't want to hide in my house, then you must remain here, out of site. Aziza will bring you food and drink. You are not to leave the tavern until they are gone. Do you understand?"

Nenshi had little choice. But in his silence, he questioned which was stronger, his desire to engage with the delegation or the need to remain unnoticed.

During the two days Nenshi had spent in the tavern, alone, he became restless. Aziza and Babak visited him frequently and told him of the day's activities. Babak omitted much of the details knowing they would pique Nenshi's interest. Aziza, on the other hand, told him everything. She described festivities held at night over countless fires; women paraded in the market and bought treasures to take back with them; and soldiers shared beer and wine with townsmen. Damascus had not seen a delegation remain as long as it did. And it was not good. It made Nenshi curious to the point that he decided to leave the tavern and get a first-hand account of events.

He put on a long cloak and a hood to cover his head. He held a cloth close to his face. Only his eyes were exposed. It was the perfect disguise. A beggar. He made his way through the streets, careful not to attract unnecessary attention.

When he reached the marketplace, in the centre of the city he looked for a place to hide and found one behind a merchant's stand. His eyes darted in every direction, consuming the sights of his people everywhere. As some of them passed by, he leaned closer to them to hear their conversations. He wanted so much to reveal himself and join in but he held back. He wanted to sit with them, drink beer and exchange stories of their journeys.

Armoured soldiers walked casually throughout the maze of tables as visitors normally would. Nenshi noticed women, few as they were, move about elegantly. Their faces were covered, yet their beauty shone through their veils. This was a special visit indeed, to have women be part of the delegation.

Behind him, Nenshi overheard two Damascenes talk about an Egyptian couple in the distance. Nenshi turned to get a glimpse. The broad shouldered and stylish officer dressed in high military fashion was slightly taller than the woman. The officer walked towards Nenshi. The woman followed behind, gentle and sublime, as the evening shadow cast by the moon, would make its path over rolling hills.

Nenshi eyed the couple as they approached. He turned to the man behind him. "Who is he?" he whispered, his voice disguised.

"I don't know what name he goes by, but he leads the entire delegation," the man said.

"And the woman, who is she?"

"His wife," answered the other man. "A beautiful woman."

Nenshi looked at the officer and then at the woman as they came closer. He stuck his head out from behind a post just enough to get a better look. The couple stood in front of the merchant's stand. They picked up pottery from the table and commented to each other. Their voices were too low to understand what they were saying. The officer, attentive to his surroundings, a sign of a trained official, turned and caught a glimpse of Nenshi. A gentle nod acknowledged the beggar's presence. The officer then gave his attention to his wife.

Nenshi moved close enough to get a good look at the woman. She appeared royal. A beaded wig fell to the shoulders and with *kohl* around her eyes. As she turned, the sun's light reflected their colour. A strange feeling swept over Nenshi. A warm sensation flushed through his body and he could hear his heart beat louder. He knew the eyes; he knew the colour. He knew the woman. He whispered ... *Sia*.

He took a step closer to draw the woman's attention. He put his hand on his chest and felt the necklace. He pulled it up to reveal it, but it was too late. She turned her back to him.

The officer walked away from his wife. He had lost interest in the merchandise. He motioned to one of his soldiers to remain behind, to watch over his wife's safety.

The woman picked up and examined a heavy clay container. Nenshi took another step towards her. This time he caught her attention. Controlled and calm, she raised her head and for a fleeting second looked at the beggar. She looked over her shoulder. The soldiers, tasked to protect her, were close by.

Nenshi stretched out his hand and took another step towards her. She placed the pottery back on the table and began to walk in Nenshi's direction. He waited until she came closer and then he stepped in front of her. She stopped and looked up. The beggar only wanted an offering.

One of the soldiers moved closer and put his hand on his dagger, strapped to his side. Sia raised her hand and nodded, signalling it was safe. It's best to give the beggar something to demonstrate Egypt's benevolence. She drew a gold coin from her pouch and placed it in his hand. For a brief second her fingers rested on Nenshi's palm. A flash of heat ran through his body like the sudden effects of a strong elixir ingested to drive out evil spirits of an unknown illness. His eyes opened wide to the feeling, the familiarity of the touch.

A voice called out. "Come Sia, it's time to return to our camp," the officer, her husband, said.

On hearing her name, Nenshi thought his heart had stopped. Was it a dream, another disturbing one, like the one he had in Thebes? It was not. The woman with whom he fell in love from the moment he met her had slipped away, once more. The woman who had always been on his mind during his time away had been taken from him, again. Would he now wonder aimlessly through love's lost world, like the Bedouins without a leader? His despair was as deep as the mines in Nubia.

Sia smiled at the beggar. She turned and walk away, like a swan's slow and eloquent swim across a placid pond. She was only a few feet away when she looked behind her. The sun's light exposed a sadness in her eyes. She turned again, lowered her head and continued walking. Nenshi removed his head cloth to uncover his face. He hoped, begged with his heart, for Sia to turn around one more time. But she didn't.

At that moment, two Egyptian soldiers, noticed the beggar, staring in the direction of the officer's wife.

"You... beggar..." called out one of the soldiers. "Move on. Go about your business." But Nenshi didn't move, as if he didn't hear or didn't care. He was still fixated on Sia and began to walk towards her. His suspicious movement alerted the soldiers even more.

"What do you want? Who are you?" asked the other soldier. Nenshi didn't reply and put on his head cloth, in an obvious hurry. The men scurried towards him navigating their way around tables. They were too late. Nenshi was gone.

They asked the merchants if they had seen the beggar. No one spoke. No one cared about beggars. The merchants went about their business squabbling with buyers.

Soon more soldiers came to the scene and commotion ensued about a beggar who appeared to want to harm or steal from Sia. One of the men ran and caught up with the commanding officer.

"What is it?" The officer, curt with his question, appeared perturbed by the interruption. Sia, stood next to the officer, leaned forward to hear the response.

"A beggar was standing over there by that stand."

"What of it?"

"He looked like an Egyptian."

"I'm certain there are vagrants here from surrounding lands, even from Egypt."

"Sir ... he acted strangely. He stared for the longest time. Beggars only want alms and then move on."

The officer was now curious. "Perhaps he's the one rumoured to be here by order of Pharaoh?" The officer hesitated for a moment and then ordered, "Find him and bring him to me. I would like to meet this man, who professes to be Pharaoh's poet."

Nenshi made his way back to the tavern. His heart raced. The flash of heat from the touch of Sia's hand caused a surge of excitement that could only be doused with a reunion.

Chapter 25

"BABAK ... I MUST LEAVE Damascus at once! The Egyptians ... they're looking for me!"

"You fool! What have you done? I told you to stay here!" Babak paced the floor, clenched his fist, angry at Nenshi's careless and selfish act.

"There's no time to explain." Nenshi removed his beggar's disguise and threw them on the floor. He turned to Aziza. "I need your help."

Aziza knew what to do. She ran to his room, gathered some clothes and rolled them together into a small bundle. Nenshi filled a flask with water. He put on his white head cloth and white robe and turned to Babak. "I need you to accompany me until I get outside the city."

Babak clenched his jaws and followed Nenshi with darting eyes as he hurried to get Nenshi's belongs from Aziza. "We'll use the back streets to get us out faster," Babak said, as he held up his hand to Aziza. "You must stay here." She folded her arms in protest. Babak ignored her disappointment. "There's a place outside the city where we can hide for a day or two. Now move ... we must get out of here."

"Let Aziza come with us," Nenshi said. "If the Egyptians track us down and get too close, she can lure them in a different direction."

Babak disagreed. The more legs on the run meant the greater risk of being caught but there was no time to argue. He nodded and motioned her to join them.

Nenshi gathered his belongings and his thoughts. He stopped at the door and turned around, trance-like; his eyes glazed over.

"Did you forget something?" Babak asked. He fidgeted, eager to get going. There was little time before soldiers would come crashing through the door.

"No, I have what I need." Nenshi's gaze, calm and steady, gave Babak new cause for concern.

"Then what's the matter? You picked a fine time for daydreaming. We must leave."

"There's something I must do first."

"You're out of your mind if you're thinking about bidding farewell to your friends ..."

"No, no ... something more important."

"There's nothing more vital than getting out of here, now!"

Nenshi walked up to Babak, put his hands on his shoulders to calm him and to get his undeterred attention.

"It's about Sia."

"Sia? You mean the Sia in Thebes? Is that what you have been daydreaming about? We must ..."

"No ... she's here ... in Damascus ... I saw her."

Babak's jaws dropped. Aziza shook her head in disbelief.

"Are you certain it was her?" Babak asked, hoping that Nenshi had mistaken her for someone else.

"Yes. It was as if we were in her garden, risking everything just to be with each other. I must see her."

"Oh my ... It's never a dull moment with you."

"Aziza, come here," Nenshi waved.

He removed the necklace and put it around Aziza, just below her collarbone to make sure it was noticeable. With a gentle touch, he placed his fingers underneath Aziza's chin and lifted, gingerly, until their eyes locked. He spoke in a controlled and deliberate manner to be understood.

"As the sun sets, I want you to go to Sia. You must find her. I have described her to you many times. You will recognize her. Make sure she's alone. Don't let anyone approach you or question you. Give her the locket. Then take her to the shepherd's well. Do you understand?" Aziza's nod left no doubt that she understood.

He grabbed his belongings and they dashed to the streets.

Soldiers casually walked about the city, as visitors would, but also kept their eyes open for an Egyptian impersonating a beggar. An incessant wind from the northwest blew through the city and brought sand. The squall raged everywhere and pelted anyone in its path, like an unstoppable army of mosquitos piercing skin left exposed. The soldiers confronted a different enemy - nature. The troop resembled a bunch of stray cats. They walked through narrow streets, turned in every direction, finally reached a dead end. The storm was a welcomed ally to give Nenshi time to get away.

Aziza waited until the storm subsided. At the southern end of the city, she searched for Sia. She found her in the company of other women in a garden. The sun rested on the horizon and time was running out. Aziza cast her lure to draw Sia away from the others. With her head and shoulders covered by a shawl, Aziza strolled about, like one of several local girls brought in to attend to the visitors. She stood a few paces from Sia and pretended to study the sweet-scented flowers. Sia cast a curious look from the corner of her eye. Aziza walked up to Sia, raised her head, casually removed her shawl and exposed the locket around her neck. Sia moved closer but Aziza covered herself with her scarf, turned and walked towards the gates. Sia followed her.

They stood alone, isolated from the others.

"Where did you get the necklace?" Sia asked, whispering. Aziza removed the locket from around her neck.

"Who gave this to you?" Sia demanded and cast a stern look. Aziza pointed to her mouth, shook her head and made short droning sounds. Sia had to rely on the voiceless girl and her own limited grasp of the signs.

"Did someone tell you to bring this to me?"

Aziza nodded again. She looked up at the darkening sky. She took Sia by the hand and pulled towards her. Sia pulled back, an unexpected jolt. She then grabbed both of Aziza's arms and thrust a demanding stare.

"Did Nenshi give this to you?"

Aziza nodded, several times, to make sure she was understood.

"Can you take me to him?"

Aziza nodded again and pointed towards the gates.

Outside the city, by the shepherd's well, Nenshi and Babak waited. A sliver of light cast what little hope was left for Aziza and Sia to appear. Once darkness struck, they would need to move on.

"Babak, I can find my way from here. You should stay and wait for Aziza. I fear for your safety if soldiers find you here with me."

"We'll wait a little longer."

"Babak, you have been good to me. You have given me a home. It is more than I could have expected from anyone but now I must leave, alone."

"And where will you go?"

"I'll follow the delegation back to Thebes. I'll stay far behind them. They won't suspect a thing."

"And then what? You'll just step into your old world as if nothing had changed? I can assure you the Egyptians will be aware of your trail behind them and before long, you'll be back in Nubia, not Thebes."

Love's swirl pervaded his thoughts. Nenshi was obsessed by his brief encounter with Sia. But he knew his preoccupation needed to be squashed. And there was little time. He didn't know whether Aziza would even find her.

"I have another idea," Babak offered. "I'll take you to a merchant friend who travels back and forth on the river Euphrates between Ur and Karchemish. You'll be safe with him until this tempest passes. We'll most likely find him in Ur."

Nenshi's eyes drooped. A gentle shake of his head was a sure sign of discontent. He was beginning to lose hope for making his way back home yet he needed to be safe. He was hoping to see Sia but the uncertainty of what she would think of him now, weighed on his mind. He felt being pulled in opposite directions. He felt as lost as when he roamed the desert, an escape with nowhere to go.

"This tempest will never pass," he said. The melancholy tone landed heavily.

Babak tried to reassure him. "Look, I know things may seem dismal but you can't let your emotions get in the way. You need to do what's most needed right now. You need to be safe. Only then can you sort out everything else."

"Perhaps you're right," Nenshi conceded. "I'll do as you suggest."

The sun's patient and steady setting beckoned the twilight. Nenshi looked to the sky; the faint twinkle of stars signalled the night to fall on the land. He turned to Babak who was pacing like a worrisome old man waiting for his son to return from a long journey.

"Shh ... I hear footsteps," Nenshi warned.

Their heads turned in every direction. They were prepared to either run or defend themselves. Shadowy images began to emerge.

Nenshi squinted and clinched his fists. As the silhouettes transformed to images, he sighed to see Aziza and Sia approach.

Aziza walked up to Nenshi, proud of her accomplishment for delivering Sia. He smiled and gave her a hug and a kiss on the forehead, like a brother pleased of his sister's achievements. He then turned to Sia.

The sun had just set, emitting red, purple and yellow light that flowed out from the horizon behind Sia. It cast a glow around her as if Anuket, goddess of the River Iteru, stepped out from the water to set a path beneath her feet. The sky's radiant colours glowed over Sia and resembled Anuket's tall plumed headdress of feathers. A gentle breeze replaced the earlier relentless wind and its warm touch on her shoulders nudged her towards Nenshi. Babak and Aziza respectfully stepped away.

The reunion reflected the uncertainty of this unexpected encounter. Their world had changed, and they now wondered if the love within them still burned. Sia broke the silence.

"You look handsome with a beard. Even as a beggar."

Nenshi smiled. They inched closer to each other. He then reached over and pulled her in to his strong embrace. The scent of her skin released an elation - the memory in her garden. His heart raced. He felt a rush through his veins.

"You're safe," she said, as she gently stepped back.

"And no longer a prisoner at the mines." He wiped her tears with his finger, cleansed her from a sorrow she could not convey.

"I have so much to tell you," she said. Her eyes teared.

Nenshi placed his finger over her lips to silence any unwanted tale that would thrust him back into the darkness of his agony. He caressed her hair. The softness evoked what had been lost, until now. He wanted to hold her but something stood in the way.

Sia moved her hands on his upper arms, near the shoulder. There was something under the sleeve, on his right side and she traced the roughness with her fingers. "What is this?" she asked.

"I've been branded with the markings of a criminal."

The words were a reminder that he had never told her about his status as a servant. He had lived with the guilt for not having told her. Instead she had learned of it from others. It was pointless to say anything now. Too much time had passed, and he feared that if he told her anything, even that he still loved her, she would not reciprocate. Time either eroded all feelings or made them a part of him, impenetrable. All he could do now was tell her that he would leave Damascus and be on the run, again.

Sia looked up at him. "You know that I have a husband."

For a moment Nenshi had forgotten about the officer, her husband, or he had discarded the thought from his mind, rejected the thought that she had found new love.

"It was a marriage arranged by my father."

Now he needed to know. "Do you love him?"

She paused, not certain which words would explain her new life. "Sometimes love comes before we are ready for it. At times it is placed before us, even out of an unwillingness to surrender ourselves to it."

The words rang deep. Nenshi realized how much had changed. In his eyes Sia seemed to be different yet in his heart he was not prepared to let it all go. Perhaps the brief encounter would rekindle the love they once shared and cherished. He took her in his arms. She let him. He leaned over to kiss her. His lips tenderly touched hers. They quivered. His silence saved her dignity.

"We must be leaving soon," Babak said as he and Aziza walked back towards them.

"This is my friend Babak," Nenshi introduced. Babak bowed his head. "And this is Aziza, whom you have already met."

"She's very courageous." Sia smiled.

"Her persistence serves her well," Babak added. Aziza shrugged her shoulders. Babak, anxious to get out from harm's way, ended the social graces of introductions. "If we stay here much longer, our lives will be in peril."

"Where will you go?" Sia asked.

Babak replied. "Nenshi must hide for a few days until the delegation has left Damascus." He was careful not to reveal details. Could Sia be trusted? "Once it's safe he'll return. Do you know where the party will go to next?"

"To a city called Gebel. Have you heard of it? Will you go there?" Gebel, in the land of the Phoenicians, had been very prosperous. Its people travelled far on their mighty ships trading and conquering. It would certainly be a place of interest to Egypt.

"Yes, I know of it." Babak said. "Plans for Nenshi's shelter are not complete. Aziza will escort you back to Damascus." His suspicious expression played on Nenshi. "I'll wait for you over there," Babak said, pointing with his eyes to the two roads that crossed one another. "Come Aziza." As Aziza walked away, she looked behind her. Her instincts took hold. Perhaps Sia had cut Nenshi from her life.

Alone, Nenshi and Sia stood in the moon's dim light. It flowed down upon them and cast two long separate shadows, alone in their own darkness. Once again, the inevitability of separation became apparent. Sia reached into her pouch and pulled out Nenshi's locket, the one Aziza used to draw her attention.

"Here ... this is yours."

She placed it over Nenshi's head. It was no longer the simple reflection of the love they shared in Thebes. Like the marks on his shoulder, it was another reminder of his plight. Disconsolate, he relinquished his hope for love. His heart let her go, for love had failed him.

Chapter 26

NENSHI AND BABAK MADE THEIR way north. The moon's light, the sacred colour of a temple's stone, lay a path on the King's Road. Tirelessly they marched not knowing if the Egyptian soldiers had given up on their search for the poet or they were right on their heels. A brief stop to quench their thirst gave them hope for safe passage.

Nenshi removed a pebble stuck in his sandal. It dug into his skin. "At least Aziza will be safe with Saulum," he said. He wiped the bottom of his foot. The small puncture from the stone let out a trickle of blood. He was not concerned.

"Aziza knows how to take care of herself, perhaps better than either of us," Babak said.

"She's had a lifetime to master it." Nenshi slipped his sandal back on.

"She can be stubborn, like a cow holding back her milk."

They chuckled.

Nenshi cast his eyes on the road before him. The King's Road was the lifeblood of the land. Nenshi remembered Tehuti speak of it; the trade route that brought paintings to Thebes from faraway places. Tehuti would buy them to adorn the walls of the temples he had designed.

By day a cloud of dust hovered, caused by trampling hooves and stomping feet. Now, in the darkness of night, the dust had settled and gave way to the usual sights and sounds. The silvery light spilled down from the moon over the richness of the land.

Nenshi imagined what lay in the distance, farther than the light could reach. He envisioned towns that depended on the road for trade. He imagined fields, cultivated with fruits, vegetables and grains that offered sustenance throughout the kingdoms. He thought of the vineyards that had provided Tehuti with his treasured wine. Yet the road, a conduit for life and prosperity, also brought disharmony and wars. Warlords wanted to control it which meant control of the access to the finest goods - frankincense, myrrh, spices, precious stones, pearls, ebony, silk, fine textiles and even gold.

The thoughts trickled through Nenshi's mind and helped pass the time in silence. He gazed up at the star strewn sky. It's purity and serenity calmed the uncertainty he faced.

Then a sound from behind alerted him. He stopped.

"What is it?" Babak asked.

"I thought I heard something."

They both turned to look behind them. Just to be safe Nenshi motioned to move to the side of the road. They lay on the ground in the tall grass and peered through the brushes. Footsteps confirmed Nenshi's fear. The sound was getting louder, their movement faster. A figure began to emerge from the darkness. Nenshi curled his body, crouched in a low position, like a cat ready to pounce on an unsuspecting mouse. He timed his move perfectly and jumped towards the image. They both fell to the ground. Nenshi stood, pulled out his dagger and looked down at the frightful face.

"Aziza ..."

Babak ran out from the bushes. "At least it's not the enemy. Or are you?" He laughed.

"You were right. She is stubborn. We have no choice. She must come with us." Nenshi smiled at Aziza, her face covered in dirt and he added, "Well ... what are you waiting for?"

They trekked over the scorched land for two days like camels in a caravan. Nenshi wondered if the monotonous grey and brown hills and the dried riverbeds would ever lead to an oasis. From time to time his eyes darted in every direction. An attack could come without warning, like a wolf's veiled approach on a lone sheep.

Aziza had brought food, prepared by Saulum, which they rationed - cheese, dates, nuts and olives, wrapped in a cloth, large enough to carry over her shoulder. It was just enough food to sustain them until they found a place for a full meal. They ate the cheese first for fear of it becoming rancid under the sweltering heat. Saulum also gave her a pouch filled with coins.

In the distance, the splashing sound of a river offered a promising sign of life. It meandered and whenever it came close to the road, they stopped to drink and refill their flasks. The small town, Hamath, appeared on the horizon.

They walked by a mud brick house. Two black curious eyes spied on the unfamiliar trio from behind a narrow opening of a fragmented door. A little girl with a bashful smile stepped out from the entrance. Farther down the road, an old woman pulled a stubborn mule and paid no attention to the passers-by.

"I trust you've been here before," Nenshi said.

"The townspeople are generally hospitable towards strangers. But follow my lead, their customs are different."

A waft of pleasant odours and laughter made its way through the opening of a tent. The hungry trio stopped in front of it.

"It's not Saulum's tavern but it smells just as good." Nenshi sniffed the air in delight. He stepped towards the entrance and Aziza followed. Babak grabbed them by the arm, forced them to stop.

"Remember, follow my lead. One doesn't enter unless first invited."

A young man came out and glanced at the three from head to toe and motioned them to go in. Nenshi walked in. Babak stepped in front of Aziza. She scrunched her face.

"Women are not allowed in," Babak told Aziza and then apologized to the man at the entrance. Aziza crossed her arms in protest.

"You know our customs well," said the young man. "My name is Akmal. I'll have some food brought out to her."

Akmal led them to a space complemented with large pillows. "Sit here. I'll bring you something to eat and you can tell me stories of your travels." Within minutes he returned with a simple peasant breakfast of bread, olives, cheese, fresh figs, jam, butter, tea and coffee. They relished every morsel they planted into their mouths.

Nenshi leaned over to Babak and whispered, "Remember, good food makes problems bearable." Babak ignored the ribbing.

After the meal, Babak stood, bowed his head and thanked Akmal for his hospitality. Nenshi did the same. Babak then reached in his pouch for coins and paid Akmal.

"May the gods give speed to your travel," Akmal said and then escorted them outside where Aziza waited. The men exchanged farewells. Akmal ignored Aziza.

Time moved slowly as they dragged their feet along the dusty road, the sluggish gait of three travellers satisfied by a hearty meal. Only casual conversation could help time move faster.

"So, tell me about your friend from Ur," Nenshi said.

"Many years ago, I went with my brother, on this very road, to sell goods. We passed through small towns, Ebla, Halab, until we reached Karchemish. We stayed for a few days during which I befriended a merchant, Harun."

"What did he sell?" Nenshi asked as he looked down at Aziza who had been walking between them. Her head shifted back and forth trying to capture the conversation.

"Nothing," Babak replied.

"A merchant who sold nothing?"

"Well ... he sold his services. Over time he had amassed a large shipping fleet that carried trade goods from cities along the two great rivers."

"The Tigris and Euphrates," Nenshi said, with the knowledge of what Soreb had taught him.

"Yes. In any event, traders would pay Harun to transfer their goods from where the rivers joined, in Ur, to Karchemish. From there they would follow the King's Road and sell to townspeople along the way."

"How often do you see Harun?"

"Not often enough. We should value our friends as we treasure our own lives. We feed our bodies; we should also feed our friendships."

This made Nenshi think of Hordekef. They had their differences but their friendship overcame them. Nenshi enjoyed hunting with him but now what Babak had said made him think of the many times Nenshi struck an animal while Hordekef's arrows disappeared, striking nothing. Nenshi reflected on the ribbing he would dole out at the expense of his friend's self-esteem. He vowed that the next hunting excursion with Hordekef would be different.

"So you trust Harun."

"Absolutely. He's a generous man. And he's good in business. In fact, he liked Saulum's tavern so much that he said one day he would buy one for himself, in Karchemish. Yes, I trust him, with my life. Like your friend ... Hor ... Hor ..."

"Hordekef," Nenshi finished the name with a smile.

Chapter 27

WHEN SIA RETURNED TO THEBES, she met with Tehuti, anxious to tell him about her encounter with Nenshi. The last time she had seen Tehuti was in the court's corridor after Nenshi's decree had been handed down.

The urgency for this visit was unusual but Tehuti didn't question it. He hid his heavy heart with his usual respectful gesture. Her presence could only remind him of what he had lost.

"Word has it you are married," he said. Sia acknowledged with a nod and forced a smile, as if embarrassed by it. "I understand it was your father's wishes for you to wed someone of high ranking in Pharaoh's military."

"It seems everyone knows."

Tehuti smiled. "Pharaoh has a way of letting people know what he wants them to know." Tehuti slouched forward in his exotic Phoenician wooden chair. He appeared older. "I'm pleased to see you." He had no quarrel with her. Like Nenshi, she was a victim of circumstance. Sia smiled, a bashful smile, and then was straightforward with him.

"I saw Nenshi," she said, then remained silent. Tehuti shot a glance. The kind that chilled a room and made it devoid of purpose and broke like shattered clay.

"What do you mean you saw Nenshi?"

"I saw him ...in Damascus."

"In Damascus?"

She told Tehuti that she had accompanied her husband with a delegation and during their stay in Damascus, Nenshi, dressed as a beggar, had approached her in the marketplace. She said that Nenshi had escaped from the mines in Nubia, but he had to flee Damascus from the heels of Egyptian soldiers. He believed he was being hunted.

"So, he managed to escape from the sand dwellers." Tehuti sighed.

"I don't understand."

Tehuti told her that he had heard about a Bedouin raid and plunder on a caravan while it transported gold to Thebes from Nubia. He told her that Nenshi was among them and in the wake of the attack many had died.

"But before all this, while he was still here in Thebes, I had made a request to grant him his freedom." Tehuti continued. "To this day, I don't know why it took so long for the petition to be presented. Nonetheless, I had made the plea even before your father had him arrested."

Sia's jaw dropped for she knew nothing of the events. A chill climbed up her back. Her shoulders shrugged. She tried to control its hold on her.

"You have no blame in this," Tehuti said. "It was something I should have done years ago. In any event, by the time the plea was heard Nenshi was already at the mines in Nubia." He paused for a moment. His hands shook, his lips quivered. "My request had been accepted. Nenshi is a free man."

The awkward silence was deafening. They shared the guilt. They had nothing in common except for the loss of a lover and a son.

"Didn't you try to reach out to the mines?" she asked.

"By the time a message reached Nubia, he had already left with the caravan. They were attacked and there was no sign of what had happened to him." The thought that Nenshi didn't know he was a free man, haunted Tehuti.

Sia's eyes swelled. The chill down her back held her captive. She moved forward in her seat and gripped tightly on to the chair's armrest to release the angst that rushed through her veins, paralyzed by the anguish.

"If I had known," she lamented. "I would have told him in Damascus. He would be here, instead of me, sitting with you." The pang in her heart brought tears to her already reddened eyes.

"Don't blame yourself," Tehuti consoled. He leaned over and held her hand. "You could not have known any of this. I kept it private. It was my fault."

He was entrapped by his own clouded judgment that for years his son remained a servant.

The sun's light broke the long and restless night. Sia got up and gazed out from her bedroom to a peaceful, calm beginning of the day she hoped would bear a more promising conclusion. The air was still. Its god, Shu, had swallowed it up and left a calming and soothing influence behind. It was a contrast to the turbulent spiralling thoughts. Shu had now retreated. A sudden wind-gust through the treetops caused them to sway in every direction.

Sia looked at the garden, plants and flowers bloomed in their magical scents, reminded her of the stolen moments she had spent with Nenshi. She could not turn back time. But she could find a way to let him know he was free. With that thought, there was only one person who was certain to help.

She scampered to dress, not considering what she wore and dashed to the market. Hordekef was sure to be there. She tracked him down, took him aside and explained everything. He was in disbelief, overwhelmed with the news. He also confessed to her, for it was his shameless act that had sent Nenshi to the mines.

"I didn't know any of this," Hordekef said. "Tell me, how is he?"

Sia told him how she met Nenshi, dressed as a beggar, in Damascus. Hordekef chucked. "He always had a good imagination and ways to escape being caught."

"Except when he was in my father's garden."

"Love had a grip on his senses. I'll go to Damascus, find him and tell him about his freedom."

"He's not in Damascus."

"But you just told me that ..."

"Yes, but while I was there with the delegation we had heard that a runaway slave was in the city. Nenshi had to leave, with a friend. Babak is his name. And with a young girl, Aziza, who can't speak."

"I'll find him," Hordekef assured her. "Someone there must know something about him. I'll find him and tell him about his freedom. I'll tell him everything. After all, he saved my life. Now I must save his."

Chapter 28

THE MONOTONOUS TERRAIN GAVE WAY to an oasis. The drab colours, nature's punishment for daring to trek through the land, was temporarily replaced by lush foliage, where at the centre, a spring welcomed the weary and thirsty.

The trekkers made their way over a ridge and stopped by the watering hole to rejuvenate their weary bodies. Babak rubbed his right eye to release the irritating grip of sand.

"Here ... let me help you." Nenshi wiped his hands on his shirt and proceeded to inspect Babak's eye. He gently pulled back the eyelids like a seasoned surgeon exploring an open wound. He then stepped back, yet still close enough to examine Babak's eye.

"Look up," Nenshi pointed. "Now look down ... look to one side ... now the other ... look up again. I don't see anything."

Babak pushed Nenshi away. The dubious instructions irritated him more than the sand.

"How can you see a tiny speck in my eye?" Babak asked.

"Can you see it?"

"No, of course not!"

"Well, then?"

"Go away. I think the heat has softened your head."

Nenshi and Aziza laughed while Babak fidgeted with his eye until he was satisfied he had removed the sand and he could see again.

"I noticed you're tiring quickly," Nenshi said. Babak's breathing, slow and deep, became cause for concern. Nenshi wondered how much longer he could endure marching through the hostile terrain.

"Don't you worry about me," Babak replied.

"But I do."

Babak ignored Nenshi and kept walking. Nenshi knew better than to challenge a man as stubborn as a mule.

Twilight was fast approaching, and they returned to the trail. From a distance they saw an abundance of trees and vegetation that sprung from the hard soil. Moments later, they heard rushing water. A twisting river murmured. It called out and invited them to consume its wealth. Nenshi and Aziza went to explore it.

Aziza stopped and kneeled to examine small flowers in bloom. On the river's edge Nenshi bent over and splashed water on his face. He cupped his hands and drank its cool refreshing offering. Rocks jutted out from the shallow water. He heard footsteps and threw a glance behind him. Aziza, ran towards him, as free as the wind blew, eager to jump into the river. Nenshi screamed from the top of his lungs to warn her.

"Aziza ... Aziza ... be careful, the water is shallow! There are rocks!"

Her excitement muffled his warning. Nenshi then stood, flapped his arms to get her attention. She pushed her legs hard against the water to run faster until it was just deep enough to jump in.

"Aziza .... Aziza ... stop ..." Nenshi cried. Aziza took another step but this time slipped and almost fell. She tried to regain balance and continued moving forward. Nenshi gasped hoping she realized the danger and would stop. But she didn't and it was too late. She slipped again, fell and hit a rock. Nenshi immediately ran to her, stepping and slipping on rocks that almost caused him to lose balance. Babak who had heard Nenshi's cries dashed to the river. Nenshi crouched over the wet and motionless body.

"Help me get her out," Nenshi cried out as he lifted her, propped her head and shoulders in his arms. Blood, washed by the water, dripped from her head.

Evening was upon them. Aziza, unconscious, lay on the ground swaddled in Nenshi's cloak. Babak wrapped her head with a torn piece from his clothing. The bleeding had stopped.

"What else can we do?" Nenshi asked, worried.

"We wait and pray," Babak said. "We are not physicians. There's a small town closer than Ebla, called Halab. Perhaps I can find my way there and get help." His tone rang sadness, disheartened by the sight of their young and helpless friend. Nenshi looked up to the sky.

"The moon is low and there's little light," he said. Not even the constellations provided its usual glow. The thought of Babak alone, surrounded by desolation, prey to the unknown, concerned Nenshi. As did the thought of Aziza lying still, perhaps never to stand again.

His eyes caught a collection of stars huddled together. He knew its name, the throne of Horus, born out of bloodshed. The patterned figure looked down on Nenshi, as if amused by human frailty.

"The gods have not been in my favour," Nenshi said. "They are displeased with me. I am dissatisfied with them."

"Nenshi ... look!" Babak grabbed his arm. "Aziza . . . She moved!"

Her effort, measured, slight as it was, offered hope. The slits of her eyes had opened. Nenshi could discern her distant gaze. He felt the emptiness, the despair. Her skin pale, her face sallow, she managed to smile with the little strength she had. She tried to make a sound and a gesture but she couldn't.

"No ... no ... you must rest." A gentle touch of Nenshi's finger covered her lips. "Everything will be all right."

Babak reached out and held her hand. He looked over to Nenshi. "The gods have heard your prayer," Babak whispered.

"I made no plea. She opened her eyes through her own strength and determination to live. The gods care not for the life of a mute."

There was little comfort in the stillness of the night. The silence made Aziza's short and heavy breaths more noticeable. Nenshi wiped the sweat from her warm face with his hand. Babak moistened a cloth with water taken from his flask and handed it to him. Nenshi's touch, tender as the pedal of a lotus, caused Aziza to open her eyes again. She reached out and took his hand. He smiled at her. She opened her mouth desperately wanting to speak, to let him hear the words in her heart.

"Shh," Nenshi whispered. "You must rest." Her head shifted to one side and she slept in his arms. Babak leaned over and kissed her on the forehead.

"We must take turns during the night," Nenshi said.

"Agreed. Let me watch over her now. Go and get water. I'll need it to dab the wound. Then you must try to sleep."

Nenshi walked to the river and sat on a rock. His heart was heavy. He leaned over, cupped water into his hands and washed his face. The coolness eroded the pain. He feared Aziza would not live to see the sun rise.

The night sky transformed to splendour. The moon brightened and its glow danced on the water. The stars flickered in the sky; their radiance bathed the barren land. Yet this was of no consolation. A familiar anger stirred in Nenshi. The same wrath he felt after he had been branded. His blood boiled to think that men were puppets made to compete with one another only to please the gods.

Gods amused themselves to see which man fell first, who was the wisest, most deceitful, cunning, foolish, brave, cowardly. It was a game they played. A selfish one. Nenshi thought of Babak, his wellbeing beginning to weaken, sacrificing himself to protect someone he hardly knew. He thought of Aziza and wondered if there was a god, compassionate and loving, who would spare the life of this child, so young, so pure of heart.

A red glow crept up from the horizon. It turned yellow and soon the land was covered in soothing warmth. Nenshi sat beside Aziza as she lay restful, tranquil, like a child comforted from a frightening dream. His eyes drooped in battle trying to fight the fatigue. The battle was lost, he fell asleep.

The next morning as Nenshi slept, Babak went to the river to catch fish for the morning meal. When he returned, he headed straight for Nenshi and shook him.

"Where is she?" he asked, frightened.

Nenshi, groggy, had no idea what he was talking about. Babak shook him again.

"Where is she? Where's Aziza?"

On hearing her name Nenshi sat up and looked beside him where Aziza had been sleeping. His panic-stricken face turned to Babak.

"She was here," he said. "I didn't hear anything during the night." He jumped to his feet and scanned the area. There was no sign of her. "Is it possible?" he asked. Babak shrugged his shoulders. Then the sound of shuffling feet caught their attention. Nenshi's face glowed when he saw Aziza walking towards them. He ran to her and hugged her. "You should have awakened me," he said and gestured. Aziza smiled and pointed to her stomach. "Hunger is a good sign of healing," Nenshi said.

"I'll cook the fish," Babak added.

Nenshi turned to Aziza. "Do think you're strong enough to keep going?" She nodded and stomped her feet, soldier-like. "Good," Nenshi smiled. "We'll leave after we eat."

They replenished their flask with fresh water and were on the King's Road again. The landscape had changed but the sweltering heat did not. Another unbearable trek loomed ahead.

"What's Ebla like?" Nenshi asked. He needed a distraction to take his mind off the heat.

"Like Damascus. The town sits at the hub of trade routes. Eblites are peaceful. They are resilient too, having fought off invaders from the north."

"Can you speak their language?"

"I've forgotten much of it. I'll teach you what little I know."

The lessons helped pass the time and made the heat bearable until, through the haze of the desert sun against the hot road, figures appeared.

Chapter 29

NENSHI AND BABAK LOOKED AT each other and then looked at the group. They couldn't tell anything about them – friend or foe, caravan or attackers. With the unpredictability of what could happen, they were prepared to face them.

"What do you make of them?" Nenshi asked.

Babak shielded his vision with his hand from the sun's light. "I can't tell from here."

As the travellers came closer, Nenshi was relieved they were not soldiers, nor were they part of a trade convoy. Women rode on donkeys, some children led sheep and goats, others carried food and necessities. New-born babies, coddled in their mother's arms, cried as loud as the bleating animals that followed. The entire scene resembled a moving village.

"A strange bunch." Nenshi said.

"They're not dressed like sand people," Babak added. "I thought I had seen every type of tribe around here but this one is very different."

A man, visibly older than the rest of them, led the clan. Two younger men flanked him and all three walked a safe distance ahead of the group.

"Take your hand off your dagger," Babak told Nenshi. "I see more men behind them. We're outnumbered. I don't want to give them reason to think of us as enemies."

The three men approached with the calm of a morning breeze welcoming nature as it awakened. The old man stood out among them. The aura of his presence drew Nenshi's attention. The weathered face, grey hair that measured to his shoulder, and his long white beard were all signs of a man who had endured a march against time. His arms, exposed to the sun, were well defined. His stature, the embodiment of resilience, made it difficult to determine his age.

"Greetings, my name is Abramu." The soothing voice and sagacious eyes captured a youthful determination. He turned to the two men standing behind him, like soldiers tasked to protect their leader. "This is Lot and Reu," he introduced, with a smile, proud as a father or grandfather or even great grandfather.

Nenshi had difficulty with the dialect, only being able to make out a word here and there. Babak, on the other hand, understood. He turned to Nenshi. "Their language is the same as Harun's, my friend from Ur." Babak had taught Nenshi some basic communication when he first spoke of Harun and now came the opportunity to learn even more. And since Nenshi would eventually meet Harun, it was also a chance to learn about Ur and the land between the two great rivers.

"Greetings to you as well. My name is Babak. This is Nenshi and she is Aziza."

Abramu glanced at Aziza, her head twisting in all directions, her eyes wide, taking everything in.

"The girl cannot speak," Abramu said.

"How do you know this?" Nenshi asked.

"Her language of the body."

"She's clever and keeps her distance. She's been this way all her life. The result of misfortune, no one to care for her and the affliction of a twisted tongue."

Aziza's defences took over. Her expressionless face examined the old man and his protectors.

"Perhaps one day she will find the words." Abramu smiled.

A woman walked up from behind. She placed a hand on Abramu's shoulder. He knew, instinctively, by the touch, who it was. "This is my wife Sarai," he said. Nenshi and Babak bowed. Aziza smiled.

Sarai was beautiful, projecting an image of grace and determination. Her subtle demeanour reflected the meaning of her name, a princess.

"It appears you have been travelling a long time, as we have," she said. "There is still time to set up our tents before the sun sets. We welcome you to join us for a meal."

The sincerity in her voice removed any doubt Nenshi might have had about the tribe. They were pilgrims not invaders. The invitation was accepted.

Lot and Reu walked back and signalled to the party to move off the road and set up camp. Everyone knew what to do; a kind of ritual they had performed repeatedly during their journey. The strongest men erected tents for the families and arrange the shaded areas for the donkeys and livestock. The younger men gathered shrubs and twigs for campfires. Women and children went to the river to fill jugs and goatskin flasks with water. Mothers milked goats to feed their infants.

Nenshi, Babak and Aziza were helpless. They would have been more of a hindrance if they tried to help. Abramu's and Sarai's tent was set up first. In short time the rest of the camp appeared, looking like a small village that had been there for generations.

With staff in hand, swaying with every movement of his gait, Lot approached. He pointed to a tent. "That one is for both of you. The girl can stay with one of the unmarried women." His tone, sturdy and serious, matched his physical stature. He had an unwavering look, like one who had just responded to a great task.

Nenshi and Babak went to inspect the tent. "It's better than what the sand people kept me in," Nenshi said. And the tribe was not like the sand dwellers that imprisoned him. Abramu's people were peaceful. They didn't display weapons. But where did they come from and where were they going? They had a single-minded determination aimed at fulfilling a purpose to their journey.

Nenshi walked around the campsite. He welcomed the cool air against his face especially after a long day's heat that emptied his energy. Not to mention the ordeal with Aziza that almost left her dead. A gentle breeze passed through him as if he had been cleansed of everything that tainted his being.

He walked past a tent where a woman sat in the sliver of shade as she held her newborn daughter, sucking on her breast. Its tiny fingers curled around her mother's thumb, as if grabbing it to make sure her mother did not turn away and release her nipple from the clutches of her lips, until milk had filled her tiny belly. Nenshi smiled as he trudged on.

He passed a group of men unloading belongings from the backs of donkeys. Some of the men waved at him as if they had known him since their journey had begun. It gave Nenshi a sense of belonging. Whatever the herdsmen knew about him was of no consequence. He was not judged nor treated as an outsider. They were his brethren. It was refreshing to be seen with clean eyes and a clean heart, as all men should be considered, Nenshi thought.

Abramu sat alone in front of his tent. He stretched out his hand and pointed to a rug, inviting Nenshi to sit with him. "The meals are being prepared and we have time to talk and learn about each other," Abramu said.

Nenshi sat on the rug and gazed into Abramu's eyes. Soreb had once said, if you look deeply into a man's eyes you will see either blessings from the gods or contemptible deception. But Nenshi had not yet gained Soreb's wisdom to ascertain a man's character simply by looking into his eyes. He was left with his own natural curiosity to determine Abramu's aspirations or follies.

"We will camp here for two nights," Abramu said. "I hope you can stay with us."

"We are tired. The rest will do us good," Nenshi said. "Babak believes you come from Ur," he added, after a short pause, not to allow his interest in Abramu to scatter like the beetles burrowing in the sand. "He recognized your language, similar to that of a friend of his from Ur."

"He's right. I was born in the land of *meso potamia*, the land between the rivers, in a town called Cutha, outside the city of Ur. As a young boy I would go to Ur with my father. He was the king's minister. One of many ministers. They were idol worshippers. I cared not for idol worshipping. Whenever I accompanied my father to Ur, I preferred to spend my time by the river, the waters that brought wealth to the city through trade. Living in Cutha was much better."

"And now you live with your tribe through lands where grass is stripped away by your flock," Nenshi said. "I have seen tribes like yours in the desert."

"But we are not wanderers," Abramu pointed out. "I had left Cutha and Ur to live in Harran, a town in the northern parts of the same river. It was my father's will. He had taken me, my wife Sarai and other members of the family to settle there."

Abramu went on to tell Nenshi that his father had wanted to go to Harran because of the swell of corruption in Ur and frequent attacks by the Elamites made life even more difficult. Harran was stable and prosperous.

"And you ... where's your homeland?" Abramu asked.

At first Nenshi was reluctance to reveal his place of birth. He had carried the weight of unearthing his past for the fear of returning to Nubia. But Abramu seemed different. Besides, sharing stories between two runaways didn't seem all that bad.

Nenshi revealed his journey - a road that meandered like an aging river, through life's struggles, the struggles of a young man who had been holding on to the past, searching for a new way.

"A life filled with experiences overflows with wisdom." Abramu said. "Yet I imagine that your toil is not over. Have faith in El, who will help you with your burden."

"El? What is El?"

"El is my god. He is the reason we left our land. I will tell you more about El tomorrow. I see Sarai coming to tell us our meal is ready."

Another god? Why must man have so many gods? Nenshi asked himself. He had learned about the gods of the Egyptians and even those of the sand people but had not known of this one. What power did this god, El, have over a man and his kinfolk to leave the prosperity of a nation and trek through a wasteland and have sand fill their mouths with never-ending dryness? Nenshi was eager to find out.

Chapter 30

THE NEXT MORNING NENSHI WAS awakened by the tingle of ants crawling up his leg. He brushed them off quickly, stood up and shook himself with the vigour of a crocodile rushing to snatch its prey. Satisfied there were no more ants invading his skin, he walked out from the tent as if nothing had happened. Babak and Aziza were nowhere to be seen so he decided to look for Abramu.

The peaceful silence in the camp matched the quiet stillness of the barren land. It was prudent for everyone to conserve their energy for the arduous trek to the unknown. Lot was among the few walking about lending a hand to men corralling their flock or helping women arranging firewood in preparation for the evening's fire. Nenshi was fascinated that a lending hand was always extended, without asking, without obligation for a return.

"Have you seen Abramu?" Nenshi asked.

"He sits over there," Lot replied, pointing to tall shrubs. "I can help you, if you need anything."

Nenshi smiled. The response affirmed the act of giving, prevalent among the tribe. "I have no need, thank you," Nenshi said. "I just wish to speak with him."

When Nenshi found Abramu, sitting with his head lowered, he was reluctant to interrupt to what he thought was a man in prayer. Nenshi's footsteps pulled Abramu out from his supplication or perhaps it was just a moment's rest.

"May I sit with you?" Nenshi asked. Abramu gestured with his hand to welcome the company. "Your son, Lot, told me you were here."

"Lot is not my son."

Nenshi's brows curled. "Forgive me. I assumed he was. He's always with you, ready to obey any of your instructions."

"Lot is my nephew. When my brother had died, I took Lot into my home."

"You adopted him."

"I never thought of it that way."

Nenshi's mind drifted for a moment thinking about how easy it was for someone to adopt a loved one without parents. Why couldn't it have been as easy for Tehuti to do the same?

"Do you have children?" Nenshi asked.

"No. Sarai is barren." The melancholy response touched Nenshi. He did not know how to respond. But since Abramu had mentioned Sarai, Nenshi needed to give advice.

"I noticed that Sarai is a beautiful woman."

"I have heard this many times."

"I must let you know that women of her beauty in Egypt are sought after. Men will do whatever they choose to have her."

"You speak unkindly of this country."

"I say this only because it appears you are travelling towards Egypt. If you go there do not let others know Sarai is your wife. The serpent's venom has penetrated Egyptian morals and you could be killed, and Sarai taken away."

"A woman's beauty has always been man's weakness which has often exposed his folly. I will keep your counsel in mind. I also trust in El's guiding hand."

Another opportunity presented itself. The mention of Abramu's god paved the way to satisfy Nenshi's curiosity.

"Tell me more about El. What does he rule over?" Nenshi asked, turning his body to face Abramu.

"Over all lands and waters, over man and beast, over all that lives and all that does not, over all that you see and all that you cannot."

"The people of Egypt believe in Geb, the god of the land and Osiris, god of the afterlife. They believe that many gods rule over many things."

"There's only one god," Abramu said, with subtle conviction.

"But you left your country and travel to places where no one knows of El."

"Yes, because El had told me to leave with my kinfolk."

"You mean he had sent you a signal of some kind."

"No. He spoke to me."

The notion of a god speaking to mortals was unheard of to Nenshi. All he had known was that gods gave signs, to be interpreted and followed with actions that favoured them. He remained silent, trying to imagine the sound of a voice coming from a god.

Abramu continued. "Earlier I had told you that my father took us from Ur to Harran. It was in Ur that El first spoke to me. His words are as clear now as when I had first heard them. He had told me to leave my father's home. Leave my land, my country and he would lead me to a land where I will prosper. Where a great nation will be born. My descendants will be as numerous as the stars in the night sky."

It was clear to Nenshi that Abramu's encounter with El had left an indelible mark, able to convince an entire tribe to follow him through unfamiliar and forsaken lands. Then Abramu cast a deep gaze to the sky. His parched lips moved but Nenshi couldn't discern the words, perhaps a prayer of some sort. He dared not interrupt. A man in prayer is deserving of intercession with his god.

When he had finished, Abramu turned to Nenshi to share his confession. "I had disobeyed El. My father ruled his tribe and his family. I had no choice but to obey him first. It was our custom, our way of life."

Nenshi now understood his words in silence, a supplication of forgiveness.

"When my father had died," Abramu continued, "I had become the head of my house and leader of my kinfolk. It was then that I had decided to obey El and take my people to the new land. El was patient with me. And what I saw in El was not the likeness of an animal, the sun or the moon, nor dark images of evil and pain. My god is not about what I chose for him to look like nor what others have carved in stone. It is what he means to me, to us, and how he wants us to see him. We must find El in each of us. As El has spoken to me, he will also have an encounter with those he chooses."

Nenshi thought for a moment. Even though Abramu's god was different from other gods that he had known, El was still the same; an image chosen to suit one's needs. Egyptian gods were created by Egyptians and the only way to gain their favour was to make sacrifices. Nenshi wondered if Abramu's god was created by Abramu only to have meaning for himself, an excuse to leave his homeland.

"But El is also demanding," Abramu continued. "He will test us and he will guide us until the peace and justice he wants for all, will live forever."

So, there was more to El than pacifying one's own needs, Nenshi thought.

How Abramu saw El was different than how Nenshi perceived the same god. What Abramu had experienced, El speaking to him, had brought him closer to his god. The intense fervour in how Abramu described El made Nenshi reflect on his own life, a life fragile and without immortality.

Nenshi believed that Egyptian gods had failed him. Everything that had happened to him was proof of it. Unlike El, Egyptian gods were never concerned about those who worshipped them. Man's everyday lives meant nothing. But El created a special bond with Abramu, by day to give him strength, by night, in dreams to nourish his essence.

Peace and justice, something Nenshi had known little of, made him think about El more deeply. An ineffable feeling stirred, as if a tremor beneath the ground shook him. The gods of Egypt demanded sacrifices in exchange for their blessings. They fought among themselves to rule over the land. El wants love, peace, justice - a god worthy of devotion.

Nenshi looked up at the sky, his eyes squinting, as if searching, longing to hear El's voice.

"El speaks to us in different ways, so that each of us can understand his message," Abramu said. "And when he does, your spirit within you will know it."

Nenshi had not known of a spirit, the kind Abramu had just described - one within him. The Egyptian soul, as Nenshi knew it, had many parts – the body in the everyday life, that in the afterlife, the personality and shadow of the soul. The spirit that Abramu spoke of lived within oneself. It was El's instrument to guide and connect with man.

El was leading Abramu and his people to a fertile land, one of prosperity and opportunity. Nenshi wondered if he too would be led to a place of inner peace and freedom. Until then, he needed to keep out of harm's way from the possibility of returning to a life of servitude. That fear, real or imagined, came to the forefront as he thought of Babak and Aziza. Perhaps travelling alone would be safer for himself and his trusted companions. But he had no idea how to approach them with the idea until Abramu provided the means.

"Your friend, Babak ... he doesn't look well," Abramu said. "I've noticed it when we met."

"He's tired from the long journey. I worry about him."

"He carries a heavy load, like a father tasked to raise his children without a wife. If he chooses, he can stay with us. Aziza as well. She can help tend to his needs."

All Nenshi needed now was to convince Babak.

Chapter 31

"I WILL NOT GO BACK with those wanderers!" Babak said, angry with Nenshi for even suggesting it.

"This long journey has reduced you to a wilted plant. You need to go home."

"Withered but not dead!"

"Look, if I could, I would go back with you to Damascus. Even if the delegation has left the city, I'm certain there are many who would turn me in for a ransom. You said it yourself. Let things calm down for a while. You and Aziza must go back."

"But how will you survive alone?"

"I can take care of myself." Nenshi took a deep breath and reminded Babak that he had survived the gold mines, the scorching desert, and shed blood in the name of freedom. He had escaped from sand dwellers and eluded Egyptian soldiers.

"I have cheated death," he said. "My ordeals have been many. I will not give up now." He put his hand on Babak's shoulder. "I won't be alone," he said light-heartedly. "I'll have Abramu's god El to keep me safe." His whimsical remark did not sit well with Babak.

"You place your trust in a god that you know nothing about? You Egyptians just love to believe in gods. The more there are, the greater success you have."

"Babak, listen to me. This isn't about the gods. I have a better chance of surviving on my own. Remember, we almost lost Aziza because we had to stay behind until she was well enough to continue. I don't want to lose either of you. You must go back to Damascus. It's best for everyone."

Reality set in. Babak's condition could jeopardize Nenshi's ability to keep out of harm's way. He conceded.

"Remember, I told you about my friend, Harun? It's best that you go to Ur and find him since he spends more time there than in Karchemish." Babak then told Nenshi how to get to Ur. Nenshi listened intently to every detailed instruction. One mishap and he could be going in the wrong direction as he had done before.

The early morning saw young men dismantle tents as fast as they had raised them. Everyone prepared to resume their journey. Ahead of the clan Nenshi, Babak, Aziza and Abramu stood alone on the road. It reminded Nenshi of the day he had left Thebes, the day he had seen Tehuti for the last time. Nenshi wondered if he would see Babak and Aziza again or if this would be a last farewell.

"Take this," Abramu said as he handed Nenshi a flask of water and a bag filled with bread, cheese, olives and fruit. Nenshi smiled, grateful for the offering. He turned to Babak and embraced him.

"Take care of Aziza," Nenshi said. He turned to Aziza. "As for you, watch over that crusty man. He'll need you more than you'll need him." Then he hugged her.

Nenshi was about to walk away when Abramu placed a gentle hand on his shoulder. The touch radiated warmth through his body with a lasting sensation like the sweet brew made of poppy seeds used to sooth pain. Abramu then raised his right hand and said, "May El be with you."

Chapter 32

NENSHI'S DECISION TO TRAVEL ALONE proved to be prudent. He was able to cover greater distance in shorter time, eventually reaching his destination.

Ur was a flourishing priest-ruled city. It attracted people from distant lands to reap the benefits of its thriving commerce. Visitors were astonished at the prosperity. The allure of astrology, writing, and craft works made Ur the hub of advanced thinking. Everyone benefited from the city's success - the rich profited from being at the centre of a trade route; the less fortunate were treated fairly; and, slaves and peasants were granted privileges. The broad avenues were a testament to the affluence; they all converged on the towering temple, the Great Ziggurat, dedicated to the moon god, Nanna.

Nenshi eventually found Harun, Babak's long-time friend. Born in Karchemish, on the northern part of the River Euphrates, he had moved to Ur, the centre of all trade. Like many, he sought wealth and adventure.

Harun wasted no time in putting Nenshi to work. Hauling cargo and keeping records of goods transported up and down the rivers helped take his mind away from thoughts of being on the run.

He had adapted well to his new surroundings, albeit temporary, as he had planned. He had quickly learned about its schools, literature, the codes of law, the splendour of the fertile land, the affluence, and the authority of priests. The city reminded him of Thebes with its welcomed confusion and fast-paced lifestyle. But Ur was not a place where he could plant new roots. His unrelenting drive to return home dominated.

The excitement of Ur and the power of the clerics over the people stirred Nenshi's curiosity. The ziggurat, situated at the centre of the city, reminded him of Egypt's pyramids and temples. He wanted to visit the magnificent structure and Harun obliged, when it was safe enough.

Harun, bare-chested, wearing a kilt-like garment drawn tightly at the waist, walked down the corridor of his mud brick building used to store goods and conduct business. He had massive shoulders and legs. Looking like two oversized barrels, one on top of the other, he barely squeezed through the entrance. His long curly black beard rolled down his chin to his neck. For most men in Ur who fashioned the style, it exemplified wisdom, strength, and social status. But for Harun, he was just too lazy to keep his face free of hair.

"Nenshi," Harun called out as he entered the room. Nenshi sat at a table tabulating records, counting goods from a list given to him by an assistant, Fazel, a young and timid scribe, always willing to please everyone. "Come with me," Harun said. "It's time we dignify the temple with our presence."

Finally, it was a chance for Nenshi to see something different than scrolls and ships. He hurriedly put away his instruments, eager for the tour.

"I'll return later to finish my work," Nenshi told Fazel who fumbled to retrieve his writing tools.

Another scribe, Emir, helped Fazel gather his instruments from the floor. Emir glanced at Nenshi from the corner of his eyes and scowled. Things changed since Nenshi had arrived. Harun had given Nenshi all the tasks that Emir had wanted and had prepared himself to do. Emir knew about Harun's friendship with Babak and so could only surmise that it was a favour to Babak that allowed Nenshi to work at Harun's business. Nonetheless Emir was bitter towards Harun for granting the work to a stranger and didn't hide his acrimony towards Nenshi. Nenshi sensed Emir's resentment ever since he had arrived.

Harun and Nenshi strolled through the roads that led to the temple. People from all walks of life were there. Musicians played customary religious songs. Anyone who appreciated the music tossed coins at their feet. Priests paraded in groups and made supplications to the gods for all to hear - *The brightness has filled the broad land. The people are radiant; they take courage at seeing thee. Shine upon us your light; bestow unto us your gifts.*

Listening to the prayer made Nenshi think of Abramu. Perhaps, as a young boy, he had walked theses same streets and had recited the same prayer. There was a strong religious presence here that kept the people together; kept them inflexible to the notion of the existence of another deity. Yet the sacrosanct walls of singular religious views were penetrated by an unknown god who spoke to a man; words so powerful that it sparked a journey to an unknown land. Why did this god choose this land to reveal himself? Was Egypt not as worthy? Was there not a admirable man in Egypt to heed a divine call? Nenshi had no answers to the questions racing through his mind. He could only wonder if El was still making his presence known, still making his words heard.

The temple complex was surrounded with festivities. Near the shrine, townspeople tended to their affairs and didn't attempt to enter it or the shrine situated at the top of the seven-tiered ziggurat. Guards prevented the curious from spying on the rituals performed by the priests. They feared that the revelation of their secret ceremonies would spark the gods to unleash their wrath. A fragrance of fresh fruits, vegetables, dates, beans, apples, onions, garlic, and turnips permeated the complex. Visitors adorned the temple with goods - ivory from the east, jewellery and lapis lazuli from the north.

"It's magnificent!" Nenshi said as he gazed up to the top of the ziggurat. The glazed facing of the walls captivated him, even though he didn't know the significance of the colours. The unfamiliar carvings reminded him of the symbols and pictures he had seen on temple facings and buildings in Thebes. "What are these?" he asked.

"The names of the kings who had ruled Ur over time." Harun said. "Each one had proclaimed himself a god."

"And what's that over there?" Nenshi pointed to a building behind the barriers.

"That's where they keep records of everything that happens here, from taxes levied on its citizens to prominent visitors, even names of criminals."

"And what's done with the accounts?"

"Who knows? The priests say the city needs to be organized. I say they like to be in control. There's probably a record about you." Harun grinned. Nenshi was not amused. He shook his head, tightened his lips, restrained himself from saying something he might regret. "Don't take me seriously," Harun teased. "No one here really cares who you are." His laughter annoyed Nenshi. "We must leave now," Harun elbowed and winked. "I want to take you somewhere else."

"Lead the way."

As they walked down the main road of the city Nenshi looked back and couldn't help but think about the countless stored records. He wondered if in fact there existed a record about a runaway slave. But he was careful not to let his obsession get the best of him. Harun was probably right. Why would Ur have a record of an escaped Egyptian slave? Ur did not care for the downtrodden in the streets, as long as they respected the laws.

Chapter 33

"ONLY THE PRIVILEGED COME HERE," Harun said. He waved his hand, palm up, across his body as if to reveal hidden lost treasures. The great hall was where the affluent came to celebrate annual feasts. Palace administrators, judges, landowners, priests and ship builders have come to start the celebration of the new moon of Spring.

Dancers kept pace with the synchronized beats from drums and rattles; flutes spread their wafting hollow tunes through the air; singers majestically united the cacophony of sounds into a creation of music. Nenshi didn't expect such pageantry.

"I like what I'm hearing," he said as his head swayed back and forth to the tempo.

"Ur loves its music," Harun said. "There's a story about a very rich man who loved it so much that he could not bear to be without it. When he died, he took his musicians and sleeping potion with him in his tomb. The potion was for the musicians of course."

"So, the musicians had a comfortable life performing for their master and when it was time to serve the gods, they followed him in death." Nenshi's sharp sarcasm drew attention.

"I never thought of it that way," Harun mused.

As they searched for a free table, they passed two scribes, arguing.

"You're a stupid illiterate Sumerian," said one scribe. "I've seen your writing and it's obvious you were not taught to hold the stylus. You call yourself a scribe?"

"I'm not illiterate and stupid," retorted the other. "I'm a scribe, son of a scribe - unlike you! I've seen your work. It makes no sense, your writing is completely illegible and when you go to divide an estate, you don't hold the measuring line while you survey the land. You are incompetent."

"I am not!"

"You are!"

The argument irritated both Nenshi and Harun.

"It seems they find it easier to criticize than to correct," Nenshi said, as he pointed to a table away from the quarrelling duo.

Nenshi positioned his seat so he could get a good view of the ceremony as it unfolded. Guests swarmed in, anxiously looking to reunite with friends. A mingling sea of old and new acquaintances flowed across the room like a boat on a river being swayed back and forth by never-ending gentle waves. Everyone rejoiced, for the first new moon announced the beginning of the agricultural year.

Nenshi twisted and turned his head in every direction to capture the excitement of the fellowship. As he scanned the room, a familiar face came into view.

"What's Emir doing here?" he asked. His forehead curled and the corner of his eyes wrinkled in suspicion.

Harun spotted Emir with less interest. "I don't know." He shrugged his shoulders. "Maybe he's accompanying one of the guests."

"I find that hard to believe."

"It doesn't matter. I want to eat. I'm hungry."

Within minutes, food and wine appeared. Harun grabbed a leg of lamb, held it securely by the bone end, clenched his teeth into the tender meat and tore away a piece. With his other hand, he pointed towards the crowd. He chewed and swallowed as fast as a wild boar devoured its catch. "Look ... over there ... an old friend of mine... the very rich widow."

"What's her name?"

"I don't remember. I just call her the very rich widow."

"You sound envious. Do you begrudge her wealth?"

"Not at all. She inherited everything from her husband. She's like many who had started with nothing and then one day they found themselves surrounded in riches. Life changes, they change, they don't look back. A lifestyle of leisure and affluence can make a person forget their roots. No, I don't object to women being rich. I object to them wanting to do everything themselves. Of course, they have rights in Ur but they do not have the schooling to master everything."

"What do you mean?"

"Only boys attend school. Women enjoy having equal rights as men, but they have not been exposed to learning."

"That's strange thinking for a land as advanced as this. Or is it just your thinking? I find them quite capable of learning. In fact, I see them involved in almost all facets of life. They come to the docks to conduct business. And it seems they're influence has also made you rich."

"That's true. You name it, they have their fingers in it."

"Get used to it Harun."

"That's my problem, I can't get used to it. My way of thinking may be old but let me tell you something - women are spending more time in business than matters of the family. Women today want status; they want recognition for things other than having children. I'm surprised that our priests allow them such liberty, allow them to have a decisive hand in many affairs."

"You're right. Your thinking is old, like you." Nenshi laughed.

They refilled their cups with wine. While they waited for more food to arrive, they drew their attention to the centre of the massive room, crowded with dancers, musicians, jugglers and magicians. An outburst of laughter came from the far end of the room where, at a long table, a group of men prepared for a drinking contest. The opposite side of the room seemed to be reserved for guests just pleased to engage in pleasant conversations.

The festivities came to a close and there was little to hold Nenshi's attention. The thought of a record about a runaway slave played on his mind that he decided to find out for himself if there was such evidence. If it did exist and Nenshi was discovered, Ur would be obligated to return him to Egypt.

"Harun ... I'm tired," Nenshi said, feigning a yawn to excuse himself. "It's been a long day. We walked the entire city and you worked me too hard."

Harun laughed. "So, you want to leave? You're bored. I know."

"Not at all. I'm simply exhausted."

Harun let out another burst of laughter. "You're not tired. You probably made arrangements to meet with a young woman."

"I don't know anyone in Ur. Speaking of which, go and spend time with your rich widow friend, the one with no name."

Harun smiled. "Go ahead, have your fun. I'll see you tomorrow."

With that, Nenshi scurried out and Harun looked around the room for the rich widow.

It was dark, except for the dim light from the crescent moon that paved Nenshi's way, undetected. He squeezed through the gates of the building that stored the city's records - messages, captured like a patient spider waiting on its far-reaching web for the next fly to get tangled. It was a simple system - fast and effective and like the spider, it never rested. A chain of towers used fire signals to relay a message; another fly was caught.

A few scribes in the building prepared messages to be dispatched the next day by an army of young and energetic boys. Nenshi heard voices coming from the upper level, from the only window with light shining through. He looked around and saw guards at the other end. He moved quickly. He pushed the heavy wooden door to open, controlled the swing so as not to cause a thud. He walked in with careful attention, ready to run out if confronted. The atrium was empty.

Now he only needed to find the room where the records were stored. The voices from the upper chambers got louder as he gingerly sauntered up the long flight of stairs. Every few steps he stopped and looked around to make sure he was alone.

In a dimly lit room, two scribes sat at a table. They drank wine instead of working. When unsupervised they always took advantage of the absence of an overseer. Working at night had its benefits.

Rolled messages were scattered on a long table, each one tied with a ribbon and an official waxed seal. Their task was to read and record what was received. Instead they preferred to drink and tell tales. One of the scribes stood and gulped a cup of wine. Nenshi moved back, away from the entrance. The scribe walked to the window and looked out.

"I'm going out for some fresh air," he said to his colleague.

Nenshi scurried behind a pillar. The scribe wobbled past him, unaware of who lurked in the darkness. The other clerk took a long drink straight from the flask, crossed his arms and placed them on the table. He had mastered making a temporary pillow with his arms. He lowered his head until it rested on them and nodded off to sleep. Nenshi waited. He heard a snore and then walked into the room; every step kept pace with each snort.

Along the longest wall were square cavities, from floor to ceiling. They all measured the same size, and all held rolled papyrus notes and cuneiform tablets. The openings were marked with the names of the places from where the messages came. Nenshi knew he was in the right room. He scanned the slots, in a hurry, looking for a clue, some evidence of a record that might point to his existence.

The scribe at the table stopped snoring and shifted his position. Nenshi turned to him, ready to move with the speed of leopard. A snore squeezed out from the scribe, then another and another. But Nenshi realized that once he began to search the records, the sound of rustling papyrus rolls and clashing tablets might jolt the scribe out of his slumber. Yet again, obsession undermined logic and he resumed his search. He randomly pulled a record with meticulous care. The marking on the roll was familiar; that of the Pharaoh of Egypt. Nenshi unrolled it, taking care to silence his action. He read it. No mention of a runaway. He rolled the papyrus and returned it to its place. He looked up at the countless rolls. It was pointless. He realized the daunting task and his obsession that had consumed him over the possibility of a record about a runaway. Harun was right, he thought. Ur does not care about runaways.

Then he heard a noise. The scribe was still sleeping and snoring. Nenshi looked towards the entrance. The other scribe would soon return. But he continued his search, one more time. If the other scribe was on his way back perhaps the long walk up the stairs would give him enough time to get out. He looked up and saw more records in a cavity with the same signs of the Pharaoh. He took a stool and carefully set it down in front of him. As he stood on it and reached up for a record, his sleeve gathered back on his arm and exposed the scars of the branded rings, the markings of a criminal.

The sound of footsteps got louder. He stepped down and quickly walked out of the room. He stood behind the same pillar that had shielded him earlier. He heard another sound, someone breathing, panting, controlling the puffs. Was there a third scribe or a guard patrolling the hallway?

Nenshi went to the end of the hall, down the stairs and out the building. Upstairs, opposite the pillar, in the darkest corner of the atrium, Emir was as obscure as a masterful thief who stalked its next victim. He had witnessed Nenshi's secret.

The next morning, Nenshi, dishevelled and tired from a sleepless night, sat at a table and stared at a bowl of fresh fruit and yogurt. He ate the fruit but left the yogurt untouched. Fazel furled his brows. He customarily prepared the morning meals since he was always the first to arrive. Emir was also at work. Nenshi found this unusual since Emir was always the last to arrive. Harun was busy in his work area organizing the day's shipments.

Just then, two men appeared. Their sudden presence raised eyebrows, especially Harun's. They were city officials. Nenshi watched with curiosity as Emir went to greet them, whispered something and went to stand behind Nenshi who remained calm yet suspicious of the visitors.

Harun turned to the men. "How can I help you?"

"We have a few questions," said one of the men.

"I am pleased to answer them. I can have my trusted assistant Fazel prepare anything you wish to see. I run a reputable business."

The other man walked around the table and stood beside Nenshi. Emir then stepped aside, having delivered the signal for the men's purpose.

"We're not here to question you about your business," the official said. "We need to know who this man is." He pointed with his eyes at Nenshi who didn't move, didn't react. His schooling in oratory could not help him now.

The other official then went to the other side, behind Nenshi. The man put his hands on Nenshi's left shoulder and pressed down impeding any movement. The other man leaned over and grabbed Nenshi's right sleeve. He pulled it up and revealed the scars, the marks of a criminal.

Chapter 34

HORDEKEF HAD REACHED DAMASCUS. THE caravan party had dispersed with everyone eager to strip themselves of the weight of cargo and exhaustion of yet another long ordeal through remote towns and villages. He stood alone on a road where the dust had soared to the sky from the heels of camels and mules creating a cloud, yellowed by the sun's light. The blanket descended, filling mouths and eyes with the dryness of the land. He licked his lips, gathered sand in his mouth with his saliva and spat it out to the ground.

"Do you need help?" a Damascene asked, one of the last men to leave the caravan. Hordekef's blank stare hinted that he had never been to Damascus before.

Hordekef replied. "It's been a long journey and I have little water left. Do you know where I can get some?"

The man nodded. "You may want more than water. There are many taverns along this road. I'm certain one of them will have what you need."

Hordekef smiled and bid farewell. The search for Nenshi was stronger than his thirst for water. He would endure the longing until he was with his friend again so that together they could celebrate their reunion over countless jugs of beer.

He walked into the first tavern on the road. It was empty, nobody in sight. Not a popular one. Disappointed, he turned around and walked out. Further down the road he entered another tavern. Unlike the first one, this was filled with patrons, noisily buzzing, like bees returning to their hive.

"If you're looking for a place to sit, you'll have to wait," said a tired waiter as he wiped his hands on his apron.

"I'm looking for someone," Hordekef said, as he looked behind the worn-out young man, hoping Nenshi was among the crowd. "An Egyptian who works in a tavern in Damascus. Do you know of him?" he asked.

"No." The curt response came without much thought. He balanced a tray full of drinks as he negotiated his way around tables. Hordekef was almost out the door when the waiter called out to him.

"Now I remember," he said. He could hardly be heard over the uproar of laughter and deafening clatter. "I think he's in Saulum's tavern."

"And where's that?" Hordekef asked, his voice, loud, crackled, like that of a boy going through puberty.

"Near the end of the road. If you hurry you might get there before the sun sets."

"Does it close at sunset?"

"No but when it begins to get dark, taverns fill with the hungry and thirsty. The streets fill with the undesirable."

Hordekef picked up his pace. Without stopping he drank from his flask, consumed as little as possible for fear of running out of water. As the sky darkened, he wondered who might be lurking like a jackal, waiting to rush at an unsuspecting prey.

He walked into another tavern and scanned the room. It was as busy as the previous one. Waiters hastened to take orders and deliver food and drinks to impatient patrons. This time Hordekef approached one of the customers. Someone enjoying their meal might be more amicable than a tense waiter.

"Forgive me for interrupting, who's the owner of this tavern?" Hordekef asked. The man's distrustful frown made Hordekef wonder if it was always so difficult to speak with anyone in Damascus or he just kept choosing the wrong ones to ask.

"Are you a taxman?" the man asked. "If you are, I have nothing to say." Everyone hated the taxman.

"No, I am not. I'm looking for a friend," Hordekef assured him.

The man took a sip of his beer and examined Hordekef up and down. "You don't look like a taxman. They come dressed in their finest clothes, their hands are soft like those of a maiden and they have no meat to their bones."

"Well, that rules me out."

"Yaakoub," said the man. "Yaakoub is the owner. He's usually in the kitchen."

"I thought Saulum owned this place?"

The man, his cheeks stuffed with mutton, shook his head. It was the wrong tavern.

Hordekef walked out into the darkness. He drew his dagger and held it by his side, prepared to use it if necessary. Alone, he would be the perfect victim, a strange man in a strange land.

He stepped into another tavern, into the safety of numbers. He went to sit at an empty table. A young waiter presented himself.

"May I help you?" he asked.

"I'm looking for a friend. Does someone work here by the name of Nenshi?"

"No. Do you want to eat or drink?" His abruptness left much to be desired. Hordekef ordered a beer to quench his thirst and hoped that placing an order would make the waiter more receptive.

"This is my first day here," admitted the waiter, apologetically. "I'll be back with your beer and I'll ask about your friend."

While he waited, Hordekef scanned the room, perchance that he might see Nenshi. His hope of finding him was beginning to fade. He noticed the waiter approach a man and whispered something in his hear. The man began to clear tables and then subtly glance towards

Hordekef. The suspicious glare made him uneasy. After all, he wasn't the only stranger in the tavern, so why was he singled out by fleeting looks? He took a long sip and wiped his mouth with his sleeve. The man casually made his way to Hordekef.

"In case you're wondering, I'm not the taxman," Hordekef said. It seemed to him that only those who frequented taverns were afraid of such collectors.

"I understand that you're looking for someone."

"A friend."

"Hmm ... a friend you say."

"Yes ... a friend."

"Does your friend have a name?"

"I have already told the young waiter. His name is Nenshi. Do you know him?" A blank stare was all that was offered in response.

"What's your name?"

Hordekef reached the end of his patience with the insolent questioning. He took another sip of his beer and slammed the mug on the table. He stood, pushing the chair with the heel of his foot.

"I have no time for this," he said and began to walk away. He turned and added, "My name is Hordekef."

"Wait. Come back and sit down ... please."

Hordekef stopped in his tracks. He wanted to leave but he needed to know for certain if anyone knew Nenshi. He turned and walked back. He pulled the chair close to the table and sat down. He peeked into the mug, there was still beer in it. He took a sip.

"Wait here. I'll be right back." The man hurried to the kitchen and shortly after he came back, followed by another man. Hordekef's eyes furled.

"I understand you're looking for someone named Nenshi."

Hordekef controlled his temper. If an altercation ensued, he was clearly outnumbered. "I have already told the waiter and your friend here."

"He's not my friend. He's my brother, Saulum. My name is Babak."

Hordekef's eyes widened, in revelation. The man Sia had described to him was indeed Babak. The pieces fit together, like stars aligned, each with its own life, presented one at a time, until the sky told its story from beginning to end.

Just then, Aziza walked out from the kitchen. Babak waved her over.

"And this must be Aziza," Hordekef said.

"Yes," Babak replied. He turned to Aziza and said, "This is Hordekef."

Her eyes widened and she grabbed a chair and sat down across from Hordekef, staring at him.

"So, where is he? Where's Nenshi?"

"He's not here." The disappointment in his tone was of no comfort.

"But Sia had told me that I would find him here."

"I understand. I'll tell you everything."

Babak waved to the waiter to bring drinks and food to the table. He told Hordekef everything that had happened. The long explanation took several beers and a full meal to get through.

"So Nenshi is in a place called ... Ur?"

"Yes. He's safe with a friend. It will be difficult for Egyptian authorities to find him. I didn't mention Ur to Sia."

"What do you mean difficult for the authorities to find him? They are not looking for him."

"I don't understand. Nenshi had told me he had been exiled from Thebes. He managed to run away from the gold mines. This and the fact he's a servant have had him fleeing from greater punishment. He was certain of it."

Hordekef sighed and took a deep breath. He understood now what had happened, why Nenshi was not in Damascus. He covered his face with his hands and swayed his head, side to side, blamed himself for his best friend's life on the run. He moved his hands away from his face, revealed the agony and guilt he had carried with him all this time. He placed his hands in front of him, leaned forward and said, "Nenshi is a free man."

Babak was visibly shaken. Aziza put her head down in disbelief. Hordekef told them about Tehuti's petition for Nenshi's freedom. But he didn't tell them that he had been the cause of the delay in granting the request. If he could not forgive himself for the selfish act, how could anyone else?

"Nenshi was right," Babak said, disheartened. "The gods have not been in his favour. He's a free man and doesn't know it."

"Babak ... you must tell me how to get to Ur," Hordekef interrupted. "I must find him. It's the only way for Nenshi to learn about his freedom."

Babak put his hand to his chin. Hordekef, alone, would have great difficulty in finding Nenshi. "We'll take you to Ur. We'll leave in two days," Babak said. Hordekef nodded in agreement.

Chapter 35

THE PRISON CELL WAS COLD and damp. The stench of urine made it difficult to breathe. Light cast into the room came from a gap between the top of the narrow thick wooden door and its frame. A guard's footsteps paced back and forth and kept an eye on the prisoners nestled in their cells. Moans and screams tried to get attention but they were ignored. The guard opened each cell door, one at a time, and peered in to make sure the prisoner was still alive. He returned to his post.

Nenshi sat on a makeshift cot, soiled, shared by many who came before him. He tugged at the ligatures that restricted his mobility. They were thick heavy ropes made from countless reeds intertwined so tightly that not even the crushing bite of a river crocodile could cut through them. They were stronger than the ones that held him down on the boat during his transfer to Nubia.

Nenshi wondered what awaited him. Perhaps the priests would decide or it was left to a vizier to deal with such matters. Whichever the case, there were few choices. He could be sent back to Egypt or back to the mines or be sacrificed in one of the city's temples. For Nenshi, all options were a death sentence.

He languished in prison, disheartened by the sudden turn of events caused by religious beliefs. The deeds of the clergy are no match for the innocent, he thought.

The morning couldn't come soon enough for the guards, bored of the same routine in guarding prisoners, like a lioness watching over her cubs. Their daily duties had ended and a fresh group, who would also become uninterested in their work, would replace them. If Nenshi contemplated an escape, now would be the time. But how could he possibly remove the ropes and get out of a locked cell?

Two men sat at a table in a room just inside the prison, close to the cells. One had his head down, sleeping, while the other kept busy shining the sharp metallic point of his spear.

"Wake up," the guard called out. "The others will be here soon to replace us. Look alive." The one sleeping reluctantly lifted his head, groaned and rubbed his eyes, heavy with sleep. He stood to stretch and shake the weariness from his body.

Nenshi peered through a crack in the door towards the end of the corridor. A dim light from their station cast eerie shadows of movements. The guards' ghostly images, against the walls of the prison, shot a jolt up his spine giving thought of many who had been imprisoned and eventually perished. Then he heard footsteps that he mistaken for those belonging to the guards coming to replace the ones on duty. A whispering voice followed.

"Nenshi … Nenshi … it's me … Harun."

Nenshi thought that the lack of sleep and lack of food and water had made him delirious. Then slowly, from the darkness, from behind a pile of dried straw used to spread inside the cells to soak up urine and vomit, Harun appeared. He pinched his nose and breathed through his mouth.

"What are you doing here? How did you get in?" Nenshi asked, in whispering shock.

"No time for that now. I need to get you out," Harun said, looking down the corridor, making sure they were not heard.

Harun tried to pry open the door with his dagger. It didn't work. Nenshi looked on, helpless. "I need to get the key," Harun said and began to creep his way down the corridor.

"You'll either come back with the key or be dragged in here to join me in this decrepit cell," Nenshi whispered.

Near the guards' station, Harun hid behind a wooden pillar. "Wait here," one guard said to the other. "I'm going outside to see if the others are arriving."

The guard who remained behind sat down and rested his head on the table. The keys to the cells hung loosely on his hip. Harun inched closer and crouched down. He stretched with his dagger to pull away the keys, but he couldn't reach. He took a step closer. The guard grunted and shifted his body. Harun pulled back. The keys were farther away. A spear was leaning up against the wall next to Harun. He took it and began to reach for the keys. The guard snored. Harun managed to lift the keys from the strap. With the keys in one hand and the spear in the other, he made his way back to Nenshi.

As Harun fumbled with the keys, trying to figure out which one opened the cell, they could hear voices coming from the station.

"It's about time you got here. Now we can leave," said the guard. A voice from the entrance responded. "I hope you're not sleeping in there or you'll be reported." The guards laughed. A tease was welcomed from a comrade. Solidarity could be mocked but not broken.

Meanwhile Harun finally managed to open the cell door. "Follow me," he motioned to Nenshi.

The prisoner next to Nenshi's cell, who had watched the escape unfold, called out to Harun. "Me too … free me too," he said.

There was no time to attempt to free anyone else so Harun handed the keys to the prisoner. "I'm sure you can manage it. But do it quietly," he said. The prisoner nodded.

As Harun and Nenshi made their way down the corridor, they heard the guards.

"Don't forget to leave the keys on the table," one guard said to the other.

"Ah yes, the keys." The other guard reached to his side. "I don't have them. Do you?"

"No."

"I must have dropped them earlier with my blade at the far end. Help me find them."

Hearing this Harun grabbed Nenshi by the arm. "This way. And hold your nose." They hid behind the pile of dried straw. The stench was unbearable.

As the guards walked past them, Harun and Nenshi crept to the other side of the stack of straw and then made their way out. The sound of shuffling feet stirred curiosity.

"Who goes there?" called out one of the guards.

"It's an escape!" the other yelled.

As they ran down the corridor the prisoner with the keys shook them to get their attention. Harun turned to see the guards trying to coax the prisoner to give them back.

"Let's get out of this smelly place," Harun said. "We have little time."

Nenshi smiled, put his hand on Harun's shoulder and said, "Lead the way."

They stood under a tree, far from the prison. Their relief to have made it out safely would be short-lived. Their getaway would not go unnoticed. It was full daylight and the city came to life. The streets filled with the usual merchants who prepared their stands of food and wears for sale.

"Here's a change of clothes," Harun said. "I can try to find you a place to stay but it won't be long before soldiers will be out looking for you. An escaped prisoner is a serious offence."

"No ... there's no safe place here for me," Nenshi said. "I don't want you to have to answer to the authorities. You would lose everything if they discovered that you had harboured a fugitive."

Nenshi had no choice. He knew he had to leave. He had to run away, again.

"You're better off going towards the mountains," Harun said. "Take this road. It'll lead you out of the city."

"Mountains?" Nenshi had no knowledge of these.

"You can't see them from here. Besides, the authorities won't suspect you will go in that direction. I'm sure you'll find a town that will be safe, then you can make your way back after a full moon. By then they will have given up looking for you."

"I'm grateful for everything you've done."

"May your god guide you to freedom," Harun said.

"I have no god," Nenshi said, with conviction.

Harun chuckled. "You can have mine if you want."

"Do you mean Nanna?"

"So you have knowledge of our gods?"

"Some. Such as El." Nenshi was now testing to confirm what Abramu had told him.

"El? We have no such god," Harun shrugged. "This isn't the time to talk about gods. You must go and so must I." Harun leaned over and gave Nenshi a strong embrace. He then walked towards the busy streets. Nenshi kept track of him as he mingled among the crowd. He then turned, pulled a tunic over his head and trudged in the opposite direction.

On the outskirts, Nenshi stopped for a moment to look at Ur in the distance - a splendid and mighty city that had given him temporary shelter. His homeland was almost forgotten and the hope of returning had become as distant as his memories. He had discovered new lands, carved new friendships. All had been placed before him by an unknown force and he didn't know why.

His journey was not complete. He had witnessed cruelty, rejection and death - the realities of life that his tutors could not have taught him. Not even the wise knew of the world that existed beyond their borders.

Every new day unleashed the challenge of another path, an uncertain destination and greater despair. The anguish inside tormented him. Looking back can be painful. Not seeing Tehuti, not hunting with Hordekef, were stripped from his life. The realization that Sia had moved on with her life had agonized him. Now he needed to move forward, to the end, to that final crossing, in search of a new life.

PART FOUR

Chapter 36

THERE WAS NO PLACE LIKE this, no connection to the kingdoms that flourished to the south and west. It stood alone. The influence from Sumer, Phoenicia and Egypt was remote. Yet it shared the humble beliefs from each of the great powers before they were tainted by human indulgence. The earth, the air and the afterlife were as important as in Egypt. Those who came from Sumer or Phoenicia adopted a new way of life. And the reflection of hospitality echoed prominently in the belief in how people should treat one another.

This was Paras – a land diverse in landscape and in the people that walked the land.

A twelve-year-old boy sat on a rock on the banks of a fast-flowing river. The land, through his eyes, was as narrow as the river, as simple as the changing seasons, as majestic as the mountains that led to green pastures.

He sat in solitude and stared at the river. He picked up a stick and threw it into the water. The current swallowed it and carried it away. A familiar voice called out to him. He turned to see his father in the distance, beneath one of the few trees on the hillside. The boy's moment of tranquillity had suddenly been transformed into guilt and fear. He ran with the speed of the river's current to meet his father.

"Haji, you know better than to wander from camp. Of all days, this one is important."

A shiver spilled down Haji's back expecting certain punishment. But there was none. The curiosity of a young boy and the desire for independence was well understood.

"Don't put your head down. You never know what might fall out of this tree and hit you," his father said. The lighter tone was more welcoming than the one that jolted him. The chuckle caused Haji to smile. "I need you to help prepare for tomorrow's journey," his father said.

"I came to see how fast the water moved," Haji said. It was his way of fighting the anxiety over the annual trek, his way of learning to overcome his own fears.

He walked beside his father, up the hill, every step was a struggle, a reluctance that pulled him back, down, towards the river.

"Father, must we cross the Bazuft again?"

It was a fear that every young boy and girl from the tribe confronted. Apprehension that even his father and his father's father had conquered. Haji was now of age to attempt the daunting task of crossing the river on his own.

"You must have courage," his father said. "You know that getting to the other side on your own is important." It was the last obstacle between the tribe and the never-ending green pastures. "But don't think of it now. The Bazuft is far from here. There are many challenges even before we get to it. And each one will prepare you for that final crossing."

The reassurance did little to appease Haji's fear. His eyes wilted at the thought of what lay ahead.

"Come now, your mother and sister need our help. Tonight, we feast with everyone. Tomorrow can wait."

Enami and Fatameh had completed their routine chores; duties they performed with unrelenting execution. Now they could prepare for the festive meal.

They walked out of their tent; their dark multi- layered skirts flapped from side to side. Their long black hair flowed down their backs, covered by a headpiece. Unlike her brother, Fatameh was now passed the age of preparation. She was ready for a new life, her own family. As a young girl she had learned how to cook and how to pick wild berries. When she was strong enough, she would pitch a tent, gather firewood, and make rugs - lessons to become like her mother, resourceful and resilient – survival skills that a good wife must have. Enami had prepared her daughter well for the role, a duty of all mothers from the tribe.

Fatameh pushed back her headscarf and began to cut and clean a lamb for the evening's meal. The scarf always seemed to get in the way when she cooked. She tied her hair back and rolled up her sleeves halfway up her arms. Now she was ready to dissect the carcass. Her strong hands made the task easy and the speed of chops and slices were evidence that she had done this many times before. The fire burned, ready to cook the slaughtered animal.

The chopping stopped. Her mother's eyes darted towards Fatameh to see what had caused the knife to silence. Had she cut herself? If she had, she would remain silent, not complain, wrap her wound to stop the bleeding and continue with her work. Fatameh smiled to let her mother know she was not cut.

As Haji feared crossing the Bazuft, Fatameh feared marriage. Life for the tribeswomen was arduous. To become a wife and mother meant accepting greater demands. And marriage was inevitable. As inevitable as the migration of the tribe moving from grassland to grassland to feed its flock of sheep and goats. As inevitable as Haji's crossing of the river.

She knew the ritual all too well. She had seen it play out countless times. Her parents would determine everything, without consulting her. They would choose the suitor, the one most suitable to preserve the family values and the tribe's traditions. She would be told only after the arrangements had been made. Her silence would affirm their decision. Strict courtship would follow, a wedding ceremony would be prepared and gifts brought to the bride's father. But for Fatameh there had to be more than the rituals, more than chores and responsibilities.

She finished preparing the lamb and placed it on a rock next to the fire. She went to help her mother fill a tall earthen jug with frigid water from the river.

"Quickly now, my child," Enami said. "The hour of the feast is fast approaching. Go see if your father and Haji are nearby. Bring more wood. Tonight, the fires must last long into the night or singing will die with the fire."

The long-awaited feast finally arrived. It was time to celebrate what life had brought, before the tribe would venture on a migration that spanned a hostile terrain and dispiriting hardships. The aroma of roasted lamb permeated throughout the camp. Fires signalled the beginning of celebration. Candles in tall brass holders, acquired through trade with local merchants, were placed strategically to provide light. Rugs of all shapes and colours, scattered everywhere, resembled a decorative quilted blanket that covered the entire land.

The food was as flavourful as its aroma - chicken and mutton; toasted bread with green onion leaves; rice seasoned with sumac, mint and salt; walnuts and raisins crushed together to make a paste eaten with flatbread; bowls of fruit nectar; and nuts floating in date juice - a bouquet that seduced the senses, eager to be consumed.

The tribe's staunch determination for survival was set aside for celebration. A fire at the centre of the campground attracted those interested in ritualistic games of good fortune. Women applauded and cheered while the men participated.

"Father, it's your turn," Haji said, always excited to see his father in competition.

"Yes, Khorram, take your place," Jalili said, who oversaw the game, a simple one, to jump over the roaring fire.

Khorram took a few steps back as Jalili poked the fire with a long stick. He swirled it around and around until it came to life. He took dry leaves and threw them into the fire and made it swell. Flames shot up towards the sky.

Khorram raised his hand to silence the crowd. The fire's intimidating blaze was taunting. He lifted his hands to the sky and recited the ritual incantation.

"My troubles and my age, I cast into your flames. In return, I ask for nothing but your warmth and brightness."

He put his hands by his waist. He was ready. Cheers spurred him on. He flexed his muscles, bent over slightly to keep balance and then placed one foot in front of the other, prepared to attack the fire. Then with a sudden burst, he ran as fast as he could. When he came close to the fire, he leaped into the air, bent his knees as high and as a close to his chest as possible and sailed over the flames. He landed on the other side, firmly on his feet. He flung his arms in the air and rejoiced. The crowd shouted in celebration of his triumph.

Ahmad, *Kalantar*, chief of the nomads, congratulated Khorram. "Good fortune continues to follow you," he said.

Khorram smiled as he bowed his head. He invited the silver-bearded sagacious leader to sit with his family. The customary visit of the *maal's* chief rejuvenated and validated the tribe's commitment - to continually move the flock to new grasslands.

"I'm pleased with you and your family. From what I have seen, your flock is much larger, twofold. And you are reliable, as your father was. I remember him well, a good friend and member of our council of elders. He has taught you well." Ahmad glanced down at Haji, smiled, put his arm around him and gave a hug. "I have seen you tend to the flock. You have learned from your father." Ahmad then turned to Khorram. "I want you to take the place of your father and sit among us at the council. You're ready and I'm confident any decision you make will be for the good of our tribe."

Khorram humbly accepted the appointment. His father would have been proud. "I hope and pray to our forefather, Bakhtiar, that he will help me serve our people," he said. Enami filled two cups with wine to honour the occasion. The two men sipped and savoured it while the others looked on.

"Wine can cheer a man's heart but the love of a family will comfort him," Ahmad said, then stood and walked away.

Khorram leaned back and looked up at the sky. Haji did the same.

"What do you see?" Khorram asked.

"Stars. Countless stars. I used to call them fireflies, far away, that didn't disappear until morning."

Khorram pointed to a group of them and explained how it predicted the start of their journey.

"One day I will teach you how to use the night sky to guide your way."

"What do the lights say now?"

"Tomorrow will be a good day and a new beginning."

Chapter 37

FINAL PREPARATIONS FOR THE JOURNEY were made before the sun draped the land with its intense rays. Each of the family members assumed their role, as they had done countless times before. Khorram dismantled the tent while Haji attended to the flock. After preparing a morning meal, Enami and Fatameh filled goatskin bags with milk and water and then packed belongings for their daily journey. Everything they had was light enough to set up in the evening and pack in the morning. They were prepared to move at a moment's notice. Even the animals seemed to know what to do. Any grass that remained would be eaten before it died from the day's heat. Man and beast shared the instinct to survive.

The signal was given for the journey to begin, a trip that would take two cycles of the full moon to complete; one that had been repeated since time immemorial. The tribe marched on - a long procession - across the desolate land, over unstable rocks. Mules and donkeys carried children along with young animals strapped to the top of their loads. Goats and sheep often strayed and men stepped out of their position to coax them back to their place.

As the flock trekked along, Fatameh struggled, hindered by her complete assembly of layered clothing. The first layer, a long chemise-like blouse fell to the hips, comfortably. The second was a sleeveless vest and long colourful skirt to the ankles. Under it, she wore straight black trousers, which protected her along cold passages. During hot days, the skirts were unbearable and made walking difficult.

Fatameh had always hated the layered clothing. Often, she imagined herself dressed like the women she had seen in the small towns when she would go with her father to trade for necessities. Women dressed in thin loose garments that swayed with their pace, seemed more pleasant than fighting layers of clothing as heavy as a load of wood she would carry to the firepit. She would kick at her skirt with every step she took. When it rained, it became even more challenging. Her wet skirt would cling to her skin and make her ankles red and raw. Every intolerable step was calculated in order to help drive the herds.

The tribe stopped near a small stream, an opportunity to replenish their drinking water. Haji and Fatameh rested and kept an eye on the flock. Then something caught Haji's attention. He tugged on Fatameh's arm and pointed. She shielded her eyes from the sun.

"What is it, a dead sheep?" she asked.

"No, it's too big to be a sheep." He took a step closer but Fatameh grabbed his shoulder and pulled him back.

"Careful." She tilted her head to get a better view. "It looks like a man!"

"He's not moving. Maybe he's dead."

"Hurry, go tell father."

Haji ran off while Fatameh carefully approached the motionless body. She looked at his features, different from the men of her tribe. He appeared strong and capable of defending himself. She leaned over and put her ear close to his mouth. She felt the warmth on her cheek.

Moments later Haji returned with Khorram.

"I think he's alive," Fatameh said.

Khorram knelt beside the man. "He's exhausted, in need of drink. Haji, tell your mother to prepare warm milk." Khorram turned the body over on its back. "He's not from our tribe." Khorram picked him up, put him over his shoulder and carried him to the camp.

Enami struck a small fire and heated a bowl of goat's milk. Khorram laid the man on blankets that Fatameh assembled in a hurry.

"Come here," Enami called out to Fatameh. "Hold him while I get the milk."

Fatameh rested his head on her lap. No man had ever been this close to her. Her eyes darted to her father. He nodded in approval. She moved the man's hair away from his face. She took the cup from her mother and poured milk into him with a gentle touch as if feeding an injured young sheep.

"Father, the tribe is beginning to move." Haji said, frantic, unaccustomed in dealing with unexpected events.

"We can't leave him here," Fatameh said, concerned about both the stranger and the tribe.

"You're right," Khorram said. "We've brought him here. He's now our guest, our responsibility."

"Ahmad will not allow a delay," Enami said. "The people will continue with or without us. And daylight is passing."

"Tend to the animals," Khorram told Haji. "Make sure they're ready when it's our turn to move. Enami, come with me."

Enami and Khorram assembled a makeshift cart, the kind used to carry the old and the sick. They tied the ends of the two long and thick sticks to each side of a donkey. The other ends rested on the ground behind the animal. A blanket was secured to the poles for the man to be placed on. It was time to fall in line with the rest of the tribe.

In the late afternoon, the tribe reached its first challenge, the crossing of the swollen Karun River. The shallow river, with fast currents and rapids, could easily carry away man or animal. By the time they reached their destination, word had spread that Khorram had with him an unexpected guest.

Khorram stood by the bank of the river. The water splashed against the shore, spilling on to his feet. He looked for the shallowest point, the safest place to cross. Here he could wade into the water and guide the man and the animals.

He observed the force of each wave and the time between them. While Enami, Fatameh and Haji blew air into each *kalak*, goatskins, of various sizes, Khorram gathered dried tree branches and made several frames. His hands worked feverishly against the little time there was to cross the river. When the *kalak* balloons were ready, he bound them to a frame and made a raft to carry his family and the stranger. A rope was secured to it and made it easier to guide it to the other side.

Haji was helped on a *kalak* and crossed the river first. On the other side a tribesman, whose flock was ahead of Khorram's, waited for Haji and helped him off the raft. The man launched it back to Khorram and then continued his way leaving Haji to perform the same task. Enami crossed next, followed by Fatameh. Next came the animals, one at a time, sometimes two or three. Enami and Fatameh removed the animals from the rafts and each raft was returned back to Khorram. Lastly, it was time to send the stranger across the river. Khorram placed him on the raft, tied him to it, and launched him to the other side.

It was a successful crossing, even though a sheep was lost to an untimely launch and a fast current. The next passage promised to be a bigger challenge.

Small fires sprinkled everywhere throughout the camp. They danced like stars flickering in the night sky. The evening was quiet and restful. Enami and Fatameh prepared a meal while Khorram and Haji sat beside the stranger. Several men and women from the tribe walked by carrying branches. They stopped for a moment, looked at the man lying on a carpet. They smiled and nodded; the affirmation of their custom to treat a man as they would have wanted to be treated.

The stranger opened his eyes. He managed enough strength to sit up. Fatameh handed him a plate and a cup of water. Their eyes met. She smiled behind her veil. He took the food from her and scanned the faces that surrounded him. In the dialect he had learned from Harun in Ur, he said, "My name is Nenshi."

The next few days proved difficult for Nenshi. Learning a new language was not as challenging as learning new customs. He was patient, grateful for being found, alive. He spent time with Haji who taught him the words to bring the flock together. Khorram tried to explain the tribe's need to move from grassland to grassland. Nenshi couldn't understand such a necessity. In his mind it was better to grow crops than lead animals to pasture.

Nenshi sat alone, wondering how he would get back to Ur and back to Thebes. Like a fish taken from a pond and dropped into a lake, nothing was familiar to him. The land had changed. Mountains replaced the desert, mules replaced camels, and sheep outnumbered people.

He closed his eyes and lifted his head just enough to feel the sun's warmth. It soothed his troubled mind. He opened his eyes just as Fatameh walked by, balancing a basket of clothes on her head.

"We'll be over there," she pointed. "My parents are collecting wood."

"I will walk ... with you," he said. He managed to find the words.

"You are learning our language with ease," she smiled.

"There are similarities in your language with others I have learned. Your customs are a different story."

"You will learn those too," she said, as she pulled back her head scarf.

Surprised, Nenshi tilted his head, questioning her action. "Is that allowed?" he asked.

"Not in the presence of a guest," she replied, smiling. "But my parents are not here to discipline me. Sometimes even I get tired of some of our customs. I have seen how others live when I have gone with my father to trade for things we cannot make. I often wondered what it would be like to live as they do."

"But I have seen women in those places wear the head scarf," Nenshi said, uncertain why clothing, so common to all women in the region, was a hindrance to her.

"I will never disrespect my parents or our customs."

"But you challenge the limits."

"To challenge how to wear a head scarf has been a woman's right, even though not many women have chosen to carry out that right."

Khorram and Enami were by the river collecting dried branches while Haji tended to the flock. Fatameh and Nenshi came to help them.

A young man approached and headed straight towards Khorram. Fatameh turned, gave an uneasy glance and resumed her work, as a discussion began only between the two men. Enami also saw him from the corner of her eye. She recognized Rustam but dared not look his way.

"What brings you here?" Khorram asked. "Do you need help?"

"No." Rustam's eyes dashed back and forth between Fatameh and Khorram. "The animals are in good hands until I return."

Their voices were too low, their distance too far for Fatameh to hear so she casually moved closer within earshot of their discussion.

"I noticed that your flock is much larger," Khorram said.

Rustam smiled, proud of the accomplishment. "It can now be divided equally between my brother and me."

"That's a good sign for a young man."

"I have prepared to be independent from my father. I'm also ready to begin a new life with a family of my own."

Fatameh's ears perked, her face creased. Nenshi watched, his eyes darting back and forth analyzing Fatameh's reaction to the conversation.

"I have no doubt your plans are in order," Khorram continued. "There are many young women who would be happy to be your wife."

"That's why I have come to speak with you." His voice softened. "I'm suited to have Fatameh as my wife."

Khorram paused, unsure of a response. Fatameh's jaws tightened. She gripped a branch with the strength to strangle a wild boar.

"My father and uncles have spoken to me about the gifts - ten sheep, four goats and a mule," Rustam said.

"That's very generous. But you know our custom. Your parents must approach me first about your intentions."

Fatameh tilted her head back. An unusual proposal indeed. Now she was curious how Rustam, overstepping his boundaries, would justify his eagerness.

"They told me they'll speak with you," Rustam assured. "I also wanted to express my thoughts."

"I understand but what makes you think you are deserving of my daughter?"

"I'm strong and hard working. I'm willing to make whatever sacrifice it takes to have Fatameh for my wife."

"Even work to keep your emotions in control?"

Rustam's face reddened from the embarrassment of his reputation. "As I said, I will do whatever it takes."

"That remains to be seen. Nonetheless, I can't make the decision at this moment."

"Or perhaps you have already decided, without Fatameh's knowledge."

"What do you mean?"

"Does he have something to do with it?" Rustam asked, pointing his eyes at Nenshi.

"Nenshi is our guest. He is not of our tribe. You know our customs."

Rustam persisted. "Has anyone else asked for Fatameh's hand?"

Fatameh wanted to turn around to make sure she heard the reply but then reconsidered. Instead she moved closer to them and hummed a tune to pretend she was not listening.

"You're the first," Khorram said.

"Then I will be considered before others."

Khorram didn't reply. His silence confirmed the questionable match between Fatameh and Rustam.

Rustam left. Nenshi noticed his eyes, angered by the disappointment, unable to convince Khorram that he was best suited to marry Fatameh. Rustam controlled his fury and walked past Nenshi, ignored him, as if he was not even there.

Enami hurried towards Khorram. Fatameh dropped her load of branches and rushed to her father. Nenshi could not make out the conversation but a look at Enami and Fatameh told him they did not approve.

"You know what he can be like," Fatameh said, her voice muffled but her eyes not without expression.

"He's a hard worker with a prominent role within the tribe," Khorram said.

"He has not worked hard enough to control his temper," Enami replied.

"The smallest incident gone wrong infuriates him," Fatameh added. "I question his actions."

Both Fatameh and Enami had made their point. Rustam still needed to prove himself. Could his sensitivities towards Fatameh's feelings overcome his temper?

Chapter 38

AT KARCHEMISH, BABAK, AZIZA AND Hordekef snaked through the streets, like three determined hyenas following their prey.

"How do we get to Ur from here?" Hordekef asked.

"My friend, Harun, the man I described to you, is from Karchemish but he now lives in Ur. He travels back and forth on the river. If he's not here, we'll need to board one of his ships and go to Ur."

They walked into a building that Babak knew as Harun's place of business during his stay in Karchemish. A man shouted orders to the workers loading a ship.

"Faster ... faster! We don't have all day. This cargo must leave within a few hours." His command put fear in their eyes. They moved faster.

"Excuse me," Babak called to the man who barked the instructions.

"What do you want?" The overseer had no time for strangers. "If you want directions, ask someone else. I'm busy."

Hordekef interrupted, not caring for his abrupt response. "We're looking for Harun ... is he here?"

"No," the man replied and threw a suspicious glare.

"Is he in Ur?" Hordekef asked, his tone rose to match his frustration.

"No. Who are you?" The overseer stepped closer, face to face with Hordekef.

"Do you know where he is?"

"Where else would he be, while we work to load his ships? At the tavern ... his tavern ... that way," pointed the man. "Just follow that road. It will take you to him."

Babak waved to Hordekef and Aziza to follow him.

Harun was surprised to see Babak but Babak was not surprised at Harun's latest acquisition. Babak introduced Hordekef and Aziza.

"Please sit. Join me. When you own a tavern, you can eat and drink like a king," Harun said as he relished a mouthful of stuffed mushrooms. "I enjoy my beer and watch how men work to make me rich."

"Some things never change," Babak said. "Don't you feel guilty? You spill your beer and they spill their lives for you."

"Now ... now ... my friend. It's not as bad it seems. They are paid better than most. Ask them? That's why I'm rich. The more I pay them, the harder they work. No one realizes this. Many do the opposite. That's why I own a tavern."

"In that case, I'll have more beer."

"And more bread and mushrooms," Harun cried out to the kitchen.

Aziza reached over and scooped the remaining mushrooms before another plate was delivered. Harun laughed as she plopped them into her mouth.

Babak explained the reason for their unexpected visit. Harun nodded; a serious look replaced the laughter.

"Harun ... I beg you ..." Hordekef nudged to get his attention. "How far do you think Nenshi might have gone?"

"I'm not sure. There are many routes to choose from."

"Is there a chance that he went along one of the rivers?" Babak asked.

"If he did, I would have known it. I sent messages to all my friends in the area to keep an eye out for him. So far, nothing."

"Is there anywhere else he would go?" Hordekef asked.

Harun thought for a moment. He filled four cups with beer. "Does she drink beer?" he asked. Aziza picked up a cup and drank the beer.

"I guess that answers your question," Babak said.

"She's spirited," Harun laughed. "She would do well working for me."

"Answer the question." Hordekef was impatient.

"Oh ... yes ... I think he would have gone away from the river. I suggested it. To the mountains."

"Mountains? Did you say mountains?" Hordekef shook his head in disbelief, shocked at the possibility. "If he has gone towards the mountains, he's either lost, gone mad or perhaps even dead." He knew Nenshi would try to find a place to hide, somewhere unknown to his captors. But this was different. This was extreme. If he were still being hunted, no one would find him because he would not survive in the mountains.

"The river is an obvious place for the authorities to look. That's why I suggested the mountains. But I told him not to go too far and search a safe place to stay for a short time."

Hordekef stood from the table and paced the room. Babak pulled at Harun's shirtsleeve to get his attention. "Nenshi's been gone from Ur for more than a full moon and you haven't gone to look for him?" he asked.

"I have a business to run. I haven't forgotten about him. Nenshi is no fool. He knows how to stay away from danger. I'm sure he's safe and when the time is right for him, he'll return."

"How can you be certain?" Hordekef asked. Harun shrugged his shoulders. "Don't misunderstand me," Hordekef continued. "We're grateful for everything you've done to help him. We're just frustrated not being able to find him. Not to mention the toll this is taking on Babak."

Harun quickly turned to Babak. "I was wondering why you looked weak and pale."

"There's nothing wrong with me. Let's just figure out a way to find Nenshi."

None of this was a consolation to Hordekef. His eyes glazed over with a sense of failure. Was this the end of his quest? What would he tell Tehuti - that he gave up because mountains got in his way? No. He came to find Nenshi and he would not stop until he found him. If Nenshi dared to go that way, Hordekef would also.

"Tell me how to get there," Hordekef said. The conviction in his voice left no room for discourse. Harun frowned, his manner of deep thought. He pushed his shoulders back and smiled.

"I know someone who can help. He's here in Karchemish. He knows the land beyond the rivers; one of a few who has gone to trade with the wanderers in the mountains."

"How do you know he'll agree to take a bunch of strangers to find another stranger through barren land?"

"I've helped him on many occasions. It's time for him to pay back the favours. Let's go. He's not far from here."

Hamid, a rustic man with no family, had travelled regularly inland away from the two rivers and had learned the pastoral ways. He had no place he called home. He preferred to travel and learn about the customs of people in other lands. He agreed to help. He had little choice. It released him from his debts to Harun.

"We'll wait for one of Harun's ships to take us to Ur," Hamid said and spoke slowly, to make sure they understood what they could encounter in such a demanding expedition. "We'll need to find a way beyond the two great rivers. We'll probably need to travel by land and follow the path of the river. There are small towns just before the mountains. I'm not sure if your friend would have decided to go beyond the towns. Nomads live throughout this area migrating with their herds back and forth from grassland to grassland."

"What if we don't find him in any of the towns?" Hordekef asked.

"Let's first get to Ur where I'll need to assemble a few men to help. We'll need donkeys and supplies as well. We can reassess the situation before we decide to go any further."

"When do we leave?" Hordekef asked. Hamid looked to Harun. They needed one of his ships to get to Ur. Harun hesitated to respond at first but realized he had to be forthright, not to jeopardize their attempts in finding Nenshi.

"I'm afraid we have to stay here for a day or two," Harun said. "The last of my ships may have just left."

"Perhaps there's still time," Hordekef said.

"Perhaps."

"Show us how to get to the docks."

Harun led the way as they meandered through the few streets that led to the docks. Their pace was not as fast as expected. Every now and then they waited for Babak to catch up. Aziza walked with him and held his arm for support.

As they reached the docks, their faces wilted to see the ship shrink out of sight. The frustration showed in Hordekef's eyes. For a moment he thought it would be a matter of time before he reached Nenshi. Now time eluded him and the prospect of seeing his friend was drifting away like the ship. His resolve was tested but not defeated.

"There must be another way." Hordekef looked straight at Harun.

"There is. But it will take longer. By caravan. Those who can't afford to move their goods by ship will go to Ur by land. I will find one."

The silence cast doubt in finding Nenshi. But they had no other choice. Hordekef had made that clear. He would search the entire land until he found him. His jaws clenched tighter than a crocodile's bite on its prey. There was hope in his unrelenting determination. Without hope they had nothing.

Chapter 39

IN THE TIME NENSHI HAD been with the tribe, he realized there seemed to be no interest in the outside world. It explained why the tribe had not progressed, as did Ur, Damascus and even his own country. Although free and independent, the people had no interest to change their ways. The only way of life that mattered, was their own. It kept them united. Unlike Egypt, consumed with power and splendour, these people depended on one another for survival. To change meant to upset the balance between man and nature.

Nenshi felt alone in a world so different from his, outnumbered by what he thought was a primitive clan. He wondered if he should have taken one of the roads that led to a village. There he would have had a chance to find his way back to Ur, to Thebes. Yet something anchored him to stay, to follow sheep, to chart the unknown. He had spent enough time among the tribe to witness their way of life; a life he was convinced could be better. Perhaps by sharing his experiences and his knowledge, they might aspire a different world.

For the time being this was his home. There were no cautious eyes to measure his actions. There was comfort in the simple life.

He walked through the camps, greeted with a nod. He passed women crouched over fires. They peered from behind their veils at the passer-by. The corner of their eyes smiled at him. Other women, unveiled, carried heavy loads of sticks and branches. A woman effortlessly made a fire. She piled sticks at the base of the pit in crosspieces. She pushed her hand through the pile to create an opening to allow a breeze to ignite the embers.

Soon the tribe was ready to march again. Nenshi walked with Haji, Enami and Fatameh behind the animals to make sure they did not stray. Haji paced up and down with his long stick and tapped at a sheep or goat to get back in line. Khorram was at the head of the pack. In the distance, in front of Khorram was Rustam and his flock. Nenshi saw him turn and eye him as he trekked on.

After several long hours Ahmad signalled to rest. It would be a short one, just before reaching a valley ahead. Nenshi sat by the side of the narrow path. He rested his chin on his chest and closed his eyes.

The migration resumed and soon the tribe found itself in a fertile valley. They stopped for several hours so that the flock could graze before reaching a mountain pass. As the animals ate, men cut and arranged grass in packs that would feed the flock during the three-day march over the grassless mountains. Meanwhile women wove rugs or gathered sticks for the evening fires. Khorram showed Nenshi how to gather grass for the animals.

"You learn with little effort," Khorram said.

"Perhaps one day I can teach you a skill from my country. A way to return the kindness you have shown me."

"We give and do not ask of anything in return."

"Unlike my people. They always expect to be repaid."

Khorram shrugged his shoulders. There was no need to compare the virtues of giving.

The chore finished, Nenshi walked back with a bundle of grass on his shoulders. Fatameh sat in front of the entrance to her tent, legs crossed and covered by her long black skirt. Her hair, long and just as black as her garb, was tied at the back so as not to get in the way. As Nenshi got closer he noticed her head and face uncovered, as she chose.

She was unlike Egyptian women, whose eyes were painted, lips coloured, bodies adorned with jewellery. A different glow radiated from Fatameh, one that shone from within, a natural beauty, not like one that was designed to draw attention.

She pulled out a handful of sheep's wool from a sack, determined to finish making the rug she had started some time ago. The bright colours of the hand-knotted and hand-spun wool stood out in front of the dull grey tent, like the iridescent tail of a peacock among a flock of drab partridges. Her hands moved with calculated precision and speed. Nenshi was intrigued.

"Your hands have eyes. They know exactly what to do," he said. Fatameh looked up and smiled, her hands still at work.

"I'm tired of carrying this unfinished rug and sack of wool with me everywhere. I'm almost finished."

She made several knots, weaved coloured strings of wool, twisted the threaded pile into another knot and repeated this throughout the length of the rug. She held it up to show the pattern that emerged from the wool and cotton threads. The rug came to life. Nenshi smiled, he beamed like a child impressed by the magic of a wizard.

"Here, this is for you," she said, proud of her gift. "The one you have is old. You must feel the cold coming through it."

Nenshi parted a gentle smile. "I'm grateful," he said. Fatameh blushed, the soft pink colour of a lotus.

Nenshi went back to help Khorram collect more grass. Haji watched over the flock. He clutched the bow that Nenshi had made for him.

"Haji go tell your mother and Fatameh to return to the camp," Khorram ordered. "We must prepare to leave."

When Haji reached the other side of a small hill, he saw his mother running towards him. Her mouth was bleeding. She grabbed him by the hand and ran back. She was out of breath and spat out a mouthful of blood. Khorram pulled out a cloth from a sack and wiped her lip. Nenshi looked towards the hill and wondered why Fatameh was not with her.

"What happened?" Khorram asked. "And where's Fatameh?"

"Two men ran out from behind the shrubs! They jumped on us, beat us … and … and … they took Fatameh!"

"Two men?" Nenshi asked. "From the tribe?"

"No … no!" Her voice quivered. "They were not dressed like us. They carried weapons … long knives."

"Invaders."

"Who?" Khorram asked.

"They might be the invaders I had told you about. Have you had encounters in the past with enemies?"

"Not often. Mostly with other tribes, like ours, looking to take over our routes."

"How did you defend yourselves?"

"Daggers. What do these men want from us?"

"Probably nothing. There is very little to gain in attacking tribes like yours. Their camp may not be too far from here."

"But what about Fatameh?" Enami asked. Her terrified stare pleaded for help.

Soon word spread about Fatameh's capture by strange men. Women gathered to console Enami. Men stood with Khorram bewildered what to do next. Ahmad tugged at his beard with his finger and thumb, a habit of his whenever he pondered about the welfare of his tribe.

"I need another man to come with me," Nenshi said. No one came forward. Was the life of one worth that of many? He then looked around to find someone to help. He pointed to Rustam, certain that his feelings for Fatameh would stir the need to find her.

"Rustam, I need you to come with me." The assertiveness left no room for refusal. The long pause suggested otherwise.

"I can't go with you," Rustam said. "My father is old. He needs help with the herd."

Nenshi clenched his jaw, Khorram clenched his fist, Enami broke down in tears.

"I'll go with you," Khorram said.

Ahmad intervened. "You realize that you may not return?"

Khorram's silence spoke for itself. Ahmad needed to remind him. "And you're aware that when it's time to move, we can't wait."

"Enami and Haji will accompany the herd," Khorram said.

"Very well. I don't agree but it's your decision. Good luck … to both of you."

Khorram then turned to Rustam. The anger in his eyes mirrored his words. "I have not yet decided who shall have Fatameh for a wife, but I have decided who shall not have her!"

"Haji," Nenshi called out. "Go get my bow and arrows."

Nenshi removed some of his clothing until he revealed only a thin shirt and loincloth around his waist. He needed to move freely, without the constriction of ragged coverings. The older women, embarrassed, turned their heads. The only time a man removed his clothes was to swim, cross the rivers or in the confines of his tent. The younger women also turned their heads but not completely. They could still see him from the corner of their eyes.

Within minutes Haji returned. "Nenshi, you have only three arrows."

"Then I'll have to make good use of them. Khorram … we must go."

Crouched, on top of a small hill, behind shrubs whose leaves had dried and sprinkled the ground, Nenshi and Khorram peered down like thieves, collaborating their next heist. Two men, in front of a tent, joked, while guarding the entrance; a feeble distraction to pass the time. The sounds from inside the tent fed their entertainment.

Nenshi turned his head in the direction of the sound. A faint sob echoed. It was Fatameh. And she wasn't alone. A voice, deep and gravelly, reverberated through the tent's soft walls. But neither Nenshi nor Khorram were able to understand what was being said. Nenshi imagined the horror Fatameh faced.

The guards looked at each other and chuckled. Khorram's face reddened with anger. He was about to charge down the hill when Nenshi grabbed him and pulled him down.

"No! That's the foolish way. Wait a little longer."

"For what? We need to free Fatameh!"

"There may be more of them," Nenshi said as he scanned the area.

"That's why we must free her now before others show up."

Nenshi studied the area. "I think most of them have left. Look over there ... you can see where their tents were ... and over there ... tracks of their movement."

"Then why are they still here?"

"The one inside is their leader. Soldiers always survey the area ahead of them. I think they've gone to explore the next place to pitch their tents. In the meantime, their leader had become aware of our campsite. He's not interested in us. We're not a threat. It's not unusual for him to take young women."

"Vultures!"

Nenshi ignored Khorram's anger. "Follow me."

They made their way down the side of the hill and then around to the back of the tent. Nenshi picked up a fallen branch covered with leaves and gave it to Khorram.

"I will hide over there," Nenshi pointed. "I want you to rustle the branch to get their attention. I'm certain one of them will come here. I'll take care of the rest. Do you understand?"

Khorram nodded his head. They took their places. Khorram shook the branch.

"What's that?" asked one of the guards. "It came from behind. I'll stay here. Go and see what it is."

The other guard removed his sword from its sheath and held it as if he was going to battle. His steps were small and controlled as he walked along the side of the tent.

"What's going on out there?" yelled their leader from inside the tent.

"We heard a noise. I will alert you if anything is wrong," said the guard at the entrance.

As the other guard reached the back of the tent, he noticed Khorram crouched, holding the branch. The guard raised his sword and stepped forward. Then the sound of an arrow whistled through the air and struck the man dead. Hearing a thud, the guard at the entrance of the tent went to see what caused the sound.

"Where are you?" he called out. No response. He called out again. Still nothing. Nenshi prepared another arrow and listened for the guard's footsteps. Nenshi pointed his bow and arrow and as the guard came around to the back, he was struck down.

The leader inside the tent would soon realize that something was wrong. Nenshi motioned Khorram to follow him.

As they reached the entrance of the tent, they stopped in their tracks. The leader was already outside with his right arm wrapped around Fatameh's shoulder and neck. He locked the back of her body against his chest, using her as a human shield. Then he shifted his body slightly to reveal a sword in his hand. Now half of his body was exposed.

"Who are you?" he demanded.

"Father ... Nenshi ..." Fatameh whispered. Her eyes widened.

"You obviously know these intruders," the man said. "Now this is interesting. Your father and ... who is this, your husband? They have come to rescue you?" He laughed. His gigantic build and grin, that exposed his rotted teeth, made for a frightful appearance.

"There are two of us and he's alone," Khorram said.

"Don't be foolish. He has a blade." Nenshi warned.

"Listen to him," the man said, as he swayed the sword in the air. He laughed again, louder, behind his thick black beard and rotted teeth. "Go back to the mountains where you belong," he bellowed. "My men will soon be back. You'll regret it if you stay."

Nenshi then prepared his weapon. He raised his bow and the last arrow he had. It aroused the man's curiosity.

"Well, well. It looks as if the mountain man has a toy. Be careful or you might hurt yourself."

Nenshi showed no fear. The man's taunt fell on deaf ears.

Nenshi focused on his target - the part of the man's body that was not shielded by Fatameh. With swift and calculated moves, he placed the arrow in the bow, raised it in position and released it. The man had no time to react. Fatameh closed her eyes and gasped. The arrow struck the man in the chest, the part of his body that was exposed. The man grunted, dropped his sword, let go of Fatameh and fell to the ground.

Fatameh ran to her father's arms. She then turned to Nenshi, reached out and embraced him.

Chapter 40

THE PASSAGE ACROSS THE MOUNTAINS had proven more difficult for Nenshi than he had expected. The abrupt clime was deceiving. Not so for Ahmad and the tribe. They had been here countless times before. And so, the trip was made during the cool hours of the morning to avoid the challenges of the heat and the mountains at the same time.

During the climb, Nenshi stopped and looked down the side. Families spread themselves farther apart from each other, to take advantage of the green pastures and allow the herds to graze.

With little warning, dreaded dust storms appeared. The horizon yellowed and huge dust clouds rolled in. The storm passed but a few hours later, another one emerged. The cycle repeated and with each storm, the winds grew stronger and stronger. Every time a tempest hit, the tribe stopped and covered themselves and when it subsided, the march resumed.

Soon the dust storms were replaced by rain. A sudden clap of thunder warned of dark ominous clouds approaching, followed by a gust of wind. Lightning and thunder swept over the valley and an unnatural eerie green colour covered the land. With every flash of lightning, the snow-capped mountains in the distance were a reminder of what lay ahead. Nenshi had never seen this kind of weather before. The sun in Egypt shone endlessly. Here, the weather would change in an instant.

The trek paused. Everyone moved to a place close to the path, where they could rest. Nenshi, Khorram and Haji were at the head of their pack while Enami and Fatameh were near the back.

"You must be tired," Enami said and handed Fatameh bread. The soft tone of a protective mother was always welcomed.

"I rest when I can, I move when I have to," Fatameh said. If she was tired, she would never show it.

"You're a strong girl."

"Mother, I'm a woman." Fatameh smiled. Her face lit up.

"You are and I should not forget that."

"May I ask a question?" Fatameh began, seeing the opportunity to confide in her mother.

"From one woman to another?" Enami's eyes gleamed - the hope of all mothers to share intimate thoughts with their daughters.

"How do you know if you really love a man?" Fatameh asked.

Enami's brows drew together. But as the only source in sharing the virtues of love, she needed to be honest with her daughter.

"Women look for love in different ways," Enami began. "Some look for a man with a strong body or one who is wealthy in flock or rich in inheritance. These are good things ... if a man has them. But if he doesn't, does it mean he is less of a man?"

Fatameh absorbed every word her mother spoke. Her eyes engrossed by the wisdom and never had thought that her mother or any of the women from the tribe held such thoughts. Their purpose was singular – to give birth to boys and perform the chores to help keep the tribe moving.

Enami continued. "If those are the things you look for in love, then those will be the only things that shall be given back. You will know if a man loves you, by looking into his eyes. They reflect his heart. If his heart is good, his eyes will tell you. A flame will glow that will give you warmth and comfort. If he lets you into his heart, you will know that he loves you."

Fatameh reflected on her mother's words that only added to her conflict, one she could not share. The tribe's culture had been so entrenched that to think of any another way of life was as remote as the next grassland. And like Nenshi, she too wanted more. She too wanted a freedom of which she had seen glimpses.

The signal spread among the families to resume the march. The next mountain range was more dangerous than the first. The trail zigzagged across the face of the mountain along a narrow path and there was room only for one person or animal. There was no place or time to rest.

The tribe reached the summit and now the route would take them down the other side. Ahmad chose eight men, strong and competent, to execute the trip. They climbed to the top with ropes and began the gruelling task of moving people and animals over the summit. Each of the men lowered ropes. Animal and human, tied, one at a time, and then pulled up and dragged over to the other side. Green pastures awaited below, and the sight gave them the strength to continue.

"When does this end?" Nenshi asked, exhausted. Khorram wrinkled his nose. It was a strange question, never considered. Nomads understood and accepted their migration. For Nenshi it was merely a mundane existence.

"After we reach the pastures below, we'll cross another mountain range that will take us to the final crossing," Khorram said.

"What's the final crossing?"

"Crossing of the Bazuft River, the last leg of our journey. Beyond it are many pastures. The animals will consume them. It will be the longest we spend in one place."

"What happens after that?"

"We begin again, another journey."

"Another journey?"

"We'll return to where we started."

Nenshi looked at Khorram, bewildered with thoughts of a perpetual cycle.

"I know you dislike our way of life," Khorram said.

"No ... it's not that I dislike it ... I don't understand it ... there's a better way to live."

"A better way for one man may not be better for another."

"Perhaps you're right and perhaps one day I'll have a greater understanding why you live the way you do."

"One day both of us may have a better understanding of each other's world. Until then, be careful of the things you say and do."

"What do you mean?" Nenshi asked, sensing caution behind the entrusting wisdom.

"Your courage and willingness to help has brought you respect among our people but there are those who watch you with suspicion."

"You mean Rustam."

"Yes, and others too. Rustam could not convince Ahmad that you are a threat to our livelihood. However, he managed to persuade others and voices against you are strong. I fear for the consequences."

"What do you mean consequences?"

The tribe was not violent by nature, unlike some of the peoples Nenshi had encountered. He wondered what form of reprimand the tribe used.

"This is new to us," Khorram said. "We have never had an outsider among us during our migration. Only Ahmad has the power to correct. Just be careful."

Khorram was right. Rustam hated Nenshi, more now than before, after Nenshi had rescued Fatameh. Rustam still longed to have Fatameh for his wife and he still had to prove his worth to her and to her parents. Nenshi stood in his way and Fatameh had grown fond of Nenshi.

Rustam planted the seed of what he hoped would be Nenshi's demise. He nourished it with disreputable accounts of Nenshi's actions and then stood back and watched as the weed spread wildly. Some of the elders had become convinced that Rustam's fears were justified.

The tribe reached the base of Zardeh Kuh, the last and greatest of the mountain ranges. Nomads and flocks assembled and prepared for a race against time. Tents were dismantled, animals rounded up and herdsmen were selected by the elders to lead the challenging climb. Khorram was among the chosen. He bid farewell to his family and was grateful that Nenshi would be able to help in his absence during the difficult crossing.

Enami led the march for her family and flock. In the middle of the line of animals, Haji followed and at the end were Fatameh and Nenshi making sure the herd kept pace. As they trudged on, they also fed the animals as best they could without disrupting the trek.

The trip was indeed difficult. Snow, something Nenshi had never seen before, made the crossing at the highest point more perilous. For a moment Nenshi stood and watched the snow, like stars in daytime, gently floating through the air, dropping softly on the land. His eyes sparkled, his face glowed, childlike, as he opened his hand and watched the snowflakes land and instantly disappear leaving behind a moist droplet.

The leader, at the head of the line, aware of his role, painfully dug a zigzag path for everyone to follow. As they removed the snow, they packed it on the outside of the track to create a protective barrier.

Fatameh frequently checked behind her to make sure Nenshi had not fallen over the side of the mountain. She looked down at Nenshi's feet, red and raw. Without losing a step in the walk, she removed her shoes.

"Here, take these," she said, as she extended her arms behind her.

"No." He tried to hide the pain.

"Take them, and give me your sandals," she insisted. "You're not used to this ... I am." Reluctantly, he took them.

Then an unusual, human-like cry startled him. A stubborn sheep that didn't want to follow the path lost its footing and slid down the mountain to its death.

"Have any of your people died during this crossing?"

"Yes, usually the weak, the old or the careless."

"And what do you do?"

"The same as when an animal falls ... nothing ... continue moving. If we find the body, we will mourn and bury it. You can see markings along the route of those that have been buried in the past."

The terrain was steep and rough. With every step Nenshi felt the stones under his feet. The pain shot up his legs. Despite the roughness, Fatameh's shoes helped lessen the ache.

Red mud caused by cold rain soon turned to snow and covered both man and animal. Men beat the animals with their sticks, women beat the animals that lagged, and young children beat the lambs and kids - the young tending to the young.

The migration had been hard, and it showed. Luckily no one perished unlike some unfortunate animals. Now, on the other side, the sun's warm and comforting rays shone on those who had survived.

Wearied bodies moved noticeably slower. It reminded Nenshi of the men, women and children at the mines in Nubia, overburdened with the weight of stone-filled sacks. Men pitched tents, women laid rugs on the ground wherever there was space and soon crackling fires gave signs of life to an exhausted tribe.

Nenshi and Fatameh sat on a rug. His feet, still frigid, were wrapped with a blanket. Fatameh made a fire.

"Are Enami and Haji coming?" Nenshi asked as he moved his feet closer to the fire.

"They're waiting for my father and will probably be here later, just before the sun sets."

"Are we trusted here, alone?"

"You know our customs well." She smiled. "Right now, this is a matter of survival not permission."

"But we're alone ... no one can see us." Nenshi remembered what Khorram had told him - to be careful of others who wanted to cause him harm. "I don't understand your customs," he added.

"Maybe one day you will. Our way is not something that can be explained, it must be lived. And don't be fooled, there are always eyes watching." She reached into a sack and pulled a piece of bread. She tore it in two and handed one to him. She poured milk into two cups.

The sun was warm and the air was still. In the distance the sound of children echoed as they rushed out from tents to play. The crackling fires swelled with golden flames. The majestic faraway snow-capped mountains jutted out from the land, surrounded by grey and white billowing clouds.

Fatameh uncovered her face to eat. Her beauty, natural and simple, radiated like the sun's glow over the fertile valley. They ate the bread and drank the milk in silence and every once in a while, their eyes met.

"Tell me a story," she asked. "Tell me about your land and how it came to be."

He welcomed the invitation to recite the story of Egypt's creation. "In the beginning, there was darkness. There was nothing but a great waste of water called Nun. The power of Nun drew out of the darkness, a great shining egg. This was Re."

Fatameh giggled.

"Why do you laugh?" he asked.

"Forgive me ... the names Nun ... Re ... they are so different and amusing."

"I suppose ... I never thought of it that way."

"Go on ... go on ... tell me more." She covered her lips with her veil to hide the grin.

"Now Re was all-powerful, and he could take many forms. Whatever names he spoke, they came into being. And so, he named Khepera at the dawn, and himself Re at noon, and Atum in the evening." He paused and looked at Fatameh for a reaction. She pressed her lips together to hold back an outburst. He continued. "Then he named Shu and the first winds blew; he named Tefnut the spitter, and the first rain fell."

Fatameh could not hold back the laughter any longer. "I can see why you're a storyteller," she said. "You can make anyone believe anything, even in laughter."

Nenshi smiled, realized how ridiculous he must have sounded.

"Do you believe in what you have said? I mean ... how the gods had created your land?"

"I've grown tired of Egyptian gods. They were created to instil fear and pain. But I've learned of a different god."

"Another tale of gods?" she asked, in a playful tone.

"Perhaps. I had met a man named Abramu. He had told me that a god named El had spoken to him." There was an excitement in his voice, a tone reflecting a discovery.

"Is El one of your gods as well?" Fatameh asked.

"El is not known to Egyptians."

"Perhaps one day he will be."

Nenshi smiled. "Perhaps," he replied. "Perhaps El will be one to replace all gods."

"Tell me more," Fatameh insisted.

"Well, this god, El, had told Abramu that he would show him and his people a new land and teach them to live in peace and freedom."

"But no one is free." Fatameh said. "I'm a prisoner to the mountains, to the grassland, to the animals. How can this El, or any god, teach anyone about freedom?"

Nenshi sensed an anxiety, unhappiness in Fatameh about her life with the tribe. He tried to ease her grief by telling her what had happened to him.

"Is that why you have the markings on your arm? I noticed them when we found you. Your arm was uncovered. I didn't know what they were - rings, burned into your skin. Only animals get branded."

Nenshi put his hand to his arm and felt the rings.

"One day I'll be free," he said. "And you? Don't you want to be free ... free from following sheep, free from crossing mountains and rivers?"

"Perhaps I too will be free." She imparted her deepest thoughts. She told him about aspirations of one day moving away from the tribe. She had only seen glimpses of a different life, when she had accompanied her father to nearby towns to trade carpets for pots or a donkey.

They sat in silence, stared into the fire as it waned and welcomed dusk, welcomed their dreams. Fireflies darted like white sparks shot from the embers and then disappeared into the darkness. Nenshi looked up at the sky. A new moon appeared. Stars filled the cloudless sky, each one called him, pulled him towards a world he believed he was destined to experience.

"Perhaps there may come a day that we can help each to be free," Nenshi whispered, in the silence of his dream. Fatameh smiled.

A cool wind cleansed all that came before it. The fire rested but a glow remained. In the distance, the sound of a stream soothed their minds with tranquillity and simplicity.

The sound of footsteps broke their trance. Khorram, Enami and Haji had returned.

Chapter 41

THE TRIBE REACHED THE SUMMER lands. Behind them, where the mass of mountains touched the sky, now were replaced by oak trees and gorges where at the bottom the swollen and icy Bazuft River passed through the valley. Gold and purple irises hint at summer pastures but the foaming, jade-green coloured river, cutting through canyons, was a reminder of what was to be expected - a most unpleasant and tense crossing.

Young girls, eager to reunite after the long journey, filled jugs by the river. Their prattle stopped as Nenshi approached. Gossip was replaced by smiles and nervous giggles. Older women gathered sticks and washed clothes. They had no time for idle chatter.

Ahmad also had his own routine. He made his way throughout the camps and greeted families. His presence gave them strength. When finished, he went to the river where Nenshi sat in solitude.

"I'm glad to see that you are well," Ahmad said. He pointed his face towards the breeze and took a deep breath.

"It was a difficult journey, I must admit. Your people are strong," Nenshi said.

"We depend on supporting each other."

"There's new excitement, now that we reached the river."

"For the young ... yes."

"Why only the young?"

"Crossing the river will prove they are ready for the next step in their lives. But for the old, it's different."

Nenshi looked at the fast-moving water, as it splashed with a taunting life of its own. He shook his head and wondered how many would not survive the crossing. To survive a long arduous journey, only to taunt the river to take your life, was inexplicable.

"I don't understand your ways," Nenshi said.

"You don't understand or object to them?"

Nenshi remained quiet. A respectful silence was better than empty words.

"We live a simple life," Ahmad said. "A simplicity by which everything is measured. It's what keeps us independent and free."

"But you're driven to find green pastures. That's not freedom and not everyone gives support when needed." He was thinking of Rustam and his refusal to help find Fatameh when she had been abducted.

"Yes, it's a battle we all face within us. We must reject the wicked and keep the good."

"How do you do that?"

"We have been created from the seed of our forefather, Bakhtiar. In his memory, we draw strength to cast aside evil."

"Is he your god?"

"He is the father of our people."

To Nenshi, whether they called him their father or their god, whether it was one god or many, it was all the same - a creation that had meaning to the people. Perhaps that was most important, Nenshi thought; a creation, a god, that meant the most to man. It was how man viewed their god and the purpose it served that brought fulfilment to life.

Ahmad continued. "Bakhtiar was a hill-man who came out from the mountains and spread his seed of goodness and life, as numerous as the rocks. We've prospered from this." Ahmad looked at Nenshi, deep in thought. "You struggle to make a choice," Ahmad said. He paused and took another long breath and let the sun warm his aging body. Nenshi watched, waited, knowing there was more to come from the old leader. "You've crossed many lands. Every step has shaped you.

Even our journey across the mountains have shaped you. But when we arrive at the summer pastures, our struggles end. Perhaps one day your journey will end and you will struggle no more."

Nenshi regarded Ahmad in the same manner as Soreb and Abramu, sagacious men whose guidance, simple yet sublime, resonated with the afflicted.

Ahmad turned to Nenshi. A smile, a nod and a straightforward truism, was all that was needed. "Remember, it is better to make choices with your mind than with your heart."

Nenshi and Haji stood on a hill overlooking the valley.

"Look ... over there," pointed Haji, towards the distant pastures. "We call it *sardsir* ... summer land. His face burst with excitement. "I know to you it's just grass. To us it is life."

Nenshi was silent and gazed at the vastness. Then the echo of roaring waters, the intimidating river below, snapped Haji's enthusiasm. The elation faded, as quickly as it had sprouted.

The last mountain range stood behind them. Zardeh Kuh had been conquered but there still remained the final crossing of the Bazuft River. Its sound of fury, its fast-moving currents captivated, hypnotized Haji. He pouted and turned away from the water, away from the lush green pastures that surrounded the majestic broad valley.

"You've crossed this many times before, haven't you?" Nenshi asked.

Haji nodded - a slow, painful acknowledgement. The sound of the roaring river, as it dashed downstream, reminded him of past attempts.

"Why are you troubled?"

Haji gave Nenshi a quick glance and then turned to the river. "When I was very young my mother carried me on a *kalak* as we crossed. As I got older, my father would put me on a *kalak* and send me to the other side. At the last crossing of this river my father had to carry me on his back, like a child, because I lost my *kalak*. It was the last one we had." Teary-eyed, Haji looked up at Nenshi. "I had not inflated the skin properly and when I threw it into the water the sack didn't float."

His careless act didn't alleviate his father's displeasure. Everything they carried with them was precious - too precious to be washed away.

"But you weren't old enough to have mastered the skill," Nenshi said.

"I'm older now, stronger. I have to inflate the *kalak* the way my father had taught me and cross by myself."

If crossing the river was every young man's opportunity to prove his manhood, as Ahmad had described, Haji showed no such pleasure. Nenshi tried to ease his fear.

"I remember the first time I went hunting. I was a little older than you. I was afraid. My tutor watched me as I placed the arrow in the bow. My hands trembled. I saw the wild pig and I aimed at it. I felt my heart thumping. I thought even the pig could hear it and would run away. Then I aimed and shot the arrow. But I missed. I turned to face my tutor, afraid of what he might do. He said, *you will have another chance to do better.* It seemed I was more afraid of failing, to make a mistake and what could happen to me, rather than what I could learn from my mistake. And so, I did what my tutor had said. From that day on, every time I went hunting, if something went wrong, I remembered what I did and I would make the next day better."

Haji sighed, a deep sigh. Perhaps Nenshi's story would lift his burden, his obsession with crossing the river. It remained to be seen if Haji had the confidence in his ability to make the final crossing.

"Look Nenshi. Look what I made," Haji said and handed Nenshi a bow. "It looks just like the one you made for me, doesn't it?"

A long and crooked stick with a knotted string haphazardly attached at each end didn't look anything like Nenshi's bow.

"It just needs a little tightening," Nenshi said. He loosened one end of the string and re-tightened the bow.

"Someday I'll make one just like yours and be as good as you. For now I'll use the one you made for me. This one can burn in the fire tonight."

"You'll need to practice first. Remember, make each day better than the one before."

"I know ... I know ... I'm going to start now ... behind those rocks." As eager as a young eagle about to leave its nest and sore to the sky, Haji ran off with his bow.

As Nenshi went about collecting and rolling carpets, a chore as mundane as watching sheep graze, Fatameh approached. She pulled the veil away from her face.

"Has my brother burdened you with his tasks?"

"Not at all. It keeps me busy."

"And out of trouble?"

"What do you mean?"

"I've heard some of the stories about you. Lies. All lies. If they only took the time to get to know you, they would think differently."

"Time. There seems to be so much of it here yet it's directed in the wrong places."

Just then Khorram and Enami appeared, followed by a tribesman and his young daughter. He held her hand, pulled her, forcibly. The anger on his face emptied into words.

"Look at this!" he said, his eyes bulged. "What is this?" He put his hand under his daughter's chin and pulled it up to expose her clumsily painted face. He then took two fingers, smudged the colours and held them up in front of Nenshi. "What is this?" He repeated, insisting on an answer.

"Those are paint colours," Nenshi said, a simple and innocent explanation. He didn't think much of the girl's decorated face, other than the paint wasn't applied very well.

"Who showed her this?" asked the man as he brought his fingers closer to Nenshi's eyes. Nenshi moved the man's arm away from his face.

"I did ... a long time ago."

A silence threatened an altercation. Khorram and Enami looked at each other, not knowing what to do or say. Nenshi explained.

"Where I come from, women, even young girls, paint their faces, around the eyes. I showed your daughter and her friends how easy it is to make the paint from stones and water."

"And so, because of you, my daughter decided to paint her face."

"I didn't tell her, or the others, to paint their faces. I was teaching them something new, how to make paint."

"Teaching? You leave the teaching to the parents and the elders. Do you understand? You keep away from us. Do you understand?" The tribesman made his point. His eyes darted to Khorram, as if blaming him for Nenshi's so-called teachings.

"Yes, but..." Before Nenshi could reply the man turned and walked away, tugging his daughter with him. Khorram held out his arm in front of Nenshi.

"Don't bother."

"Let it out of your mind," added Enami. "Some men are not approachable."

"I was only trying to teach them new things," Nenshi said, apologetically.

"We understand," Enami said and returned to her chores. Khorram nodded, in agreement. Nenshi wondered if they actually understood or had they chosen to merely appease him. He wondered if he had done the right thing, to show others a different life.

He thought of the young girl's father, who scorned him for teaching girls how to make paint for their eyes. He reflected on Enami's indifference to his innocent act. And then there was Rustam, determined to have him banished from the group. Perhaps even Khorram regretted saving him from near death. Ahmad's words sprung to mind, telling him that decisions should be made with the mind not the heart. Now Nenshi questioned which of those had caused him to do the things he had done.

In the distance, Nenshi could see Fatameh, churning fresh yogurt. The time he had spent with her during the migration had filled the emptiness inside his. She looked up and saw him smiling. She smiled back.

He carried the rolled carpets to Enami. She asked if he had seen Haji. Nenshi shook his head. He knew Haji was practicing with his bow but kept it to himself. Just then, a boy's cry startled them. It was Haji.

"Mother ... mother ... mother..." he shouted as he ran towards her, chased by a man. Khorram heard the commotion.

"What is it? What has happened?" Enami asked, frightened, examined Haji for injuries.

A tribesman suddenly appeared. "I'll tell you what happened," he said, short winded. "He struck one of my sheep with this." He held up Haji's bow.

Khorram walked over to Haji and put his hand on his shoulder. "Is that true?" he asked. His sternness was expected in the presence of another tribesman.

"Yes ... but it was an accident," Haji said. He was now more terrified of his father than the tribesman. "I was aiming at rocks. The bow went in a different direction."

Enami, mother-like, tried to explain and placate the irate man. "He's just a boy playing with this thing. He doesn't know how to use it."

The man was not convinced. He stood, arms folded, unsympathetic.

"Did your sheep die?" Khorram asked.

"No but its leg will take long to heal. It will not be able to keep up with the rest of the flock."

"I'll give you one of mine ... of your choice ... and I'll take your injured one."

The offer calmed the tribesman. "It is fair. I accept," he said and then threw a scathing look at Nenshi and tossed the bow at his feet. "This is his fault! If it wasn't for him, this would not have happened."

This time Nenshi didn't defend himself. It was pointless. Sometimes the ways of the unwilling can cloud what is reasonable.

The rest of the day passed without incident. Nenshi hadn't seen Khorram for most of the day. "Where's your father?" he asked Haji. Haji shrugged his shoulders and continued to groom a donkey.

Fatameh, overheard Nenshi. "I saw him go into the elders' tent," she said as she approached. At first, he thought nothing of it. They would certainly need to meet to discuss the crossing of the river. "Rustam went in too," she added.

"Rustam? But he's not one of the elders."

"Not yet. Perhaps his cunning ways will help him secure a place among them."

His mission to spread the seed of malcontent towards Nenshi would certainly find reward. Nenshi retreated to his tent. An ominous feeling crept through his mind. The shadow of uncertainty loomed over him. The time had come. He heard the sound of footsteps approaching and then a voice called to him. He walked out to find Khorram, his long face sombre.

"The elders wish to speak with you."

Nenshi did not challenge his friend. There was no merit in challenging what was expected. He glared up at the red moon that painted the evening sky with blood-like vengeance and then turned to Khorram.

"I am ready."

Chapter 42

THE RAGING FIRE DANCED IN the centre of the black goat-hair tent. Flames leapt randomly mimicking the movements and uncertainty of those summoned to cast judgment. Nenshi sat staring into the fire. It is not until a man is measured by his peers that he has come to know his allies and his enemies.

Nenshi raised his head and raked back his hair with his hand. His eyes held a troubled gaze. Beads of sweat rolled down his face caused by the fire's heat or by the anxiety that burned inside. He knew why he had been summoned yet refused to be deterred. The meeting was more than just a gathering of the elders in preparation for the crossing of the river.

"Let us begin," Ahmad ordered.

Men scurried for a place to sit. Their shadows, thrown against the walls of the tent by the fire's light, tangled and brewed a gloomy mood about to spill. The council of elders welcomed the meeting. The elite members came to share their scorns and opinions for it was time to put an end to the unrest that spread like oak trees along the foothills of the mountains. Now, in the tent of justice, men were assembled to make decisions purely based on tradition.

Nenshi closed his eyes and listened to the increasing thumping sound of footsteps. The respected members herded in. He remained motionless except for his eyes, blinking, uncontrollably as he stared into the fire. He took a deep breath. His chest expanded. His expression, stalwart like a warrior as if prepared to face his enemy, reflected the conviction of his existence.

Being punished for falling in love with a freewoman should not have happened, he thought. He was convinced of it. He had been looking forward to the freedom that Tehuti had promised, if it had not been for his own careless acts and striking Sia's father. Not even escaping from the gold mines in Nubia brought him closer to realizing his freedom. And now he was following sheep instead of following his own path.

"Do not feel estranged in this tent," Ahmad said. He looked at Nenshi who sat across from him, separated by the fire. Ahmad's voice remained strong and assertive, as it should be that of the *Kalantar*, leader of one thousand nomads.

Nenshi squinted, looked past the fire. He tried to get a good look at Ahmad, to read his expression - friend or foe. The fire's light obstructed any hint of the leader's demeanour. Ahmad had planned it this way, where to sit, a roaring fire, kept his distance, detached, not to let his manner betray him. The fire waned for a moment. The barrier had weakened enough for Nenshi to look straight at Ahmad.

"I'm not a stranger," Nenshi said. "I have travelled with you long enough to learn your customs." True, he had learned much about the tribe. And they had learned much about him and the land from which he came. He had spent long hours among some of them, even Ahmad. At times the fires would die before their conversations. It was the few that protested his involvement. Those, he avoided. Voices among the protestors grew to overshadow those who expressed gratitude for learning new ways.

The cacophony of clattering voices needed to be quelled. "Quiet!" Ahmad said, with a commanding tone. The muttering was silenced, replaced by the sound of the crackling fire. The last of the council members walked in and took their places. As the tent filled with men, so it filled with the pungent odours from their perspiring and overworked bodies.

The fire weakened. Bearded faces, seething eyes, compassionate smiles, all pointed towards Nenshi. How could the rift among them be narrowed in such a crucial time?

Ahmad continued. "I had no intention for this meeting to be called. Yet I knew it was inevitable." He chose his words carefully. He didn't want to influence a decision, yet he wanted to leave room for compromise, concerned about the tribe soon to make the final crossing of the Bazuft River. This, the last leg of the tribe's migration to green pastures, was always met with uncertainty. The crossing of the treacherous river would cost lives, as it did every year. The inexperienced suffered the consequences and Nenshi was among the vulnerable.

Preparation was important. And now the tribe had to deal with what to do about Nenshi. Ahmad dedicated his efforts to the welfare of the tribe and its flock, not to the fate of one man. Yet Nenshi's fate was as important as any other in the tribe.

"Some members of this group have approached you about your actions," Ahmad said. "Many questioned why you insisted on imposing your lifestyle on them, even our children. These actions were not seen to be favourable."

Ahmad referred to the well-known events - Haji's bow and arrow, the girl's painted face, stories about prosperous towns and cities - yet all told without malice. Nenshi remained silent, only now he realized his actions had caused concern among some of the people.

A man took a long stick, poked the fire and caused it to come to life. Shadows fought the fire's flames for attention. Khorram sat alone. His first decision, as the latest member of the elders, would be to judge the man whose life he had saved. Would he let the guilt for bringing him to the tribe darken his judgement? Perhaps he should have left Nenshi in the wilderness. He might have had a better chance for survival. The two looked at each other with merciful eyes, yet for different reasons.

Nenshi then looked away and stared back at the fire. Flames stretched up, in desperate search of an escape from the surrounding hostility. It raged with an intense heat. Drops of sweat rolled into his eyes. He blinked repeatedly and fought the penetrating and burning salt. He wiped the sting away and continued to stare into the fire for what seemed to be forever. The fire began to wane.

The shadow of a figure, by the entrance, stretched along the floor and faded as it reached Nenshi. With arms crossed, Rustam eyed Nenshi. Nenshi knew that Rustam had started the rumours that planted seeds of mistrust that eventually led to the acrimony among some of the tribesmen and the call of the elders. Nenshi had found it more difficult to share his world with anyone, not knowing who cared to listen or who fueled suspicion. And Rustam, a man in pursuit to marry Fatameh, would fashion stories, a guise to get rid of the obstacle that stood between him and the woman he sought to possess. Now, his plan was almost complete.

A young boy walked into the tent with a load of dry tree branches. He dropped the load near the fire. He picked up a log and stretched out his arms towards the burning fire. But he couldn't reach. A man saw the boy struggle and nudged him to step aside. The man took the branch and plunged it into the centre of the fire. He added more logs. Flames roared. Faces that melded with the black walls of the tent began to emerge again.

Among the tribesman sat the man who had accused Nenshi of teaching his daughter how to make paint used by Egyptian women to add colour to their cheeks and eyelids. Nenshi also spotted the man who was angered when Haji accidentally struck one of the herdsman's sheep. Others, eager to cross the river were impatient, hoping for a fast judgement. There were also those who had welcomed Nenshi and had guided him in learning skills he had not been taught to perform.

Nenshi now understood the call for the meeting but he was not prepared for his fate to be determined by men whose lives were only driven by ritual. He took a deep breath. He would let his decision be known, not to acquiesce to theirs, no matter what they decreed.

He stared into the fire. The heat, the blaze, reminded him of the land from which he came. Egypt was a distant place. Yet the memories and the journey that had brought him to this new land were as fresh as the lotus flowers that adorned the place of his youth.

His mind drifted for a few moments, clouded with every step of his long and demanding passage across the serpentine bridge into manhood. The cacophony of sounds among the elders melded with his memories. Together they created the same feeling when he was among the sand dwellers, drinking and becoming intoxicated from their bitter beer and potent wine until he had lost all self-control.

The fire raged no more. Only embers kept it alive and no one moved to revive its fury. As it faded, so did the memories and journey that flashed through his mind. His daze was shaken by a sudden gust of wind that caused the walls of the tent to flap intensely like an eagle's wings in full flight. He regained his composure only to feel the darting glares from the men that had accused him of imposing his lifestyle on theirs.

The accusations from those who disagreed with his actions, were enough to anger any man but Nenshi remained calm. He pulled his shoulders back, lifted his chin with the subtlety of an eloquent nobleman and gathered his thoughts. He would not allow men whose lives were driven by survival determine his fate. It was now his time to speak.

"I cannot fault any of you for the way that you think about me," he said. "I forgive the accusing tongues for they have been led astray by selfish aspirations." Eyes widened. It was a defence they did not expect. "You are content to live as you do. You take flocks through rugged lands; you draw homes high above the clouds in the cold white sand and you push forward against a relentless wind. Admirable qualities for a band of men and women whose world has been shaped by grass and mountains. And even though I would not take animals across mountains nor want to feel the rain while I sleep nor care to walk, barefoot, in the cold white sand - I have respected your customs. Yes, I tried to show you, to teach you, how others live, perhaps in the hope that you might change some of your ways. I was wrong."

There was a long silence. It was an admission of guilt. The burnt logs from the fire crumbled and caused ashes to spew into the air. A log was thrown in and flames swelled with a vengeance. The acrimony burned in its wake. Voices clamoured, increased to an almost uncontrollable climax. The tent filled with confusion and remorse.

Rustam's jaw dropped. He had wanted to create chaos. Instead, he had caused a man, an outsider, to praise the ways of a nomadic tribe. He stared at Nenshi, stared into his eyes and saw the reflection of the fire that burned brightly - a fire from within.

The heat from the roaring fire made Nenshi's mouth dry. A man offered a flask of water and Nenshi took it to quench his drought. He then closed his eyes for a moment. His mind filled with thoughts that swirled and overflowed like a tempest in search of a place to land.

Ahmad raised his hand to calm the commotion. It was quiet again, a silent invitation for Nenshi to continue.

"Your forefather Bakhtiar, whose teachings and wisdom have survived for generations, has laid the foundation of your existence. Man must observe the words of their god in order to move forward as one, in peace and harmony." Nenshi stopped to take another sip from the flask. Its soothing sensation washed away any bitterness he might have harboured.

He looked at the fire that refused to die. He stood and declared his decision. "There were times during this migration that I could have turned around and perhaps find my way back home. But something kept me here." He was thinking of Fatameh when he said this but dared not to express it. The bond that grew, anchored him to the connection between them. Each, in their own way, wanted freedom. He continued. "I knew one day I would be called to defend myself. Even though I cannot and will not abandon my convictions, I cannot and will not condemn your way of life. I will stay to help Khorram and his family cross the river. I owe much to them, for saving my life and helping me through all of this. But once I reach the other side, I will leave them and leave your tribe. Tomorrow will be my final crossing."

A deep sigh lifted the weight from his shoulders. Yet he felt no sense of liberation. Instead he was filled with deep remorse knowing he would leave behind the woman he was beginning to fall in love with.

Men whispered amongst themselves, some relieved of any guilt they would have had to endure over a decision to cast him away. Others pitied him for enduring ordeals he had never known only to go back and face them again.

Nenshi stood, gestured a respectful nod, and walked out.

Chapter 43

AN OAK TREE, BY THE river, stood out among the others. With few blossoms, purple tube-shaped clusters, it was a sign of old age. Nenshi sat under it. If the tree could speak it would recount stories of every nomad that crossed its path. Stories of endurance, challenges, excitement. Now it had a new story to tell, unlike all others; of a pitied man who travelled from a land where the sun ruled to a place as dark as his life had become. As with all its stories, the tree with its ancient branches, had a parting message - all things of the earth change, all things of essence do not.

"May I sit with you?" Ahmad asked. He came as a friend, not as the *Kalantar.* Nenshi welcomed him with a smile.

"When Khorram had brought you to us, you had sand in your eyes. Every grain was like a serpent spitting its poison. You tasted the dryness of the desert; you heard its call of death. Your skin was dry like the sand and your body was heavy as rocks. I knew, for a man to live through all this, he must be guided by the essence of his being."

The words sounded familiar. Nenshi remembered Abramu who had also talked of a life-force. He had called it *spirit.* Two old and wise men, as far from one another as the land was to the stars, yet both shared a common language.

Ahmad continued. "Our worlds are different. We have spoken about it many times. Our life does not centre on power and prosperity. Your people have conquered others and have taken from them what they wanted. They spend much time building magnificent dwellings, only to house but a few. You change only to serve your desires. We change to serve our basic needs. We adapt according to what comes before us - too much rain, we take shelter; too much snow, we stop; too little grass, we move on. It is simple."

Indeed, the simplicity, as Ahmad described, had never occurred to Nenshi. He now realized that change could not be avoided. Ahmad and his people responded to the necessities that were presented.

"What about the life-force? What is it?" Nenshi invited Ahmad to go deeper.

"It's a simple reminder of how we live and how we should live. It encourages us to live in harmony and when we do, the rain, the snow and what little grass we find are all easier to accept."

Ahmad put his hand on Nenshi's shoulder. Warmth passed through his body, the same warmth when Abramu had done the same. Ahmad then stood, walked away and disappeared into the sun's light.

Nenshi picked up a mud-covered stick from the ground and walked to the river. He sat on a large rock and stared at the water rushing downstream. He closed his eyes and thought of what Ahmad had told him. He had misunderstood the tribe. These people, barren of any progress, did not know of a world beyond their tents. It was all they knew - seclusion, mountains, trails and they were proud of the life they led, simple and tranquil.

Nenshi turned to the sky. His heart longed to be elsewhere. The gods had taken him out from his home and given him no reason for his journey. As Sheikha, the divinator had foretold, life, as he knew it, would change.

The jade-green coloured river swelled. Its foam splashed against the rocks and a sudden gush of water burst into the air. Nenshi could hear Abramu's voice echo inside. *Your spirit will know and you will delight in the bond, the covenant, with El ... When he speaks to you, you will know it.*

Nenshi was released from his struggles, now free to choose his path. He gripped the mud-covered stick, raised it over his head and flung it into the river. The mud loosened and soon dissolved into the water. The stick was cleansed. All the afflictions he had endured were lifted and washed away. Now he needed to find his way back to Ur and then possibly back to his homeland.

Chapter 44

EARLY MORNING. THE SUN BEGAN its climb from the horizon and the warm air bathed the faces of the wanderers as they prepared for the final crossing of the Bazuft River. Fatameh walked up to Nenshi who gathered belongings and secured them for the crossing. She wanted to hold him and be held by him, to reach up and caress his face, stroke his hair between her fingers and to feel his strong arms around her. She suppressed the sensation, the longing.

"I heard from my father that you have decided not to cross the river," she said, her voice subdued, her eyes deep as the waters to be challenged. Nenshi turned. A trace of a smile suggested his heartbreaking decision.

"It's best for everyone," he said. Fatameh wasn't convinced. The tone of his voice masked the tone in his heart.

"Is it? Best for you? For me?" Her eyes teared and she turned away.

"Sometimes two worlds, no matter how close they become, cannot be bridged," Nenshi whispered.

Fatameh wiped her cheeks with her veil, turned to Nenshi and said, "It's not always a bridge that connects two worlds."

Nenshi remained silent, the orator was stymied. Fatameh knew that Nenshi's decision was final. But he offered a glimmer of hope. "Perhaps one day our worlds can reunite. I have learned over time that anything is possible."

"I hope that day is closer than imagined." She pulled back her veil for Nenshi to see her smile. "So how do you plan to go back?"

"The same way I got here."

"There's a better way. After we cross the river everyone will travel towards the grassland. In the opposite direction, further in from the river, there are roads that lead to towns. I have been there."

"That's better than going through the mountains."

Just then Enami appeared, an untimely interruption. Fatameh looked at her, uncertain of the expression behind the veil. At least her soft tone did not create discord.

"The time for the crossing is approaching," she said. "We must be ready. Nenshi, may I ask you to help Khorram?"

"It's my obligation," he replied and smiled. As he walked away, he caught Fatameh's disconsolate glance. She then turned to her mother.

"I thought Nenshi was getting accustomed to our ways. He doesn't have to leave."

"You have grown fond of him. I know."

There was no point in trying to disprove her mother. The look in Fatameh's eyes confirmed it. "I hope he finds his way back," she said.

"I suppose if you could, you would be his guide."

"I would be more than just his guide," she replied. "You know how I have felt about being trapped in this life. There is more out there than sheep and goats. I have seen it. You have seen it."

"You have always stood out among others; a flower among shrubs. You have always been a good daughter. You need to find your own way in life. And I would not stand in your way."

Fatameh smiled. She had made up her mind. It was time to choose her own road.

Khorram explained to Nenshi how the crossing would be made. Timing was most important. They would first observe how the river moved, watching the waves. As they retreated to the side of the launch, the level of the water would rise. At that instance, that precise moment, the *kalaks* would be sent across. Animals, attached to the them, went first, to test if they would float. The natural motion of the water would carry it to the other side. If the *kalaks* were sent in too soon, all would be lost.

"You must remember, if the river carries anything or anyone away, let it go. You will never get it back." Khorram's emphatic advice was ingrained in Nenshi's mind.

"Have you thought about where you will go after we cross the river?" Khorram asked.

"Fatameh told me there are towns along the road."

"She knows them very well."

"Then she would make a good guide."

"No doubt she would. And I would not object, if that's what she chose."

Soon the banks of the river filled with animals and people. Nenshi stood and watched men throw animals into the river, cautiously and with calculated steps. People jumped in and held on to the inflated bags to keep them afloat. Nenshi realized why only the young became excited about the crossing - the most capable relished in the challenge, the old would be left to die.

One at a time, Haji brought a sheep, goat or donkey to the river where Khorram took over and planned the timely push. Occasionally, he would stop as a sheep or dog floated downstream, hardly visible from being tossed around by the current. Only the sound of its yelp identified what had been carried away.

Enami stepped close to the river's edge. She secured two air-filled bags around her waist. In one timely motion, Khorram hurled her into the water and she floated to the other side. Fatameh was next. Nenshi helped her tie the bags to her waist. She winced.

"Is it too tight?" Nenshi didn't think he had secured it tightly, forgetting his own strength.

"A little," she acknowledged and placed her hands over his as he adjusted the rope. "Nenshi, I'm afraid," she whispered.

His eyes crimped at the edges. He had never known her to fear anything.

"You've done this before," he said.

"But you haven't. I'm afraid for you."

"There's nothing to fear," he asserted, confident of his ability.

Fatameh, not convinced, held his hand, leaned towards him to whisper something. Nenshi tilted his head. As she bent over, about to whisper her secret, Khorram called out, "Fatameh, come here. It's your turn." Fatameh looked over to her father and then back at Nenshi. He smiled and squeezed her hand to reassure her.

Within minutes, she was safely on her way across the river.

Haji was next. His hands shook as he inflated a sack. His thoughts drifted back to when he had attempted the crossing and failed. He didn't want to repeat the mistake he had made. He didn't want to disappoint his father, again. He looked around to see if his father was watching. Luckily, Khorram and Nenshi were busy inflating sacks.

He took a step into the water. He felt a large rock under his foot and used it to balance himself. Then, as he tried to tie the *kalak* around his waist, the sack slipped from his grip and fell into the water. He reached to grab it but lost his footing on the rock and fell in. He screamed.

From the other side of the river Enami and Fatameh heard his cry. Enami called out to Khorram and pointed to Haji in the water. She gasped. She was helpless. Khorram turned and was terrified to see his son being pulled by the current. Instinctively he stepped into the water, then stopped. A rush of water pushed him back.

Arms flailed desperately as Haji tried to keep himself afloat. In desperation he reached to grab whatever he could - branches, boulders that jutted out from the water. But he wasn't strong enough to hold on. He drifted further away. The river had come to life, to augur misfortune.

Nenshi heard Enami's calling and saw her pointing towards Haji. Khorram ran along the shore to catch up to him. Fatameh looked on in fear as Nenshi waded into the river. It deepened without warning. His only chance to save Haji was to step out on the rocks. Then he thought of what Khorram had told him earlier - *if the river carries anything or anyone away, let it go.* But Nenshi couldn't accept the senseless loss of human life.

"We can save him!" he shouted to Khorram. "I need your help!" He then ran far enough along the shore and waited for Haji.

Khorram stood still, eyes fixated on his son. Nenshi called out again for help as Haji was getting closer. Khorram then moved quickly to join Nenshi. Enami and Fatameh were running along on the other side, trying to keep up to the horror as it worsened.

As Haji got closer, Nenshi waded into the water, until he was waste deep, knelt and prepared to grab him. The water swelled and a wave hurled itself against him. He was pulled into the river but managed to stand up, breathless, gulping water. He grabbed on to a large rock that jutted out from the water. Then another wave struck, caused him to almost lose his balance.

He wiped his eyes and targeted Haji. Khorram, now stood close to Nenshi, and watched. Nenshi maneuvered himself to make sure his footing was secure, his timing perfect. Then as Haji came within an arm's length, Nenshi lunged and grabbed him by the arm and pulled him out.

"Khorram … hurry," Nenshi yelled. Khorram ran into the water, clutched Haji and brought him back to shore.

As Nenshi stepped off the rock, to make his way to shore, another wave hit. Again, he lost his balance but this time he fell in. Khorram heard the splash, looked behind him and saw Nenshi in the water. He left Haji on the shore and stepped out on the rocks. Nenshi mustered all his strength to fight a strong current and held on to a large rock. Khorram got closer and dropped to his knees.

Nenshi lifted his arm out from the water and shouted out to Khorram, "Give me your hand!"

Khorram stretched as far as he could. As Nenshi tried to grab Khorram's hand, he felt the current pull him away. He then made one quick move for Khorram's arm and managed to lock his hand on to his forearm. Nenshi felt a hard tug through his arm and shoulder. He sprawled out and held on to a rock with his free hand, as tightly as he could. The water attacked him from all sides. All he could do was try to breathe and hold on.

But his grip began to slip. His face surfaced. He gasped for air. The desperation in his eyes spoke to his helplessness. A wave covered them both. When it receded, so did the pull in Nenshi's shoulder. He no longer was holding Khorram's forearm. The current pulled Nenshi away faster and faster, farther and farther, until he disappeared. Fear of the inevitable became a reality.

But Nenshi managed to stay afloat. Waves tossed him in every direction like leaves caught in a whirlwind. His legs tired from endless kicking. He gasped for air, repeatedly. He was alone, no one in sight to help him. By now Khorram would have given up on any effort to rescue him.

Moments later the waters had calmed. It was the opportunity for Nenshi to fight his way back to shore with what little strength he had. But, suddenly, an undercurrent pulled him down as if a creature, a giant water snake, took hold of its next helpless victim, determined to devour him. But it didn't. The waters calmed. The creature moved on.

He tried to swim towards the shore but the river's flow made it difficult as it dragged him downstream. Ahead, a fallen tree strewn across the water from the shore, offered hope. If he could grab on to the trunk or a branch, he might have a chance. But another wave engulfed him. Water blurred his vision and filled his mouth. He gasped.

The tree seemed to rush towards him, faster and faster. Broken branches jutted out like spears ready to impale whatever came in their way. He concentrated on the tree, fast approaching. When it came within reach, he stretched out and his hands locked on to a thick branch. But the waves did not yield and fought him at every turn, determined to take his life. The branch began to slip from his grasp. He fell back into the water. He reached and grabbed the branch again but this time it cut into his hand. The water reddened with his blood. He pulled himself back up, with the little strength he had, and he straddled the trunk. He latched on like a child embracing his mother, clutching the only safety he knew. He dragged himself, on his stomach, along the trunk of the tree until he reached the shore. He stood, walked a few steps and then fell to the ground. He had defeated the river.

Further upstream, where the tribe completed the final crossing of the great river, Fatameh stood alone on a small hill. She gazed beyond the rocks and rapids as far as she could see. Tears filled her eyes. She couldn't hold them back. If only she had told him, before the crossing, that she loved him. If only she had told him what was in her heart, she would not be pouring her tears into the river.

As she looked past the rocks and trees along the shoreline, she noticed something moving. It was the image of someone, walking and then falling to the ground. Her heart began to pound. She wiped her tears to clear her vision. She recognized the image. It was Nenshi. Her eyes sparkled in the sun's light; her thoughts lifted with the freshness of the cool air passing through her. She lifted her layered skirt just high enough not to get in her way as she ran towards him.

At the bottom of the hill, behind a tree, Rustam watched. He saw Fatameh fixating her stare at the image and run along the shore. He followed her.

Chapter 45

NENSHI'S FACE PRESSED AGAINST THE wet ground. The mouthful of mud was better than swallowing water. He wiped his arm across his face to remove the dirt. Then he tore the sleeve off his shirt and wrapped it around his hand to stop the bleeding. He moved his other hand around his head and neck to make sure he was not cut. His hand passed over his neck. The necklace was gone. It had been washed away, forever.

A breaking sound of twigs caught his attention, but he was too tired to move, to turn around. Mud squished by feet, made him wonder if Khorram had come to rescue him, as he had done before in the wilderness.

The sound got louder. He wiped his eyes and face with his forearm. He squinted, blinked repeatedly. Then a figure emerged through the beams of light through the trees.

"Fatameh ..." She walked up to him and fell into his arms. Her tears spoke of the happiness to see him alive. "How did you find me?" he asked.

"It doesn't matter. You're safe."

They sat under a tree. Nenshi shivered from the cold water. Fatameh removed her long shawl and spread it over his shoulders. He smiled.

"Well, now what do we do?" he asked.

"Do you remember, before we crossed the river? I had something to tell you," she said, gazing into his eyes with excitement.

"I had almost forgotten about that." He smiled and nodded his head.

"I want to be with you, to go wherever the roads lead."

"But your family ... your mother ... she will not be able to go on without you ... and your father ... and Haji ..."

"They have known my wishes for a long time. I could no longer live the life of a nomad. Their hearts will be heavy. I will carry their sorrow with me forever. I hope in time the pain will pass."

Nenshi held her and kissed her. His love for her would help to heal the sadness in her heart. He felt the moisture of her tears as her eyes emptied and the tears touched his cheeks. Nenshi wiped her sorrow from her face, gazed deep into her eyes, raw with pain and said, "Your life is now with me."

Suddenly their tranquil embrace was broken by the sound of twigs breaking.

"Is it an animal?" Fatameh asked.

"No. It's the sound of footsteps."

Just then, Rustam appeared.

"It's your fault," he said, eyes burned with rage.

"Rustam, what are you doing here?" Fatameh asked.

He did not reply. He held a dagger. Instinctively, Nenshi slid his hand down his side for his dagger. He had forgotten he had no weapon. He tried to mollify Rustam's anger. "I have just survived crossing the river. You know that I have no intentions of staying with your people."

But it was pointless. Rustam was obsessed, obdurate to any rational thought. "It's your fault," he repeated. "It's your fault."

Fatameh intervened. "What are you talking about? What fault does he have?"

"It's his fault that your father has not agreed for you to be my wife."

"It's not just up to my father nor my mother to decide." Her voice resonated an anger to the suggestion that she was just a pawn at the whim of tribal customs.

Rustam took a step closer towards Nenshi who could see the veins in Rustam's hand swell from squeezing the handle of the dagger. "If I cannot have her, neither can you."

Nenshi nudged Fatameh aside. Incensed, Rustam lunged at Nenshi who fell to the ground. Rustam pressed down on Nenshi's shoulder with one hand and raised his other hand in the air. He aimed the point of the dagger at Nenshi's throat. Fatameh screamed. Rustam's eyes seethed with the venom of a serpent.

Nenshi reached up and locked his hand on Rustam's wrist and tried to push it away. An enraged man has the strength of a lion. Nenshi locked his foot on Rustam's chest and pushed him away. The dagger flew from Rustam's grip. He picked up a tree branch and swung but Nenshi sidestepped the blow. He swung again and this time struck Nenshi on his left shoulder. The scream echoed through the hills. Rustam picked up the dagger.

As Nenshi stepped to the side, Rustam lunged at him again. The blade tore through Nenshi's shirt, grazed his skin. Nenshi then grabbed Rustam's wrist, pushed as hard as he could and they both fell. They struggled, each one tried to gain control to deliver a final, lasting blow.

Again, the dagger flew out from Rustam's grip. Nenshi picked it up, grabbed Rustam by his shirt and pinned him to the ground. He put one knee on his chest and rested the blade on Rustam's throat, ready to push it through his neck. Rustam was helpless. Fatameh looked on in horror.

"What are you waiting for? Do it!" Rustam said, conceding his loss. "I am just another life for you to take."

Nenshi gripped the dagger's handle as tight as he could. He took a deep breath and lifted his body slightly to add his weight to the thrust. He had total control. He looked at Rustam, his eyes lifeless; he had accepted death. Then Nenshi felt something come between him and his victim. His hand did not push the dagger, as if an unknown force made time stand still. A sensation burned in his chest and then slowly subdued, releasing the tightness in his muscles.

A voice then made itself heard - tender, compassionate. Nenshi thought of Abramu and what he had told him - *We must find El in each of us. As El has spoken to me, he will also have an encounter with those he chooses.*

Now, Nenshi too had been chosen and the voice beckoned a new beginning, saying, *do not kill the innocent.*

Nenshi looked at Rustam, whose eyes were now closed waiting for his death. Nenshi pulled back his arm and released the pressure of his weight on Rustam. Killing did not serve any meaningful purpose. He tossed the dagger to the side. Rustam slowly opened his eyes.

"Go," Nenshi said. "Go back to your people."

Rustam stood, visibly shaken that his life had been spared. Nenshi watched as he ran into the wilderness, as fast as a caged hare just released from its captivity.

Nenshi walked over to Fatameh. They embraced, held each other tightly. He looked at her with fresh eyes, those of a new man.

"There has been too much bloodshed, too much injustice in my life," he said. "I will not live this way any longer."

A cool breeze swept over him. The sky's light, blue and grey, shone through the trees, it's beam found its way to him. In the distance he could hear the sound of the fast-moving river splash against the rocks, a reminder of its power, an unforgiving force. But there was no greater power than the voice that had commanded him to spare the life of a fellow man.

While the tribe rested, allowing their flocks to graze in the summer pastures, Khorram, Enami and Haji stood together just outside the camp. The crossing had been completed. A few sheep and goats perished. Haji's determination to cross alone prevailed. After he was rescued, he strapped on his *kalak*, secured it tightly, waited for the right moment and then jumped in. Khorram had seen him take an important step towards manhood.

Fatameh had not been seen after the crossing and although no one reported the loss of human life, concern grew for her safety.

"Look … over there," Haji said and pointed.

"It's Rustam," Enami said. He was making his way back to the tribe, dejected and humiliated. He almost walked past them when Khorram put his hand on his shoulder to stop him.

"Have you seen Fatameh?" Khorram asked.

Rustam turned his head in the direction in which he came. He then resumed his walk back to the camp.

Khorram scanned the area back and forth. "I can see her," he said, pointing. Enami squinted trying to catch a glimpse.

"I can see her too," Haji said.

Finally, Enami recognized her. "I see her."

"She's with someone," Haji said.

Khorram recognized the figure. "It's Nenshi."

"He alive!" Haji's excitement brought relief. "They're looking at us. They can see us. I'll go get her." As he took a step, Khorram grabbed him by the shirt.

"No," he said. "She's not coming back."

Realizing Fatameh's decision, Enami's eyes filled with bittersweet tears.

"Sooner or later, she would have left us," she said. "The hunger for a new life was too strong. She has found love and a new life."

"He's a good man," Khorram said. He then raised his hand in the air and waved. Enami and Haji did the same.

In the distance, Nenshi and Fatameh waved back, then turned and walked until they disappeared into the sun's light.

The warm air and hot fire quickly dried Nenshi's clothes. They sat close to the fire in casual conversation, planning what to do next. Nenshi mentioned wanting to go back to Ur. Fatameh had not heard of Ur, but once they reached one of the villages where she and her father had gone to trade, someone would certainly be able to tell them how to get to the city between the two rivers.

Fatameh reached down to a sack she had brought with her. "This is yours," she said and pulled out the carpet she had made for him. He chuckled and took it from her, pleased to have it again. He placed it on the ground.

She leaned forward, closer to the fire and closed her eyes. The reflection from the fire cast a glow on her face. She opened her eyes, tilted her head and glanced over to Nenshi. Her eyes, soft and inviting, locked on his, which glowed with a flame that imparted warmth and comfort, a flame that invited to be held, a flame that led her into his heart.

Nenshi moved closer to her. Their eyes met, a gaze that penetrated deeply. His heart beat fast and hard, as it had never done before and a sensation passed through his veins that warmed his skin. He then pulled her into his arms with a soft embrace. Then his muscles tightened to hold her closer. She put her arms around his shoulders. Together they reclined on the rug like two petals from a rose gently floating until they touched the ground.

He lay on top of her, her arms wrapped around him, pulling him in. He pressed every part of his body against hers. They kissed, with a passion unknown to either of them. He caressed her face and her arms. She kissed his neck, his shoulders and the two markings. They found love.

A new moon appeared surrounded by countless stars. A cool wind cleansed all that came before it. The fire still burned, soothing two bodies with the tranquility and simplicity of a new life.

Chapter 46

In Ur, Hordekef was eager to continue his search. He and Hamid made their final plans. Babak listened. It was all he could do since he could not go with them because the journey would take a heavy toll.

"Where's Aziza?" Harun asked, his hands balanced trays filled with food. "She must be hungry."

"She's exploring the city and probably getting into some kind of trouble," Babak said. Harun laughed. He had become fond of Aziza, amused by her antics.

Fatameh was right. Traders in a small town gave directions to Ur. After a day's rest they made their way to the city. Nenshi looked for anything familiar that would remind him how to get to Harun's buildings. He pointed to a narrow street.

"I have never seen anything like this," Fatameh said, as she twisted and turned like a drunken peasant in awe of the splendour that surrounded her. Crafted works were displayed everywhere, people paraded in rich attire and the temple towered in the distance.

Suddenly a hand reached out and grabbed Nenshi's arm. Beggars, thieves, he thought, they're everywhere. He turned ready to defend himself. Instead, he looked down at big eyes staring at him.

"Aziza!" he shouted. He took her into his arms and squeezed tightly. Fatameh removed her veil and smiled. She remembered Nenshi had told her about Aziza and his friends.

"What are you doing here?" he asked. She gestured in uncontrollable excitement. "Slow down." Nenshi held her arms for a moment to calm her. She took a deep breath. She began again to speak to him with the gestures he would understand.

"Babak ... he's here with you?"

She nodded and then gestured there was someone else.

"Saulum? He's here too?"

She shook her head. She puffed out her cheeks and expanded her arms. Nenshi crinkled his eyes and shrugged his shoulders. Aziza put her hands to her chin and wiggled them. Fatameh giggled.

"A big man with a beard. Harun."

She nodded several times and then again expanded her arms.

"Yes, yes. You already told me. It's Harun."

Aziza shook her head. Her face scrunched and she put her hands on her hips. Then she repeated the same gesture.

"There's someone else?" Nenshi asked. Again she nodded. Nenshi had no idea who she was trying to describe.

"Why don't you take me to them, and you can introduce me to this other person. But first I want you to meet Fatameh." He smiled like never before. "I'll tell you all about her on the way."

As soon as they entered Harun's place of business all heads turned.

"Nenshi!" Babak cried out. He ran to him and landed a big hug.

"You look like a new man," Harun said. He walked over to Aziza. "You're an amazing young girl."

Nenshi then looked over and saw the man Aziza had tried to describe. His lips quivered; his eyes teared. He took a deep breath and sighed. He wondered what might have happened to his friend. Now the thoughts he had carried with him were released, the question answered. He glanced over to Aziza. "So, this is the other man you tried to describe." She nodded.

Nenshi walked up to Hordekef and the two embraced like two brothers who had longed to be together again.

"I'm happy to see you," Hordekef said.

"And I'm glad you have recovered from your injury."

"The pain I had from the injury pales compared to the anguish I have carried inside."

"What do you mean?"

Hordekef told him how he had hidden the petition to set him free. The accident had further delayed him from taking it to the scribes.

"Forgive me," Hordekef said, pained by his actions. "Our friendship is more important than the envy that consumed me."

Nenshi put his hand on Hordekef's shoulder. "I don't fault you for what happened. Nor do I carry anger, for anger only brings more anger." He smiled and so did Hordekef. Nenshi then took Fatameh's hand. "I want all of you to meet Fatameh."

Stories were told over dinner and long into the night. Food was plentiful, so was wine and laughter. Hordekef, in his boisterous way, re-enacted their journey from Karchemish; how he hung on to a donkey as it tossed him in every direction. They roared with laughter. And Nenshi described his journey, as only a storyteller could. All the while, Fatameh had her arms around Aziza, who had never known a mother's embrace.

They filled their cups and toasted to friendship, old and new, to a new life that had yet to begin. They cherished the reunion.

"So Nenshi, how does it feel to be a free man?" Babak asked, as he stretched his arm for Harun to fill his cup.

Nenshi savoured the thought. His eyes, transparent to the spirit within him, sublime to the sensation of the discovery, took his cup of the elixir of celebration, smiled and said, "Freedom ... so tenuous, yet so precious. I paid the price, now it is mine!"

They cheered; they drank. Hordekef stood and raised his cup and announced, "Soon you'll be back in Thebes and you can choose to live as you please."

There was apprehension in the thought of returning to Thebes. Nenshi's life had little significance there and Tehuti had willingly set him free. The excitement had faded, now replaced by a new life. The burden, the desire to return, that Nenshi had carried throughout his travels, had been lifted.

"My journey is complete," Nenshi said. "I've survived slavery and cruelty and I stared down death in the desert and mountains. I defeated the might river. The lands that I crossed bare the humility of my true existence." He then reached over, took Fatameh's hand and said, "Yes, we will go back to Thebes, to be with Tehuti, my father. But, only for a short time. My friends, Egypt is not our home."

The realization of his new direction in life came without surprise and without a heavy heart. He was grateful for their friendship and their courage to risk their lives to find him.

He looked at his friends, their eyes reflected the acceptance of his decision. He took a deep breath, smiled and said, "There's a new life for us in Uru Salem. El waits for us ... to live with love, justice and freedom." There was a silence. They understood his calling.

Nenshi then looked to Aziza and said, "And you can come with us."

THE END

With all the vileness in his possession
Man attempts to change the world.
Goodness he transforms into evil,
Kindness he shapes into cruelty,
And love he dissipates as he chooses.
But he will never change the one thing
That is most dear to God.
For the spirit - like God Himself - is eternal.

Vince Santoro

About the Author

Vince is an Italian-born Canadian who grew up in Toronto, Canada and now lives in Pickering, a suburb of Toronto, with his life partner, Elizabeth. He has two children, Julia and Philip, both paving their road in life.

Strong family values, sports, and education at a private boy's school, helped to shape Vince. Graduating with a degree in History and Behavioural Science, led to his fascination for Egyptian history.

After completing his studies, he set his eyes on Europe and played professional basketball in Italy. When he returned home, he decided to hone his writing skills by studying Journalism and had several articles published.

Then came the next challenge - to write a book. His debut novel, The Final Crossing, has been a labour of love, one he had worked on for many years. It reflects life experiences, woven into a story that inspires and entertains. Perhaps even see the world in a different way.

Find out more about Vince at vsantoro.ca

Author Photo by DorisVess Photography

CPSIA information can be obtained
at www.ICGtesting.com
Printed in the USA
LVHW112318300622
722526LV00004B/257